BEAUTY

Other Books by Sheri S. Tepper

A novel by

sheri s. tepper

a foundation book

DOUBLEDAY

NEW YORK LONDON TORONTO SYDNEY AUCKLAND

BEAUTY

To Malcolm Edwards,
who is wisely
responsible for
these empty pages

A FOUNDATION BOOK

PUBLISHED BY DOUBLEDAY
a division of Bantam Doubleday Dell Publishing Group, Inc.
666 Fifth Avenue, New York, New York 10103

FOUNDATION, DOUBLEDAY, and the portrayal of the letter F
are trademarks of Doubleday, a division of Bantam Doubleday
Dell Publishing Group, Inc.

BOOK DESIGN BY BONNI LEON

Library of Congress Cataloging-in-Publication Data
Tepper, Sheri S.
    Beauty / by Sheri S. Tepper. — 1st ed.
        p.   cm.
    "A Foundation book."
    I. Title.
PS3570.E673B4   1991
813'54—dc20   90-22305
                                                    CIP

ISBN 0-385-41939-2
ISBN 0-385-41940-6 (pbk.)
Copyright © 1991 by Sheri S. Tepper

FOREWORD

[In the pages that follow, there are certain interpolations written by me, Carabosse, the fairy of clocks, keeper of the secrets of time. When I stand on the bridge above my Forever Pool, I see all past and future things reflected, near or far, dim or plain. If I invite others to stand beside me, they too may see.

That which we do, we do because we see.

This journal is written by Beauty, daughter of the Duke of Westfaire, recipient of many pleasant gifts. Though it is regrettable that no one gave her the gift of intelligence (a gift not highly valued in Faery) she has a practicality that often makes up for that lack.

Intelligent or not, she is the coffer that hides our treasure.

Intelligent or not, Beauty is all our hope.]

THE JOURNAL

of

BEAUTY

daughter of

THE DUKE OF

WESTFAIRE

Getting started on this writing, I cut five different quills and ruined them all. Father Raymond finally cut this one for me. I told him he must, since he gave me the book as a reward for good progress in Latin, rhetoric, and composition, and for going a whole month without complaining. Now I have a place to write all the things I cannot say to anyone, except to Father Raymond, and sometimes he is too busy to listen. It is my intention to tell the story of my entire life so when I am aged I can read it and remember everything. Old people often do not remember things. I know because I have asked them, at least the ones around here, and they usually say something like, "Beauty, for heaven's sake, child, I just don't remember."

If I had a mother I would ask her. I never knew my mother. That is probably as good a place to start as any.

1
MY LIFE IN WESTFAIRE

I never knew my mother. My father never speaks of her, though my aunts, his half sisters, make up for his silence with a loquacity which is as continuous as it is malicious. The aunts speak no good of her, whoever she was and whatever has happened to her, specifics which they avoid, however much ill they find to mutter about else. I have always thought they would not waste so much breath on her if she were dead, therefore she is probably alive, somewhere. *De mortuis nil nisi bonum,* Father Raymond says, but that only applies to dead people.

When I was very young I used to ask about her. (As I think any child would. It wasn't wickedness.) First I was hushed, and when I persisted, I was punished. Nothing makes me angrier or more intent upon finding out things than having people refuse to tell me. I don't mind when people don't know, not really, but I hate it when they just won't tell. It's not practical, because it just makes others more curious. It was the aunts whispering about things that started me upon the habit of listening behind doors and dallying outside open windows. Father Raymond reproaches me for this when I confess it, though he admits it is not a very great sin. It was my own idea to confess it because it felt slightly wicked, but perhaps curiosity is not really a sin at all and I need not feel guilty about it. I will try not confessing it for a while, and see.

Sometimes I hear my mother's name, Elladine, and references to "the Curse," or "the Curse on the Child." The Child is presumably me. If I had known what a curse was during my more tender years, I might have been irremediably warped or wounded. As it was, I knew no more what a curse was than what a mama was, except that most children had not the one, but had the other, and that I had had both without getting any discernable good out of either. Now that I am older and know what a curse is, though not the particulars as they may relate to myself, I am used to the idea and I do not find being cursed as frightening as I probably should.

(I know I am being loquacious. Father Raymond says I am very loquacious and affected. I don't really think I am affected, unless it is by the aunts, and if it is by the aunts, how could I help it? All these words are something I was born with. Words bubble up in me like water. It is hard to shut them off.)

I have resolved to find out all about Mama (and the curse) as soon as I can. So far I have not found out much. I do know that Mama was very beautiful, for one of the older men-at-arms said so when he told me I look much like her around the eyes though the rest of me seems to be purely Papa. Papa is an extremely handsome man, and therefore I am very beautiful. It is not conceit which makes me say so. It is a fact. One must face facts, or so the aunts are fond of saying, though they don't do it at all. They say many things they don't do. I've noticed that about people. The fact is that I shall be ravishing when I grow up if I continue in good habits and do not take to drink.

Aunt Lovage, I regret to say, is a tippler, though the other aunts are quite abstemious.

Father Raymond took over teaching me when I was ten or eleven years old, but my earliest memories are of an education supervised by the aunts. I learned cookery from Aunt Basil and wines from Aunt Lovage, sewing from Aunt Marjoram (who was herself educated by the Sisters of the Immediate Conception at St. Mary of Perpetual Surprise) and music from Aunt Lavender who, though tone deaf, plays upon the lute with great brio and a blithesome disregard for accuracy. She refers to her style as "spontaneous," and urges me to emulate it.

I have found I can play the right notes quite as easily as the wrong ones, though to satisfy Aunt I do flap my arms rather more than the music requires. I am quite talented in music. I am told I sing nicely.

When I was four or five, Aunt Tarragon taught me my letters in order that I could read improving works and be confirmed in the faith. Some of the writings I like best do not feel very improving, though whenever Aunt Terror is around I pretend I am reading religious books. I was confirmed when I was nine, rather late in life, truly, though Father Raymond considered it soon enough. Even then I thought some bits and pieces of doctrine were unlikely at best. Aunt Tarragon is very pious. The other aunts call her the Holy Terror—a play upon her name. They say things like, "Where's the Holy Terror gone?" and collapse in silly laughter.

It was my grandfather's notion to name his seven daughters after herbs, a black mark in the heavenly score book which was no doubt wiped clean by his death or enslavement at the age of seventy-four while on his way to Rhodes to offer his services to the Knights Hospitaler of St. John. We are a long lived family, so Papa says, and Grandfather was still very hale and fervent at that age. Grandfather's ship was blown off course in a storm and was taken subsequently by Mamluks, so Grandmama was informed by an escaped survivor. From what Papa and the aunts say about him, I doubt Sultan al-Maluk an-Nazir had any pleasure of Grandfather.

Luckily, Grandfather's demise or disappearance came long after he brought home the builders who saw to the reconstruction of Westfaire Castle. Some say the architects were pagans from the Far East, and some say they were inheritors of the Magi, but they could not have been anything evil to have built so beautiful a place. There is no other castle like it in England; there may be no building like it in the world. Westfaire is without peer. Even those who have traveled to the far corners of the earth, as Father Raymond did in his younger years, say it is of matchless beauty.

Grandfather's first wife had no sons and two daughters. They are eldest of my aunts, Aunt Sister Mary Elizabeth and Aunt Sister Mary George, who are nuns at the Monastery of St. Perpituus in Alderbury. The sisters do not visit us often. I believe they took holy orders simply to escape being called Tansy and Comfrey, though it is possible they were summoned by God. Sister Mary Elizabeth was rather infirm when I last saw her, though it is likely Sister Mary George will go on forever, getting a little leaner and drier with every passing year.

Grandfather's second wife had no sons and five daughters. Aunt Lavvy, at fifty-eight, is the youngest of them. Aunt Love is sixty. Aunt Terror is sixty-two. Aunts Bas and Marj are twins of sixty-five. I am almost sixteen, and the difference in our ages (as well as their reticence about things I want to know) seems an impenetrable barrier between us. They often fail to perceive the things I perceive, and this makes communication between us exceedingly difficult. I cannot say that there is more than a superficial affection on either side of our relationship. Father Raymond talks about filial duty, but it seems to me there should be something more in a family than that.

Grandfather's third wife, my father's mother, died soon after Grandfather vanished, of grief it is said, though in my opinion she died of simple exasperation. I sometimes imagine what it would be like to be wife to a man and mother to a son who are always off on pilgrimage, as well as being stepmother to seven daughters, all of them considerably older than I. I would die of it, I think, just as Grandmama did. She was only fifteen when she married Grandfather, after all, and about thirty-five when he was killed. What had she to look forward to but decades more of the herbal sisters, all of them dedicated to eccentric celibacy? Buried among all those stepdaughters, Grandmama would have been unlikely to find a second husband, especially since there was nothing left of either her dowry or her dower. Grandpapa used everything rebuilding Westfaire: all the dowries of his three wives, all his own money, and all the considerable fortune he had somehow obtained in the Holy Land, about which people say very little, making me believe Grandfather may not have been quite ethical in amassing the treasure. Grandmama was left with nothing to attract suitors, and death might have seemed a blessed release. At least, so I think.

I spend a lot of time thinking about people. If one leaves out religion, there is very little to think about *except* people. People and books are just about all there is. I don't have anyone much to talk with and only Grumpkin to play with, so . . . so I spend a lot of time thinking. It comes out in words. I can't help that.

I do read everything I can get hold of. Books and my own

writings are a comfort to me in the late hours of the night when all in Westfaire are asleep but me, and I am awake for no reason that I know of except that my legs hurt (Aunt Terror says it is growing pains) or the owls are making a noise in the trees, or my head is full of things I have do not have enough words for yet— there must be such things!—or my chest burns as it sometimes does, as though I had swallowed a little star. It burns and burns, just behind my collar bone, as though it were trying to hollow me out to make a place for itself. I do not know what it is, but it has always been there.

So, I sit up in my bed with the bed curtains drawn tight, the candle on one side and Grumpkin snoring into his paws on the other, and make lists of new words I have heard that day or write pages to myself about all the things I do not understand. Grumpkin lies on his back with his tummy up, his front feet folded over his chest or nose and an anticipatory smile on his face, as though he is dreaming of mice. I wish I could sleep like cats do.

2

DAY OF ST. PATERNUS, BISHOP, CONVERTER OF DRUIDS, APRIL, YEAR OF OUR LORD 1347

When I was quite young, about eight or nine, I purloined some boy's clothes from a line near the woodsman's hut, leaving a silver coin in their place. I had gone out of my way to steal the coin, too, because I had no money of my own, and I thought that though God might forgive my robbing the well-to-do, he would not forgive my increasing the distress of the poor. Dressed in these uncouth garments, dirt on my face, and with my hair twisted up under a grubby cap, I presented myself at the stables asking for whatever work Martin, the head groom, could give me. I am fairly sure Martin knew who I was, but we both preserved the fiction that I was a boy from the countryside, one Havoc, a miller's son, whom Martin employed in order to take advantage of youthful enterprise. If we had ever been found out, I would have sworn on the Holy Scripture that he was guiltless, so grateful to him I was, and I believe he relied upon my protection in the event our game was discovered.

It was in the stable I learned to ride long before the aunts had me dressed in voluminous skirts and perched upon a sidesaddle, one of Grandfather's inventions. I do not think the sidesaddle will catch on. Most women ride sensibly astride, and I cannot imagine their giving it up for something both so uncomfortable and of such doubtful provenance. According to the stable boys, the sidesaddle was designed to protect a maiden's virginity, while risking the maiden's neck. Risking rather much for rather little, I thought at the time, though of course I knew nothing practical about the matter then and scarcely more today.

Martin sometimes asked me to exercise the horses and take them down through the little wood to the stream for water. It was there I first met the pointy-eared boy. He came strolling out of the copse, introduced himself as Puck, and asked my name. When I told him Havoc, he laughed. "I know that's you, Beauty," he said. When I asked him what he was doing in *my woods,* he told me he was keeping an eye on me for someone. I assumed Martin had sent him, simply because I couldn't think of anyone else who might care to have me looked after. After that, I saw him every now and then. Once in a while he would tell me stories. They were not like the stories anyone else told. He spoke of God, but not as Father Raymond did. Some of the things he said sounded greatly like blasphemy to me, and I told him so. I assumed he was some woodcutter's son, told off to watch me whenever I left the stables, which wasn't often because that's where things were going on and people talking about things I might not have learned about otherwise.

It was in the stables that I learned about animal procreation and saw enough of stable boy anatomy to draw certain useful parallels. Though the boys' equipment suffers by comparison to that of the stallions, the similarity of function cannot be ignored. I think it odd that the aunts have never said anything about this matter. There are a great many things they simply do not discuss with me. They did not even tell me about the way of women, and when it happened I thought God was punishing me for having certain feelings about a certain person by letting me bleed to death. It was Doll who found me weeping and told me it was all very ordinary and had nothing to do with sin.

Doll is Martin's wife. Doll is short for Dorothy. She was named for St. Dorothy who was a virgin martyr known for her angelic virtue. Doll says she wishes she had been named for someone a little less angelic and a bit more muscular. She is one of the women who keeps the castle swept and the cobwebs pulled down, and that takes muscle. I'm sure she has always known what I was up to in the stables, but she has never told on me. Doll and one of the other women make clothes for me, too, and I thank God for that. If it were up to the aunts or Papa, I'd always be dressed in things out of the attic made for ancient female relatives in their latter years. Doll and Martin are my first two friends.

My third friend is Giles.

Giles is one of the men-at-arms. He is a year or two older than I, well-grown for his age, very broad in the shoulder and slender though well-made in the hip and leg. He has a frank and open countenance and much soft brown hair which falls over his forehead at odd times, making him look like a much younger person. His eyes are blue, deep blue, like an evening sky. His lips . . . He has very nice features. I have had certain thoughts about him from time to time, thoughts which I have not even told Father Raymond about, because I would blush to do so. Besides, I don't have any polite words to use because either there aren't any or no one has taught them to me. I know how the stableboys talk, but Father Raymond definitely would not appreciate that. Nonetheless, when I see Giles, I think of the stallions and their way with the mares, and I get all flushed feeling.

Also, I see the way he watches me sometimes—Giles, not

Father Raymond—which lets me know he feels those same feelings. He is of good birth, but he is only a young man without fortune or rank, and there is no question about his being a suitable prospect for the daughter of a duke. He is not. I know that, and he knows it as well, but he is nice to me. He is thoughtful and kind and has never, even by so much as a word, done anything improper toward me. Sometimes, after a lengthy rain, I will find my bench in the garden carefully dried off and a rose laid upon it. I'm sure it is Giles who does it, but he doesn't say anything, nor do I. Still, he is my friend. He would not act so otherwise.

My other friend is Beloved.

Her mother calls her Beloved, though her name is actually Mary Blossom. She is the daughter of Dame Blossom, an artisan freeholder, a weaver, in the village. Dame Blossom is very much respected by everyone because she is a midwife and can heal wounds and set bones. If there is trouble, better get Dame Blossom and stay away from doctors, everyone says. It's true. From time to time one or the other of the aunts has consulted a physician, and all the great scholars ever did was sniff at their piss, bleed them dry, and give them some dreadful mixture that—so says Martin—would kill the old ladies off a few years before their time. Beloved is my personal maid. She is also my friend and almost certainly my half sister, almost my half-twin.

Not that Beloved is the only young one running about the castle who looks a lot like me. Everyone pretends not to notice, but I would have to be blind not to see. When two mares who do not look alike throw foals that look exactly alike, you know the same stallion has been at them, so it's clear my Papa has been at Dame Blossom. That was sixteen or more years ago, of course, when she was younger and prettier. I remember her when I was a little girl. She was quite slender and gay then. She has put on weight since, and become very grave, which is a suitable style for a respected matron.

So, Beloved is my half sister, born on the same day I was, and she looks enough like me to be my twin. Sometimes I love her and sometimes I hate her because she has a mother and I don't. We sometimes dress up as each other and Beloved will take my place in the castle, in the dining hall or sewing with the aunts, and they never know the difference. She can spend all day in the castle without anyone guessing that she isn't me. But, if I go down to the village pretending to be the weaver-woman's daughter, Dame Blossom takes one look at me and says, "Beauty, it isn't nice of you to tease me this way. Go tell my silly daughter to come home."

That always makes me feel like crying for some reason. Maybe because she always knows right away I'm not Beloved. You have to notice people to be that sure about them. Though I have thought that maybe it is because she can see the burning thing in me. I know Beloved doesn't have one of those, because I asked her. She wondered if it was like dyspepsia, and I told her it was not.

•
3
•

DAY OF STS. PETER AND JAMES, MAY, YEAR OF OUR LORD 1347

Yesterday my father, who is thirty-seven years of age, returned from pilgrimage to Canterbury—he has already made pilgrimages to the tombs of St. Francis of Assisi, St. Martin of Tours, St. Boniface at Fulda, and St. James at Compostela, as well as to Glastonbury, Lindisfarne, Walsingham, Westminster, St. Albans, and all places else where there are relics of note. Immediately upon his arrival, he told us he intends to marry again. He told us his intended wife will arrive shortly with a small retinue, and that they will all stay for the betrothal ceremonies. Her name is Sibylla de Vinciennes d'Argent. I detested her from the moment I saw the miniature of her that Papa insisted we all admire.

You must not think this rejection of a stepmama is pro-

voked by hostility toward another woman who will take a beloved mama's place. I have heard tales like that, but I don't
know whether I would have loved Mama or not; she has given
me no opportunity to find out. As for Sibylla's taking my place
in my father's affections, she can't take what I have never had.
Though I am almost sixteen, he has done none of the things one
expects of a loving papa. He made no provision for my education, merely leaving me to the mercies of the aunts. If Father
Raymond hadn't taken me over, I should be as woefully ignorant about many important things as they. Papa has made no
effort to arrange a marriage for me. When I've raised the subject
with him, he has said, "Wait until—well, until you're sixteen,
Beauty. Then we'll discuss it." Not likely! I can count upon the
fingers of one hand the number of "discussions" I've had with
Papa, count them and quote them from memory.

"Ah, Beauty," he says. "Doing well with your studies/
cooking/music/herbary?"

"Yes, Papa."

"Good girl. Always do well with your studies/cooking/mu-
sic/herbary."

Once in a great while, when I have been greatly troubled,
I've gone all the way to his rooms to talk with him. This isn't a
journey to take lightly! Starting in my rooms, which are off the
long corridor behind the kitchens, I go up one flight of stairs to
the corridor outside the small dining hall. This is the tall one
hung with crusaders' weapons and banners and with paneling
carved all over with birds and flowers and fish. Then I go
through the little suite between and into the large dining hall,
an even taller room, where the ceiling is decorated with stone
rosettes dependent from the multiple arches, each like lacework,
where the long wall is one tall window after another—all looking over the garden with the apricot tree that Beloved and I get
all the fruit from because the people in the kitchens always
forget it is there—and the other walls are hung with tapestries
telling stories of gods and goddesses, most of them naked. At
the far end of this dining hall, I come out into the great hall,
under the dome. Father Raymond says it is not unlike a cathedral dome, though smaller. Since I've never seen a cathedral, I

see it as the inside of a lovely shiny melon, pressing up toward the sky, round windows set about it like gems in a ring, poking up in the center to make the high lantern visitors say they can see from miles away as they approach on the north road. They look for it, they say, as the first sight of the most beautiful building in the world!

The floor of the great hall is marble, laid in designs. When I was little, I used to play there, walking along the designs as though they were paths in a garden. From the great hall, two curving stairs follow the walls up behind a graceful stone balustrade, joining at the center before three arches with statues of veiled women set beneath them. No one alive made the statues. Grandfather brought them from a country across the sea from the Holy Land, from a man who had dug them up from an ancient city, and Papa says Grandfather did it because the architects of Westfaire told him to. From either side of the arches, other corridors lead left and right, and at the far end of the leftward one, up another flight of curving stairs, are Papa's rooms. All the floors, except the one in the small dining hall, which is made out of tiny woven strips of walnut wood, are laid in mosaics, ribbons and leaves and flowers and fruits bordering all the walls. It's hard to walk over them without stopping to look at them. It's hard to climb the stairs without listening to the way my clothes trail along the steps, the way the smooth stone feels under my hand. It's hard to go anywhere in Westfaire without stopping and staring, sometimes for a long, long time. Besides, it's just a very long way to Papa's rooms, so I don't go there very often, only when I'm desperate.

And when I do go, when I get there, I knock on **Papa**'s door and call, "Papa, may I talk to you?"

"Not now, Beauty," he always replies over the sound of female giggles. "I'm very busy just now. Later on, perhaps."

Now that is what our filial relationship amounts to! I don't think that's enough of one for the new stepmama to threaten.

I am not jealous of whatever attention Sibylla may receive from the aunts, either. I heartily hope she will take my share along with her own. They pay entirely too much attention to me, all the time, without being in the least comforting or kind.

No, my revulsion at the idea of a stepmama is not jealousy. It arises from the pictured face itself, a pale, rather long face with a simpering mouth over large teeth and with something thoughtfully devious about the eyes, the kind of face that might result if a rabbit mated with a weasel.

And perhaps I am jealous of the fact that she will be mistress of Westfaire Castle.

No, that is *not* honest. If I am going to write things to remember when I am old, I should at least tell the truth. I am sickened at the thought of her being mistress of Westfaire. Though I have always known it will be my fate to marry and leave it, still I love Westfaire hopelessly. I love the lowe of sunset on the lake at our back, the blossoming trees in the orchard close, the gentle curve of the outer walls resting in the arms of the forest. I love the towers, the shining dome, the delicate buttresses, and the lacy windows. From a hill not far away (we always go there on the first of May to collect herbs and wildflowers) one can look down on Westfaire and see it whole. Whenever I look at it thus, the burning within me grows into a fire, closing my throat, catching at my heart, as though Westfaire and I burned with the same holy light. If I turn in time to catch the aunts staring down, their faces have a look not unlike mine, though not so pained, as though they, too, love the place so much they cannot bear to leave it. I've always refused to think about leaving Westfaire, but it is probable my dislike of Sibylla comes from nothing more than simple grief at what she will gain and I will inevitably lose.

Feeling beauty must be rather like feeling arms and legs. Some of the old men-at-arms talk about losing an arm or a leg in battle and how, ever after, one feels it is still there, even while one grieves over the loss. So I know it will be when I lose Westfaire. I will feel it in me forever, even while I grieve endlessly over losing it.

I still don't want to think about that. Instead, I keep telling myself that a wedding offers to be an interesting event which can be anticipated with an observer's relish of novelty. It will not make much immediate difference to me, personally, so I can resolve to enjoy it as spectacle.

[I find it interesting that she feels the truth, without understanding it in the least.

I said as much to Israfel and he remarked that it would be better if she didn't understand it. "Much of life," he said to me, "depends on our being ignorant of reality. If we understood reality, we would never go on."]

.
4
.

ST. MONICA'S DAY, MAY, YEAR OF OUR LORD 1347

When I wrote that Papa's marriage would make little difference to me, personally, I had failed to perceive Sibylla's capacity for inventive malice.

She arrived yesterday with her mama and assorted female relatives in a great bustle of boxes and flutter of veils. They trotted briskly through the castle, visiting each of my aunts in her own rooms, which are in various parts of the castle, though not in the long wing where Papa lives, which is virtually empty. We had all assumed the visitors would be quartered there, where the extravagant, lacy vaulting reaches its perfect expression (says Father Raymond) and the tall windows admit the most light. The rooms are comfortably furnished with high, enclosed beds and plenty of benches and hangings and carpets. Besides, in expectation of company, that wing had been given an extraordinarily thorough cleaning. Doll has been at it for days.

Our assumption was mistaken. According to Sibylla's mama—a woman who always looks as though she has a mouthful of something nasty which only courtesy prevents her spitting out—Sibylla could be happy only in the rooms near the kitchens which I have occupied since my earliest memory. It was not, in her mama's words, fitting for Sibylla to be housed too near her intended bridegroom lest some indecency occur prior to the blessing of Mother Church. I turned my mind from the indecency which would undoubtedly occur subsequent to that blessing. Far better, Sibylla's mama went on, for Sibylla to be as far from her intended husband as possible, in the bosom of the aunts, getting to know them better.

Strangely enough, I was rather cheered by all this. It was pleasant to be given a reason for hating her, and this immediate assault upon the daughter of the house by the putative bride told me how right I had been. The rabbit *had* mated with a weasel, and that right gladly. I was furious, of course, but justified. Beloved and I whispered about it, resolving upon mutiny, after which I smiled at the committee which was delegated to approach me, aunts and all, and declined to move.

Aunt Taragon had a few pious words to say concerning Christian resignation and turning the other cheek. I suggested that she convey this message to Sibylla, for whom it could do nothing but good. While this was going on, Beloved hid behind my bed curtains and made faces at me behind Aunt Terror's back. When she left, we collapsed on the bed, giggling. Though Beloved was supposed to be my maidservant, I never ordered her to do anything for me. What she did, she did because she wanted to, such as caring for my clothes because sometimes she wore them while I wore hers.

Aunt Basil was the next to arrive and remind me I had always thought my rooms were so near the kitchens that the smell of aged grease overcame the spices in the clothes press. I suggested she tell Sibylla, who would no doubt change her mind about wanting my rooms. Beloved and I had another giggle over that.

Aunt Lovage came to promise me (or rather Beloved, since by that time we'd changed clothes and were being each other) a bottle of a very special vintage and a picnic on the sward. Beloved suggested we have the bottle and the picnic anyway. This was not a particularly clever rejoinder. Beloved and I look exactly alike, but I am much cleverer. I tried to teach Beloved to read and write, but she isn't interested. She doesn't even care. She sometimes watches me reading and studying, and she says it is a dreadful burden being clever and well-schooled, and she is glad she does not have to carry it.

Aunt Marjoram promised to make me a new cloak, but Beloved told her my old one will last years yet. It will, though it is already faded. Perhaps I will make myself a new one.

And finally, Aunt Lavender promised to play a new song for me, one she had learned from a traveling minstrel. I was being myself by then since it was late afternoon and Beloved had gone home. Since I had spent more time with the minstrel than aunt had and already knew all his songs, I declined.

I had thought they might appeal to Aunt Sister Mary Elizabeth and Aunt Sister Mary George, but Papa gave them no time for that. In the afternoon Papa sent a servant to bring me to the small room where he does business with his bailiff, and there he told me to get myself moved by dark or he'd send me to Alderbury to join my two eldest aunts as a nun.

I would move, I said gayly. I would move happily. I had always felt my rooms were rather too close to the kitchens. What had given Papa the idea I was reluctant to move? I dimpled and curtsied, then rounded up three serving maids, including my old friend Doll, and made a clean sweep of it before Sibylla or her mama could say a paternoster, being sure that everyone heard me chirping happily away about the whole thing.

There were no rooms left except the ones in Papa's wing, including the suite we had intended for Sibylla. All the rooms there were huge. The corridor was obviously one used frequently by Papa's . . . friends, whom I did not want to meet going and coming. I sat on my baskets and told Doll that was the last place I wanted to go, feeling quite put out now that my little drama had been played and Sibylla had been installed where I had lately been, in my cosy rooms beside the garden, with my carpet and my bed curtains.

"There's the room your mama used sometimes," said Doll. Doll is older than most of the other servants, and she was present when my mama was still in residence. "Up in the dove tower," she said, raising her eyebrows up under her hair and jerking her head back. Doll is stout and red-cheeked and has

more energy than any five other women. She stood there, looking at me intently, hands on hips.

The dove tower is slender and tall, the tallest of all the
castle towers, its top decorated with spiky finials and a long pole
for flying banners. Around it the white doves make a constant
cloud of wings and a liquid tumult like water falling into a
fountain.

"Up in the dove tower, then," I agreed, and we all went
back through the hall and wound ourselves here and there
through little side passages until we came to the tower door. It
screamed when we opened it, like a goose being killed, and the
dust on the stairs puffed under our feet as we crept up, round
and round and round until we were dizzy. The door at the top
hung loose with great nails sticking out of it, and the room itself
was filthy with bits of bird nest and veils of spider web. Doll
sent a girl to ask Martin to come up and fix the shutters and the
door, and he did that while one of his boys unstuffed the chimney and two of the women scrubbed the floor and walls and
another one swept the mess down the stairs. Martin threw the
carpet down into the yard, for it was eaten to rags by moth and
mouse. The doves from the cote below had made somewhat free
with the space, but under the dirty coverlet the bed was all
right, and so were the bed curtains we found in the carved armoire, once they'd been shaken free of dust and well brushed
and hung. I cleaned out the armoire myself (finding something
interesting in the process) and put my clothes in it. Then I sat on
the chair and felt important. It has arms! Only Papa and Aunt
Terror have chairs with arms. Everyone else sits on benches or
stools. While I sat there, I examined the thing I'd found in the
armoire, but there wasn't time really to figure out what it was,
so after a time, I put it under the chair seat, which lifts up to
make a storage place, and told myself I would examine it later
on.

Doll showed me the privy closet over the moat. The door is
in the wainscot beside the fireplace. I'll have it all to myself. I
can see the lake through the little windows. The tiny panes of
glass are quite intact and clear now that the bird droppings have
been washed away. There are three windows in a row, and the

middle one goes all the way to the floor and opens on a balcony where a kind of pole juts out over the stableyard. Martin calls it a spar, and says he'll fix the pulley and put a rope on it tomorrow, so that water and firewood can be hauled up from the stableyard below. By late afternoon everyone was finished with the cleaning and went off, leaving the room neat and sweet-smelling with my lute hung on the wall, a pitcher of water and a bowl to wash in on the chest, a kettle by the fire for hot water, the woodbox filled, all my things tucked away, and me here alone, looking around at the sky like a bird from its nest.

Without a carpet or rushes, the floors will be very cold. Without tapestries, the walls will be even colder. Still, the hooks are still there to put wall hangings on, if I can find some, and the worst of the cold weather is over. It will be warm enough for a night or two, until Sibylla leaves and I can steal my carpet back from my old room. I must stop writing and go down to supper.

Though we made a noisy enough bustle getting the tower room cleaned, it seems the tower is so high and remote no one heard us. None of the aunts noticed where I went; they all spoke as though I'd moved into a room in Papa's wing. I suppose Sibylla and her mama think that's what I've done. At table this evening she peered at me as a chicken does at a bug, acting very discontented and disappointed, as though she had been counting on my making a fuss about moving, perhaps, which would have given her something to complain to Papa about. Poor fool woman. She doesn't know Papa.

"All settled?" he asked them vaguely, not waiting for an answer. "Good. It's always good to get settled." Then he went back to talking with Father Raymond about the pilgrimages he intends to make before and after the wedding while Sibylla sat there, caparisoned like a tournament horse, playing with a slice of overdone venison and staring at the back of his neck. I thought of telling her that's mostly what she's going to see of him. The back of his neck as he plans some journey or the back of all of him as he rides away.

[The device Beauty found in the tower room was one I, Carabosse, had left there for her: a clock. It has my name on it, and I hope it will serve as an introduction so she will not be completely surprised, later, when we meet. We plan for her to leave Westfaire, which is conspicuous now and will be even more so, and go to another place, a hidden place where she is unlikely to ever encounter the Dark Lord. Thus far, things are progressing precisely as Israfel and I expected they would, as the Pool showed they would. The immediate future is usually quite clear in the Pool, and we had foreseen Sibylla. We had anticipated the succession of events leading to Beauty's occupation of the tower. I had even foreseen her pleasure in it.

What I had not anticipated are my own feelings. I fear I am growing fond of the girl. She has something none of her fairy godmothers gave her, something that came entirely from her human heritage. It is a kind of courage. An indomitability. Like a buoyant little boat, she pops to the top of every wave. Loquacious though she is (and Father Raymond was perfectly right about that), even a little arch at times (and why shouldn't she be? Most of her aunts have exactly that manner), still, she has something attractive about her. Perhaps it is the outward sign of what we did to her, Israfel and I.]

•
5
•

ST. ETHELREDA'S DAY, MAY, YEAR OF OUR LORD 1347

After Sibylla left, in the days between the betrothal and the wedding, which is supposed to take place very soon, I got the tower arranged to suit me. Martin and I stole my carpet from my old room and replaced it with one out of the attic. Laid over a nice layer of straw, it made the floor much warmer. We could find no wall tapestries in the attic, but we did find some painted wall cloths up there, blue background with a design of little starry flowers in silver, quite good enough to take the chill off the stone. Also, Martin put up a new firewood rope.

After that, I had time to really look at the thing I found. It is round, like a wheel, about as big across as the palm of my hand, and as thick through as four of my fingers held together. It has four little feet like lion's paws. It is made of shiny metal which could be gold, for it is very heavy for its size. The round front is made of glass. Under the glass are nine numbers, Roman numbers, set in a circle. The numbers start at the top right with fourteen, and go on around the circle to twenty-two, which is at the top. There is a lacy golden arrow starting in the middle and pointing to the fourteen. Well, actually pointing about halfway between the fourteen and the fifteen.

On the back of it is a place like a keyhole, but there is no key. On the top is a handle, like two dragons, fighting or kissing or just being heraldic. And that's all.

Except the noise it makes. I can only hear it at night when things are very quiet, but I can hear it then. The tiniest ticking, the faintest crepitation, like something very small inside there, breathing or tapping its toe.

Oh, on the front of it, twining all around the numbers is a design of leaves and vines, and I think they are meant to spell out letters. Sometimes I look at them for a long, long time, trying to make the letters out. Two, I'm almost sure, are Ss. Two, I'm almost sure, are As. I think there's a B and a C, but I can't be sure. Since I don't know what it is, I call it my mysterious thing, and it sits on the chest with my other things.

I like the tower very much.

As it happened, Papa had gone off somewhere before the aunts even found out where I am living. When they found out, there was much consternation, buzzing, and confabulation. The aunts wanted to know who suggested such a thing?

No sense getting Doll in trouble. I told them it had been my own idea.

More wide eyes, open mouths, and thrown up hands. More fussing and steaming and orders to move here, move there.

"My mother lived up there," I said to them at last. "If you want me to get out of it, you'll have to tell me why!"

Which settled them down in a hurry. Not one of them is willing to say why or what or when. Since Papa is off viewing decayed bits of saints' bodies, he isn't available to offer an opinion. Aunt Sister Mary Elizabeth and Aunt Sister Mary George, whose thoughts on the matter were solicited by Aunt Terror in a thick letter sent by messenger, have replied that they are unaware of anything ungodly about the tower room. This sent the aunts into a frenzy of calculation, trying to decide whether either of the elderly nuns was present at Westfaire at any time when my mother was here.

I stood it as long as I could, and then I went to Doll. "Doll," I asked her, "tell me what this is all about." I've asked her about my mother many times over the years, and she has always shaken her head at me. Still, the last time I'd asked had been a long time ago, when I was a child.

"Be my gizzard's worth," she said. "Be worth my life and soul if they found out." She wrung her hands, one in the other, trying not to look at me.

"Not from me," I swore, spitting in my hand and making a cross on my chest with ashes from the cookfire.

She wrung her hands again, staring over my shoulder. Finally she gave a kind of sigh and a shrug and said, almost in a whisper, "When your papa insisted on makin' a great celebration out of your Christenin', she invited some relatives of hers, and when your papa found out about that, they fought about it. I don't know what it was about because I couldn't hear anythin' except them yellin'. Then, when the Christenin' was over, your papa took you away and gave you to a wetnurse down in the village, then he locked your mama in her room up there in the tower. He nailed the door shut, and he went up every day to yell at her through the door, tellin' her the whole thing had been her fault and she'd had no business marryin' him without tellin' him.

"What did he mean?"

She flushed and twisted her hands together. "It's not something I'd speak of, Beauty. Besides, I don't know for sure. None of us common folk knows for sure. Third day after your mama was locked up, your papa got no answer when he yelled at her, so the carpenter jerked the door open and they found her gone."

"Jumped?" I asked, thinking Doll knew something she

wasn't telling me. Her face was red, like she was holding something back, but I didn't want to push her too much or she'd refuse to talk about it at all.

"Too high to jump," she said.

"Went down the firewood rope."

"Your papa took the firewood rope down first thing he put her in there."

"Flew away?" I offered as a jest, watching in amazement as Doll crossed herself.

"There's those that say she did exactly that."

"I did get christened, didn't I?" I asked, wondering why Mama had made such a fuss about it.

"Of course you did, silly," she snorted, going back to her cleaning, obviously not wanting to talk about it anymore. Needless to say, this has given me a great deal to think about.

·
6
·

ST. LADISLAS DAY, JUNE, YEAR OF OUR LORD 1347

Yesterday Papa came back from his trip full of plans for the wedding, which he seems in a monstrous hurry to accomplish, and this has given the aunts something else to worry about besides where I am housed. None of them chose to be the one to tell him I am living in the tower, and I'm certainly not going to tell him.

The weather has been having a sulky spell, with gloomy clouds and chill rain. I've kept the shutters closed and a fire going, to make a warm shadowy space. What with the wall hangings and the carpet and the low ceiling (though it is vaulted up from five stone piers to join in a carved rosette high in the middle), it stays warmer than my old quarters did, even though the fireplace is a tiny little thing next to the door where the stairs go down behind the one straight wall. Though it took him several days to get used to it, Grumpkin has come to like the tower room, both for sleeping and for prowling about on the balcony. I love it. I can practice on the lute without anyone's hearing or learn new songs or read, all by the light of the fire with the one candle making strange shadows.

Which led me to my discovery. This afternoon I saw that a shadow on the chimney piece looked exactly like a face. One of the stones was a nose. I went over and stroked it, watching the shadow of my hand, feeling the nose shake a little. The stone was loose. I fiddled with it and jiggled at it until it slid out into my hands, not heavy at all. It was only a thin piece shaped to fit into the front of a little space. And behind the stone was a box.

I took the box out, replaced the stone, and sat down before the fire to look at it. The box is well-made of a pale satiny wood, and though it has a keyhole, it wasn't locked. Inside was a packet of needles and three hanks of thread, a ring with a carved stone, and some tightly rolled sheets of parchment. These I unrolled and found the top sheet was a letter directed to me.

> Dear Beauty:
> Since you have not had a mother's love, my child, I believe you deserve at least a mother's explanation.
> I did not leave my own country with the intention of marrying anyone like your father. I met the duke quite by accident; he wooed me with great ardor; I fell under the spell of his passion.
> As it happens with my people, from the moment of the wooing, my memory of my past existence was dimmed. I was first enveloped by your father's encompassing desires and later smothered by his overwhelming aunts. The former caused me to lose my memory and virginity, though temporarily; the latter have caused me almost to lose my mind. I hope this is also temporary.
> Time passed and I learned that I was pregnant. I was not unhappy about this. As I grew large, however, your father began

to absent himself. I should say, absent himself more frequently, as it is common knowledge in this household that your father is a libertine. As I grew larger yet, he left me completely to myself. Among my family, celibacy restores both memory and virginity, a useful attribute under certain conditions—if one wishes to trap a unicorn, for example. To say I was horrified at what I had done is to say both too much and too little. I regretted the liaison as being beneath my dignity, but at the same time, I delighted in the prospect of having a child. Children have a very special meaning to our people.

Then you were born. Your father planned to have you christened. I considered this unnecessary and demeaning. His religion is stealing our birthright, day by day and year by year! Why should I take part in it! However, your father insisted not only upon the ceremony itself, but upon making it a cause for semipublic display.

Since all your father's aunts would be attending this ceremony, however, fairness dictated that my own aunts be offered the same opportunity. They would have been mightily offended otherwise.

I let the letter fall into my lap as I considered these confusing words. How very strange. I reread the first of the letter, but it made no more sense the second time. I shook my head and went on.

I did not invite Aunt Carabosse. She came uninvited! For some inexplicable reason of her own, she laid a curse upon you, my child. Upon your sixteenth birthday you were to prick your finger upon a spindle and die.

I crushed the letter to my breast in sudden horror. My sixteenth birthday was only days away. I forced my eyes back to the parchment where it trembled in my hands.

No one heard this except your great aunt, Joyeause, who was standing beside the cradle at the time. She came to me after the guests had departed to tell me she had modified the curse as best she could. The curse now implements as follows: "When Duke Phillip's beautiful daughter reaches her sixteenth year, she shall prick her finger upon a spindle and fall into a sleep of one hundred years, from which she will be wakened by the kiss of a charming prince." Or perhaps it was Prince Charming. I have been much upset by all this and did not pay proper attention to what she was telling me. No one knows what Aunt Joyeause has done but me—and you, if you read this letter before your birthday, as I am confident you will do for I have set a timely discovery spell upon it.

[Most of the above is nonsense. Joyeause did overhear what I said, since she was closest to me at the time. What I said was that the duke's daughter would be pricked by a spindle and fall into an enchanted sleep. All that bit about the hundred years and the prince is pure invention. I never said the child would die, and if Joyeause tried for a thousand years she couldn't change one of my spells. Joyeause has always been a dilettante.]

Your father, already offended by Carabosse's attendance at an event to which she was not invited, became outraged. He raved at me, and I had no time to remonstrate with him before he dragged me off to this tower! He says he has hidden you away and will hide all the spindles in the castle, perhaps all those in the dukedom. He castigates himself for marrying one of my race, and me for being what I am. Men are like that. They marry for reasons that have nothing to do with what they expect from matrimony and then damn their wives for not being what they want later. They marry for beauty and charm and sex, and then expect their wives to be sensible, parsimonious and efficient.

Now that memory and virginity are restored, I need not remain here to be insulted. I choose to return to my ancestral lands.

My powers at the moment have been considerably diminished by the time I have spent here, and I cannot find you to take you with me. You will find this letter when you are old enough. If you cannot come to me before the curse takes effect, come as soon thereafter as you can. I have left you the means to do so. Keep safe the box in which you find this.

I put down the letter and wiped my face where the tears were running down, making an itchy mess of my eyes and nose. I did have a mama. And evidently I was not to die on my birthday, though the fate Grandaunt Joyeause had planned did not seem a thrilling alternative. I could not understand how Mama expected to see me after the curse, since even mothers did not, as a general rule, live more than one hundred years. The letter continued briefly on a separate page.

My dear daughter, too long separated from me, be assured of my affection. *Come to me with all haste before you grow any older.* I will await you with a joyous heart.

Your loving mama,
Elladine of Ylles.

You can imagine my amazement. I was struck by how clean the parchment looked upon which all this had been written. It could have been delivered that very afternoon. The more I looked at it, the more I thought that in a sense it had been delivered that very afternoon. After reading the letter several times, both pages of it, I replaced it in the box and the box in its hiding place, sliding the stone carefully into place. Set well in, it cast no protruding shadow. I could only believe she had left it sticking out so that I would see it. It had been put there for me, and me alone, to find. Mama.

I climbed into my bed, pulled the bed curtains shut, propped myself upon my pillows, and pulled the coverlets up to my chin. This was something that required thinking about, though thoughts were slow and reluctant to come. The first one to emerge teasingly into the forefront of my mind was that even though the letter had been written almost sixteen years before, my mother was alive, just as I had always supposed. I thought of Beloved's mother, how she had known at once I was not hers, and something lurched in me, just behind my breastbone.

My next thought was that Elladine had said she had left me the means to find her, though I could not imagine what she meant. The contents of the box included only the ring, the packet of needles and the three hanks of thread. Which led to the fleeting suspicion that Mama, however lovely, might not have had all her wits about her. This would explain the aunts' attitude, certainly. Even women as reconciled to the holy will as the aunts might bridle at having a madwoman in the family. It would also explain papa's locking her in the tower, since such is known to be the fate of madwomen and madmen whenever madness and towers occur in appropriate contiguity. Towers, or, in a pinch, attics.

The letter, however, far from seeming the ravings of lunacy, had been odd but well-reasoned. I was sure that Mama was not mad. Absent, yes, and for reasons that seemed sufficient to her, but not mad. I would have to figure out how to find her.

My final thought was that the name of the wicked aunt was Carabosse. The two adjacent Ss in that name reminded me of something. I got my mysterious thing off the chest and looked at it. One of the letters could be a B, and another an R. Is this the gift she gave me? Is it her name upon it? And if so, what is it?

["Wicked aunt" indeed. I confess, that hurts to read.]

7

My thoughts and worries concerning my own future have been somewhat interrupted because the wedding guests have started to arrive. The day after I found Mama's letter, Weasel-Rabbit and her entourage came down the roadway on horseback and in two carriages, followed by an enveloping cloud of dust. Other parties arrived thereafter, both large and small, some of them with marquees they have set up in the meadow as though they had come to a tourney. All the aunts have moved together into one suite, and their rooms have been reserved for various countesses and barons. Poor Father Raymond is dithering about, trying to remember where he put the festive vestments. The wedding is to take place in our own chapel; the abbot from St. Paternus (a great, rich, important abbey down the lake a bit, near the main road to London) will officiate. Father Raymond will assist him.

Down in the kitchens, the head cook is screaming at the kitchen boys and having the tantrum he usually has whenever he has to cook for more than just the family. The whole place smells of roasting meat and baking cakes, spices and stewed fruit. There will be a banquet each night, three nights running, with the abbot attending the banquet the night before the wedding.

I have resolved to be very good, for the sake of my soul. Aunt Tarragon always goes on about the state of my soul, much more than Father Raymond does, which is odd. Over the past few days I have stayed out of Weasel-Rabbit's way and out of the aunts' way and out of Papa's way in the easiest manner imaginable, by putting on my boy rags and working in the stables. Besides, that lets me see what kind of horses everyone has and whether they look well-treated or not. Weasel-Rabbit has horses which look ill fed and badly groomed, not at all consonant, I feel, with her rather extravagant equippage. Her carriages have tall painted wheels and a suspended, woven bed with soft pillows to sit upon, very elegant. Such carriages would indicate (though the matter had certainly not been discussed with me) that Papa is marrying into a fortune. Since I can not see why anyone would willingly marry Weasel-Rabbit otherwise, it explains a great deal. Supporting five half sisters takes a bit of doing all by itself, and helping get up a new crusade (which Papa talks of from time to time) is frightfully expensive. Just maintaining Westfaire involves constant outlay. Papa needs a wealthy wife, though I can't figure out why such a wealthy woman should have such poorly cared for horses unless she is at the mercy of idle grooms simply because she does not know the difference.

•

8

•

ST. BERTHA'S DAY, JULY, YEAR OF OUR LORD 1347

The preliminary banquets went quite well. There are enough minstrels about that Aunt Lavender has not felt called upon to entertain us upon the lute. Indeed, all five aunts-in-residence spend most of their time with Sibylla's mama, and I am left largely to myself.

There was one noteworthy encounter in the cloister garth this afternoon. I had gone down to the chapel with Grumpkin, not intending to pray, you understand, but simply to see if Father Raymond ever found the vestments he was looking for. He had. They were stored in a chest in the muniments room and he had finally remembered putting them there himself. While I was talking to Father, Grumpkin fell asleep on one of the prie-dieux so I knelt down at the next one. The chapel was so peaceful, the light in it so rarified and the smell of it so—well, the chapel has a certain smell, though only I seem to be aware of it. I have asked Beloved about it, and I have asked Doll, and even the aunts, but none of them notice it. Perhaps it is only the candles or the incense, though it seems different from that to me. More illusive. Less natural. It is very pleasant to me. It makes me want to go on sniffing at it, as though it were a flower.

At any rate, the chapel smelled so whatever-it-is that I prayed a small prayer and determined to behave myself and not absolutely hate Weasel-Rabbit. I knelt for some time getting this resolution firmly in mind, and then Grumpkin woke up and meowed to go elsewhere. I have noticed that cats are little impressed by religion. We went out of the cool, gray light into the brightness of day. Grumpkin was trailing along as usual, batting at my skirts, when we confronted Sibylla coming out the passageway that leads to the kitchen gardens. She took one look at Grumpkin and let out a howl one might have heard as far as Alderbury. "A cat," she screamed. "A cat."

I should have thought the matter self-evident. There is nothing uncatly about Grumpkin. He is a red and cream-colored tabby of most ferocious mien, and I picked him myself from among the litter the stable mouser kindled three years ago. He is called Grumpkin because his furry eyebrows make him seem always frowning or, at the least, very thoughtful about things. He is indeed a cat, and the matter does not usually occasion remark.

"Get it out of here," screamed Sibylla. "It'll have to be killed. I can't bear cats."

I seized Grumpkin up and went off in the opposite direction, trying very hard to hold on to my resolution not to hate her. I think perhaps I could have persevered in a state of grace if Weasel-Rabbit hadn't gone immediately to Papa, demanding Grumpkin's execution.

I'm not sure Papa even paid much attention. So far as Papa is concerned, horses are simply things one rides upon and dogs are simply things one hunts with and cats are simply animals that infest the stable and are tolerated because they dispose of vermin. I don't think Papa has ever had a pet, but if he ever has, he has long since forgotten it. I'm sure the fact I love Grumpkin never entered his mind. At any rate, he listened to Weasel-Rabbit and then told his scribe to take care of the matter. The scribe told one of the men-at-arms, and the man-at-arms, laughing, mentioned it to Giles. Giles knew how I felt about Grumpkin, even though I'd never said a word to him about it. Well, he watched me, sometimes, so he would know, wouldn't he? People who really look at you do know how you feel. Giles told the other man he'd take care of it and came to find me. He bowed, quite formally, and explained the situation. We talked it over, with me trying very hard not to cry and mostly succeeding, and Giles suggested that he take Grumpkin down to the stables to live with Martin for a time and then report the cat disposed of, which he would have been, in a sense.

Since the feelings I have about Giles are often very hot and tempting ones, I usually try to stay as far away from him as I can. Usually I manage it fairly well, but this time I was so grateful to him about Grumpkin I did not stand a distance from him. I stood very close, where I could smell the warmth of him, and handed Grumpkin to him, telling my good cat to be patient and wait for me. Giles touched my arm when he took Grumpkin from me, not meaning to, I think. I can still feel the place he touched.

All of which made the whole matter even more troublesome and upsetting! It seems that Weasel-Rabbit was determined to take everything away from me. First my room and then my cat! I tried to think what else I might have that Weasel-Rabbit would want, but I couldn't think of anything at all, which just shows how naive I was. The rest of her plan emerged late this afternoon, before the final banquet.

I am not supposed to go into the small anteroom adjacent to the muniments room, which is between the small and large dining halls. The anteroom is a cosy warm place where Papa's steward and bailiff and the scribe work during the daytimes and where male guests sometimes retire after dinner to play at dice or cards or chess and talk about their travels in ways they cannot do while the aunts are present. Hidden behind the tapestries is a little oriel window, covered over because it lets in the cold, and under it a low seat just large enough for me. Sometimes I go there to hide. It is the one place no one has ever found me. If one can bear the boredom of hearing the same stories over and over, one can learn quite a bit about swiving and having one's pleasure and what men of Papa's sort think of various classes and types of women. I have learned that men talk about women quite a lot, when they aren't talking about hunting or fighting, though considering that they use the same words and the same expressions for all three things, perhaps there is not much difference.

I hid there because I wanted to be alone. I was upset over Grumpkin; I was upset over how I felt about Giles; I was trying to· keep my resolution, trying very hard to exercise Christian forbearance, which Father Raymond constantly suggests that I do. At any rate, there I was in the oriel window when I heard voices through the tapestry. One, which I had learned to know well, was Sibylla's mama. The other I assumed was the abbot, for Sibylla's mama cooed at him in a tone she uses only with royalty and people of importance.

"Sibylla feels that she cannot take responsibility for the girl, Your Reverence. We have all heard about her mother." The words "her mother" were said in a very low, meaningful voice, the same tone of voice in which Aunt Tarragon talks about certain bodily functions, as though they were both repellent and inevitable. "Sibylla will undoubtedly bear children. She would not want those children exposed to . . . well, you understand. Sibylla feels, and I must concur, that it would be wisest to send Beauty to the convent where her aunts are. She can be with her kindred there. As a nun, she may perhaps expiate some of her mother's . . . well, you understand."

Evidently the abbot did understand. He hemmed and hawed, but he said he would discuss the matter with Phillip, Duke of Monfort, Westfaire, and Ylles, that is, Papa, and see if something couldn't be arranged.

Sibylla had not been content to have only my room and my cat. She also intended to have my future.

Somehow, without even intending it, I found myself back here in my tower room, at my work table with a new quill, a pad of ink, and a bottle of water. Spread out before me was the

second page of the letter from mama, which I had rolled backwards to make it lie flat. Mama's writing is not unlike my own.
We both write a fine, curly hand. There was plenty of room at
the top of the page, and the words seemed to flow out of the pen
of their own accord. "This first day of July, year of our Lord,
thirteen hundred and forty seven." The wedding was scheduled
for the following day, the fifth. Dating mama's letter back to the
first allowed four days for the letter to have been on the way
from somewhere before reaching me. When the ink was dry, I
folded the parchment up and addressed it to "Beauty, the
daughter of Duke Phillip of Monfort and Westfaire and the
Lady Elladine of Ylles." I sealed it and marked the wax with the
signet ring from the box. It shows a winged being which I take
to be an angel.

I feel rather glum as I look at what I am to wear to the
banquet, a dress provided by Aunt Lavender which has all too
obviously been made over from something previously worn by
someone else. It has achieved a pallid limpness much like that of
the cleaning rags which are always drying on the kitchenyard
wall.

I must not succumb to vanity. It does not matter how I
look.

9

LATER, MIDNIGHT

As I was about to put on the limp dress, Doll knocked on my
door and came in with a gown. It was of heavy India silk, the
color of a deep pink rose, worked with silver and seed pearls at
the neck and at the edges of the full oversleeves. Beneath the
long sleeves were tight sleeves of silver cloth and the underskirt

was of silver cloth as well, with roses embroidered in a border at the bottom. It had belonged to my mama, Doll said. All this time it had been folded away in clean linen in one of the attics, awaiting an opportunity to be worn again.

I looked across my room to the dress provided by Aunt Lavender. It was poor, ugly stuff, compared to this. Doll saw my glance and nodded.

"I saw what you were goin' to wear," she said. "Thought it wasn't nice enough. Your mama'd have a fit, seein' you in that. All her clothes are up there in the attic, and you should make use of them."

"Did you like my mama?" I asked Doll.

"Nicest lady ever," she said. "And I don't care what they all say, she wouldn't kill herself."

Well, I'd never thought she had! But there was no time to talk about it, for Doll set about getting me dressed and doing up my hair in a knot in back, with part of it flowing down. Most of the women would be wearing wimples and or headdresses with peaks or wings and veils flowing from them. I hate headdresses because they muffle up my head, but then I wash my hair a lot and most women don't. Washing the hair is dangerous because it fevers the brain, they say, but I'd never noticed mine being anymore fevered than usual.

"There now," Doll said when she was finished with me. "You look a lot like her around the eyes."

I caught her eye in the mirror, and we stared at one another, each knowing exactly what the other was thinking. She had piled my silver-gilt hair up, making it look plentiful and curly. She'd told me before that my eyelashes were as thick and black as Mama's, and my mouth curved just the way Mama's did. The dress fit like a glove, so I knew I was built the way Mama was, too, slender in the waist and nicely plump other places. I even guessed I knew why Doll had found the dress for me. She had got me up to look rather like Mama to remind Papa of Mama because Doll didn't think Mama was dead. I smiled at her and winked. She winked back.

There was no pocket in the pink gown, but it had long, full

oversleeves. I broke the seal upon the letter and pinned the letter inside my sleeve.

When I came into the hall, Papa gave me a puzzled look, as though he might have seen me somewhere before. After a bit his face cleared and I knew he had remembered. Then he looked at Weasel-Rabbit for a while, frowning. I could see him thinking that his second wife was a paltry substitute for his first. All the aunts gasped when they saw me, but they didn't dare say anything with the abbot right there at the table. I simply smiled and sat in my place. So there we all were: Sibylla and her mama and my papa and five aunts, also the abbot and Father Raymond and a little princeling from somewhere as guest of honor, looking at me with admiration and saying courtly things. As luck would have it, I was sitting between the princeling and the abbot.

My friend, Giles, was at a table just below me. I saw him watching me, and I blushed and nodded at him, letting him know I thanked him for what he had done. Father Raymond saw me see Giles, and he saw me blush and nod. I know because his brow furrowed up, the way it sometimes does, and he looked first at me, then at Giles, several times.

I waited until everyone was eating hungrily and the musicians were playing and the wine steward was going around for the second time. Then I said to the abbot, quite loudly, "Your Reverence, I have the most amazing news. Today I have received a letter from my mama."

Silence. Everyone had heard me but Papa, who was busy telling Aunt Terror about a pilgrimage, and everyone stopped chewing or talking except Papa.

I said, "It's the most wonderful thing, Your Reverence, though I'm sure you've heard many wonders in your life. I brought it to show you." And with that I tugged it out of my sleeve and spread it out on the table, using his wine flagon to hold it down flat. Everyone was whispering to everyone else. Weasel-Rabbit had gone dead pale. Her mama had little sweat beads all over her forehead. The princeling was very attentive, ready to enjoy whatever happened.

The abbot read the letter. He handed it to Father Raymond. Father Raymond read it, flushed, and gave it back to the abbot, his mouth in a funny little quirk as though he couldn't figure out whether to laugh or frown. The abbot read it again, mumbling it out loud, then it went to someone else. By this time, Papa had some idea that something was more than merely a little wrong.

The abbot rose to his feet. "I cannot unite in matrimony a man who already has a living wife," he said, loud enough for everyone to hear him well below the salt. He got Papa's attention at last. "Your daughter has received a letter from her mother. It is dated only four days ago, and thus we know you have a wife still living."

"Impossible," said Papa, going very pale.

"Ridiculous," said one or two aunts.

"I knew it," cried Aunt Terror. "I always knew she'd come back just at the wrong time!"

I need say no more about the banquet. Papa was so angry he could not speak. It wasn't an hour after I had come back up to my room that I was startled by the carpenter nailing my door shut. Over the years that poor door has had more than its share of spikes driven through it.

"You thankless wench," Papa cried. "You'll not go off like that flighty witch, your mother."

I feel I have achieved considerably more than I had intended. Disrupting the marriage seemed a good idea, merely to get even with Sibylla. Making Papa furious at me wasn't part of the plan. Papa gets so silly when he gets furious. He puts people in the dungeon and then just forgets about them. We used to have a perfectly marvelous goldsmith who made the most wonderful things. Papa got irritated at him and put him in the dungeon. A month later, Papa wanted the man to make him a new salt, but when they took him out, he was almost dead and didn't recover. Papa was fully capable of going off on another pilgrimage and just leaving me locked in the tower to die. Then, when he got back, having happened on an advantageous marriage opportunity for me, he'd probably ask, "Where's Beauty?"

Remembering what Doll said about the time Mama was nailed up in here, I went out and took the firewood rope down from the spar and coiled it up under my bed. Then I lighted a splinter at the coals of the fire and the candle from the splinter and read Mama's letter again, the first page. The page I had used ended up with the princeling. He purloined it from the abbot, probably intending to take it back to court and share it with everyone, including the King. On reading the first page over, the story of the curse sprang out at me.

Maybe I've reminded Papa of the curse and he has nailed me into the tower to protect me!

It would be nice to believe that, nicer than believing he has shut me up to starve out of pure pique. However, if Mama's Aunt Carabosse managed to get to my christening without an invitation; it is unlikely she would be forestalled by my being locked in a tower.

I do *not* want to spend the next hundred years lying in this tower room, waiting for some prince to happen by, however charming he may be. The idea is intensely unpleasant and frightening!

Now Papa is down in the stableyard, shouting at Martin. I can see him through a crack in the shutters, pointing up and yelling, while Martin holds up the lantern and shrugs his shoulders as though to say there hasn't been any rope there since I moved in. Good old Martin.

I may as well get a night's sleep. There is nothing I can do until tomorrow.

[We had foreseen all this, down to the details of dress and the menu served at dinner. We had looked deep into the Pool, Israfel and I, and we had foreseen it all.]

10

Early this morning, before light, I got dressed up in my stable-boy's clothes (the latest of the several sets I've had since I was eight), put the firewood rope back on the pulley, and let myself down into the stableyard after first letting down all the things I thought I'd need, including Mama's box. I have always had a good head for heights, gained through climbing tall trees on a dare when I was very young, which is a good thing for the tower is extremely tall. Almost as though we'd planned it, Doll and Martin were waiting for me.

"I thought that's what you were thinkin, missy," Martin said, wrinkling his nice face at me. "Clever girl. Just like your mama. She was clever. Nice, too." Then he handed me Grumpkin who settled down in my arms and began to purr.

"Doll," I asked, "did my mama leave anything for me here in the castle? Did she leave money for me or anything. A map, maybe?"

"I never heard of any such thing, dearie," she said. She sometimes called me "dearie," though no one else did.

"In the letter, she said she'd left me the means to go find her, but I don't know what she meant."

Doll looked at her feet and turned red in the face and squirmed her hands around in her apron. Martin said, "Tell her, Doll. Somebody's got to tell her."

"You mean about Mama being a witch?" I asked, flushing. "Papa said that when he nailed my door shut."

"She warn't no witch," said Doll, firmly.

"What was she then?" I asked. Looking back on it, I was frightfully stupid, but I really hadn't figured it out. It's not the kind of thing that ordinarily occurs to one.

"She was a fairy," Doll said. "And I heard the abbot talkin' to your aunts this mornin' about havin' your papa's marriage set aside because a fairy can't enter into holy matrimony, anyhow.

I've never heard that was so, but you know who gave the abbot that idea."

I did know who had given the abbot that idea. Sibylla or her mama, one or both. A fairy! I should have realized that myself! How could her aunts have been anything but fairies to go about making and changing curses. And how could she have escaped from the tower if she were not a fairy herself? It certainly explained the attitude of the herbal aunts. Fairies would be repugnant to my aunts, I suppose, totally concerned as they are with food or drink or religion. Mama's being a fairy also explained why Weasel-Rabbit wanted me shut up in a convent, and it helped explain Mama's letter. When she'd gotten involved with a mortal, she'd lost her memory of being a fairy. I suppose that's about the only way a fairy could survive married to someone like Papa, or married to any mortal. She could accept it only as long as she didn't remember anything else. Then when Papa had gone off and left her, she'd gradually regained her memory, that and the other thing.

"Am I—am I half fairy?" I asked Doll and Martin. "Does that mean anything?"

They looked at one another and shrugged. It was the kind of question I couldn't expect them to answer. In fact, the only one who might be able to answer it was Father Raymond.

"Never mind," I said as I turned and left them. I found Father Raymond at last, sitting in the orchard close. I remember the bees making such a sound when I asked him if he knew. He gave me and my boy's clothes a long look, maybe wondering how I'd escaped, but then he smiled. Father Raymond sometimes had a very gentle smile for such an old, creased face, like a sweet stalk of sunshine growing through rough clouds.

"Yes, Beauty, I knew your mama was a fairy," he told me. "She didn't tell me before she married your papa, because she didn't remember. Later, she did tell me, when the matter of your christening came up. I intended to discuss it further with her after the ceremony, just to set her mind at rest, but Duke Phillip had her locked away before I had the chance."

"Why did Mama object to my being baptized?" I asked.

He pursed his lips and made the *hmming* noise in his nose

that he makes before he answers complicated questions. "I've always understood that fairies were made when the angels were. Long before men, at any rate. There has been conjecture that there's been some mixing, since. It's said that Cain's wife was a fairy. Since the Scriptures give us no account of God creating him a human wife, it stands to reason he must have married something else, and it's unlikely an angel would have lowered herself so. On the other hand, if people have inherited fairy blood, it would explain the fascination . . ." He looked off into the distance. "Your mother had some other objection. She said something to me about the church stealing her birthright. . . ."

Mama had said that in her letter, though I did not know what she meant. "What about my baptism?" I reminded him.

"Oh. Well, fairies, being separately created, were not tainted by the original sin of our first parents, so baptism—for them—wouldn't be necessary. So much of what the Lady Elladine had to say was correct. On the other hand, if the duke is your father, and I have no real doubt of that," he blushed, obviously remembering that Papa seemed to have sired half the children in Westfaire village, "you are half mortal, and that half needed to be baptized, which your Mama had not considered, and it was properly done."

"Holy water and the white cloth around my head and everything?"

"Exactly so. Exorcised, annointed, and the chrisom bound round your head."

"Are they Christians?" I asked him. "F . . . that is, my mother's people? Or are they infidels?"

"Well now," he wrinkled his brow at me. "I don't think that question would mean much to ah . . . them. If they are immortal, then they don't die. If they don't die, they don't fear hell. If they don't fear hell, then they aren't stained by sin. If they aren't stained by sin, why would they need to be Christians? Or you can argue it frontwards to the same effect. The question of their being infidels doesn't apply, does it?"

Which just shows you that even though Father Raymond was old and a little dithery he was still capable of reasoned argument.

[Which just goes to show you how much sheer fantasy exists even outside Faery.]

"Then Mama wasn't trying to keep me from being a Christian?" I asked. "When she told Papa it wasn't necessary?" There was more to this than he had told me, but I had no idea what it was. Mama had seemed to blame religion for something to do with her people, and nothing Father Raymond had said had explained that.

"I think it more likely she just made a oversight in theology," Father Raymond said. "She thought it wasn't necessary, forgetting you were half mortal. We can't blame her, after all. I don't imagine fairies spend much time studying catechism. In any case, I was there and I heard your fairy aunts giving you some very nice gifts, and you've always been a very good girl, so don't worry your head about it."

"What nice gifts did they give me?" I asked, though Mama had already told me.

"Oh, they gave you a good nature, for one thing. And charm."

I hadn't known about those, particularly the good-nature one. Sometimes I didn't feel at all good-natured.

"By the way, Beauty," he said. "I wanted to be the one to tell you that Giles has gone away on a journey for me."

"Giles," I said stupidly. "Giles?" wanting to cry.

"He'll be away for a year or so," he said, watching me intently. I didn't say anything. After a moment he asked, "Is there something you need to tell me?"

I just stared at him, hating him. Then not hating him, just blank inside. There was a hole there that nothing would fill, ever. Father Raymond had done it for me, because he thought it was best, but I wished he hadn't.

I shook my head at him, "No, Father." I had nothing to tell him, nothing at all. There was a lump in my throat, and I could hardly get the words out. There was nothing I wanted to tell him ever again.

"Well then," he said, trying to be comforting. "Well then."

By the time Giles comes back, I will either be dead, or married, or asleep for a hundred years, or gone off looking for my mama, and who knows if I will ever return.

.
11
.

[When Elladine of Ylles had written her letter to her daughter, my hand had helped move the quill. Not that Elladine is incapable of either writing a letter or loving a daughter, but when she writes she is prolix and when she loves she is sentimental rather than sensible. She gave no thought to what would be involved in loving a half mortal child. Elladine is like others in Faery who have taken the easy way. Like Joyeause, she dabbles. Power is painful, in the getting and the keeping, and Elladine has never thought it worth the pain. So, she flutters and travels and glamorizes and enchants and now and again falls in love, sometimes with mortals. Knowing this, I inserted some words in her letter and removed many others and put the box in her hand already equipped.

Israfel and I were counting on the love of a child for its mother. We had no mothers; we have born no children; so we take the matter largely on faith, but we counted on it nonetheless. Beauty would long to see her mother, off she would go to the place we'd prepared for her, a place remote from the real worlds, a place where the Dark Lord would not think of going for any reason, in short: Chinanga.

Chinanga is one of the imaginary worlds, well off the mainline of invention. It had taken me a long time to find it, and I'd been looking for it. No one who was not looking for it would be likely to stumble over it. Elladine would get there only shortly before Beauty herself arrived (Israfel and I had arranged that, as well); once there they could get to know each other, safe in a place time could not touch. So we planned.

Further, we planned—deviously, dangerously—for Beauty to leave

Westfaire without anyone knowing she was gone. She would make use of the things in the box, and when the time was right, she would be ready!

Unfortunately, we had overlooked who she is and what she is carrying and what Westfaire is, as well. We overlooked the forces that bound them together!

Beauty did not make ready to go off in search of her mother! Instead, she found reasons for delay!]

ANOTHER TIME. ANOTHER DAY. I DON'T KNOW WHEN, YET.

In the days that followed Giles's departure, while I was still supposedly nailed into the tower, I moved freely about the stables, fretting about the three significant events soon to occur: my approaching birthday (which I was determined to survive without being victim of the curse), Papa's postponed marriage to Sibylla (to take place when he got matters straightened out with the church), and my departure in search of my mama, happenings that would occur, I presumed, more or less in that order even though I *knew* I should forget about the birthday *and* the wedding and just *go,* now, while I had the chance. Good sense said go, voices in my head said go, dreams said go, but my stomach said stay.

I found myself making excuses to go into the great hall and look at the dome, excuses to walk along the walls, peering at the mosaic floors, excuses to go upstairs and downstairs, slowly, listening to the sounds, smelling the smells. I found myself crying at odd moments at the thought of leaving Westfaire at all, and besides, as I frequently told myself, it is hard to plan a journey when one has no idea where one is going.

I'd never felt quite so alone and lost before. Always before, in the back of my mind, Giles had been there, sturdy and dependable. I'd always known I could go to him if there was real trouble. Or, Father Raymond had been there. Now Giles was gone, and since Father Raymond had sent him away, I couldn't count on him either. Papa and the aunts were just useless. Martin didn't have time to help. Doll was busy, bustling around, directing the other maids who were carrying water up and chamber pots down. I grabbed her arm and made her listen to me.

"Mama said she left me means to find her, but all she left me was this box," I told Doll. "I can't find anything helpful in it." I showed it to her. She looked at it and its contents, quickly, between doing two other things, at the packet of needles and at the signet ring with what I now recognized as a fairy on it and the three hanks of thread: heavy brown, medium black, and fine, silken white. She shook the box to see if there was anything else inside, but there was no secret compartment. It is just a wooden box, and not a very big one.

"If the Lady your mother said she left something for you, then she did," said Doll. "And if this box is all you have, then this box is what she meant. You keep it safe. Sooner or later, you'll find out what it's for." She turned away from me to tell a new servant not to use the Duchess's Staircase, which is what they called the wide curving graceful flight which comes up from the great hall.

"I wish I knew what to do with it," I complained, wishing Doll would pay attention to me. Wishing somebody would.

"Well, you could sew with it," suggested Doll, glaring at me. "That's what people usually do with needles and thread, and it would keep you from bothering me while I get this work done." She ran off after the new maid, who'd gone in the wrong direction.

My feelings were hurt, but the suggestion made sense. I went into one of the attics and scruffed around, discovering some lengths of black tussah silk, probably left over from Grandma's time. I took them and a handful of nuts and some dried apples into the empty stall I'd been occupying to keep me out of the aunts' way and sat myself down on a pile of straw to sew, which was one thing I'd learned to do pretty well in sixteen years, believe me. In the winter there's not much else to do. I've done enough cushion covers and mended enough tapestries to stretch from Westfaire to East Sawley, plus all the hours spent with Aunt Marj mending bodices or starting new tapestries that won't get finished for a hundred years. I told myself that if the curse got me, and if they went on working while I was asleep, the tapestries might be finished in time for my awakening a century from now, in 1447. The fifteenth century!

For the first time, I realized what that meant! If I slept for a hundred years, all the aunts and Papa would be dead. Papa would probably die before Sibylla did. With him gone, Sibylla would probably store my sleeping body in a cellar somewhere, if she didn't go ahead and bury me, out of spite! And then, when Sibylla died, who would come after her?

I imagined Westfaire abandoned, wrecked, sold off to pay Sibylla's debts, and I wanted to scream. And who was going to take care of a sleeping person for a hundred years? I simply couldn't see Sibylla or her children caring whether I lived to wake up or not!

I made myself stop thinking about it by laying out the fabric and the thread and measuring both carefully to see whether there was enough to make a cloak. Straight cloaks are very easy. Father Raymond taught me the pattern, because they're almost the same as the monks wear, except the monks' don't open down the front. First you cut one flat piece as long as from your shoulders to your heels and wider across than your shoulders, for the back. Then you cut four more pieces, the same length and half that wide. Two of these are for the front. The third one gets cut in half, and then each piece folded in half again for sleeves. The last one gets cut in half, and one of the halves gets folded with one end sewed shut for the hood. The hood piece gets gathered on at the neck, which is the hardest part, and if you're not careful it leaves an ugly bunch of puckers on the inside. If you want to get fancy, you can use the other sleeve-sized piece to make pockets. Since I had a lot of time on my hands, I got fancy and made great deep pockets on both sides. By noon, I had it mostly done except for sewing braid around the hood and down the front to finish it off. I'd used the sides of the cloth, what Dame Blossom calls the self-edge, for the edges of the sleeves and front, so all I had to hem up was the bottom. I heard Doll's voice outside, so I put it on and went out to show her.

I stood there, turning around for her to admire me, and she looked right through me at Martin and said, "Where's Beauty?"

"Don't know," said Martin. "Haven't seen her since this morning early."

"The whole herb garden met and decided they didn't dare let her out of the tower because of her Papa," said Doll. "They say he'll be home for her birthday celebration and he'll let her out then."

I walked a little closer to Doll, flapped my cloak arms at her. She didn't even blink.

"But then they decided she might starve by then," Doll went on. "They're in there now, tryin to decide what to do about that."

"How do they expect to feed her?" Martin snorted. "Send nut meats up by pigeon?"

Martin didn't see me. Doll didn't see me. They weren't pretending not to see me; they really didn't see me. It took me a moment, but I finally realized why. The black thread had sewn a cloak of invisibility, which is something a fairy gift might be expected to do. It was all perfectly logical. I went back in the stall and took the cloak off, wrapped it in the sack I'd brought my things down in, then came out again carrying the mostly finished cloak wrapped in a neat bundle.

"There you are, Beauty," Doll said at once. "Your aunts decided they couldn't let you loose without making your father murderous at them, but they're not planning on letting you starve, either, though you'd be a bit hungry by the time they agree on how they'll get you fed. No point in having Martin haul you back up there, far's I can see. Do you want to hide out here in the stables or up in the servant's quarters? There's empty rooms up there."

I said I'd stay in the stables, as it was airier and cooler than the attics where the maids lived, though the flies were much worse. The fact that the aunts wouldn't turn me loose made me very curious as to what was going on, so I went around the corner, put my new cloak back on and wandered into the castle to hear what I could hear. Not surprisingly, no one noticed me. No one at all except Grumpkin, who insisted on trailing along, batting at my skirts just as he always did. Fairy things don't impress cats. Fairy things and holy things. Cats are, perhaps, a separate creation.

I drifted along to my old rooms near the kitchen, wanting to know just what Sibylla was up to, and a good thing I did, for the little Weasel-Rabbit was up to nothing good.

"She has to die," she was snarling to her mother as I sneaked in through the slightly open door. "Duke Phillip's daughter must die."

She disliked calling me, "Beauty," I'd noticed. She usually referred to me as "Duke Phillip's daughter." There were certainly a lot of people wanting me dead. Evil fairy aunts. Wicked stepmothers.

"I had thought," her mother said in a fussy little coo, "I really had thought that having her enter the convent at Alderbury would be sufficient."

"Not at all," said Weasel-Rabbit. "I've spent all morning going over things with Phillip's steward. In the marriage agreement between Phillip and Elladine, she tied up her dowry for her children. If that girl goes into a convent, the convent will claim Elladine's estate as dowry. They certainly won't let the girl into the convent without one!"

"I thought their marriage could be set aside!"

"If the marriage is set aside, the Duke will have *no* right to the estates in Ylles. If there had been no marriage, there could have been no dowry. If the one did not exist, certainly neither did the other!" Sibylla stamped her foot in vexation. "No, the only way is if she dies. With her dead, Phillip will inherit everything she owns."

"Why is it so important? Surely there is enough here . . ."

Sibylla laughed, a long, mirthless laugh. "Oh, Mother, we have miscalculated most stupidly. There is little or nothing left here. Affairs are in a shocking state. The estates in Ylles and Castle Westfaire itself are virtually the only property the man has not pledged to the moneylenders. The only reason he hasn't pledged the estates in Ylles is that he has not been free to do so. Beauty seems to own them, though I believe she is not aware of that fact. The Duke never talks to her about anything, thank

God. He scarcely knows she is alive except when she annoys him. He will not grieve greatly when she is gone."

I found myself crouching along the wall, my face wet. I knew what she said was the truth, but it was very hard to hear.

"It is unheard-of to pledge land," Sibylla's mama whined. "No nobleman of honor would pledge land. Why has he not sold his villeins their freedom instead? Or pledged the crops?"

Even I knew the answer to that question, but I remained silent, wiping at my eyes, as Weasel-Rabbit answered.

"He has done all that. I think he would have sold his soul if it had brought him a few guineas. Evidently there was an indebtedness left from the rebuilding of Westfaire in a previous generation. Phillip's father speculated in order to clear this indebtedness and succeeded only in increasing it. Phillip himself goes to shrines and prays for a fortune. He feels only divine intervention will save him."

"Perhaps we had best try again, with someone better off."

"We haven't the time or money to try again," snarled Sibylla. "The estates at Ylles have good revenues, and though we have not seen them, undoubtedly they will do well enough!"

"Ah," said Weasel-Rabbit's mother in a discontented voice. "I suppose it must be done before Phillip finds out your own dowry is as much fakery as the wealth he promised us. He won't be impressed by hired carriages for long."

Well, well, I thought as I wandered out into the corridor again. Here was a pretty mess. Papa wanted to marry a fortune. Sibylla wanted to marry a fortune. Both pretended to have one, and both were as poor as lackeys. Who had the fortune? I did. Or rather, Mama did, since she was alive and well, assuming she was alive and well, which I did assume. Though there had been no recent word of her (despite the letter I had misdated), I simply knew that she had suffered no harm. Something inside me declared this to be incontrovertibly so. She was waiting for me, and I had to go to her.

As I was lost in contemplation, Sibylla came out into the hallway and let out a screech to wake the dead. Grumpkin was there, playing with an invisible something, and Sibylla shrieked for someone to come kill the animal at once. I swept him up, hiding him in a fold of the cloak, and went back out to the stables while she had hysterics behind me, screaming about a cat that had disappeared. My only thought was that my life wasn't worth a fig in that place.

"Where is Ylles?" I asked Martin.

"Eels?" he queried. "In the river, Beauty, some seasons. And in the sea others, so I hear."

"Not the fish, Martin. The place. A town, maybe?"

Doll came out just then, so I asked her as well. She didn't know.

"Mama signed her letter 'Elladine of Ylles,'" I told her. "That means it has to be a place, somewhere."

No one knew. I told Doll to ask Aunt Terror and Aunt Basil, but neither of them had ever heard of Ylles, except as an adjunct to Mama's name, and they got quite offended at being asked by a servant. So I went to the anteroom where Papa's steward keeps things. He wasn't there, or the scribe either, for which I was very grateful. The man always wanted to touch me, just a little. Hand on wrist. Arm against arm. Brushing against me in the hall. You know the kind of thing. Whenever I smiled at him, he melted down into a puddle and just lay there, quivering with inarticulate desire. There is something intensely repugnant about people wanting you in that way. That is, unless you want them back.

I could find nothing that helped. So far as the contracts were concerned, none of them gave direction to Ylles. By the time I had looked through all the dusty scrolls that seemed at all likely to tell me anything, I was starving.

I stopped in the kitchens to sneak some supper. Cold game pie and a lump of cheese out of the firkin in the storeroom. In the stables I chewed and stared at the other hanks of thread, a brown one and a white one. The brown thread was heavy and waxy. It looked familiar to me, and after a time I figured out that it looked like the thread the shoemaker in the village used. Thread to sew leather, which could mean anything at all. I had no way of knowing what. Something kept teasing at me, as though someone might be trying to whisper words in my ear, and I shook my head in annoyance. If I was half fairy, it had to be my bottom half, for my head told me nothing useful. I put the thread down, and found myself picking it up again. Put it down, pick it up. At length I got tired of thinking about it and went to sleep in the hay with Grumpkin curled up beside me.

[I have said elsewhere that Beauty is not particularly intelligent. The sewing kit was the simplest, easiest method Israfel and I could think of to let her seek her mother with the magical powers to which she was born. She has already sewn a cloak; common sense should dictate that the other threads will sew other magical garments! Stories of such garments are current in every hamlet! I cannot recall ever having felt quite so frustrated before. She will need the other garments very soon! I keep whispering, "Use the thread and needles," but all she does is yawn!]

I was so weary from it all that I didn't wake up until the middle of the night when I heard people shouting. They were shouting because the dove tower was burning. Of course, I wasn't in it, though no one but Doll and Martin knew that. Except for my carpet, nothing I treasured was in it, which was a good thing because there was little enough left of the tower when the flames were finally extinguished.

I went to Father Raymond, being very cool and dignified, and told him I'd escaped sure death because I hadn't been in my room. I said I believed Sibylla had set the fire. I told him why. I said my life wasn't worth a rotten apple in that place anymore, and I was going away very soon to join my mama. I said that, once I was well away, he could tell everyone I'd gone on a pilgrimage. That would prevent Sibylla laying hands on my dowry lands. He asked me where, and I said I wasn't sure, but I'd figure it out when I got started.

"Oh, Beauty," he sighed at me. "I suppose I might have expected it." He reached for my hand, but I stepped away from him. He had sent Giles away without talking to me about it, and therefore he was no longer really my friend.

"I'm not going until after my birthday, though," I said in a formal voice which only shook a little. "Which is day after to-morrow."

"If you're determined to go, I should think going before would be safer," he advised me. "Just in case there's something to the curse. Or another fire."

"There is undoubtedly *something* to the curse," I said, "Just as there is undoubtedly *something* to Sibylla's burning the tower. However, I will simply not be driven from my home before I am ready to go!" The truth was that the thought of leaving made me so panicky and scared I couldn't do it. I kept putting it off, until this, until that.

"What shall I tell your aunts?" he asked. "They'll wonder why you aren't dead?"

"Tell them I escaped certain death through a miracle. An angel wakened me and opened the door to let me out." I thought I was being pert, but he told them exactly that. Sometimes I think Father Raymond doesn't take things as seriously as he pretends to. Except love. He saw I loved Giles, and he took that seriously. I did love Giles. I do love Giles.

Between the fire and Father Raymond's mention of the curse, I decided it was time to make a few defensive plans. While Sibylla and her mama muttered in the corner and I sat safely among the aunts, being exclaimed over for having occasioned divine intervention, I came up with a stratagem.

The working of it was dependent upon the fact that Beloved knew nothing at all about the curse. It was not something that had been generally discussed (though the aunts had whispered about it when they thought I couldn't hear). Even I had not known of it until I read the first page of Mama's letter, but no one knew about that page of the letter but me. Add to this the fact that Beloved adored parties. She loved being "me." As a result, on the following day, she eagerly fell in with my plan that she play my part on my birthday in order that for a few hours I might escape—so I told her—the edge of Sibylla's tongue. We had spent hours talking over every aspect of the Sibylla matter, and Beloved liked her no better than I did.

Papa was to be home for the celebration. Of the neighboring nobility, a few of the nearest had been invited to a modest banquet in honor of the occasion. Beloved and I spent some time going over the guest list so that she would know who they were and how to address them. She loved to speak the affected Frenchiness of the aristocracy rather than the uncouth but lively tongue of the common people, and she did it so well that no one knew she had not been reared in the castle. We shared this ability of mimicry, she and I, which we must mutually have inherited from Papa, though I had never known him to make use of it.

Very early on our birthday morning, she came to my room —the room I was using in Papa's wing, though I had slept in the stables overnight, just to be safe—and put on my clothes. I told her to be careful of her language and not to look for me until dark. Then I went out, put on my cloak and waited halfway down the Duchess's Staircase to see what happened. As I had more or less expected, by midmorning Beloved was being fussed over and adorned and prepared for the banquet, while the aunts peered into corners (looking for spindles no doubt) and made little cooing calls to the Virgin for protection against evil as they fingered their missals in their pockets.

Grumpkin was not fooled. He knew who was who, and he insisted upon following me about in a worried fashion, so I tucked him into one of the deep pockets, his large, scowling face peering out, visible to me but invisible to anyone else. Though he was a big, heavy cat, I preferred to do this rather than shut him up in the stables. Later, of course, I was to thank God that I had done so. God. Or someone.

[Not I! Israfel and I had never concerned ourselves with her cat!]

Afternoon came. The guests began to arrive for the banquet, which Aunts Lovage and Basil had arranged to be held in the late afternoon or very early evening in order to allow the guests to get home before full dark. The aunts buzzed about in a flurry of hospitality, and I saw Beloved, momentarily ignored, looking annoyed, as though she had a pain. I saw her yawn and lick her teeth. I followed her as she wandered back through the large dining hall and opened the door leading to the enclosed garden outside the high windows.

I knew then that her expression had been the result of simple hunger. She had been so busy being dressed and fussed over, she hadn't had any lunch, and now she was starved and had remembered the apricot tree in that garden. We'd spent many stuffed and sticky July afternoons there, fighting the wasps for the fruits. The moment the door opened, I smelled them, heavy as incense, more fragrant than I had ever known them to be before.

Grumpkin muttered something and put a paw on my hand. I stopped to hush him before following her. "Be still," I said. "You don't want her to know we're here." Then I went out after Beloved, arriving just in time to hear a fading burst of cackling laughter and catch a glimpse of a pair of burning eyes disappearing in midair.

[I had let myself be seen. Now surely *she would leave Westfaire and go in search of Elladine. I had put the thread in her hands a dozen times! Surely now she would go where we had planned for her to go, where we could protect what she carried, forever if need be. I faded into invisibility and remained there, watching, mentally urging her to go.]*

Beloved was facing me, weaving a little on her legs, a look of faint astonishment in her eyes. Though she could not have seen me, her right hand was extended as though to hand me something. It was a spindle, precisely as it had been described to me: a spiky thing that looked rather like a spinning top. I put my hands behind my back. The spindle fell even as I moved toward her, and she went down with it, crumpling, knees and hips and then shoulders and arms, falling in a loose pile, like washing. I kicked the spindle thing away and knelt beside her. Her face was quite peaceful, as though she was sleeping, as indeed she was, though a sleep of a strange and terrible depth. Her breast barely moved. Her skin was chill. A pallor had fallen over her skin so that she seemed to be carved of ivory.

For a moment, I could not think at all. My mind was blank. I straightened Beloved out, pulled her skirts down and folded her hands on her breast, my tears spotting the satin of her bodice. I left the spindle where I had kicked it, not daring to touch it. I hadn't really. . . . I had thought the curse wouldn't function if it couldn't find me. . . . I had never considered that. . . . Or had I? I didn't know. Had I planned it, or not? The wording of the final curse referred to "Duke Phillip's daughter on her birthday." She was as much his daughter as I was. It was her birthday as much as mine. I had known that!

I fled back through the dining room, seeking help, and was sent sprawling when I tripped over the body of one of the footmen lying beside a trayload of scattered flagons. In my daze, I assumed he had seen what happened to Beloved and had fainted. Even when I reached the hallway and began to find other bodies, I did not immediately realize what had happened. Only when I found Aunt Lavender fallen prone across her lute did I realize that the malediction had been modified by Aunt Joyeause not only to send Duke Phillip's daughter to sleep, but to include everyone at Westfaire. I had worried about what people would do with a princess who slept for a hundred years! It seemed they would do nothing at all, for she was not to sleep alone. When she regained consciousness, a hundred years in the future, all her court would still be around her, though it was not Beloved's court, but mine.

I found Doll and Martin asleep in the stables and Dame Blossom asleep at her loom. In the village, everyone slept. The shoemaker and the tailor and the potter and the tanner and all. I howled for some little time, as frightened as I have ever been, while I ran about through the barns and stables, the armory, the dormitories of the men-at-arms, the kitchens, the granary, the orchards, through every house in the village by the walls. Everyone was asleep, guests and all. Every living thing. The cattle in the byre were asleep, and the chickens in their pens, and the swine, the piglets laid out like rows of barely breathing bottles at their mother's swollen teats. Wasps slept on the fruit on the sunlit walls. Spiders slept in their webs. The weevil slept at the

heart of the rose. Papa's dogs lay indolently in the sun, as unmoving as the painted wooden saints in the chapel.

And in that chapel Father Raymond slept beside Papa—
who had arrived home only that morning—both of them on a
bench, propped upright by each others bodies. Papa's mouth
was open and the faint, infrequent breaths hissed across my ear
when I leaned down to shake him. I inadvertently dislodged him
so that he fell sidewise, onto the bench, but his sleep did not
break, nor did that of Father Raymond when I clung to him,
wetting his surplice with my tears. He held a piece of paper in
his hand. Evidently something he and Papa had been looking at.
It caught my eye because I saw my name on it.

It was addressed to Father Raymond. "Tell Beauty that I
love her forever," it said. "Tell her I honor her always. Tell her I
would never have done anything to hurt her. Tell her no matter
what distance separates us, I will love her still." It was signed by
Giles. Father Raymond had not shown it to me. He had shown it
to Papa! I hated them both for that, but I could not stand there
doing it. I put the letter in my pocket and ran on.

The sleepers included even Sibylla and her mother. I found
them in the scribe's office, lying atop Mama's marriage contract
in an uncomfortable looking heap. I left them that way, hoping
when they woke they would have cramps. Of all living things in
all the lands of Westfaire, only Grumpkin and I were free to
move about because we were cloaked in magic and invisible to
the enchantment. Grumpkin wanted to leave my pocket, but I
did not dare let him go.

I cannot remember what I did then for a while. Though a
few other guests had been expected, none arrived. It was as
though the castle had been set aside from mortal lands. The sun
sank slowly, and I with it. For a time I huddled on the stairs,
crying, Grumpkin patting my face with his paws and making
the small, trilling noise he makes when he seeks catly companionship, his love call. I clung to him and wept. I reread Giles's
letter and wept.

Tears changed nothing. Eventually, my eyes dried and I realized I had no choice but to go. There was no way I could stay
in this place. No way I could maintain myself. I made myself

think carefully about going away, made myself consider calmly the things I would need to take with me, gritting my teeth so hard that later my jaws hurt. I needed money. The keys to Papa's chest were around his neck, and the coin he had available, poor though Sibylla had said he was, was locked in the chest in his room. Also in the chest were two warrants making claims upon usurers in London, and I took them both. Papa or his man-of-business had evidently tried to delay the final reckoning by deferring payment of current expenses and putting current income into the hands of the Jews to collect interest. Usury was a sin for Christians, but then so was lust, and Papa had not balked at that. I think anything done to excess must be sinful, including pilgrimages, but if so the poor man was paying for his sins. If he had not neglected Mama, I kept telling myself, none of this would have happened.

The aunts had some jewels, which I did not hesitate to purloin. They would not need them for one hundred years, and I needed them now. There was the Monfort parure of emeralds and diamonds that Papa intended to give Sibylla for a wedding gift. I took that, too, though I suspected the gems might not be the real ones. Surely Papa had sold them, poor as he was. I wondered how much Papa had received for the jewels when he had sold them and what he had spent it on. If, indeed, Grandfather had not sold the emeralds in his own time and put the money into rebuilding Westfaire.

The last thing I did before I left was to drag Beloved in from the garden. I could not carry her up the stairs into my tower room, which seemed most fitting, but then, what is fitting at such a time? Where are Sleeping Beauties supposed to lie? Towers come inevitably to mind. Towers or perhaps bowers or enchanted tombs of glass. I could manage none of them. Half fairy or no, I had no powers that I was aware of. Perhaps my mama would have managed better. Besides, the tower was burned and there was nothing there except my mysterious thing, sitting untouched upon the window ledge, with charcoal all about it.

As it was, I got Beloved onto the table in the small dining room and covered her with a brocade hanging, bringing it neatly up under her chin, placing a cushion under her head, doing what I could to make her long sleep a comfortable one. I wondered if she would turn over in that sleep and found myself giggling hysterically at the thought. "I'm sorry Beloved," I cried. "Sorry!"

It was pure hypocrisy. Suppose I had known what was going to happen, wouldn't I have done the same thing again? I may even have known what would happen without admitting it to myself. Even then I caught myself thinking, better Beloved than I. She would be thrilled to be awakened by a prince, and why not? It was a far finer fate than a weaver's daughter could ordinarily expect.

As I stood looking at her, I was aware of two things: first, that Westfaire was redolent of that odor I had always associated with the chapel; and second, that there was an aura of glamour which flowed from Beloved's form in a swelling tide. When I went out into the hall, the aura came after me, a shining mist of silent mystery, an emanation of the marvelous. Every stone of the hallway throbbed with it, giving my footsteps back to me like the slow beat of a wondrous drum or some great heart that pulsed below the castle, making the very stones reverberate with its movement. Above me the lacelike fan vault sparkled like gems; through the windows the sunbeams shimmered with a golden, sunset glow. Once outside, I looked up at the towers and caught my breath, for they had never seemed so graceful. Over the garden walls the laburnum dangled golden chains, reflowered on this summer evening as though it were yet spring. In fact, springtime had miraculously returned. In the corners the lilacs hung in royal purple trusses, and roses filled the air with a fragrance deep as smoke.

All around me beauty wove itself, beauty and the strange, somehow familiar smell of the place. Westfaire became an eternal evening in an eternal May, the sun slanting in from the west as though under a cloud, making the orchards and gardens gleam in a green as marvelous as the light in the gems I carried. Slowly the sun moved down, and I feared it would not rise again on Westfaire for a hundred long years.

I took myself away from the castle, across the wide gardens

and lawns to the tall inner walls built when the castle was re-
newed. Outside these walls the moat reached around from the
lake on one side to the lake on the other, filled by its waters.
The heavy bridge was down. My footfalls thudded on the tim-
bers as I crossed, then fell silent in the dust of the village street.
Little shops and houses huddled in quiet, thatch glowing like
gold, walls flushed by sun. Beyond the village lay the paddocks
and the commons, and past them the outer walls, all that was
left of the first Westfaire, built so long ago that men had forgotten when—low, massive ramparts with squat watchtowers and
a fanged portcullis—and beyond that the final bridge and the
road leading to the outside world.

I went out, hearing my lonely footsteps, remembering the
sounds of carriages and horsemen, listening in the silence for a
sound that did not come. Beyond the last bridge, at the limit of
the castle lands, I stopped in amazement to confront a waist-
high hedge of briar rose which rustled with savage and implaca-
ble life, pulsing in the smell of magic as it grew ever taller. Was
this part of the curse or part of the amelioration? To either side
of me the hedge stretched in a wide circle, enclosing the outer
walls, reaching back on either side to the shores of the lake,
hiding what had always been my home.

I pushed my way through, crying out as the thorns tore at
my arms, thankful for the thick fabric of the cloak I wore. Once
outside the limits of the enchantment, I took off the cloak and
changed my clothes. It would not do for a woman to walk about
on the roads alone, though it was safer in the country than in
the cities, where gangs of youths roamed about seeking unprotected women to abuse and ruin. I had already decided to wear
my grubby boy clothes, which would attract no one's interest.
Then, tears still running down my face, with my hair twisted up
under a grubby cap, and with everything I owned in a sack over
my shoulder, I went away from there. At the roadside not far
distant stood a pale arm of stone which emerged from the forest
in a tumbled wall topped by a rock shaped like a cat's head.
Under that rock was a little cave Grumpkin and I had discovered
long ago. We called it the cathole. It was a place to secrete trea-
sures, a place for Grumpkin to hide in, a place I had hidden in

once or twice myself as a little child, though I had outgrown it long since. Now I stopped and put most of the wealth I carried inside it, stopping the opening with a few head-sized stones well wedged into place with smaller bits of rock. The aunts had often warned against the robbers at large in the world, robbers and ruffians and villains of all sorts. Hiding a part of what I had would save it against later need.

I kept some coin in my sack. Though they might not be real, I kept the emeralds wrapped up in rags: collar, circlet, two brooches, and a bracelet. I kept one warrant on a usurer. The rest of the jewelry and coin and the other warrant, I secreted away. Once this was done, I started on my way again, wishing I had a horse. It had been a weary and frightening day.

As I came from behind the stone, I saw a shattered gleam of sun on the flower-gathering hill, as though a man in armor had moved and reflected the light. I thought of Giles, my heart leaping up. He had known I needed him and had come home! Grumpkin cried, and I held him in my arms as I ran toward that gleam of light, telling myself it was Giles, it couldn't be Giles, perhaps it was only a knight, but perhaps he had a spare horse he might let me ride, or even a horse and saddle I might buy. I had not gone far before Grumpkin snarled, sensing presences I did not. He would not have snarled at Giles.

[We had not foreseen this! We had planned on Mary Blossom taking Beauty's place, but we had not foreseen this!]

The men and women I came upon were doing something incomprehensible. They moved among contrivances, among strange apparatus, boxes which hummed and winked and made noises like the midnight peeps of startled birds. There were five persons, some men, some women, though it was hard to tell which were which. They were clad much alike, and my impression of maleness and femaleness came more from stance and stature than from any other regard.

I saw them before they saw me. I should have stopped, turned, gone somewhere else, but it is a measure of my distraction and pain that I simply kept walking, mouth open, eyes fixed on them, wondering vaguely who they were and what they were doing on the May flower hill.

[Nothing in our calculations had included this! These people came from a time the Pool could no longer reach, a time beyond the veil, where I could not see. . . .]

"Did you get time lapse shots of the hedge?" the oldest of the men cried, his voice urgent.

"Time lapse, hell," answered the tallest, heaviest man, his eye fixed to the end of the convoluted box he held upon his shoulder. "It's fast enough to show without lapse. Look at the damn thing! It's fairly crawling into the sky!"

I turned. The hedge had grown up behind me and was now higher than my head. Tendrils at the top reached upward like hands, clutching at the clouds. I felt a sob pressing upward and choked it down. Now was no time to give way, however much I needed to do so.

"What are you doing?" I cried, stepping from behind the bush.

[I actually reached out to stop her, but she moved too quickly.]

They turned, mouths open, staring. Almost simultaneously, two who had not spoken before said:

"Oh, shit!"

"That's torn it. Hell!"

Not a polite greeting, considering everything, though not necessarily hostile.

"What in the bloody hell are you doing here?" asked one of the women in an offended voice. "There's not supposed to be anyone here!" Her accent was strange. It took me a moment to figure out what she had said.

I shook my head, almost unable to respond. "Coming home," I mumbled. "From market."

I saw them mouthing the words, having the same difficulty I had had in understanding what they heard. Evidently my tongue was not their native speech.

The oldest man turned to one of others, throwing up his hands. "What do we do about this, Alice?"

"How the hell am I supposed to know, Martin," the one called Alice replied. "If this shows up on the monitors, they'll have our guts for dinner."

"What's your name, boy?" Martin asked. His gray hair was combed back from his face, almost as short as the woman's.

"I am Havoc, the miller's son," I mumbled. It was the name I had used with Martin since I was tiny. There was no time or need to invent another.

"Damn," he said again, thrusting parts of his apparatus into cases. "Jaybee, you got enough footage? Bill, ready? There are only minutes left."

The man addressed as Bill turned his face toward me, grimacing. He was shorter than I, the height of a child, with hair the color of ripe apricots, and he wore the same kind of singlet and trousers as the others. "Ready," he said, staring at me with something like pity in his eyes.

I did not understand the word "footage."

"Janice?"

The other woman looked into the eyes of her contrivance and nodded. "Plenty," she said in a cold voice. Her hair was white as snow, but she was not an old woman. Her eyes when she looked up at me were hard and black, like fowls' eyes.

"What are you doing here?" I wanted to know.

The white-haired woman laughed, a quick bark of laughter. "A documentary, boy. We are recording the vanishment of magic from England—and from the world. Now, do you know any more than you did before?"

"That isn't true," I said, shaking my head. "No."

"Not yet," she smiled. "But soon."

The one called Jaybee stared at me as he had been since I came from behind the bush. His jaw moved restlessly, like that of a boar pig, and I resolved to stay away from him, for tushes or no, he had that look to him which says all pigs are sows to him. "We need to get rid of this kid," he said, glaring at me. "I'll do it."

"No!" shouted the Alice one. "Killing him would show up on the monitors. Don't! We've only got a minute left."

Jaybee sneered at her and grabbed me by the shoulder. When he jerked me, my hat fell off and my hair tumbled down. He shouted, then laughed and grabbed me up from behind, one great hand clamped on each arm near the shoulder, holding my arms tight as he turned me toward a thing standing behind us, like a great barrel with a door in it. On my shoulder, Grumpkin snarled and scratched at him, but he paid no heed. Both of us were thrust through the door and the others tumbled in after us, all of them shrieking at Jaybee, telling him to put me out, and him fending them off while holding onto me.

Alice staggered to a certain part of the barrel where there were buttons and a flickering of light. She bent over them, muttering. Then we were all twisted inside out. I was. I presume the others were, for Janice cried out and then cursed. Grumpkin screamed. So did I. It felt as though I were being slowly torn apart from inside by rats.

[As was I, for I took hold of the thing she was in and went with her. Or tried. A barrier stretched from the bottom of the world to the top, from side to side. Impenetrable. My powers were absorbed by it, like a sponge. I could not move it. I could not get through. I was being sucked dry, sucked out, killed. I felt Beauty leaving me and could do nothing about it at all. And then she was gone. What she carried was gone with her. All our hopes gone. I was still there, sitting on the hill and weeping when Israfel found me, I who had not wept since the fountains of the deep were sealed.]

Then everything stopped. Quiet came. The pain went away. The others began to stir and bend and mutter. And the little man, Bill, opened the door into the twenty-first century.

12

MY LIFE IN THE LATER CENTURIES

·

"I want her," said Jaybee. "She's mine." His fingers were making holes in my arms.

"No," Alice snarled at him, her voice like a whip. "You've gotten us all into enough trouble. You were a stupid fool to drag her along. They're already watching you! Risk your own life all you like, but you're not going to get me killed. Get out of here! Do something to distract the guards at the door, and maybe they won't see there's an extra person!"

"Let Bill take her," said Martin. "Nobody'll bother Bill. I'll see to the guards." He pushed me at the little man and then walked away behind the scowling Jaybee, talking loudly, gesturing, making people look at him.

Bill held me by one wrist. He gave me no time to see anything. I had an impression of grayness, of round things like lance shafts hung across a wall. All sounds echoed, dwindling away in reverberations, as though we were in a great stone hall. I remember a mighty clamor of voices. Some were ours and echoes, but there were others. One of the women said, "Get that animal out of sight. Hide her hair."

Choking down a curse, I put Grumpkin under my shirt and held him there, feeling his ragged breathing against my belly and his claws in my skin. Bill bundled up my hair and pushed my cap down on my head. He must have picked it up when it fell off.

"Now! The guards are looking the other way! Get her out of here, hurry."

The little man pulled me along with amazing strength. He was not much larger than Papa's fool, but he was very powerful. He dragged me up a flight of stairs that clanged under our feet like swords upon armor.

The women were behind us. One of them said, "God, there's a pop-patrol." I heard it as one word, "popatrol." I looked for it, thinking it must be some kind of dangerous animal, but saw nothing except heads and legs, people moving in all directions, up and down and across, all dressed alike, all looking alike. The surface we walked upon was full of tiny holes. Another such surface was above. There were feet above us, tramping down on us, thousands of feet. Below us were the heads of people, moving fast or slow, thousands of heads, arms swinging below them, feet at the bottom, and below them, more heads and arms and feet. There were people on all sides. I wanted to scream. I think there were beggars, for some of the people rattled canisters beneath our noses as they cried, "Fidipur, fidipur."

"Get off here," the woman said from close behind.

Bill jerked me to one side. We ran down a corridor that moved beneath our feet, weaving through clots of people moving more slowly. I stumbled when the corridor ended, only to be hauled up and dragged onto another one. There were several more corridors that moved slow or fast. People stared at me curiously. I lost my footing and fell down and was jerked upright by my panting escort. Suddenly we were standing on an unmoving surface in front of a door. Bill put his hand flat on a place at the side of it. The door opened, and we were inside somewhere with the door shut behind us and the noise mostly gone, though I could still feel it rumbling in my feet. I felt the scream bubbling in me.

"Home-sweet-home," said Bill. Much of what he said was unintelligible, and I've doubtless got a lot of it wrong, but I know he said "home-sweet-home," because he always said it, whenever he came in.

"And what's your name again?" he asked me.

I swallowed the scream and started to say, "Havoc." No point in that. He knew I was a girl. "Beauty," I said, in a kind of mumble, trying to see on all sides of me at once. I would not have called it home-sweet-home. It was tiny, half the size of my tower room, full of complicated surfaces, with more of those ropes on the walls, very straight, like lances. When we brushed them with our bodies, they clanged.

"Mind the pipes," said Bill. "You'll knock off a steam valve, and then where'll we be?"

I shook my head at him, signifying I did not know either where we were or would be or what a pipe or a steam valve was. I must have looked frightened, for he became less cheerful and tried to soothe me. "It's all right," he murmured. "Just sit down and relax. Sit down. It's all right."

Grumpkin heard him if I did not, for the cat came out from under my shirt all in one movement and crouched at my feet yowling.

"He's hungry," I said. I knew he was, because I was. We had not eaten during all that grieving time at Westfaire. And now—I had the feeling much time had passed.

"What do they eat?" he asked me, pointing to the cat.

I could not imagine anyone not knowing what cats eat. "Milk," I told him. "Meat. Eggs. What any animal eats."

"Milk," he said, laughing. "Meat. Eggs. Ha, ha. Ha."

It was not amused laughter. It was bitter laughter, the kind Papa's fool sometimes got up to when he remembered his wife who had run away with his children.

"You don't have any?" I asked.

"Have none. Have never seen any. Would not know any if I saw them."

"What do you feed your animals? What do you eat?" I asked him in amazement.

"We have no animals. We couldn't have both animals and Fidipur. We eat orange one and two. Green one through four. Red one through five, though I don't much care for three. The original white series, all ten of them." He turned to open a door in the wall and take from it a bowl of things. Wafers. Little flat cakes. Orange ones, and dead green, and pottery red, and white, with numbers stamped upon them. He waved the bowl at me, offering. "It doesn't take much to feed me, so I've got more than I need. 'Balanced protein and fiber with all necessary vitamins and minerals.' "

I didn't know what he meant, but I took a green thing and nibbled at it. It did not taste like anything, and yet I could not honestly say it tasted nasty. I would not have thought it was food, yet I could tell it would stifle hunger. I gave a piece of it to Grumpkin. He sniffed at it, crunched a bit of it, then yowled again.

"They go better," Bill said, "if you have a bit of water along with them. White one and two actually have taste."

"I would prefer beer or wine to water," I said.

"Ha," he muttered. "Ha, ha. Ha."

"You have no beer or wine?" I guessed. Only fools drank water. One could grow ill, drinking water.

"No wine. No beer. Nothing that takes food to make. The food must go directly to Fidipur."

A god, I thought. Some kind of religious being? Perhaps an ogre or dragon that demanded sacrifice? Had I fallen among the heathen? Or were they Christians still? I felt it might be danger-ous to ask that question.

"And you have no meat or milk?"

"That would take grain, also, which must go directly to Fidipur." He gazed at me. "How old are you."

"Sixteen," I replied, honestly enough. As of today, I was sixteen. Only, of course, it wasn't today.

"Oh, God," he sighed. "A minor."

"No," I told him. "I am a miller's son." I wasn't, but Havoc was, so to speak.

"I mean you're not yet eighteen," he explained. "In our society, you're not considered a full citizen until you're eigh-teen."

"What am I then?" I asked.

He shrugged. "A person we don't want to come to the at-tention of the pop-patrol, that much I know. If they find you, they'll find you don't have an implant. Then they'll wonder how anybody could get here without an implant. Then they'll question you with the truth machines and find out how you got here, and then it will be my neck. Mine and the rest of the team. They'll claim Janice did sloppy research, or one of us fouled up on the trip, and it'll be the disposal chutes for all of us. There wasn't supposed to be anyone around while we were filming. We can't be seen, not that far back, or we risk upsetting history, changing it! No one was supposed to see us."

If I had not subverted the curse, there would not have been anyone around. His trouble was my fault, if anyone's. "Tell me again why no one was supposed to see you?" I asked.

He explained at great length, waving his arms and striding to and fro across the tiny room. It had to do with history, with changing things that had already happened, which might change other things in the now. He used words I didn't know. Permutations of the possible. Linked events. Making a closed loop that would pinch off. I didn't understand much of it. He glared at me and shouted, "I don't know what to do with you. Jaybee and Martin expect me to put you down the disposal chute, but I don't want to do that. We'll have to talk about it and decide."

"I think you should put me back where I was," I said, trying to keep calm. "I don't like it here."

"Ha," he muttered. "Ha, ha." He went on striding, talking, muttering, waving his arms. After a time, I grew weary and my eyes closed. It had been long since we had slept, Grumpkin and I. I heard the little man talking, through a veil, as though he were far away.

Then his hands were on me, gently enough, pulling off my shoes, taking off my cap, feeling my chest.

I sat up, my hair spilling down my back.

"You're a very pretty girl," he accused me, putting his hand back on my chest to make sure I was a girl. "We have very little prettiness anymore, and that makes you noticeable, which makes things difficult."

I drew away, offended. "Actually," I told him through a fog of weariness, "I'm a duke's daughter." I don't know why I told him this. Perhaps it was because I had just been wakened. Perhaps it was to reassure myself that I was really myself.

He buried his head in his hands. "That butcher, Jaybee. He's sick. The things he does, the way he thinks! Not that Alice is that different. She's the only one who can handle him. They both ought to be put down the chutes, but he's a genius, so they don't, they haven't, and now he's dragged you along, they'll put us all down the chutes. What am I going to do?"

"Put me back," I suggested again. "I won't tell anyone. No one would believe me, anyhow."

"I can't," he said. "I don't have an authorization code. We can't use the machine without an authorization code. Even if I could use it, I couldn't put you back at the same time. The tolerances aren't close enough. If we make a closed loop, it will pinch off and everything will collapse!"

He wrung his hands for a while, then told me, "Go on, go to sleep. I've got to think. I've really got to think."

I lay sidewise on the bed I was sitting on, a narrow bed to be sure but no harder than the one I slept upon in Westfaire. Grumpkin lay beside me, munching on the strange biscuit with an expression of remote disdain upon his face. I took a fragment of the biscuit and put it in my mouth, letting it dissolve there. It had sustenance in it but no pleasure. I could live on it, but if it were all there was to eat, I thought living might not much be worth it.

.
13
.

The day after my arrival, Bill went away, returning sometime later very strange in his manner. "All for nothing," he cried at me, as though something had been my fault. "Why wouldn't you let us finish it?" He slammed around the tiny place for a while and then went out again, giving me an intense, wondering look as he left. When he returned, he was giggling and staggering a little, happier, for some reason. He seemed to have forgotten whatever had bothered him before, and I did not ask him what the trouble had been.

In the days that followed, I grew to know the untaste of the biscuits and the boundaries of the tiny room all too well. It had many folding places in it: a folding place to wash, a folding place to relieve oneself, folding places to store things. The bed slid into a pocket, the table slid into another pocket, each thing became something else. Bill went away each day, telling me to stay out of sight. He locked the door behind him and unlocked it when he returned. There was no window. I complained of this, and he told me the room was deep inside a great redoubt; windows would merely have looked into other rooms. There were no windows anywhere, he said, for there was nothing for them to see but more rooms and more rooms. He taught me to use the screen, instead, and gave me a great pile of "documentaries" he had helped make. They made my head hurt, but I watched them nonetheless. It was something to do. I learned to understand the language of the place that way, watching the images on the screen as they flowed and danced. It was my own language, more or less, though strangely changed. Often it was easier to understand the printed words that surged across the picture than the spoken ones.

There were other films, as well. I could watch some of the "porno-mance" ones, but the "horro-porn" ones I could not watch. Jaybee had filmed some of them. I threw them down the disposal chute, but every few days more were delivered from the supply chute. There was no end to them, each one full of pain and blood. I learned very soon there was nothing beautiful in that place. Even the things they watched were not beautiful. There was no contrast between beauty and ugliness. There was only ugliness.

I suppose it was more practical for them. If there had been any beauty at all, people might have wanted that instead. As it was, they didn't know there was any such thing, so the lack did not bother them. I knew, though. I hurt all the time with such a longing. My chest burned, as though I would die of it.

Grumpkin learned to make his mess on paper, which I threw down the disposal chute thing where my own waste went. Everything worn out or used up went down the chute, said Bill. His name was William, William Picte. "Pic-tee," he said, spelling it for me. He was a writer of what he called scripts, which I learned were stories for the pictures I had watched on the machine. He was a man of mature years, thirty at least. He came up to my shoulder. His hair was the color of apricots, and his skin was very pale, covered over with freckles. The hair on his body was the same as the hair on his head. I saw it when he washed himself. He had nowhere else to go to wash himself. The room we were in was the only room he had. We slept together on the narrow bed, our heads at opposite ends. He did not try to do anything to me, and I was grateful for that.

"Take me with you," I begged him one day when he was about to set out. "I want to see something else."

"There isn't anything else," he told me. "It's all like this. Except for Fidipur's farms, but nobody can go there except the people who work there."

"Let's go to the ocean," I suggested. "To the sea." I had never seen the sea, but Papa had, many times.

"There isn't any sea," he said. "Except the farms for Fidipur."

"A forest then," I begged, growing frantic. Sometimes I thought if I had to spend one more day in this little closet I would die. "Take me to the forest."

He shook his head. "You don't understand. There isn't any forest anymore. No forest, no prairie, no mountains, no jungle, no swamp, no animals, no birds, no fish. It all went to Fidipur. This is all there is. Rooms like this one. Full of people like me."

"Where do you go when you go out?" I begged.

"To the area supply station to get the daily ration of food wafers," he snarled at me. "I get the same as a full-size person, which is why there's enough left over for you. Then I go to the area work station to check in each day so they will know I am still alive and my room occupied. Then to the area water station to punch in so they'll know I'm still alive and using water. To the required school for continuing education, which is a laugh, because there's nothing left to teach anyone that matters. There aren't any books; they take up too much room. There aren't any teachers. There's one technical university, and only the people who run things get to send their children there, so they can keep on running things."

"You do that every day?"

"Except the sabbath. On the sabbath I go to the required

religious observance of my choice. We're very religious, hadn't you noticed. Ha. Ha. Ha."

None of it was reasonable, so I thought he lied. One day I opened the door and stepped out. There were people everywhere, small people. I hadn't noticed the first time, but almost all of the people were small. Still, they filled up the moving corridors and stairs. All of them wore much the same sort of clothes, and it was hard to tell men from women. Some of them saw me looking out, and stopped to stare, muttering, the noise level rising like a disturbed hive. I was afraid the noise would bring some official to see what was going on. I went back in, hastily, and stayed inside after that.

All this time the thing inside me kept flaming away as though it had to burn its way out. It wasn't pain, it wasn't that kind of burning, but there was such a dreadful urgency about it. I felt stretched thin. Like parchment stretched around a flame, trying to contain it, getting hotter and hotter all the time.

Even though he had said there was no wine, Bill came home another time acting giggly and happy, as though he had been drinking. If there wasn't wine, there was something like it, because his face was flushed and the pupils of his eyes were tiny, like dots. He giggled at me, like a drunken baby, waving his finger, and took a box out of one of the hidden closets. The box had women's clothes in it, and he put them on. There were stockings like cobwebs, but full of holes, a silky black blouse, a red and black striped skirt, a slim underbodice without sleeves. Around his shoulders he wrapped a fleece, a sheepskin, with the wool out, as though it had been fur, then he staggered around on high-heeled red shoes. All the things were old and stained, like the clothes the aunts had given me to wear.

I told him the things weren't very nice.

"I know," he said. "Oh, I know. Women don't wear clothes like these anymore. We all dress alike. Men and women. Nothing silky anymore. Nothing lacy or soft. Just these," and he pinched up a handful of the trousers he had discarded, the harsh wrinkled fabric of them pulling up in mountain peaks beneath his fingers. "I brought the silky clothes back from a time-trip, a long time ago. When we went to take pictures of whales."

I thought he would have liked living at Westfaire. My father wore soft things, velvets and satins. "Please take me home," I begged him. "You can go with me. There are many nice fabrics at home. You would love the gowns."

"Beauty," he said to me, pushing me down on the couch and squatting on the floor in front of me like some great lady frog, the soiled silk lying in loose folds on his flat chest. "Listen to me. I am a member of a work crew. The work crew is assigned to make certain kinds of films, like the ones you've been watching. There are five of us. Alice Fremont is the travel technician. She takes us places to film things. Martin Duboise is the director. He tells the cameraman—Jaybee Veolante—what pictures to get. He usually talks to me about that also, because I write the scripts, the words, you know?"

I knew he did. I had seen him at work, at a fold down place with a screen to show words and a thing to print paper.

He said, "Janice Saintjohn is the researcher."

I asked him what that was.

"Researchers find things out. They learn about other people, other places, other times. The researcher tells us where we might be able to get good film. The director decides if we'll do it. I write the script, Alice takes us there, Jaybee photographs it. We do maybe three stories a year, and that's how we earn our keep. Until they assign us some other story, we can't go near that machine. I don't know how to run it anyhow. Alice would have to run it."

"Ask Alice to run it," I demanded. "You said I'm dangerous to you here. So, I'm dangerous to her, too. Ask her to run it and put me back where I belong."

Some days I thought if I had to eat one more of those wafers or spend another day shut up in this cell called home-sweet-home I'd die. I burned and sweated and tried to keep from screaming. One morning, after I'd been restless and nightmare-ridden half the night, I woke up with an idea. I don't know why I hadn't thought of it before. As soon as Bill left, I found the sheepskin thing he had worn around his neck and some scissors he used to cut his scripts and piece them together and I cut the fleece to make a pair of boots.

I knew how to do it. I had watched the shoemaker in the village many times. I knew how to cut the sole and make the upper part and sew the two parts together. It would have been better if I'd had some stiff leather, but on the other hand, stiff leather would have been hard to sew without the right tools. The sheepskin was very soft. I put the wool part inside. I used the thick needle and the heavy brown thread from the box my mama had left. It had come to me in the night what the thread was for. It was shoemaker's thread, so it had to be for seven-league boots. It had to be. Seven-league boots which would take me back to my own time!

When they were done I put them on, and my cloak, with my things in one pocket and Grumpkin in the other, and I opened the door and went out into the hall. "Take me to my mother," I said, closing my eyes and waiting for the boots to work.

When I opened my eyes, there were people standing all around me, staring at me. The boots hadn't worked. The cloak didn't work! They could see me!

I got back inside and fell down on the hard, narrow bed and cried. I was still there, still crying, when Bill got home.

He made me tell him what I'd tried to do.

"You little fool," he sneered at me. "There's no magic left today. The fairies are all gone, and there's no magic left. Put those things away, and don't do anything so foolish again. If someone official had seen you, you'd be down the chutes by now!"

We lay on the bed, head to toe, and I listened to the sound of the world. A clangor, a constant sound of metal, distant and yet all around me. It was like being inside a gong, gently struck by an erratic wind, the reverberations coming and going without rhythm or predictability. Over that the sound of voices, a buzz, a hum, like some great hive. Over that the sound of feet, shuffling, stepping, never together, never marching, but moving endlessly up and down the corridors of the world. One listened and listened, waiting always for something significant in that sound. Some voice one knew. Some sound one recognized. There was never anything but the constant roar of everyone, everything, closing in and closing in. I put the blanket around my ears and wept while Grumpkin licked my eyes.

I cried so hard and so long that Bill said he would bring Alice to talk with me. Next time he went out, I waited for a long time walking back and forth, back and forth, like the lion one of Papa's friends had brought back from the Holy Land with him, to and fro in my cage as he had gone to and fro in his, action that his body demanded even when his mind was hopeless, to and fro until he died at last, his feet stretched out and worn through to the blood beneath, as though he had walked himself to death, trying to get home.

At last voices spoke outside the door. I hid myself in the disposal closet until I was sure it was Bill. The woman Alice was with him. So was Jaybee Veolante. He stared at me. I realized almost at once that my hair was down and my singlet was tighter than the shirt I had worn when he saw me. He grunted, and I thought again of a boar pig.

"So," he said as his eyes devoured me, "what've you been up to with her, Billy-boy?"

I found my shirt and put it on. The way he looked at me was frightening. As though he wanted to swallow me. Which was not unlike the way the woman was looking at me.

"You remember Alice," Bill said to me. "Alice Fremont?"

She was a little older than he, I thought. Her face was pale and thin, like the carved face of a saint sanctified through many stringencies, but alive and hungry withal. She was looking at me hungrily, too, and I shifted uncomfortably.

"I told Alice what you suggested," Bill said to me. "About her taking you back. Us, back."

"Us," sneered Jaybee. "All or none."

"Jaybee, uh, overheard us," Bill explained. "He wants to be included." He shifted nervously, watching Jaybee from the corners of his eyes.

"Included, right." Jaybee's jaw moved as though he were chewing something. His teeth made an audible gnashing.

Alice sat down on the bed. Bill pulled a seat out of the wall and sat confronting her. Jaybee lounged against the door, as though to prevent anyone escaping. I stayed where I was, with Grumpkin behind my legs, his head against my ankle.

"Before we technicians do a trip with a team," Alice explained, "we always do a check-trip, to be sure the machine's working right. The check-trip is always a hundred years, give or take a few. The tech is supposed to be the only one aboard during the check-trip. That's part of the reason we only go a hundred years, so if something's wrong with the machine, only the tech gets abandoned, and the time is recent enough a person could probably get along."

Bill slumped on his chair. "What are you saying, Alice? Tell me what you're saying."

"I'm saying, any tech can get into the complex anytime to make a check-trip. If I could get you in there with me, I could take you back with me."

"A hundred years?" I asked. "That's no good! I want to go home! That's what? Seven hundred at least, isn't it?"

"Seven hundred forty-two," she said. "There's no way to do that. The machine is energized for trips over a hundred only on receipt of a trip-authorization number from the powers that be, but it's always on ready power, that is, energized for a hundred years—roughly. Zero to one day takes a lot of power. That's what they call the Present Horizon. It takes enormous energy to get into that time because nothing is settled yet. People don't know what the hell is happening in the present. Some things that happen are inconsequential and get forgotten almost immediately. Some things that don't happen are thought to have happened; they get recorded or have consequences, and then people think they remember them. The present is fluid. It has to settle before you can travel in it.

"From one day to ninety-eight point something-or-other years takes almost no power, so they keep the machine hot. That's the Recent Past, and we don't fool with it, either, because we'd be in the lifetimes of living people. Still, it's cheaper keeping the machine powered for the Recent Past than shutting it down between trips and having to power it over the Present Horizon again."

"So you're saying we could go back to the 1900s?" Jaybee asked.

"Talk to Janice about it," Alice suggested. "There are rumors that a lot of people have gone back. We know some have because we've talked to them ourselves when we've been there."

"I met one once," Bill said. "When we did the first shots on the whales. She told me she had come back."

Alice nodded. "I've heard some researchers say it's the last good time. The last years before Fidipur."

Bill stared at me intently. "It would be better than here."

"Yeah," Jaybee muttered. "If we end up there. But we could end up dead. There's guards on the travel-complex. Alice may have a permit, but they won't give me one."

"I said it would work *if* I could get you in," Alice said. "I'm not talking anybody into anything. Bill asked me, I didn't ask him."

"You'd stay?" I asked her. "You'd stay there?"

"Damn right," she said, glaring into my eyes as though determined to find something I didn't know was there. *"If* I can figure out a way to sneak us down there."

"Janice finds things out," I said. "Bill told me so. Ask her to find out who goes where the machine is."

"Janice?" Alice wondered.

Bill looked up alertly. "She might want to go along."

"She'd drag Martin in."

"No," said Bill. "That's why she might go. They broke up not long ago. He said she was getting weird and filed for separate quarters. Haven't you noticed how they've acted? She's become very strange and religious."

"Then she might want to go." Alice shook her head, ran her fingers through her short hair. "She might. Who's going to ask her?"

"I will," said Bill.

The others said a few more words, then left. As he was going out, Jaybee turned around and gave me one more stare, a long, swallowing look, as though he'd like to hit me. Or eat me.

Bill brought Janice to the home-sweet-home later on. I was

asleep when they came. They talked in whispers, and I never really woke up. I was dreaming about Westfaire, and I didn't want to wake up because in the dream I knew if I wakened Westfaire would vanish forever. So I let Bill and Janice talk without letting go of the vision, knowing when Janice left they had come to some kind of agreement. When I woke up, I remembered this very clearly, but there was no one to tell it to but Grumpkin. Grumpkin looked sick. His fur was dull. His eyes looked bleary. He needed outdoors. He needed it no more than I. My legs were jumpy. My skin was breaking out in spots. I dreamed of trees. The burning in me was getting so bad I thought I'd turn to coals and die.

A day or two later, Bill came home with two suits of stiff green clothing that went over everything and closed up the front with fuzzy stuff. He had me put one on. Then he told me Grumpkin was too likely to attract attention, so I'd have to put Grumpkin down the chute. I told him I'd kill him if he ever said such a thing again. We ended up putting Grumpkin in the sack, along with my cloak and things. Bill didn't want to leave his woman clothes behind, but I told him he could buy all the woman clothes he wanted where we were going and I'd even buy him a new fur to make up for the sheepskin I'd cut to pieces. I still had the emeralds, so buying a sheepskin shouldn't be that difficult. I cut a hole in the sack for Grumpkin's nose. The cat growled, but he stayed put. I think he knew I was trying to get us home.

When we went out, there weren't as many people as usual. Bill said it was between shifts. Somewhere along the way, Jaybee joined us. We went down stairs and around corners. I didn't recognize anything or anyone from before, but then everyone looked alike. Almost everyone was the same size, their hair was cut alike, they wore the same clothes, they had the same dead, no-expression blanks for faces. We came to a gate with two men outside who were dressed a little differently, in high-buttoned jackets and hats with metal trim on them.

"Cleaning crew," Jaybee said in the bored voice everyone used.

"You're early," one of the metal-hats complained.

"We're late," said Bill. "Should have been here last shift. There's a stalled walkway down toward the nine-hundreds and everybody's jammed up."

The man nodded without paying any attention and let us through. Inside were more corridors and stairs, and then Alice came out of a room and walked along with us. She was carrying a little bag.

"Janice is already down in the control room," she said.

She was there when we arrived, dressed as we were. She nodded at us, then we all moved out into the huge, high room where the machine was. I hadn't really looked at it from the outside before. It looked like it was made out of rock, like a great tub carved from stone. The door of it clanged behind us. Alice pushed some buttons. My insides came out through my nose, and then back in again.

"Quick," said Alice. "We've only got seconds."

Bill opened the door and we all fell out. When we turned to look behind us, the machine was shimmering, then it was gone. In its place was a signpost pointing ten miles to a place I had never heard of.

"Nineteen ninety something or other," Janice murmured. "In what used to be the States of America. And God help us."

[We found her! We feared she had gone forever, except we could feel what was inside her, pulsing a little, like a faraway heart still beating. We knew she was still alive, for I could feel her life, just as I could feel that life dwindling. All we could do was lurk along the borders of that time and hope she would come out. Oh, the pain of living where there is no magic at all. Even humans need a little of it. The Holy One, Blessed be He, knew that. Perhaps it is why he put both our races here to begin with.

Never mind. We've found her. We know where she is. She is in a time of little magic, but there may be enough. We can reach her, slowly, slowly, setting our lures, readying our hooks. We will draw her back to us!]

14

JULY 1991

We joined the homeless, many of whom are from the twenty-first and slightly later times. Janice said it was odd the authorities of the 1980s never caught on to the fact that the homeless sprouted rather suddenly. Time-travel was perfected in 2080, and the hundred-year limit means that the homeless began showing up in the 1980s, many of them with limited communications skills, covering up by pretending to be crazy. There's a secret finger sign we travelers use among ourselves to tell each other that we're what we call "comebacks," and there are enough real 1980s homeless that we comebacks can hide among them without difficulty.

Evidently the people in this time decided to knock down all the poor people's hovels because they weren't nice enough and close all the asylums for crazy people because they weren't perfect either, but the people who had lived in the hovels and the asylums didn't have any other place to go, so now they live under bridges and places like that. I think we did it better back in the fourteenth. At least we didn't knock down hovels just because they were substandard. It seems to me substandard is better than nothing.

Anyhow, Bill and the rest of us took advantage of the situation by seeking shelter in an almshouse run by the Church, which did not surprise me at all, though the first time I attended Mass I was considerably astonished. The priest did the whole thing facing us and speaking English, which is what the language is now called. Evidently no one uses Latin anymore. I thought of all those sessions with Father Raymond and could have cried.

Jaybee and Alice and Janice had a big fight, and then Jaybee and Alice left for some big, big city where they can both sort of disappear into the mob. I was so glad when Jaybee went. It was like smelling rain after a long dry spell, just to know he was gone. Bill and Janice have signed up for job training here. You have to, or they won't let you stay in the almshouse, that is, the shelter. After a few weeks of being tutored by Bill in arithmetic and by Janice in geography and current history, which I know nothing about (Bill shakes his head and tells me not to believe half of what Janice tells me), I will be sent to school.

AUGUST 1, 1991

Everyone went out to look for work today. They left me in the shelter, by myself except for a few other people who had just come or were too ill to go out. Two of them were a woman and a child who came last night. They were both very pale, very thin, almost like stick people, and the little girl seemed very sad.

I went into their cubicle to see if I could talk to them, maybe cheer the little girl up a bit. The two of them sat on their bed, scarcely moving. On the table was an almost untouched plate of food someone had brought them, the knife and fork laid side by side, a glass half-empty beside it. I got the little girl to play with me. At least, I sat her on my lap and told her stories. She leaned into me, as though she needed the warmth. She put her head against my chest and smiled a tiny smile. I wondered if she felt whatever the burning was. It hadn't been quite so bad since we'd come to the twentieth, but I could feel it, so maybe she did, too.

I told her the story about the gypsy and the prince, and I ended it, "So they lived happily ever after."

"Ever after," said the woman. "Together."

I had not heard her speak before. Her voice was dreadful, like a mechanical echo, with nothing vital in it at all.

"We loved each other," she said. "We said we would be together ever after, together."

"Who's she talking about?" I whispered to the child.

"Daddy," the child whispered back, putting her cheek against my chest and smiling, as though she heard something inside there.

"But the chutes were full," her mother said in her cold,

quiet voice. "We were going together, but the chutes were full. Full all the way to the top, the furnaces gone out, bodies jammed in, rotting, stinking, bones sticking out . . ."

"Daddy and mommy and me were going down the chutes," the child said with wide eyes. "To happyland."

I looked at the woman in horror. Her face was very still, her eyes were still. Her mouth moved and the words came out, but there was nothing behind them. It was as though she were dead, already, and the words were bats fleeing from her coffin.

"But we couldn't go, couldn't go, couldn't go," she chanted. "So we walked away, down the corridors where the sidewalks slept, down the aisles where the rot lay thick, down the stairs where the stink rose up like paste, gluing itself inside our lungs, down and down to the room where the machine was, humming to itself, the little machine."

"It was very tiny," the child said. "Only big enough for Mommy and me. Daddy knew it was there. He turned on the big engine that gave it power for more than a hundred years, and he put us in and shut the door. And when we opened the door, we were here."

"Down, down," the woman crooned, "down, to happy-land."

I asked the child to come away with me, and after a while she did. Her name was Elaine. She had a lovely laugh. I asked her what year she had been born, and she said 2108. She couldn't remember what year it had been when she got in the tiny machine, but she looked about six to me, which would make it about 2114. We stayed in the corridor, playing ball, playing hide-and-seek.

The last time she hid, I could not find her. Finally, I went back to their cubicle to see if she had gone there, and she had. She was lying beside her mother on the bed. Her mother's hand was still upon the knife, wet with Elaine's quiet blood. Deathwords came from the woman's mouth, a terrible singing, "Down . . . down . . . down . . . to happyland."

I screamed, stood there screaming, screaming until it hurt. The people who manage the shelter came and took the woman away. They wrapped up the little girl's body in black stuff and took it away. Someone gave me a white pill and a glass of water. They said the woman was mad. That she should have been locked up long ago.

I did not tell them that the woman had been locked up, locked up all her life; that in the time she had come from, everyone was locked up forever.

•

AUGUST 12, 1991

Bill brought back a set of his documentaries with him to use as examples of his work. He had to claim they are speculative fiction in order to use them in seeking a job, but evidently they're good examples of his talent, for it didn't take him long to get a position writing for a television station. Janice got work, too, at a library, and then we three rented a house on the corner of Wisdom Street and Seventh Avenue. It's a house about the size of the pigpen at Westfaire.

However, it has flush toilets, which I like, and a garbage disposer. I also like hair dryers and tampons. I do not like telephone salesmen and the way everybody has dogs they let empty themselves just anywhere. In my time commoners didn't have dogs, they couldn't have fed dogs, they'd probably have ended up eating the dogs. I don't like the noise people are allowed to make with radios. It does not sound like music. It sounds savage and makes your ears ring, and afterward it is hard to hear when people speak.

I have a room of my own, with my own things in it. I put my cloak and the boots and Mama's box at the back of the closet shelf. Grumpkin sleeps on my bed. I don't like all the concrete and no trees. I do like hamburgers and french fries and Pepsi, and the kind of chickens they have now with all the meat on them. In the fourteenth, chickens were very skinny and tough. I hate the way the world smells. On balance, I would go back in a minute, but since the boots don't work, I don't have that choice, I'm trying to seek the good in the time I'm in.

From a television show I learned that people like Bill are called transvestites and that Janice is probably frigid (though maybe she's just a religious fanatic) and Jaybee is probably a psychopath. The aunts would have had a fit if they had ever seen the things they talk about on TV, but I think it's good to have words for things.

Everything is all right, except for the dreams I have about the little girl in the shelter. I dream I am with them in the twenty-second. I dream I am trying to find a chute which is not already stuffed full of bodies. I dream I am singing: down, down, down to happyland. And I wake up choking.

.

AUGUST 15, 1991

I met a neighbor girl my age. She's a senior at George Washington High, the school I'll be going to next month. Her name is Candace Maclear, and everyone calls her Candy. She's very friendly. She says I'm really rad, which is good, and offered me some coke (to sniff) and spent all day teaching me to fix my hair. She says I talk funny, so I'm concentrating on sounding more like her.

.

AUGUST 17, 1991

I told Bill about Candy offering me drugs, and he warned me about it when I go to school in two weeks. Everyone here uses them, he says, and it's hard not to. He talked about "peer pressure," which seems to mean letting other people run your life for you. I had enough of that at Westfaire!

.

AUGUST 20, 1991

Candy's brother told me her boyfriend really goes after girls with long hair, and Candy's afraid he'll take to me. I've seen Candy's boyfriend and, believe me, she hasn't anything to worry about. His hair stands up in spikes and he has pimples. I look at him and I think of Giles. I look at all the boys here and I think of Giles. I wonder if they're all like this!

•

AUGUST 21, 1991

Everything here in the twentieth seems very temporary. Nothing lasts. Friendships don't last. Love affairs don't last. Marriages don't last. I've seen men here who people tell me have been married four or five times, and their old wives aren't dead, either. People even change what sex they are, and there are people coming to the door all the time trying to get me to change my religion and be born again, though I haven't gotten used to being born the first time yet. Wouldn't being born again imply I didn't trust God to have done it right the first time?

Even though I was mad at him, I wish Father Raymond were here! Janice did get born again, last week, and there's no living with her. I finally had to tell her I am a Catholic and please leave me alone. She got very angry. She doesn't approve of me and she doesn't approve of Bill. She says he's being sinful to dress up like he does. I can't see why. He isn't hurting anyone, but Janice says God intended men to wear trousers and women to wear dresses. I look at pictures of Greeks and Scots and aborigines and Jesus, and I can't figure out how she knows that!

•

SEPTEMBER 6, 1991

Well, I've been to school. I know who sells crack and who fucks who and which teachers are gay and who has AIDS. Nobody has asked me to do any arithmetic or geography at all, so that was a waste of time. I am taking classes in literature and biology and Spanish. Bill and Janice decided these were the safest subjects for me.

Bill took one whole hour to tell me about sexual diseases, and maybe it's a good thing he did. I do not want any of their diseases, though, after eavesdropping on a table of boys at lunch, I don't think I'd be tempted anyhow. They were talking about this girl they got drunk or stoned and then they all did it, watching each other. They were laughing at the way different ones had done it, making comments about how long it took this one or that one, like the stableboys used to hang over the paddock, watching the stallion serve the mares, giggling and pointing. I wonder if that has anything to do with male bonding?

In the fourteenth, we dreamed of chivalry and courtly love. I remember the oaths of fidelity the young men-at-arms used to offer their ladies, and they were no older than these high school boys. These guys don't offer anything. It's like the women they hit on are sacrifices to some kind of god that only boys worship. Most of the boys here remind me of Jaybee, though I'm not sure why.

The twentieth makes me feel very lonely. This isn't my place. When I remember how beautiful Westfaire is, was, when I remember Giles, I want to cry. I choke, my chest burns, I get the hiccups and have to lie down. The worst part of living here is that nothing is beautiful. There must be something beautiful in the twentieth, and maybe I just haven't seen it yet, but the way everyone acts, this is all there is. Magic doesn't work. There is no other way. Some days all I want to do is cry.

[Some days all I want to do is cry! We keep trying to lure her, and she keeps ignoring us. I have thought of sending Puck. He says he can get there. The problem is, his doing so might draw attention to her. The Dark Lord may be watching the Bogles. We don't know who he's watching! Puck's going there might show up like a meteorite, burning across the night. Israfel keep saying, "Patience, Carabosse." Patience! I don't think he sees the irony of that.]

.

OCTOBER 4, 1991

Today I think I figured out Fidipur. In social studies class the teacher commented that the recent famines in Africa are only the beginning of what may turn out to be worldwide famines of varying degrees of severity. Then he showed us a film of black people in Africa dying in large numbers and another one about the hole in the Van Allen belts. (Father Raymond would be fascinated!) The teacher explained that very soon the world would warm up and get dryer, that food would be harder to produce, and "We won' be able to fidipur, 'cause there'll be millyuns and millyuns of 'em."

Fidipur! Feed the poor. The way he said it was exactly the way the beggars in the twenty-first had said it. I asked Bill to explain it to me, and he told me about population growth and the Catholic church and acid rain and cutting down the rain forests to grow more food. Everyone argues about it, he said. Economists and businessmen say nothing is going wrong. Ecologists and population experts say the end is coming. While they argue, things keep changing until we get to the point of no return, sometime during the next hundred years. After that, there'll be no more out-of-doors because every square inch of land will be needed to produce food, and that's why, in the twenty-first, all the people had to be shut up in great tall, half-buried towers where they couldn't move around and interfere with Fidipur's farms.

I said, sensibly I thought, that God gave man the duty to take care of the world, not a contract to wreck the place, and Bill laughed the way he does, ha, ha, ha.

The comebacks say everything starts breaking down sometime late in the twenty-first, with Fidipur's farms playing out and people getting pushed down the chutes a hundred thousand at a time and all the machines breaking down. Elaine may have been the last person who came back, and she came in about 2114.

Bill says the handwriting is already on the wall, we're already doomed. Janice says he shouldn't say "doomed" when so many people will be alive and being fed, so he asked her why she left the twenty-first if it was so great, and she got mad at him. There are tear spots all over this page, and I can't stop.

•

OCTOBER 7, 1991

I've stopped thinking about Fidipur. You can't think about things like that all the time. Your body won't let you. Everytime I started to cry about it, my chest would burn like a bonfire. It got so I was afraid to think about it at all. So, I'm trying to think

about other things, about trying out for cheerleader—which
seems kind of dumb, but all the good-looking girls do it—and
going to football games and things like that. I am trying to do as
Father Raymond used to suggest and seek the good. Things
wouldn't be too bad if Janice would just stop talking about religion and let me alone. I wish I could be nicer to her about it, but
her religion is so ugly! So mean!

*[We go on transmitting these urgencies, but they have not the volume of
the constant music where she is; they cannot be heard above the traffic noises.
There are so many distractions in the twentieth, she doesn't hear us. If she
would only decide to be a nun! I think possibly we could get through to a nun.]*

•

NOVEMBER 15, 1991

Yesterday we had a special kind of event at school. The event
was called "Career Days," and they had people from all kinds of
jobs and professions come speak to us about their jobs. One of
the men was our teacher's brother, an author, Barrymore
Gryme, only he told us all to call him Barry. I've seen his books
in the school library, but I've never read one. After the session,
when the students were leaving the room, he asked me what my
name was. I told him, Dorothy, because that's the name Bill and
Janice and I had decided on, after my old friend Doll. We knew
enough to realize I couldn't call myself Beauty, not in the twentieth.

"You don't belong in Kansas, do you?" he asked me with a
funny smile.

I didn't know what to say, so I just smiled back.

"No, you're the Emerald City all over," he said. Then I
knew he was talking about that movie with the singing girl and
the straw man. The Yellow Brick Road one. I'd seen that in the
twenty-first, about fifteen times.

"Not that Dorothy," I explained. "I was named after an old
friend."

"Where do you live, old friend Dorothy?" he asked me. I
didn't want to be rude, so I told him. When I got home that

night, there were flowers for me in the living room, from him. Bill was puzzled, but Janice was furious.

"What have you been doing when you're supposed to be at school," she shouted at me. "What have you been up to?"

I guess my mouth dropped open, because Bill told her not to yell. When I saw his name on the tag with the flowers, I was just as puzzled as Bill was.

"I only said about six words to him," I said. "And there were lots of other people around."

"Where, around?" Janice demanded.

I told her, at Career Day, at school, that he was our teacher's brother, and after a while she believed it. When I told her his full name, then she was as puzzled as Bill.

Bill nodded, his mouth pursed up. Then he sat me down at the desk and made me write the man a nice note, saying thank you for the flowers but I'd sent them to a hospital, because I wasn't allowed to accept gifts from older men. Bill thought it was "appropriate."

.

NOVEMBER 17, 1991

I told Candy about the flowers I got from Barrymore Gryme. I said I couldn't understand why he'd do that, and she got bright red in the face and said, "Honestly, Dor, you're so dumb it's just unbelievable." And when I asked her why, she said look in the mirror for crysakes.

Well, I've known for a long time I'm beautiful, but that doesn't explain anything! He's too old for me, and I'm sure too young for him. Candy thinks I ought to have an affair with Barry Gryme.

I told her she was crazy.

She says just wait. Her aunt told her virginity gets to be more and more of a burden the older you get. She told Candy you get to the point where you don't decide whether you like someone enough to make love to them or not, you only get to the point of wondering whether they're good enough to give it up for. "Aunt Becky says you quit wondering when and start wondering if," Candy said.

Should I have an affair because of Candy's aunt?

[As if Israfel and I did not have enough to worry about already!

We were standing at the Pool, trying our best to get through to the twentieth, when Israfel remarked that, as our magic weakens, the power of the Dark Lord strengthens. I had known that, of course, though I had not let myself consider it deeply. Our departed brother took terror and pain as his portion. It was always a part of what we did. Magic is a perilous thing, and it has its horrifying aspects, but we have always worked with and around these aspects, not making them the focus of our art. The Dark Lord has taken these to the exclusion of all else. He works in pain and prurience, lust and death, ramifying these until they fill his whole canvas. Discontent with his own efforts, he selects minions among men to develop these themes further. Is Jaybee one of these? Is Barrymore Gryme?

Has this man been set upon her, like a hound set upon a hare? We have been so careful. We have done nothing to draw attention to her, letting it seem that she has done everything out of her own motivation, out of her own desires. She has left no magical trail behind, like the slime of a snail, for some inimical creature to follow. Surely, he can't know?

So I say to Israfel, and he to me, trying to convince ourselves.]

NOVEMBER 20, 1991

I got a Barry Gryme out of the school library and tried to read it. I read two hundred pages, then I had to quit because it scared me to death. Everything in it was hopeless and terrible. People kept being mutilated or eaten or destroyed. It was full of sex, too, but there was no pleasure in it. It was . . . it was a lot like the horro-porn films in the twenty-first. If lots of people read things like this, there's something terribly, terribly wrong. . . .

CHRISTMAS MORNING 1991

Bill and Janice are still asleep. If I were home, I'd be in church, watching Father Raymond moving around at the altar, smelling the incense, hearing his voice with the Latin rolling out, seeing the candles flicker. I'm homesick. There's nothing to do about it, so I'm watching one of Bill's documentaries.

Water, gray and cold, with lights in it as bubbles, rising, bright shadows in the water and vast distances, with everything moving and shifting, so there is no up or down. Singing in the water. Deep, organ tones, one, then two together, then a third. Soft, hurting sounds.

Bill's voice, his deep voice, the one he uses when he does the narrations. "These are the last whales, and this is their last song. Though they are unaware of it, this pod of whales is the last of the great sea creatures to swim the seas of earth. Cells have been saved in the hope that some future time will allow their regeneration, though as things stand today such hope seems dim and distant."

The organ voices again. Incredibly sad. Jaybee's camera focuses on an eye set in a great wrinkled socket. The eye looks at me. Oh, there's knowing there. They know. They know they are the last. All these seas are their tears, they have wept them all. All the oceans of earth are made up of tears. Whale tears, elephant tears, the tears of forests, the tears of flowers, the tears of everything beautiful cried out to make oceans.

We come up. We fly up through the water, we rip through the surface scattering droplets in all directions, we skim over the waves like a flung spear, toward the farms, skeletons on the horizon, with huge blades rotating, with solar collectors like blinding sheets of white fire.

"Fidipur's farms," says Bill's voice. "Here, suspended over the deep, are the mighty wind- and sun-powered pumps that bring the cold harvest of the sea to the surface, where it is dried, powdered, and shipped to the great landside factories of Fidipur."

Ships going and coming, being loaded and leaving, zipping into the loading docks empty, one after the other, by the hundreds. Like beetles. Like wood beetles. Eating everything, all, until nothing is left.

Back across the water, down to the whales again, this time slowly, letting us see them. Their bones show through their flesh. Their eyes are deeply sunk. The thin calf nuzzles its mother hopelessly. There is no milk. They are starving. Fidipur has taken it all.

I'm crying. Janice is calling me to breakfast. I'm not hungry. It's Christmas, but beauty is dying. We're gobbling up the world. I don't ever want to be hungry again.

·

JUNE 1992

Graduation. At first I didn't think I'd go, but I did. Bill and Janice came, too. We all wore those silly hats and the rented gowns and paraded up to get a piece of paper which isn't even really our diploma. We'll get that later in the mail, after the office checks to see we don't owe any money or library fines or anything. So, big deal, I thought, that's over, so now what will I do?

I got a phone call from Barry Gryme. He wanted to know if I was old enough yet, and I told him no, I am only seventeen, and I don't go out with married men anyhow (Janice found out he was married), and he said he was divorced.

·

JULY 1992

I bought another one of Barry's books, to see if I could read it all the way through. I got about a hundred pages into it and then I had to stop.

I've seen people die. I saw the goldsmith Papa put in the dungeon, when he was almost dead. He had been my friend, and I saw him when they took him out, saw his bones showing through his skin, and the sores on him, and the places the rats had chewed him. I saw a thief whipped to death once. I've seen men hanged. It's horrible, seeing that, but not as horrible as this book, because in this book, you're supposed to *like* seeing it, *like* reading what happens to the people. You can tell the way it's written you're supposed to kind of lick it up, like something juicy.

[We tried again. She was in such a downcast mood, we thought she might hear us, but she didn't. I'm considering sending Puck through to her. She knows him, and possibly she could accept him without headlines resulting: CALIFORNIA GIRL SEES CREATURE FROM OUTER SPACE.

Israfel says be patient just a little longer. I have just about had it with Israfel!]

CHRISTMAS 1992

A letter came for me, from Jaybee. I'd almost succeeded in forgetting Jaybee. The letter was gibberish, but frightening gibberish, and it was illustrated with photographs.

At first I couldn't tell what the photographs were. They looked like abstract art, fascinating compositions, dark, light, black, white, with ribbons of red. Then I saw that the dark was shadow, the light a woman's breast, the ribbon of red . . . well, it was blood, wasn't it? You could see the knife, the edge of it, making a design against the nipple. I began to make out what all of the photographs were, flesh, manacled flesh, cut flesh, an eye, half open, staring unbelievingly into the lens, lips which looked swollen with desire until you saw they were bitten half through.

If you turned them upside down, they were fascinating abstracts. Only when you looked at them closely could you see what was really happening. They were mostly pictures of one woman. Sometimes pictures of several. Well, I knew about that kind of thing. I'd taken a psychology course at school. Knowing about it didn't make it less sick, less hateful. I burned them. I didn't know what else to do!

The pictures somehow reminded me of Barry Gryme. Last month he called me to ask if now that I'd started college I was old enough to go out with him. I told him I didn't think I'd ever be old enough, and he laughed. He said he needed to know what I meant, would I just have coffee or a beer with him, so I said yes, I'd have a beer with him between classes the next day.

He showed up, which kind of surprised me. Seeing him sitting there, I tried to switch gears, tried not to be just a college girl, tried to be me, Beauty, someone who knew things he would never really know. He's not bad-looking. He is a charming, funny man. He's full of little jokes and amusing stories. Finally, he asked me what I've got against horror writers.

I said there was real horror in the world. Disease and starvation and torture. I said we needed to feel revulsion for these things, needed to be galvanized into action against them and against all poverty and pain and injustice, but that his books merely made us accustomed to horror, as a recreation.

He wasn't listening. He was looking at my face, at my shape, smiling a little smile to himself, his head cocked. He was thinking about going to bed with me.

I stopped talking. After a moment, he said, well, his books were popular; they made a lot of money, which bought a lot of nice things; people liked being scared to death, so why not?

One of the teachers came by just then and greeted him by name. Barry got up to go speak with him about some seminar he was doing.

I sat there, wondering why not. I knew there had to be a reason, but I couldn't say what it was. Maybe it was that I knew the world was going to end fairly soon and he didn't. All his horror was going to come true. Here people were, bustling around, speaking of the dangers, creating committees and movements to Save the Whales, Save the Forests, Save the Rain Forests, Save the Condor. How could *these* people become what I had seen? But they would.

They would become habituated to horror. They would read it, see films of it. They would soak it up. It would deaden the sense of terror they needed to stay alive. They would catch a kind of leprosy of the spirit, an inability to feel. I mean, I've seen some of that already. They had a terror they call the Holocaust, and because people are so determined it mustn't happen again, they keep banging on it and banging on it until people have stopped paying attention. The more you talk about it, the oftener you see it, the more it loses its power to shock, its power to disgust.

And in the end, unable to feel terror, mankind will go, we will all go down, down, down to happyland.

"Thank you very much for the drink," I said to him, when

he returned to the table. "I'm sorry I couldn't explain better what I meant, but I don't believe you know what horror is."

He got a teasing smile on his face and reached for my hand. I whipped it back, as I would have whipped it from the hand of Death himself. He looked in my face and whitened at what he saw there. I was surprised that he, writing what he does, seemed not to have seen real terror before.

[Jaybee Veolante. Barrymore Gryme. Israfel reads and peers as I do and turns away, sickened. We have already sent Puck, telling him to stay out of sight. We tell ourselves not to panic, that these men may be merely men, not creatures of the Dark Lord, that they may be attracted to her for her physical beauty alone. Israfel has stopped telling me to be patient.]

.

NEW YEAR'S, JANUARY 1, 1993

Outside the window I hear singing in the street. A drunk, I think, on his way home from a twenty-four-hour celebration. I am not going to the window to see. I am afraid to go to the window. Instead, I sit here in the Wisdom Street house with Father Raymond's book resting on the table, one bloody hand holding it in place while the other plies the pen and mops at my nose, trying to make it stop bleeding. I think it may be broken.

I am writing to keep from screaming.

Bill is dead. I don't know exactly where Janice is; she said she was going to visit friends somewhere over the holiday and won't be home until day after tomorrow.

Bill has . . . had a gun somewhere. I went looking for it and came upon my cloak and boots and this book instead. It was too late for the gun anyhow.

Short recess there to wash off some of the blood. This is all so stupid and terrible.

Bill and I were having a quiet New Year's Eve. Almost midnight, someone knocked on the door, and Bill went to open it. Jaybee came in, looked at me, and said, "I've come for you, sweetie."

I could tell he was drunk. Bill got in front of me and said, "Here, now, Jaybee. Let's talk about this." That's all he had time to say.

Jaybee reached out and snapped. . . . Just that. Bill's body was there on the floor. Jaybee didn't even change expression. Then Jaybee knocked me down and pulled off my clothes and hit me and raped me. He kept turning me over, coming at me from the front, then from the back, over and over. I fainted, finally. At least, I don't remember anything for a while. Then he went away. He took Bill's body with him, wrapped up in a blanket, like laundry. The last thing he said when he left was, "Thank me nicely for cleaning up the place, sweetie. I'll be back in the morning."

[Puck has to have arrived by now! Oh, why did we wait so long? He must be there. He must!]

Sweet, kind Bill. Dear little man. Oh, he loved it here where he could dress in lace and silk and satin and velvet. He would put on a recording and dance, all dressed up in his heels and stockings and smooth, slick underwear. I gave him teddies for Christmas gifts. Teddies and lace panties and garter belts. He was so kind to me. When I cried because I was lonely, he told me stories to make me laugh. When I cried out at the future of the world, he told me nothing was certain, not even death, and I should never give up hope.

He was the size of a child. He had delicate little wrists and ankles, a thin little neck, like a tiny woman. He was strong for his size, but he was tiny! Jaybee broke his neck with one blow of a great ham hand, broke it and laughed, and then kicked him where he lay.

I don't remember very well what I did right after Jaybee left. I hunted for the gun; I've said that. I found the book, and Mama's box, and my cloak. The warrant on the usurer was there, and the emeralds. The box and the cloak almost pushed themselves into my hands, as though someone were actually handing them to me.

Then anger came, out of nowhere, like a fever. I shook with

it, burned with it, bathed in it, soaked it up, wanting nothing
else. All I want to do is kill him!

I came to myself crouched over the book here. Anger will
have to wait. I'm too sick and weak to plan vengeance, let alone
execute it. My nose is battered. There are great bruises on my
face. I think one or two ribs are cracked. And the pain in my
groin feels as though he pushed a knife up me. I'm bleeding two
places down there, too.

I have to get myself together. I have to calm down. To calm
down I have to go home, really home. I need quiet to think in.

Something made me start thinking of home, like someone
whispering memories in my ear. Maybe it's because I need to
escape. Jaybee said he would come back, and I know he will. If
stay here, he'll find me. He's inescapable.

So I can't stay here.

LATER:

The boots were in my hand. I couldn't remember picking them
up, but there they were. They hadn't worked before, but now?
Only it wasn't before, was it? It was future, not past. Now? I
didn't know. I thought, maybe they will work. I put them on. I
put on the cloak. I put the book in the pocket, and Mama's box.

I went to the window and pressed my eye to the slit in the
curtain. There were some people out there, milling around, singing drunkenly. Jaybee was standing on the corner watching my
windows, an expression of amusement on his face. I could read
that face. He intended to do it again. As soon as the people
moved away, he planned to come back in here.

I ran to find Grumpkin. On the shelf of my closet were the
boy clothes I had arrived in. They went in one pocket and
Grumpkin in the other. He hung there, paws and head protruding, wondering what was happening, growling a little as he
caught my mood. As we had arrived together, so we would
depart together.

I had just fastened the cloak when the knocking started: a
soft, insistent, teasing knock on the door. I stood in a corner,
paralyzed. He called me. "Beauty?" Softly, sweetly. "Beauty."

Sickness and terror rose in my throat and Grumpkin

moaned in his throat, almost a snarl. "Shh," I told him. "Be still Grumpkin, my cat."

"Beauty?" Jaybee called again. "Let me in or I'll break down the door." He laughed, a liquid, bubbling laugh, like molten lava, molten lead, searing in its vile heat. "I'll huff, and I'll puff, and I'll blow your house down!"

He would. I knew he would, but I couldn't move. He would huff, he would puff, he would blow my house down. All my safety he would rip away. He liked to do that. I leaned down and touched the boots, but still waited, as though I had to *see* him do it. No. It was because I was so afraid the boots wouldn't work. Until I had tried and failed, I could hope. Once I had tried and failed, there would be no hope.

He kicked in the panel of the door with a splintering crash. His hand came through the hole, releasing the latch. Then he was in, grinning, whispering, "Beauty? Beauty?"

"Go!" a voice said in my ear.

He didn't see me! He went past me and didn't see me! He went through the living room into my bedroom. I heard the closet door slam against the wall. He was calling, "Beauty, Beauty, Beauty," as though he was calling a dog or cat. "Don't make Jaybee mad," he sang, like a spell, like an enchantment. But he didn't find me so he became angry, angrier still as he searched everywhere.

"Go!" said the voice again.

I tiptoed toward the broken door. Behind me I heard crashing and breaking. Anything I might have treasured, he would wreck. I heard the shattering, the bellows of rampaging fury.

I got out, onto the sidewalk, onto the lawn. Someone had heard the noise and called for help, for there were sirens at the end of the street.

"Boots," I whispered softly, praying I had not miscalculated, "take me home."

I took a step. A whirlwind bent down to take me, and I heard Jaybee running past me on the walk. The world spun and dizzied. I was standing on a street corner I recognized, not a block from the house. There was a newsstand beside me and the papers in it were dated August 13, 1981. Only ten years. I trembled. It was probable Jaybee could not find me here, but it was a long way from where I wanted to be. Grumpkin meowed in the pocket of my cloak. Someone coming along the street looked at me, then away, then back again, as though they saw me but not quite. Jaybee hadn't seen me because of the dark, the shadows. In the daylight, he would have.

"Go," whispered the voice, gently.

"Boots," I whispered again, taking another step.

I was on another street corner, in the midst of a huge crowd. Soldiers were marching in the street. People were screaming and throwing paper. "What year is it?" I asked a man from behind him, hoping he would not turn to answer. He gave me the answer over his shoulder.

"Nineteen forty-five," he cried. "Nineteen forty-five."

"Boots," I sighed.

The next stop was in the early years of the century, then the century before. Each time the boots surged more strongly upon my feet, and I knew that as I went back, the power grew stronger and stronger. There had been none of it in the twenty-first, and little enough in the twentieth. By the time I reached the sixteen hundreds it was strong enough to carry me the rest of the way home. When I said "Boots," there was only wild wind and bent time and the shriek of ghosts sucking all the air away. I gasped. There was nothing to breathe. Everything was dark and bloody red inside my eyes, and then only dark.

[*And then only dark, thank God. We stood looking down at her, only now beginning to breathe again.*

"Is she all right?" asked Israfel, leaning down to put his hand on her breast. Can he feel what is there, inside? "She looks . . . she looks drawn very fine."

"We need to get her to Chinanga," I told him. "To the place of safety we planned for her! Now she'll go to find her mother, and all will be well. If her mother is still there!"

"Oh, Elladine's still in Chinanga," said Israfel. "So far as she's concerned, no time has passed at all. I wish Beauty didn't look so tired."

"She's been through hell," I snapped at him. I leaned down and smoothed the hair back from her brow. Beauty. My beauty. Poor child.]

15

I wrote the last few pages when I woke up at the first light of dawn, on a weedy road looking up at the hedge of roses, now some sixty or eighty feet high. When I sat up, I felt dizzy and weak, but the feeling passed, so I pulled out the book and wrote of Jaybee's wrecking the house and my escape while I could still remember everything. It gave me something to do and stopped my wanting to scream or run or do something else loud and foolish. I wrote until I was too tired to write anymore, then I lay back down for a while, the cloak tight around me, and did not wake again until the sun was halfway up the sky. I dreamed someone came and told me I looked tired, smoothing the hair away from my forehead. Perhaps it was my mama.

When I awoke the second time, I saw the cat's-head out-cropping of stone not far down the road. Beyond that pinnacle was the hill where we had gathered flowers when I was a child, where I had first met Bill and the others. To my left was the old well we called the shepherds' well, where the flocks were watered on their way to market in East Sawley. Nothing looked the same, and yet everything looked familiar—oddly familiar, as though I had only remembered it wrongly. The pinnacle was too short, the hill too low. The trees were too huge, too vast. There were no trees like these, anywhere, anytime. I leaned against one of them, feeling the scratchy roughness of the bark. No. There had been trees like these, once. It was just that I hadn't seen them for a very long time.

I slipped off the boots and rose to my feet, putting one hand toward the hedge to help myself and withdrawing it with a howl of pain. The rose-wall was furred with thorns, small ones and large, an upholstery of needles. The four-petaled pink blooms were sweetly fragrant, though the scent was faint, more like a smell remembered than one present, like an old sachet, left long in a linen drawer, remini-scent. I turned to see an old horse grazing nearby, one eye watchfully on me. When I moved, he turned to stare at me, ears forward, not yet sufficiently surprised or frightened to move away.

I played games in my head, saying words to myself to see if I knew what they meant. Retreat. Regroup. Realize. Resume. The horse whickered at me, coming forward with its neck stretched out, nostrils wide. I put an arm across his back and together we walked away from the hedge. When I looked back, I was unable to see the top. It seemed to arch away from me at the height, and the farther I walked, the taller the green mass stretched into the sky.

Under the cat's-head stone, I searched for my fortune. There were flowers growing between the stones, and a silver-leafed shrub grown well down among the rocks I had used to stop the hidey-hole. It was clear I had returned some little time after I had gone. The rocks had to be levered out with a dead branch, and they came unwillingly, bound about by roots. Inside the hollow was a scattering of coins and gems, but no sign of the leathern bag that had contained them. A mouse, I thought, finding signs about: a whole company of mice. I picked the coins and jewels up and put them into my sack, feeling here and there for the warrant I had left behind. Parchment, it had been. To a mouse as goodly a chewable as a leather bag! Then something rustled under my hand and I pulled the parchment out, dry and whole, not badly stained, nibbled only at the edges. Perhaps the small creatures had not liked the flavor of the ink.

After retrieving my belongings, I trudged up the wildflower hill, turning at the top to look down on Westfaire as I had done a hundred times in my childhood. There was no Westfaire. There were no towers. No high banners whipping in the wind. Nothing there but an escarpment of green, a great whale-back of verdure, a monstrous and overgrown mound, a spined and impenetrable barrow of roses. If one did not know what was under it, one would think it merely a hill covered with thorns, not worth the scratches it would take to explore.

Something shoved me. I turned to find the old horse nosing at my sack. He whickered at me. I stroked his soft muzzle and he pushed his nose into my shoulder.

"I have no grain. Will you be ridden? Saddle or no?" I
grasped a handful of mane and drew him toward a rock, climbing upon it and leaning across his back. He made a sound, almost of pleasure. I slid a leg across. He waited. I lowered my
weight upon him, fully expecting to be tossed onto the rocky
ground. Instead, he turned to look at me, as though asking,
"Where do we go now?"

"Down the River Welling is a little hamlet called Sawley
Minor," I said aloud to see how the words sounded, trying for
the remembered words and accents of this time. "Where the
miller lives. Let us go there." When I had played at being Havoc,
the miller's son, Sawley Minor had been the place I imagined as
home. If I received no welcome at the mill beside the Sedgebrook, the abbey lay only a little farther down the River Welling, and beyond it the village of East Sawley. East Sawley was a
village of some size, occupied by woodsmen and sawyers, and I
could undoubtedly find lodging there. I nudged the horse with a
leg, showing the way, and he moved slowly down the hill in the
direction I had indicated.

When the horse moved, I felt the pain in my groin, like a
knife. Jaybee had torn me there. There were raw places, and I
could feel warm stickiness on my legs. Getting on the horse had
started the bleeding again. I shook with fear and rage and loneliness, and the horse turned his head to fix me with his round,
incurious eyes. "My enemy isn't here," I said, convincing myself. "He doesn't have boots, so he can't get here without the
machine, and he'd have to go back to the twenty-first to use the
machine, and he probably wouldn't dare do that even if he
could. Besides, he could not imagine I have returned here. No
one knows I had the means to do that."

Grumpkin stirred against my thigh, like a hand, stroking
me. That reminded me of Bill, and I felt the blood leave my face.
Bill knew. No. Bill didn't know I could come back, that is, he
didn't believe I could come back, but he didn know I thought so.
Pray God he didn't mention it to Jaybee.

Then I remembered Bill was dead. Jaybee had killed him.
Bill wouldn't mention anything to anyone.

"My enemy isn't here," I whispered again, blinking rapidly

to make the tears drain away, keeping my voice flat and level. "Not in this time. Not in this place. Take me somewhere, good horse, where we may rest."

We ambled down the road while the sun moved toward noon. The blood caked on my legs, and my trousers stuck to my skin. When the sun was at its height, we reached the place where the Sedgebrook fell into the Welling beside a tumble of stone and the shattered remnant of a great wheel, moss-hung where it stood beneath the sluice. Scattered among the trees were the stalks of old chimneys and a soggy rubbish of thatch. Sawley Minor was no more. There was no one in the place and nothing to show why they had gone.

Grumpkin crouched beside the water, a paw extended to catch whatever might be swimming there. The horse nibbled at the tall grass beside a broken chimney. I took off my clothes and washed myself and my trousers and changed my underwear and put a folded twentieth-century sock between my legs to keep the blood from coming through my clothes. In this time there were no napkins, ready-made in a box. There were no tampons. At my next "flowering" (Aunt Lovage's word), I would have to go back to rags, worn and washed in cold water, then dried and worn again, as Doll had taught me.

The horse and I drank long at the sluice while I wondered what to do next. Though there was no one at the mill, the road that led beside the ruins was still traveled. There were hoof-marks in the muddy verge, and the grasses at the edges had been bitten back by hungry beasts. It led to the abbey and on to East Sawley, and there would be someone, many someones, at either place. We turned down it, the horse, the cat, and I, moving slowly in the shadow of the leaves.

As we rounded each corner, I found myself looking for the abbey. I had been there a few times, with Papa and Aunt Terror. It had not seemed a lengthy journey, even to a child. When I saw it at last, however, I did not recognize it for what it was.

Empty walls by the lakeside. A few carved pillars, with branching tops, like trees turned to stone. Steps leading upward to a floor littered with blackened, shattered beams and a sooty altar stone. The chapel had been there. The burned beams told of fire and the roof falling in. Around this wreck stood vacant halls where men had once worked and prayed, weedy fields they had once planted. Beyond the chapel floor, in the cemetery of the abbey, lay row on row of crosses, a hundred new ones where once there had been a few dozen old ones.

I slid off Horse's back and walked between the stones of the tumbled wall. Beyond the fallen rock, roses were blooming. Here the abbot's garden had stood. Papa and Aunt Terror and I had had wine and cakes on the pillared porch where briars now tangled themselves beside the steps. In the center of the garden was a fishpond where lilies had bloomed, the roots brought home from distant lands by a crusader, so the abbot had told us. The pond was muddy now, sodden from recent rain and rank with vines.

I heard a sound and turned to see a skulking figure dart away behind a pile of stone. "Hey," I cried. "What happened here?"

There was no answer. I waited where I was, and after a time, an old face peered around a corner. I started toward it and was waved away.

"Stay away," he cried. "Stay away from me. Bring me no death. Stay away."

I stopped. "What happened here," I called again. "Did the place burn down?"

"Dead," he cackled at me, his eyes squinched almost shut. "Dead, all of them. All but half a dozen. Then the fire. Then the ruin. Then those that were left went away to Wellingford, all but me. I'll stay, I told them. Stay and guard the abbey."

"Dead?"

"Where've you come from, boy, that you don't know dead? With the Black Death dancing among us like the vintners upon the grapes until we are squoze, trampling us like the threshers on the straw until we are winnowed. Dead they all were, the abbot among them. Swollen and screaming and dead." He came out from behind the corner, a thin old monk in a ragged habit, capering like a goat and making a thin, screeching sound of lonely agony.

I knew of the Black Death. Of course. I had read of it, heard of it, repressed the information, somehow never dreamed that it had touched anyone I knew. And it had come here! And where else?

"Are there many dead in the nearby towns as well?" I asked. "In the hamlets and villages?"

"Everywhere," he cried, jigging up and down in his fear or fury. "Everywhere. And half of all the world is dead of it, too. Stay away from places, boy. Hide you in the forest. Hide you deep where nothing comes on you. Else you'll join them all. . . ." Something sounded deep within the trees, and he leapt like a startled deer and darted away. When I turned back from the sound, he had gone, leaving me with my dilemma still.

I had no time to nurse it. What had sounded in the trees was a horn, and what emerged from the trees was a hunting party, two lords, a few huntsmen, and a pack of spotted hounds. The men carried boar spears, so I knew they had been after wild pig, up Trottenham way most likely. I stood aside, humble as salt, and let them come.

He who came up with me was a stone-built man, thick through as a tree. "Ho, boy," he said to me with a bit of threat in his voice. "How came you by that horse?"

I bowed, as common people did. "I came not by it, master," I said. "It came by me. I was on the road, and it came up and nuzzled the sack I carry. When I told him I had no grain, he cared not but bid me ride anyways."

"That's Miller Sedgebrook's horse," said one of the huntsmen. "Miller's been dead over a year."

"Him and all his house," said another. "But one son who'd gone away."

I marked down that the miller had a son who'd gone away. Named Havoc, most likely. "Me," I said. "I've come back."

"Likely the beast was wandering," said the first huntsman. "Lonely for humankind."

"He seemed lonesome indeed," I said, looking at my feet.

"Did no one teach you to take off your cap before your betters?" the lord asked. "And what happened to your face?"

"Aye, s-s-sir," I stuttered, "but I've got my supper in it, and a man beat me, sir, and robbed me." Which was true enough.

He had stolen my virginity and my best friend and all my peace. He had robbed me well enough.

Though I had spoken without thinking, what I had said made me cry and them laugh. They felt amused and sorry for me, both at once.

"Get up on old Sedgebrook's horse and come with us, then," the lord said. "You can have a bite of supper that's better than you'll find under your cap, at least, and a place to sleep while you heal."

I gestured at the ruined abbey. "The old one there told me to stay far from people, sir, lest I die."

The lord nodded. "Ah, and well enough he'd have told you last year, boy, or the year before. But there've been few deaths this last twelvemonth, and we've hopes the thing is done with."

"The Black Death, he said?" I wanted confirmation.

They gave me curious looks, and I thought I'd better say less and listen better. Evidently the matter was so well-known it occasioned no comment.

"It seems to have been everywhere," I added, hastily.

They agreed it had indeed and bid me again to ride off with them, which I did, though well behind as was respectful. If I was to keep up my boy's disguise, I'd need to cut my hair shorter or braid it up tightly. The men wore theirs almost to their shoulders, but if I'd taken off my hat, mine was down my back so I could sit on it, which was what had betrayed me first to Jaybee. If they'd seen that, they'd not have long accepted me as a boy.

The place they took me was Wellingford House, a goodly manse set some distance from Wellingford village and with no walls about it. Papa had always called the lords of Wellingford plain fools to have no defenses, but from what was said on the ride, they had survived the Death better than most other places. When I saw the place, I thought I knew why. Whether I'd heard of the Death or not, everyone in the twentieth knew that rats and mice and fleas carried disease, a thing unknown in my own time. Wellingford House was as clean a place as I have seen in that time. Since there were no close walls to hold it in, the stables, kennels and barns were well away from the house with much clean garden between. The house had no rushes on the floor, and maids were kept busy sweeping morning and night. In most lordly places, even some parts of Westfaire, the floors were a midden of old rushes, bones, dog offal and droppings, and other, even more disgusting, dirt. Janet, the chatelaine of Wellingford House, would have none of that, and I saw only one rat the whole time I was there, and that was near the granary.

Janet was a termagant against fleas, as well, with much beating and sunning of clothing and much fleabane strewn in the presses. As a result of all this cleanliness, few of them at Wellingford had died. I was not introduced to those who were left, but I was sent to the kitchens, which is as good as an introduction. Never was a cook yet didn't like to talk, so I'd been told by our cook at Westfaire, and in the Wellingford kitchens I found out a good deal about the people, especially after the woman there had seen my battered face and come to feel sorry for me.

The lord was Robert of Wellingford, eldest son of the old earl who'd died some time before. His lady was Janet, and they had four children living, the youngest only three. Robert's two younger brothers lived on the place as well, the youngest, Richard, in the manor itself and the middle one, Edward, in the Dower House, which was some distance away across the park. There was some shaking of the head and pursing of the lips when they talked of Edward, "Naughty Ned," they called him, "One For The Ladies," who was always "Setting A Bad Example For The People." Janet had told him he must go out of the manor house to the Dower House, where he could have his doxies out of sight and mind.

I nodded and slurped my soup and dipped my bread and begged a bit of meat for Grumpkin and a swatch of hay for the old horse, which was really my horse if I was the miller's son, and asked questions about the countryside. Wellingford village and East Sawley, it seemed, were still there, though the latter was much depleted by the plague. All around the countryside places were in ruin, and there was nobody left to build them up again.

"Sir Robert's been looking for masons and builders for over

a year now, to put the abbey back together, but there's no men to be had. In the cities, it's worse! There's no one left to do anything at all. We've only enough here to work the fields and the flocks, as is, and there's places hadn't enough men to put seed in the ground! Come harvest time, people'll go hungry, mark me!" She, plump as a pigeon, bustled around the fire in a way that made one doubt hunger existed. Still, if she was right, if there weren't enough people left on the farms to plant grain, hunger would come. I shivered and took another mouthful.

"Sir Robert planted extra this year, so's he can give doles come winter," she fretted. "But it won't be enough. Nothing will be. When the people died, the oxen wandered off, and the horses, like the one you found. Some are probably out there, wandering, but many have been killed and eaten by the poor and the homeless. So, even if we had more men to plant more fields, we'd have no more plowbeasts. And the people, wandering about, taking refuge in old places, they make fires and burn the places down, not meaning to, just out of carelessness. The mill, that's how the mill went. And the abbey. And nothing tastes like anything at all, either." She put her hands on her ample hips and glared at me as though I might have occasioned the plague without knowing it. "There's been no spices all this year. The traders died, too, just like everyone else. We're lucky to have a priest about to keep us in the grace of God; most places have none at all."

I thought of Father Raymond, asleep at Westfaire. It was no time to think of Westfaire.

"What's the year?" I asked, ignorant country boy that I was. "I forget."

"It's the year of Our Lord thirteen fifty," she said. "So says our learned priest. And no Death this year, which makes it a good year, boy, whatever else happens." She gave me more soup and a pat on the head.

I had spent a year and a half in the twentieth, but three years had passed here since I had left. So much destruction and death in three little years.

"If everyone's looking for workers, then maybe there's

room for me here?" I asked. "I'm thin, but I'm strong. I'm good with horses. I've done stable work since I was eight."

"I'll tell Sir Robert you want to speak to him," she said.

She was good as her word, and the lord spoke to me the next morning, giving me my keep and space in the stables and a tiny wage for my work, as well. Considering everything, it seemed a good place to stay. Grumpkin agreed. The smells of the horses and the hay spoke to him of home. He made himself a nest in the loft and lay there much of the day, like a lion glorying in his past and future conquests, while I groomed horses and mucked out the stalls and rubbed oil into leather, just as I had used to do long ago, with Martin. He had schooled me well, for no one found fault with my work.

It was a strange time, that next time. Despite all the death around, I felt safe. Despite that the country was in ruins, I felt at home. Despite that I had to hide my hair and my body—easier then, in those loose smocks and unfitted trousers than it would have been in the twentieth—I felt myself. Anger left me, slowly, until I was able to acknowledge what had happened. It had happened, I said to myself. I had been defiled and terrorized, but I was still alive, unmutilated, sound in body and mind. My body had healed. Vengeance, I promised myself, but there was no hurry. I could take a time to simply be Havoc, the miller's son. I had been away, I said when they asked. I had not known my family was gone until I came to the mill itself.

"I didn't know the miller had another son than the three who died," the Lady Janet said.

"Oh, yes," someone said. "He had another son, but I've forgotten what it was about the boy."

"He sent me to his sister when I was only a baby," I told them. "I've been there since." Who was to say I lied? Let them think what they would think anyhow, that Havoc had not been born in wedlock, that he had been the miller's son but not of the miller's wife.

Each day started with a bite of bread and a draft of beer in the kitchen, this through the kindness of the cook who said I was still a growing boy, for others of the servants and serfs got nothing until later. Then exercising the horses out on the meadows, staying away from the sheep and the cows so they would not be scattered by the dogs who came running after the horses, their tongues lalloping out of their mouths as they ran. Then grooming, and feeding, and taking care of the saddles and bridles. Some of the leather was worked in gilt, and the oil would strip it away, so it was mincy work with a little brush and a rag. The other stable hands hated it for their big hands were clumsy with the tools, so I did most of it myself. It was quiet. There was no one about.

Dinner at midday was bread and beer again, and salad or a bit of fruit and a bite of stringy mutton sometimes, or a piece of boiled fowl, sometimes juicy, sometimes powdery from being in the soup so long, tasting like the memory of chicken. Then there was hay to pitch up from the wains, or stalls to muck. Sometimes Grumpkin would bring me mice, strings of them, laying them out on the stable floor like toy soldiers. He was learning to be a real stable cat again.

Supper was in hall, everyone there except the kitchen servants, and me at the bottom of the lowest bench of all, quite content to be there, even though I had lice. No help for it. No way for a stableboy to avoid other stableboys, no way to get a hot, soapy bath in the washroom off the kitchen, no way for me to let my hair down until night, when they all slept and I was alone in my loft. I itched all the time, but I was content to be there, nonetheless, listening to the singing sometimes when a jongleur came through, listening to the lords and ladies talking in their stilted French with English words dotted through it like raisins in a pudding, while the rest of us bellowed away in that same English, soon enough to be the language of us all, I supposed. Since they'd spoken something like it in the twentieth, clear enough that it was the tongue to survive.

In the stables, I'd met Lord Richard and Lord Edward: Naughty Ned. Of the two, Ned was the more interesting. Robert and Richard were both sticks, nice sticks, but sticks all the same, dry and twiggy and given to crepitant stretching when they dismounted, every bone making its own little complaint. Ned was full of the juices of life, wild and rideaway, with lips that fairly dripped honey, even to those in the stable. They had not lied about him. He did have his ladies, no better, as cook said, than they ought to be, a new one every few days or weeks. They were not doxies, really. They were widows mostly, women of a certain class who took only noble lovers and accepted "presents" rather than payment, living from invitation to invitation.

Everyone talked about Robert's demand that Ned get himself married. Ned said no, and Robert said yes, and it had been that way for a while. Even Lady Janet had put her voice to work on him, explaining how people were needed to work the estate and how it was everyone's responsibility to produce children.

Ned only laughed. He'd stand in the stableyard, telling the head groom about it, saying he scattered his seed far enough, it wasn't his fault it didn't grow. Scattered among the tares, muttered the chaplain, giving him long penances when he confessed. I was outside, praying. I could not confess, for I did not trust the priest as I had Father Raymond. He might well tell on me.

I asked about Giles. Sure enough, he had returned—one of the men-at-arms knew of him—but had gone away again when he found Westfaire mounded with roses. That night I wept, wondering where he might be and how I might find him and whether I dared have the boots take me to him. He could be anywhere in the world. He could be married. I was afraid to find out.

It was a time, a few foolish weeks, during which I returned to the sureties of childhood.

It stopped abruptly one day when the cook asked me, "Havoc, how long have you been here, now? Five weeks or more? And not stepped foot in the chapel for mass yet or gone to confession. . . ."

Five weeks. Surely not. And yet when I counted up, it was true. I had been there five weeks. My mouth dropped open in sudden realization.

I had, using Aunt Lovage's word, "flowered" only two weeks before Jaybee had attacked me. I had not "flowered" since. Aunt Lovage talked that way when she was a little drunk. Which, come to think of it, was better than the other aunts who hadn't talked of it at all. It hadn't mattered that they hadn't told me however. What I hadn't learned in the stable or from Doll, I'd learned in school, in the twentieth, about things like this.

Things like this. Things like probably being pregnant. I wanted to howl, couldn't howl, not with the cook there, bustling about, not in that soapy, hot-watery place, all grease and yeasty smelling. I wanted a howling place, a place of my own.

Evening went, and I went with it, mounted on my old friend, Horse, and with Grumpkin on my shoulder. I went back to Westfaire by the light of the moon, determined to get inside those roses. I remembered the water gate, where the lake ran into the moat. I remembered a time Martin and some of the other men had gone to clean it out, and Havoc had tagged along. They had gone under the stone bridge which stood at the shoreline and through a gate into the moat itself. Roses, so I thought, could not grow on water.

By the light of the moon, I went out into the lake, then waded up to my neck, holding Grumpkin on the folded cloak above my head, my shirt making slithery motions around my thighs. Nothing but roses on the shore, piled into pinnacles and towers, massive ramparts and flowery battlements, roses and more roses. But in the water, nothing. I saw the shape of the bridge, covered with thorny green. Below the bridge, roses draped down to the very surface of the lake, but behind those canes was a gaping hole where the water flowed in. I waded, pushing the canes aside with padded hands. Under the bridge, only water and the soft lop lop lop of it against the curving mossy sides where it flowed. At the inside end was an iron grating, like the portcullis above. That was to prevent people bringing boats into the moat from the lake. I had no key, but the bars were far enough apart that I could slip between them.

Which I did, scratching myself on the rusty iron and discomfiting Grumkin a little. I stroked him while he growled and clung to me, as though I were a tree. There were slippery steps leading up to the little door in the corner of the wall. I went up, and through, and came out dripping wet in Westfaire.

So strange a place. Surrounded by darkness. Only open at the very top, so that the moon shone in, silvering the stones.

Within the roses, nothing had changed. Everyone was sleeping still, just as I had left them. I sat down and howled, holding onto my cat, crying my heart out, letting the stones hear my grief. Certainly no one else heard it.

"Mother!" I cried. "I'm pregnant!"

No wind in answer, no song of bird. Not even the squeak of a bat, high in that moon-tunneled darkness. Silence and sleep. I stood amid watching shadows and wept.

[We stood in the darkness and watched her, Israfel and I. I think I cried, I who have wept only once since the fountains of the deep grew dry.

"She was supposed to go from here, into hiding," I said. "To Chinanga, where no one could hurt her!"

"Yes," Israfel nodded. "But she needed a little rest first."

"Perhaps we could take it out of her and hide it somewhere else," I said.

"We'd kill her if we tried," said Israfel. "It has grown into her. She permeates it, now. You can't get it out without killing her."

"Is the Dark Lord looking for it yet?"

"He has been looking for it since he was born. He simply doesn't know what it is."

"And he has not found it yet."

Israfel shook his head to tell me no, the Dark Lord had not found it yet.

I think people sensed it in her. I think Jaybee and Barrymore Gryme had sensed it, without knowing what it was. Perhaps the Dark Lord had sensed it as well, though he had not found it yet.

"Can we wait until she has the baby?" I asked.

"We must," said Israfel. "Since it was fathered by someone who may be a minion of the Dark Lord himself, who knows what it is likely to be," he said. "She cannot have it in Chinanga. She would remain pregnant forever in Chinanga. She could have it in Faery, but everyone would talk of it and the Dark Lord would surely be curious about it. Better that she have it here, where it will evoke no curiosity, where it will only be another birth among these fecund humans. If it is a monster, we can protect her from it."

"Poor child," I said. I had said that several times recently. Briefly I wondered, if I had known her before we did what we did, would I have done it?

"Yes," said Israfel, reading my mind. "You would."]

There was no answer to my cry. I tried again. "What am I going to do?" Still no answer. The shadows looked like robed figures, watching me. Almost I expected them to speak, but they did not. Instead they wavered, as in a breeze, and became only shadows.

What could I do. Go back to the twentieth. Stay where I was. Go somewhere else. Oh God, oh God, where was Father Raymond? Where was Doll? Asleep, deep asleep.

In the twentieth it wouldn't be much. Women had children all the time, married or not. As Candy would say, not enough to shed two tears over. Except he was there, Jaybee. Wouldn't he love it, making me pregnant. Wouldn't he strut, cock of the walk, cock of the dung heap. Wouldn't he whisper to me, stroking me like a cat, Beauty, Beauty, come with me, Beauty, or else. . . . And what would he do to a child?

I couldn't. I would rather die. Not merely words, those, but truth. If dying were the choice, then I'd do it. Drown myself out in the lake. Swim out until I couldn't swim any farther, then go down, choking, just for a little time, into swimmy depths.

Not to know how it all came out? Not to know where Mama was? Not to know whether it would be a boy, or a girl. Or neither! There was a thought!

Abortion. I could go back and have an abortion! Go to some other place. New York, New York, the wonderful town. Chicago. It didn't have to be the States of America, it could be London! I didn't need to have it. It could be ripped out.

I howled.

I didn't want it to be ripped out. I didn't want it, either, but I didn't . . .

Didn't . . .

Don't, I told myself. Don't do anything. Don't decide anything. You're too tired and upset. Go up to your room and sleep, here in Westfaire. Wrapped in your cloak, you're safe. Sleep.

I did. I went up the winding staircase to my own tower room, finding it miraculously repaired, all signs of the fire gone away. I started to lie down on the bed but found myself lying there already. Someone had brought Beloved up from the room far below where I had put her. Somebody had put her in the tower, where romance and glamour demanded she be. The fairy aunts, like enough. I would have done it had I been all fairy. On the chest beside her my mysterious thing made its quiet noise, and I looked long at it, convincing myself the lacy arrow had moved. Not much, but some. It was now exactly halfway between the fourteen and the fifteen.

"Oh, shit," I said, leaving it there to go thumping my way down the stairs, down to Aunt Lavender's room. She was asleep on the floor. Her bed would be empty, dust free and sweet scented by the herb she was named after. As it was, for Grumpkin and I lay down there, wrapped in the cloak, and slept, deeply and dreamlessly, until morning.

Morning was as strange as night had been. Everything was lost in a green murk. Only at noon, with the sun straight overhead, was there any light, for the roses went up to make a great chimney, open at the top. I could look straight up and see clouds passing, birds flying. "Mama," I called again, thinking she might be about, for perhaps she had helped to move Beloved, "I'm pregnant!"

No answer. Perhaps Aunt Joyeause had moved Beloved. Perhaps they had all come together, riding on doves, to repair the tower and set things properly, as on a stage, and then had gone far away again, where I could not follow for I knew not where they were.

Grumpkin meowed at me, saying he was hungry. In the dairy I milked a sleeping cow and we shared the milk. In the kitchen we found a meat pie and shared that. It was enchanted and therefore did not taste as though it had been sitting there for three years. The smell was still there, and the aura flowed down from the tower. I was in my cloak and did not fall asleep. I put a flap of it over Grumpkin as he ate, and he did not fall asleep, though I thought of setting the cloak aside and lying down there in that familiar place, to sleep for a century or so.

What did I want to do?

I didn't want to go back to the twentieth. It was too uncomfortable and too ugly and too threatening.

I wanted to stay here, where I was.

I didn't want to have a bastard child. Life is very hard for bastard children, even when they aren't called that. Even in the twentieth, life was hard for them.

Well then. I would need a husband. Preferably a wealthy one. Preferably a charming one. Preferably . . .

"I have decided our future," I told Grumpkin at last. "We're going back to Wellingford House and seduce Naughty Ned."

·
16
·

I am not an accomplished seductress. I am not a seductress at all. At Westfaire, no man would have dared say a word to me about such matters or even make a gesture toward me. In the twentieth there were words and gestures in plenty, but I rejected all of them, too frightened of diseases to risk getting involved with anyone, perhaps, or, perhaps, simply not interested. Still, I knew well enough how babies were planted. What I had not learned at the stables in Westfaire or at school in the twentieth, Jaybee's assault would have shown me. If Naughty Ned were to be convinced my child was his, I would have to get him to bed with me soon as might be.

And just to bed would not be enough. He would have to want to marry me as well. Unfortunately, there was no reason under heaven he should want to marry Havoc the miller's son. Havoc who smelled. Havoc with his lice and his dirty skin and his filthy boy's clothes.

I considered stealing women's clothes. Often the maids put Lady Janet's linens out to air, and I thought I could make away with some of them, leaving a petticoat or two half over the hedge to suggest the wind had blown them away. Lady Janet was twice my size, however, as well as being shorter than I. And even if I took the underthings, I would still need a gown. No one at Wellingford was my size, and none of the girls in the village nearby had nice enough gowns. I could not even make myself a gown, for how would I hide it from my stable mates while working on it?

After a time the obvious answer came to me. There were ladies' clothes aplenty at Westfaire. If one of my mother's gowns had fit me, then all would fit me. I made another midnight expedition to bring some of them out—a few of the dozen I found hung in the attics—and I hid them away in a kind of cubby over the stable, still wrapped in the sheet I had carried them in. I would have been able to do none of it without the horse God had sent me, so I thanked Him by renaming the beast Angel.

Next it was time, so I thought, to find out what kind of women Naughty Ned preferred. Every night for a dozen nights I went to the Dower House, invisible in my cloak, seeking the answer to that question. There were four ladies during those dozen days. One left the first night I watched. One came then for three days. One came then for seven. And one was still there when I stopped watching. At the end of that time, I asked my question still, for the ladies were nothing alike. One was a blonde, two were dark-haired, one had hair the color of carrots. One was slender, two voluptuous, one skinny as a rake. Their eyes and mouths and skins were different as well. I conquered my blushes to watch what they did in bed as well as out of it, or beside the bed or on the way to it. It was nothing any two acrobats could not have done better with less sweat, though possibly with less enjoyment. Though, come to think of it, Naughty Ned had not seemed to enjoy it that much. He had been lively and yet, if I interpreted his look correctly, somehow uninvolved.

There was the one woman who had stayed seven days. He had taken her to bed less often than the others, but she had stayed with him longer than the others. She, though not astonishingly clever, was the wittiest of the lot. Seeing this gave me a faint ray of hope. The time came, as I had assumed it would, when the current lady went away, and there was not yet another lady to take her place. There was not another lady because certain messages had been intercepted or sent mistakenly to people who knew nothing about them. Havoc had been invisibly busy, arranging that letters should go astray.

When the last lady departed, Havoc volunteered to get up at dawn and heat the water for doing the wash, which was done in the same tub and the same room as people bathed in, when they did. It was Beauty who bathed in the water while it was hotting, however, well before dawn and no one knew about that. I washed my hair, as well, and combed the nits out of it before wrapping it up in rags because there are no curlers in this century. The rags I hid under my cap, and I dirtied my face in case cleanliness should cause suspicion. Faces are easy to wash.

When nighttime came, I washed my face again, combed out my dry hair to let it hang in a foamy golden cloud down my back, put on one of Mama's gowns and my cloak, and sneaked away across the meadows. At the Dower House I took off the cloak, hung it carefully over the terrace railing, where I could find it again, and walked down the terrace to the room where Naughty Ned always sat at his ease after his evening meal. I knocked. He came to the tall window himself and let me in, his face a perfect picture of surprise.

"Good evening, Edward," I said. "I am Beauty, the daughter of the Duke of Westfaire. I have come to keep you company and tell you tales to allay your boredom."

Then I sat down by the fire and told him the future of the world. I was witty. I was amusing. I laughed gently and forestalled his advances. I drank but little wine and kept my wits about me. When the bell in the Wellingford chapel rang for Matins, I excused myself and left him there, disappearing into my cloak on the terrace. He came out after me, searching, calling my name. I ran away, down the long terrace and home across the meadows, just in time to put my gown away, get on my boy clothes once more, and catch a scant few hours sleep in the hay.

It had been, I told myself, done as well as I could do it. When I saw how well he liked the wittier lady, I remembered a book I had read in school in the twentieth. It was called the Arabian Nights, and it was about Scheherazade who told clever tales for a thousand and one nights in order to avoid being put to death. I had nowhere near that long. If I couldn't fascinate him sooner, the whole thing was hopeless anyhow. Going to bed with him would not accomplish what I had in mind. He had done that over and over again with many women without wanting to be married to any of them. And though he had tried several times, out of habit, to interrupt me by suggesting something improper, I had always put him off and gone on with my tales. I thought possibly the mystery would reach him where the carnality hadn't.

As Havoc, I watched that day as Edward set off to ride to Westfaire, which was known by most local residents to be under an enchantment. I heard Edward talking about it with the men who were riding with him. "An enchantment of roses," is the way he put it, sounding excited. That evening, when he returned, he looked scratched and frustrated. One of the men told the head groom that Lord Edward had not been able to penetrate the roses around Westfaire though he had repeatedly tried! I considered it a hopeful sign.

That night I put on the second gown—I had brought only three from Westfaire—and went to the Dower House again. Again I told him tales until Matins, and again he pursued me when I ran away.

On the third night I took my cloak in with me, set it beside me on the chair, and in the midst of my discourse sighed and interrupted the tale. When he asked me why, I told him I was under an enchantment. That until I was married to a man who would ask me no questions, I could appear only after dark and the barrier around Westfaire would remain. I said this twice, being sure he understood it, before I directed his attention to a spurious spy at the window and disappeared while his head was turned. He looked around him wildly, cursing and crying my name. I had done it as well as it could be done, I told myself again, making my weary way home across the fields.

The fourth night I did not go at all. Nor the fifth.

On the sixth, I returned in the gown I had worn when he saw me first. He was stalking up and down on the terrace outside his window, clenching and unclenching his fists, muttering and sighing. This was a good sign. I took off the cloak and sighed loudly, myself. The moment he saw me, he went to one

knee and asked me to marry him. I turned away, thrusting out
one hand as though my maidenly modesty had been deeply
surprised. He begged. I looked at my hands and wrung them
dramatically. He begged the more. At last, on an expiring sigh, I
said yes. I would meet him at the Wellingford chapel at dusk,
three days afterward, and marry him there.

He would have time for second thoughts. So did I, when I
was awake enough to have any thoughts at all. Lord Robert
cursed at me for being asleep in a horse's stall, and Lady Janet
told me to wake up when I dozed against the side of the steed
she was mounting. Mostly I thought that I did not want to be
married. I would not have minded if Giles had been there to
marry me, but I did not want to marry Ned. What I really
wanted to do and had set out to do was find my mother. I
longed for a mother. Someone to tell my troubles to, a shoulder
to cry on, a sympathetic hand on my forehead, a voice saying,
"There, there, dear, we'll work it all out." I thought of using the
boots, assuming they would take me wherever she was, but the
thought of going to my mama pregnant! She had told me to
come to her at once, before I grew older. Coming to her in my
present condition did not seem appropriate. It would be like
going home in disgrace. Despite my fretfulness, that night I
slept like one dead, and in the morning woke to hear the news
everyone was babbling. Lord Edward was going to be married in
three days, but he would not say to whom.

I went in my cloak to keep watch on him that night. There
were no ladies at the Dower House, nor on the night that followed. It appeared he really intended to go through with it.

The Wellingford chapel was a small one, large enough for
the family and servants only, served by a resident priest who
said daily masses and took care of christenings and burials. Also,
three monks had been taken in from the abbey when it was
destroyed, and it was they who rang the bells for the holy office.
The chapel was set in a graveyard, and there were Wellingfords
buried all around and beneath it, the whole place smelling a bit
of sanctity and dust and rot, as well as of incense and tallow.

I did not go openly. I went in my cloak, ready to flee if
something appeared amiss, and I stood on the porch for a time,

looking in at the people. The priest was there, looking grumpy.
So were various members of the family, irritably glancing
around to catch a glimpse of the putative bride. Ned **was** there,
jumpy as a cat, darting glances at the door every second or **two**.
The priest gave up his unpleasant look to yawn. Ordinarily,
Ned and I would have pledged our respective properties and
exchanged rings in the church porch. I had no property to ex-
change, or at least none I was willing to use as dowry. Ned
would have to take me as I stood.

I put the cloak down in the porch and walked slowly down
the center aisle. Everyone stared at me and murmured. I pretended not to notice the admiring looks cast my way by some of
the gentlemen and even a few of the ladies. I had done what I
could to look well. There were summer flowers twined in my
hair. I had returned to Westfaire for yet another dress, the pink
one I had worn at the banquet the night before Papa had intended to marry Weasel-Rabbit. When the priest asked my
name, I told him in a clear and carrying voice that all might hear:
"Beauty, daughter of Elladine of Ylles and the Duke of Westfaire, under an enchantment which can only be broken by marrying an uninquisitive man."

Ned looked into my eyes and swore to honor and keep me.
He whispered in my ear that he would be uninquisitive. He
would not ask questions. He trembled when he took my hand. I
looked at his chin and pledged to render him my duty, wondering betime what Father Raymond would have said about all
this. Father Raymond had had definite opinions about the sacrament of marriage, and I concluded he would have been disappointed in me, taken all in all. The priest babbled a great deal of
comfortable Latin and we took the sacrament together. Ned
kissed me, delicately, as though I might break. I curtseyed to his
older brother, to Janet, to his younger brother, to other members
of the family. Janet gave me a hug, rather quickly, as though she
were afraid the enchantment might rub off on her. We left the
chapel and walked across to the manor house where the kitchens had been steaming since noon, preparing a feast.

"We didn't have time to prepare anything elegant," said
Janet. "Or to think of a proper gift."

"I was given a proper gift," I said in what I fondly hoped were mysterious tones. "A young boy, seeing me approaching the chapel, told me he would give me his dearest possession as a gift for my wedding. The gift is a cat called Grumpkin, he is in the stables, and I would like him brought here."

Someone went for Grumpkin, coming back later rather the worse for wear with my poor cat in a sack. I cursed myself for stupidity in letting anyone else go in my place and turned him loose, giving him a saucer of cut up fowl on the floor at my feet.

"We couldn't find the boy, ma'am," I heard one of the servants saying to Janet.

"He told me he was leaving," I said, my words carrying over the clatter of the diners. "Going away. Never to be seen in these parts again."

It was true, then, so far as I knew. What need had the wife of Edward Wellingford for Havoc, the miller's son.

Remembering what I had seen in the Dower House as a voyeur, I made no effort to compete in innovation or athleticism with the women Edward had consorted with in the past. It was no lie to pretend virginity. It was no lie to pretend shyness. I felt them both. When, on the third or fourth night after the wedding, Edward made love to me at last—I having held him off till then out of a genuine feeling of revulsion which I managed to overcome at last only by much purposeful wine-bibing—I felt nothing much except discomfort and relief when it was over. Jaybee had evidently unsuited me for the enjoyments of the flesh, though thereafter, knowing what to expect from Edward, it became easier. I knew it was supposed to be a pleasant experience. Out of curiosity if nothing else, I had read in the twentieth how a woman can assure that it is pleasant, but I felt no impetus toward talking with Edward about it or doing what in the twentieth would have been called "working at our relationship." It would have been a lie. I did not want to work at the relationship because I did not love him. I came quite to like him as the days went by, but I did not discern in myself even so much affection toward him as I had often felt toward Bill or so much as I felt toward Grumpkin. Edward did not know me and never would.

Our relationship was built upon a fiction. It was shallow and, I feared, temporary. I could not visualize myself staying at Wellingford long after the child was born. The child itself, I could not visualize at all.

Still, I was carefully gentle and kindly in my mood, receptive in my manner. So much was owed the man, after all. I took my wedding vows as seriously as I might for what time I had. He liked me to look lovely, so I made a point of that. Even when I became, all too soon, swollen as a melon, I could smell sweet as any garden and wear flowing things that rustled gently.

We rode. He insisted I ride sidesaddle, which I hated. My grandfather's invention evidently had gained some little reputation among the neighboring nobility. We read together, he evincing delight that I knew how to read and write, which, indeed, I did better than he. I told him stories, things I had experienced, things I had heard of, and he was mightily amused, wondering how I had come by such a store of tales. I made up a lie about my father's fool, that he was a widely traveled creature with a retentive memory who had fed me on stories from my childhood. It was more or less true. The fool had fed me on stories, right enough, though they had mostly been of a less than salutary kind that made the women he had known the butt of his evil humor.

When we had been married about four months, Edward came in from riding one day to tell me that the roses mounded Westfaire still, that the enchantment remained. He looked hurt.

I was prepared for this. I told him that we knew half the enchantment had been removed, for I was able to appear regularly in the daylit hours, but that since complete lack of inquisitiveness was the *conditio sine qua non* there must be some kernel of curiosity in him still, which prevented the entire enchantment from being broken. He flushed, and I knew I was safe from further conversation on that matter.

Time wore on through the winter to the early spring, and the baby was born. It was early, of course. I made much of that when labor started, saying no, no, it could not be yet. I need hardly have troubled. In that time, babies often came early and were too tiny to live. Often they died. I thought I would die, wished to die, wished I had stayed in the twentieth where there are drugs for such pain, almost screamed out for my boots to take me there, but was drowned out by the midwives' exhortations to breathe, to breathe, to push, to push. I screamed and breathed and pushed. There was a squall, followed by bustling to and fro, then the tiny swaddled creature was laid on my arm while someone messed about between my legs, cleaning up. There was much clucking over the afterbirth, in which the midwives purported to read signs and portents of both good and evil, but they soon gave over and set things to rights. I thought of Aunt Lavvy as they sprinkled oil of lavender about and burned sweet resins in the candles to kill the mudflats, seaside smell of birthing. When Edward was allowed in, we were clean and sweet once more, and he gazed at us both as he might have gazed at heavenly angels.

"What shall we name her," he asked in a whisper, his hand gently upon my arm.

"After my mother," I told him. "Elladine. That was my mother's name." I wanted to love the child. I wanted to remind myself that children need a mother's love.

He added a string of family names, and a day or so later she was taken to the chapel by Janet to be christened. Though she was one-quarter fairy, I made no mention of the fact. My own christening had started all this mess. Better the baby get by as simply as possible with Robert and the Lady Janet as her godparents and the blessing of Holy Church to guard her through life.

After that, time seemed almost to stop. I tried to nurse her myself, rejecting the wet-nurse from the village. I rather liked the feel of it, liked being close to her. The sight and sound of the tiny fuzz-covered head so tight against me, the little star-shaped hands pushing like a kitten's paws, the toothless pink mouth agape like a bird's, all were interesting. Then one morning when she was about two weeks old—it was midmorning, actually, with the sun casting westward beams along the wall at the edge of the heavy curtains—as she was nursing, she opened her eyes and looked at me and it was Jaybee's look, greedy and violent. Her mouth clamped down on me as though strong fingers pinched me. There was blood on my nipple. I gave a cry, and the maids came rushing in. I told them to fetch the wet-nurse, that my breasts would no longer be enough for the child, keeping my voice as calm as I could though inside I bubbled with hysteria. He too had bitten me there. He too had drawn blood.

[*"Now," I said to Israfel.*
"Wait a little," he said. "She is coming to it of her own accord."]

Thereafter they brought her to me once or twice a day, to look at. She was everything tiny, precious, holdable. Everything fragile and sweet. And yet his eyes looked out at me from the infant face, as though he lay within the infant mind, waiting. After that, I could not touch her without an instinctive aversion, a revulsion. The wet-nurse fed her; the nursemaid changed her napkins; and Edward adored her. Seeing his face above the child was like seeing the spring sun rising over the fields. He was so full of love it shone from him.

Edward hovered over me, too, but, as was thought proper in those times, did not invite me to his bed for the forty days I lay with the bedcurtains drawn, seeing neither the sun nor moon until time came to be churched. Father Raymond had always said the churching of women was a ceremony of thanksgiving for a safe delivery, but at Wellingford it seemed quite another thing. There, so the midwives said, a woman was considered unclean and unholy by virtue of the blood she had shed in giving birth, and only the priest's words said over her put her in a state of grace once more. While there were some at Wellingford who disbelieved such nonsense, Lady Janet believed it wholeheartedly, and it was her way the wives forced on me, whether I would or no. In some other time or place I might have made a fuss, but since Edward and his kin were kindly and generally well-disposed toward me, there was no point in making them uncomfortable.

At the end of the "lying in," I went to the chapel, all muffled up in the traditional veils, to take a seat near the altar and have the priest read psalms over me to compensate for my having offended God by bearing a child in holy wedlock. The "chapel smell" was very strong that day, as it had been the night Ned and I were married. I still couldn't identify what it was. When the priest had finished, I was supposedly free of the world again, able to look upon sunshine and stars. I did not tell them I had been sneaking out of bed nighttimes to sit in the window watching the moon and longing for something I could not quite name. My own mother, I think. Someone of my own, at least, who could explain to me what I was feeling. Despite all my good intentions I could not love my own child. It horrified me that I saw Jaybee's malevolence in that tiny face. She was half me! Surely my half counted for something! Often though I convinced myself of that, when I saw her, when she opened her dark eyes and looked at me, I saw only violence and terror and felt only a memory of pain.

In addition to her fears about newly delivered women, Lady Janet also feared the babe would be taken by fairies, so there were maids about day and night, hovering over the cradle. Janet told tales of babes snatched away with changelings left in their place. No one said why fairies preferred human children to their own, and I considered it unlikely. I had seen one that Janet spoke of and knew him to be no changeling but a poor idiot, what the twentieth called a Down's syndrome child, born to a woman in her forty-fourth year, but there was no point in arguing the matter with Janet. It would do little Elly no harm to have loving people about her, even for a spurious reason.

Though I kept her at a distance from me, she had no lack of caring hands to help her and gentle arms to hold her. Ned played with her as if she had been a novel toy, doing peek-a-baby and pat-a-cake until both he and Elly were helpless with laughter. More than once I surprised on his face an expression of grateful wonder, as though there were something in being a father he had neither expected nor dared hope for. As for me, I wavered between resentment that the babe was not the child of someone I loved and thankfulness that at least she bid fair to be beautiful and not apish as Jaybee's child might well have been.

Remembering what I had learned in the twentieth, I took such precautions as I might to be sure I did not conceive again. Luck or God was with me. Almost a year went by and I did not kindle. Remembering Ned's boistrous talk before our marriage about having scattered his seed widely without issue, I began to think he might be sterile. I wished I knew for sure, that I might give up the counting of days and the playing of games, pretending to have headaches or other infirmities to keep him at a distance betimes. Still, the thought gave me some hope that Elly would be our only child.

I took to riding a good deal, for exercise, and to get away from the house. I went often alone, preferring that to being pursued by panting stableboys mounted on fat carthorses, for the master of horse would let them ride nothing better and there were no men to spare to keep an eye on me. One day I had ridden out early, going up into the hills, and I came to a ridge where one could look down, over the burned abbey and the lake and across the lake to the mound of roses where Westfaire slept.

I didn't see the man there until I had dismounted. He moved, and it startled me.

"M'lady," he said. "Do not be afraid."

Oh God, I knew that voice. I turned and went toward him, he looking across at me, at first in curiosity and then, almost, in terror.

"Beauty!" he cried.

"Giles!" I screamed in return. Oh, he was the same, the same. He had hardly aged at all. The same light brown hair, though it was cut short, as though he had spent much time under helm. His eyes were the same when they looked into mine.

"You can't be," he said firmly, like a man turning his back on an enchantment. "Oh no, you can't be!"

"No, I am!" I cried. "I really am. It wasn't me who got enchanted, Giles. I was outside!"

He took my hands. He pulled me close to him and I felt the thunder of his heart. It was the first time he had ever held me, and everything in me turned warm and molten and, oh, I lusted after him. I wanted him, there, then, on the patch of grass beneath that tree. I put my arms about his neck and kissed him, the kissing burning like a fire. We kissed one another, turning our heads this way and that, as though if we found the proper position we could somehow transcend our separateness and become one person, fused at the lips.

"No, no," he gasped at last, putting me away from him. "This is not proper. You are a virgin girl. . . ."

I laughed. I reached for him, clung to him, said I wasn't. I was married, a mother, married to Edward of Wellingford. I babbled, holding on to him like a cat to a tree. He went white. He loosened my hands. He backed away from me.

"Married," he whispered. It was as though he had said, "Dead."

I stopped talking and looked into his eyes. There was no lack of love there, but I knew that, when I told him I was married, I had lost him. Giles was an honorable man. He was a religious man. He was a chivalrous man. I had lived so long in the twentieth, I had forgotten about honorable, chivalrous men. But Giles was! Not merely in words, but in deeds. He would no more cuckold another man than he would strike an opponent from behind, for such would not be virtuous, and he longed for virtue. Would he have obeyed Father Raymond and gone from me else?

"Giles . . ." I whispered. "Oh, Giles. Don't leave me. I need you."

He warded me off, as he might have warded a curse. "I love and honor Beauty, the only woman I will ever love," he said. "But she whom I loved was a girl whom I had the right to love." He went away from me, turned and ran for his horse, and I think I heard him sobbing as he went.

I screamed his name. I stood there, screaming his name, the tears running down my face. I threw myself on the ground and wept. When I looked up next, he was gone. I thought I might have imagined him, but then I saw him, far below, riding full tilt across a clearing, away, away.

When I could, I returned to Wellingford, to Elly, to Ned, to my life. I felt that I had died, and only my shell was there.

As Elly had grown, so had Ned's love for her. He loved me, too, but as he might love an ornament, a thing fragile and fair which he might brag of having, a thing barely utilitarian. He owned a crystal cruet some knight had brought from the Holy

Land, and he spoke of that cruet much as he spoke of me. My lovely Beauty. My Beauty without compare. And then, "Mother of my Beloved . . ."

When he said that, something cracked. Anger spurted out like blood from a new wound. So, I was the mother of his beloved. I was always something to do with someone else's beloved. Edward's beloved or my father's beloved. And Giles, my beloved, would not have me because I was the mother of Ned's beloved. I went to my bed and cried, and the longing to get away began to grow in me. The longing for someone of my own kin possessed me.

I remembered that while a year and a half had passed in the twentieth, three had passed in the fourteenth. I wasn't sure how old I was. Was I seventeen? Or nineteen? My mama had said to come before I got any older, but I was older. Still, if I spent some time searching for Mama, it might seem only a little time to little Elly and to Edward, for time was different in different places.

I wrestled with my conscience as Jacob wrestled with the angel of God, paining myself in the sport until I could not sleep at night. I wandered about the place all that night, half the night spent traversing the walk to the chapel, there and back again. I went through the still room stores, counting and recounting the cordials, the jams. Through the cellars, totting up the wine. Through the linen closets. As I was counting the linens, it became too much to bear. I locked the closet and went to the nursery.

She was asleep in her cradle beside the fire. The heat had made her rosy. Her hair tumbled in dark curls about her head. Her thumb was in her mouth. Her eyes were shut, but I knew if she opened them, I would see Jaybee once more.

["Now," I said. "She is coming now."
"She is," said Israfel. "At last."]

I was wearing a simple kirtle. I snatched up my cloak and took my boots from the pocket, dropping the linen closet key deep into the pocket as I did so. I traded the boots for the shoes I had on, putting the shoes in the pocket also. As I went out the door, I picked up a sunshade one of Edward's craftsmen had made for me. It would do to keep off the sun or rain and to keep dogs at a distance. Outside the front door, I said, "Boots, take me to my mama."

The vertiginous darkness swept me up in its embrace. I heard Elly crying from a great distance, a brief, pained cry, and then I knew nothing more.

.
17
.

CHINANGA: TIME UNKNOWN, PERHAPS TIME IRRELEVANT

When at last the darkness passed and the boots were still, I stood on a spit of sand that extended like a finger into an expanse of water which seemed, at first glance, to be limitless as the sky. It was full day with a hot sun half hidden behind rising mists. Behind me dark trees full of noises and vines thrust up through the water to make a shimmering wall. Before me the water moved slowly, glossed with metallic lights and sullen ripples. Across the flow were other trees, laced with more vines and echoing with fainter though similar noises, the water going away among them to sheen the buttressed trunks with dancing reflections of greeny light. At a considerable distance to both my left and right, the trans-riparian growth curved inward to join the closer jungle behind me. The curve informed me I sat on the inner shore of a sweeping bend in a great river.

The nearer trees were decked with orchids, their cloying fragrance spiced by scents of lemon and clove. Though the perfume beckoned, the jungle did not welcome, nor did the water. The scene was not there to be entered but to be observed, like a splendid backdrop for some as yet unplayed drama. Seen thus, with the sun filtered through rising veils, the scene was one of somber loveliness, of profound melancholy, of aching nostalgia, as though I—or everyone—had known this place, in youth, or in dream, or in richest imagining.

I had told the boots to take me to my mother. If she were anywhere near, her presence was hidden from me. Given that I still wore the boots, I could have gone striding off in search of her, but all directions seemed equally magnificent and mysterious, and along with the heady fragrance of the orchids and spices came the stench of swamps, an odor which recommended caution.

Time in this place was not equivalent to ordinary time. Hurry had little meaning. Impatience had none. I resolved to wait upon matters. The cloak hid me well enough that I was not afraid of predators; the sand spit was dry and warm; I had set out not long after supper and I had eaten reasonably well. So I sat down and waited, bringing my book up to date, letting the slow surge of the flood before me lull me into a daylong doze broken only when a tribe of quarrelsome monkeys came down to drink. The water was silent. *Altissima quaeque flumina minimo sono labi,* Father Raymond had been fond of saying: deep rivers are quietest. He usually said it when the aunts were chattering. Or when I was. This river was quiet enough to be very deep.

When something changed at last, I sensed it only gradually as a remote dissonance adding itself by tiny increments to the sounds of birds and monkeys. A splashing sound. A clattering yet liquid noise. Something upon the water, or within it. Something far off to my right and slightly behind me, in the direction of the water flow, coming upriver though as yet hidden by the towering screen of trees.

Should I become visible or remain invisible? Should I appear miraculously out of nothing? I considered the alternatives without moving as I watched the bow of a great riverboat emerge from behind the jungle, a tall, many-decked boat with two huge wheels at its sides, thrashing its methodical way against the flow, its decks cluttered with folk. In this case invisibility would not aid me. I slipped off the cloak and boots and stood forth in my simple gown to summon attention with my ruffled sunshade.

It was some time before anyone saw me, then everyone saw me at once. The ship shuddered as it changed direction. The riverboat's whistle screamed, making me put my hands over my ears. A small boat was put over the side and came darting in my direction like a water bug, walking upon its oars. The two rowers ran the little boat up onto the sand and then sat in it staring at me as though I were some kind of exotic animal, though I was no more strange in my way than they in theirs, they being dwarfish and dark-skinned men with narrow ears.

"My name is Beauty, Lady Wellingford," I told them. "I have been abandoned here and need transportation to the nearest town or city."

They muttered. I understood them well enough for they spoke a kind of bastard Spanish with a great deal of Latin in it. At last one of them got out of the boat and offered to carry my baggage. I smiled prettily and let him, somewhat astonished to find I had baggage. We got into the boat, they pushed off with the oars, and we went skimming over the water toward the riverboat, which beat slowly at the current, holding itself in place.

The lower deck protruded fore and aft of the upper ones, making the upper decks look rather like the upper layers of a wedding cake set down upon an uncompromising loaf of something darker and more practical, pumpernickel, perhaps. The lower deck carried cargo. The upper ones carried passengers. So much was obvious from the faces peering at me over every rail.

I ascended a ladder to the second deck, then had only time to straighten my skirts before being confronted by the captain, a gold-bedecked, large-headed, stocky person who might as well have been carved out of wood for all the solicitude he expressed.

"Ma'am!" he said, in a threatening tone.

I repeated my self-introduction in a lingua franca of my own, what Spanish I remembered from school plus Latin and a smattering of Saxon and medieval French, at hearing which he glared at the sand spit as though it had been guilty of hatching me of its own malicious will.

"Never before!" he asserted. "I've been ferrying people, man and boy, so many years I can't count, and never before has there been anyone picked up along the way."

"I have some resources if it's a question of payment," I suggested.

He shook his large head, drawing his brows together, considering what this might imply. At last he said, "No need. Traveler in distress is enough reason to stop. Got an empty cabin, so no difference." And he stalked away, muttering mysterious oaths in what I took to be Hebrew and Greek, shaking his head, plunking his stumplike legs down as though to force them through the planks. Despite his assurances, I did not feel welcomed.

There was time to catch only a glimpse of the other passengers: some, behind a barricade, burly and small, brown-skinned and dark-haired, dressed fancifully in what appeared to be ethnic garb; others, walking about the deck, lighter-skinned, dressed in uniforms or simple gowns. It was a colonial group, obviously. The ruled and the rulers.

While those behind the barricade stared and pointed, one of the boatmen led me to the empty cabin, a small, cool room with a wardrobe and dressing table along the inner wall, a narrow, netting-canopied bed, and shuttered windows looking out upon the deck. It was there the captain joined me when he had had time to compose himself and become more cheerful about my rescue. The intervening moments spent alone allowed me time to decide upon a story of kidnapping and abandonment. I had been taken from my home, I did not know by whom. I had been left upon the sandbank, I did not know where. Some of it was more or less true, and the rest could not be disproven.

The captain shook his head at all of it, while claiming he was delighted to be of service. His name was Karon, he told me, and the boat was the *Stugos Queen,* currently bound for Nacifia in the land of Chinanga, which country surrounded us. He asked me if these geographical locutions sounded at all familiar to me, and I could only reply honestly that they did not. I had expected to be in Ylles. I had expected to be in Faery. Perhaps this was Faery. Certainly it was not Ylles.

"Is the land of Ylles near Chinanga?" I asked.

"By St. Frog," he said, "do they have their own land now?"

Wondering if I had heard the oath he had used correctly, I let the matter go. He evidently did not know of Ylles. He led me out upon the deck and introduced me to my fellow passengers before conducting me upon a tour of the vessel. The passengers were more than merely interested in me. I gained the impression that matters in Chinanga were not always amusing. One very old and wizened lady held my hand long in hers, cocking her head to get a good look at me. "Hello, a beauty," I think she said. Surely she could not have said, "Hello, Beauty," for I was introduced as Lady Wellingford. She smiled engagingly, but her manner was a little forbidding in that it was quite intense and focused. She was a stranger, and yet with something familiar about her, as though her voice or face, perhaps, resembled someone else's. Someone I had known well.

The forward hold, said the captain, was full of raw rubber from the plantations downriver. The after hold was stacked with sacks of coca leaves and coffee and stalks of plantain, swarming with flies. At the extreme upriver end of the voyage, she would take aboard exotic fruits and wines from the sunny hill plantations of Baskarone, sent down through Joyafleur.

"Baskarone?" I asked. The word set up a strange reverberation inside me, that almost-recognition I had felt for the old woman. "Baskarone?"

"Our neighboring country," he said. "Up there." He pointed upward with a peculiar gesture. I assumed he meant at a higher altitude, though the river mists prevented my seeing mountains, however close they may have been.

We stood at the rail together. The Stugos was in flood, he said, as it was at least half the time, but the torrential waters were more moody than usual even for floodtime, full of strange eddys and streams of bubbles emitting violet fogs. The crew, he said, seemed to be spending half its off-duty time at the river altar on the taffrail, propitiating one or another of the water devils or begging St. Frog to protect them.

"St. Frog?" I asked, wondering once again if I had heard him correctly.

He nodded. "We bought relics of St. Frog from the Cathedral of Helpful Amphibians last time we were in Nacifia." He scratched his buttocks reflectively, wondering out loud if it might be worth the trip up a tributary river to a particular one of the mighty falls at the very border of Chinanga where one might make an offering at the shrine of Our Toad of the Intermittent Torrents, perhaps, or to Saint Serpent of the Sandbanks.

I was reminded of my father. "Is such a pilgrimage thought to be efficacious?" I asked wearily, a question I had many times asked Papa.

He shook his head gloomily. "Don't know," he replied. "Some say yes, some say no."

He might have explained further, but he was hailed by a crewman and left me to go to the lower deck and put his ear to one of the hatches, listening, no doubt, for the rubber or coca leaves to declare themselves. I knew then that he had lied about what was in the holds.

I stood at the railing, asking myself whether I should put on the boots and go in search of Mama. The old woman stood next to me, as she was to do often in the succeeding days.

"Have you come here to meet someone?" she asked me, a little surprisingly, for surely Chinanga was not the crossroads of the world.

"I have come here to meet my mother," I said. "But I have no idea where she is."

"We arrive in Nacifia in three days," the old woman told me. "You will undoubtedly be able to find out where she is, in Nacifia. Someone there will know."

I thanked her and she smiled at me, a smile of particular pleasure and joy. Nothing in our conversation explained her expression, and I went to my room thinking her even more strange than I had formerly done.

Strange or not, she had told me the truth. On the third day, just before dawn, the dome of the Cathedral of Helpful Amphibians in Nacifia loomed against the fading stars. Our arrival time, which may well have been purposeful, allowed the whistle to be used to maximum effect. While I watched our approach from near the rail, my hands held tightly over my ears, Captain Karon hauled on the whistle rope, hunching his head down between his shoulders to keep the reverberations from rattling his skull. The resultant howl was enough to wake the dead. Certainly the noise could do nothing less than bring the sleeping town to attention.

When he had hauled on the rope a few more times, sending great clouds of pigeons reeling skyward from behind the dome of the cathedral, to be turned into flying rose petals by the pink light of dawn, he evidently felt he had let off enough steam that he could tell the stokers to leave off, rake down, and tie the valves open. By the time we docked, the town was stirring like a disturbed anthill. I spied more than a few rude gestures aimed in our direction. The captain only grinned and hoisted his round belly over the top of his trousers, stroking it with one hand as he might some imperfectly tamed animal, raising the other in an ironic salute in my direction.

I went down onto the lower deck and looked about me with the keenest interest. The passengers were a motley lot, their oddities more evident than usual thus assembled in contiguity to one another, and their crated belongings were odder yet. Armadillos plated in gold and decked with jewels; chickens in shades of vivid emerald and aquamarine; turtles, their eyes awash with lugubrious tears. There were even stranger figures upon the pier, leaping men and women with painted faces, cavorting among the crowd in manic lunges. I pointed them out to the old woman, who was standing beside me. She habitually stood beside me. As though she did not want me to be out of her sight.

"From the clownery," she remarked, pointing to a brightly painted building along the river as she tapped her head with a meaningful gesture. "Every now and again they escape."

"Do you know Nacifia well, madam?" I asked her.

"I have explored it," she said. "Prior to choosing it as my place of residence for a time. I have a little house on the hill, there, up the Street of Immaculate Intentions. Perhaps you will visit me there."

"Perhaps, madam," I murmured.

"Captain! Ho, captain!" The call came from the pier, slightly below us and to our right. Captain Karon craned his neck to see the person waving her flowered umbrella at him. I had not seen her approach, though she was worth the seeing now she had arrived, a full-bodied and bright-haired woman, skin glowing ivory in the creamy shadow of her highly domed parasol. Her voice was softly rounded, an amorous moo, so solid and smoothly finished a sound that it seemed to writhe itself toward his welcoming ear, probably tickling all the way down as it demanded attention.

"Mrs. Gallimar!" he shouted in return, taking off his gold-bedecked cap and stumping toward the gangway where passengers were already clotting up like ants on a mango, waiting to disembark. Captain Karon slid behind the barrier and down the gangway to meet the lady on the pier. This was no doubt the lady he had mentioned to me—and to everyone—so frequently during the voyage.

She spoke clearly, making no effort to avoid being overheard. "Oh, Dear Captain Karney. Here you are again, but so late!" She tapped him on his chest with an extended forefinger, the finger bending backwards like that of an oriental dancer, flexible as cable, as she looked up at him through fringed eyelashes with an expression of admiring coquetry. "I expected you weeks ago." Her voice lowed, like that of an amorous bovine; it sinuated like a snake—a veritable cow-python of a voice.

The captain flushed and shifted from foot to foot, as though aware of a sudden warmth in various parts of his anatomy. I wagered idly to myself that Mrs. Gallimar, with her smooth skin and her smell like a garden full of flowers, had that effect on most males. "We're right on time," he objected. "Not even a day late."

"Oh, but I was so eager!" She tapped him again, smiling up at him with wide and innocent eyes. I knew those eyes. Candy had had such eyes. Such eyes made a practice both of flirtiness and of not noticing men's response to it. It was a way of telling them not to presume upon what seemed to even the most iron-groined among them to be unmistakeably sexual signals. This contradictory manner probably left most men as it left Old Karney now, opening and closing his hands helplessly and with a distinct shortness of breath. Mrs. Gallimar was, not to be too vulgar about it, a tease. I had seen teases in the twentieth. I put my hand up to hide a knowing smile as she cooed at him. "I'm going with you when you leave!"

He was dumbfounded. His doubt showed in his face, for the lady nodded her head, slowly and emphatically, signifying that he had not misunderstood her in the slightest. "I have to go upriver, Captain. To Novabella."

"Novabella?" He could not help his faint grimace nor I my start of slight surprise. From what I had been told, it was not a town for the likes of Mrs. Gallimar. Novabella, in the crew's opinion, was not a town for anybody much.

"The Viceroy is sending me," Mrs. Gallimar confessed. "It seems there's a gallivant eating the people there, and I'm to take a provisional permit."

"A permit?" he breathed, as though he could not believe it.

"I know it's hard to credit, but a permit it is." She nodded, her lips pursed in a serious and childlike expression, her eyes saying that though one could hardly believe it still it was true.

"A permit," he said again, trying the consistency of the words to see if there was anything believeable in them. During the days of our voyage the matter of permits had come up more than once. Permits, I had been told, were mythical creatures, less common than gallivants. There were bodies lying unburied for generations in Chinanga, for want of permits. There were bastard great grandchildren of couples who had hoped to marry but had not, for lack of permits. To obtain a permit! Ah, what had happened to occasion this?

"How many people has the gallivant eaten?" the captain asked.

Mrs. Gallimar burrowed in her tiny purse, digging a chipmunk tunnel through the contents, bringing out a tiny leather covered notebook with a mother-of-pearl pencil at one side, leafing through it reflectively to find her notes. "Two children," she said sadly. "And at least one adult person. And it has bitten the left buttock and part of a breast off a woman married to

someone important." She shook her head as though wondering
at the novelty of it as she put the notebook away once more.

"But a permit!" the captain said, still in awe.

"I know." She nodded, seeming to admit the weirdness of
it, the notion that a permit even in the abstract would be strange
enough without having one in the absolute to deal with.

"So you'll be coming along," he breathed.

"I'll be coming. As well as Colonel Esquivar, just in from
the jungle, going to hunt the gallivant. And Mirabeau, the chaperone."

"Aha," said the Captain. "*That's* it! They've found one!"

Mrs. Gallimar nodded. "I think so. What else would move
the Viceroy to issue a permit? They must have found one."

I shifted my position to get the sun out of my eyes, deciding in that moment that I wished to be introduced to Mrs. Gallimar. With the old woman trailing behind me, I went to the
gangway and, with a barely audible "excuse me," slid behind
the barrier as Captain Karon had done.

"Well, we'll be leaving tomorrow," the captain was saying
as I, we, approached. "Or maybe the day after that. As soon as
we can discharge the cargo."

I smiled at the captain. He bowed in my direction. I asked
to be introduced to the lovely lady of whom I had heard so
many fascinating things. For a moment Mrs. Gallimar's hand
rested in my own as the captain mumbled, "Mrs. Gallimar, Lady
Wellingford. Lady Wellingford, Mrs. Gallimar." The old woman
behind me said, "Ahem," and the captain began again. "Mrs.
Gallimar, Senora Carabosse; Senora Carabosse, Mrs. Gallimar."

The old woman's name brought me up short. Surely I had
heard it before. Surely I had seen that name somewhere.

I was given no time for reflection. Mrs. Gallimar expressed
a belief that meeting me was one of the most exciting things
that had ever happened to her. Her eyes ate at me with tiny
glances, she nibbled at me with her ears, almost twitching at
every word I uttered. She wondered if I had breakfasted, and
when I told her I had not, she invited me to accompany her to
her house, for if the *Stugos Queen* was to leave soon, she would
need to see to her packing. She left the captain with a last titil-

lating stroke of her fingers along his arm, and we sauntered up the cobbled street down which she had come, back to the gentle amenities of a little pink house set behind a sheltering wall on the south side of the Street of Immaculate Intentions. Behind us the old woman stumped along, disconsolate, watching me as though she were a fish and I a fly. When Mrs. Gallimar and I went into Mrs. Gallimar's house, Senora Carabosse went on up the street, glancing at me over her shoulder.

While breakfast was being prepared, we sipped passion fruit juice as Mrs. Gallimar toyed with a pet ocelot. The ocelot had been a gift from Colonel Esquivar himself, Mrs. Gallimar remarked, seemingly to the ocelot. The colonel had recently recovered from being poisoned by his wife, the Viceroy's sister, monstrous Malisunde, who was a notoriously inefficient poisoner. It was said the colonel had more to fear from his mistress, the Viceroy's wife, despicable and fecund Flatulina, who had threatened to batter him to death and would no doubt be aided in the attempt by the elder half-dozen of the colonel's numerous bastards. Such a fate had been long predicted. It would scarcely come as a surprise, even to the colonel himself. Did I think such an end was likely?

Unprepared for her including me in the conversation she had been having with her pet, I took a moment to reply that I had not really considered the matter.

She went on to say that very shortly the Viceroy's palace would make the formal announcement of the hunt for the gallivant. Everyone would begin to wonder, just as the captain had, why the Viceroy would have issued the permit at all. By nightfall there was not a creature in Nacifia who would not guess that the people of Novabella had found the virgin. The one everyone had been hunting for. So Mrs. Gallimar told herself and the ocelot, while the ocelot watched me and I watched both of them, listening.

"The virgin?" I asked. Something within me trembled, as a glass will quiver, in resonance with a distant bell.

"A virgin with a difference," she replied almost in a whisper. "The Viceroy has been seeking one for a very long time."

"A virgin with a difference? What difference would that be?"

"One wonders, doesn't one. One has all kinds of strange ideas."

Her softly voiced ruminations were interrupted by the arrival of breakfast, brought in by the two maids, Dulce and Delice, upon a wheeled table and set in the large bay window overlooking the garden. I smelled muffins and my mouth watered. We sat at either side of the table to confront a platter of tiny delicious sausages and breakfast breads oozing with fruit.

As we sat down, I asked, "Have you lived in Nacifia long?"

"As long as one does," she replied. "Sometimes that seems very long indeed." She gave me tea.

"You know, I should suppose, almost everyone?"

"Oh, my dear Lady Wellingford, not almost but definitely everyone. Some better than others, of course, but yes, everyone. Each last wee babe, each tottering elder. And why not? Hasn't there been time enough to know them all?" She passed the tiny buttered muffins, and I took several.

"Does the name Elladine mean anything to you? Elladine of Ylles?" The muffins were spread with sweet butter which clung to the tongue like a lover's kiss. Why was I thinking of lover's kisses?

She thought, furrowing her brow delightfully. "What time-of-life person are we speaking of. Would she be a young-appearing woman?"

I nodded. Elladine would surely be a young woman. Did fairies ever grow old?

"Her appearance?"

"Ah," I murmured. "Very lovely. Very lovely indeed. Rather like me around the eyes."

She examined my eyes, shaking her head firmly. "No, my dear Lady Wellingford. There is no one like you around the eyes in all of Nacifia. I could not be mistaken about that."

I sighed. She passed the marmalade. We went on to speak of other things. She told me while in Nacifia I must see the cathedral, the marketplace, the clownery.

Our enjoyment was interrupted by a firm knock at the

door. A moment later, the caller was announced: Licencee of the Bureau of Public Morals, Chaperone First Class, Roland Mirabeau.

Mrs. Gallimar composed her face into an expression of dignified pleasure and rose to greet her guest. He entered, bowing, and stood up to reveal a face which would not have disgraced a classic sculpture. He had stature and presence, a curly moustache and eyes that glittered. I was introduced. He bowed again. He took Mrs. Gallimar's hand and expressed his compliments. Mrs. Gallimar seemed unstimulated by this encounter, and I wondered why.

She signaled to Delice that another chair should be brought to the table and a third place laid.

"Senor Mirabeau," she began.

"Roland," he instructed with a polished smile, which was only very slightly peremptory, as he took a cup of tea. "Though we have not seen one another for a time, lovely Mrs. Gallimar, still, we are acquainted."

"Roland," she began again, returning his smile with one of her own. I knew that smile. Captain Karon had described that smile, the smile flirtatious, which had been known to conquer whole regiments of men while they were merely marching past.

The chaperone assumed an appropriately spellbound expression, but the mechanics of this process were as entirely visible to me as they were to Mrs. Gallimar. Though the face before us went through a series of calculated adjustments indicating enchantment, its owner was not, in fact, enchanted. Mrs. Gallimar recognized this fact as quickly as I did. Her mood changed, and with it her manner. The smile flirtatious was tucked away. "This gallivant," she said in a businesslike voice, "seems to be causing a good deal of trouble."

The chaperone sat back in his chair and said calmly, "Indeed."

"It must have been very difficult for them to obtain even a provisional permit," she said.

"Undoubtedly the people of Novabella offered a sufficient inducement," the chaperone replied, accepting her offer of a cuscumbre muffin. "As you and I both know they must have done, Mrs. Gallimar. Let us not trifle with one another. I have come to inquire what your part in all this may be."

"I am to convey the permit to Novabella," she said. "Prior to providing it to the Gallivant Committee, I am to ascertain that all is as it has been represented. The Viceroy wishes me to do so."

"Is there some doubt that the gallivant has indeed eaten the children it is said to have eaten?" he asked innocently. "If so, how will you be able to tell whether they met their fates by being eaten rather than by some other equally dismembering cause?"

"There is no doubt about the beast. As to the other matter, I will ask questions," she said. "The Viceroy trusts me to come to the truth of the matter. I am confident of my abilities in this regard. Still, you may expect to be paid your proper fee."

"Oh," he said casually, biting into a bit of brown bread, "The fee is the least of the matter. It distresses me that the Viceroy does not think me capable of ascertaining what I am sure you are also being sent to ascertain, Mrs. Gallimar. He wants to make doubly sure that she's truly a virgin, doesn't he."

Mrs. Gallimar flushed, only slightly. "Perhaps the Viceroy felt that . . . well, a woman would be better qualified."

"Nonsense," he said crisply. "Any graduate of the Bureau of Public Morals Institute of Chaperonage is quite capable of knowing on the instant whether One is or One is not."

"Perhaps he is sending me, dear Roland, to keep her company on the return voyage." Mrs. Gallimar pouted prettily and cast her eyes toward her tiny shoes. There was a moment's uncomfortable silence.

"Is it permitted to ask," I inquired, "what sort of difference this virgin is to display?"

Roland's perfect lips lifted slightly away from his white teeth. "Difference, dear Lady Wellingford. How can one define difference. The virgin is to have it, else she will not do. Were she lovely as the dawn and pure as the spring rain, I would still find nothing there of interest to me unless there is also *difference.*"

The words set up that odd resonance once more. Something

I had heard. Something I had seen. Where had I, myself, encountered reference to a virgin with a difference?

So musing, I almost missed Mrs. Gallimar's grumpy response to the chaperone's comment. "I quite understand," she said.

I felt that I, too, was beginning to understand. Roland Mirabeau was unmoved by women, by any ordinary woman, by any except an extraordinary woman. Mrs. Gallimar knew this, though her customary manner had caused her to overlook it for a few moments. Roland was, in fact, unteaseable, therefore of little interest to her.

He took another bite of brown bread. "We can hope she is as represented, Mrs. Gallimar. If she is, I will know it." He snapped up the last bite with a click of his teeth and a quick lick at his lips. "Since our departure is imminent, I will take my leave, lovely Mrs. Gallimar, in order to put my baggage in order and assure that it is properly stowed."

He bowed himself away from us both, murmuring, "Lady Wellingford, such a delight," while Mrs. Gallimar sat unsmiling and annoyed. I thought as I made my own farewells that for a woman of Mrs. Gallimar's disposition Roland Mirabeau would not be an amusing companion on a lengthy voyage.

["I had hoped to get to know her," I said to Israfel. We sat across from one another in my house on the Street of Immaculate Intentions. We were drinking tea.

"She looks at you and is afraid," he replied. "She senses your interest in her and is put off by it. Your acquaintance is too new. You have offered her your friendship too soon."

"I shall persevere," I told him severely. "Too soon or not, she will need me."]

.
18
.

Aboard the *Stugos Queen,* I put on my cloak and went into Nacifia to see all those things Mrs. Gallimar had recommended I see. If we left upon the morrow, there might be no other opportunity to investigate the city.

I went first to the Cathedral of Helpful Amphibians, which was beautiful, outside and in. Though the materials were not ones Gaudi could have used, the place reminded me somewhat of pictures I had seen in the twentieth of a Gaudi cathedral. I sat down near one of the pillars, crystal carved into the likeness of a jet of water, leaping toward the sky. The whole cathedral was a fountain in stone. It was lit from high green windows with a dim, liquescent light, and in the side chapels statues of the helpful creatures sprawled or lay or climbed, each after its own nature.

I took off my cloak for coolness sake when I sat down. It was not long thereafter that I was surprised by a voice behind me saying, "Is there anything I can do for you, daughter, or are you merely sightseeing?"

"Ah . . . Father," I murmured, turning about so I could see him. "Sightseeing. Yes."

"You're the lady rescued from the sandbank," he smiled at me as he came to sit beside me. "What do you think of our cathedral."

"It's very beautiful," I said honestly.

He nodded in agreement, beaming at the pillars.

"At home," I said, struggling for truth without complication. "At home we would think it strange to dedicate a cathedral to . . . ah . . . amphibians."

He seemed slightly startled. "What would you dedicate a cathedral to?"

"A martyr, perhaps," I suggested. "An angel?"

"Were they made by the Creator?" he asked.

I nodded that they were.

"Well, so are these," he said with some asperity, gesturing around him. "Are some parts of creation more worthy than others in your homeland?"

I told him yes, that in my homeland (thinking of the twentieth and twenty-first) only humans were worthy of anything at all. All else was disposable.

He shook his head over me, speechless, his old face suddenly lined with horror. He made a gesture in my direction, which I recognized as being one of aversion, one of fear.

"I didn't say I believed that," I cried.

He made the gesture again, and tottered away into a side chapel where I could see him kneeling at the altar of St. Frog, murmuring in a heartbroken tone. I slipped on my cloak once more, saddened by his rejection.

My next stop was at the clownery, where I wandered invisibly down long hallways, watching the inhabitants at their work or play or whatever it was they were doing. One inmate was packing cockroaches, one hundred to the bag. I do not think the insects were dead, though they were very quiet. Another inmate was constructing a large bust of the Viceroy, so the label said, out of what appeared and smelled to be dung. A third inmate, with the aid of a tall ladder, was writing her autobiography on the walls of the place. She had covered four stories of one stairwell and had extended her tale out into the reception area, where two walls were already covered with obscenities. I followed her story back in time until I reached a door to the roof, where a group of attendants were having morning coffee. Even read in reverse, it had been a novel of violence, abuse, incest, and horror.

I stood on the roof listening to the attendants, who were mostly interested in discussing the fine points of their latest soccer series. When I went down the stairs again, the walls were clean. Another inmate with bucket and brush was washing them, as he sang a lovelorn lament. The inmate with the bags of insects had given them to someone else, who was letting them go. The sculptor was asleep in the shade of his gigantic construction, while six or seven others carried the substance of it away in wheelbarrows. Each madness had been unmaddened.

I made my way next to the macabre heights of Mont Osso Negro where the citadel stood. I had a mind to look upon the Viceroy of this place. I found him striding through arched corridors in search of his daughter Constanzia, whom, as his bellows of rage and accusation testified, he suspected of dalliance with the young men of the garrison. Before his iron-booted feet, legions of scrub women scattered to one side or the other, squawking like chickens, except for one aged crone who scuttered along beside the Viceroy on all fours, attempting to slosh soapy water in his path while muttering, "Beast. Hideous beast. Inhuman dog. Ingrate," calumniations of which the Viceroy took no notice. His long, white face was set in an expression of obdurate annoyance, one, I was to learn, of his two customary expressions, the other being a vacuous stare of terminal ennui.

When his invective became boringly repetitious, I left off following him and went in search of Constanzia herself, a quest which the boots made simple. She was hidden in one corner of the long, vaulted library loft, reading a leather-bound volume with the word "Forbidden" stamped on its cover in age-faded ink. The book was mildewed and fly-specked; the pages were yellowed by time. Still, the gold leaf of the title gleamed bravely in the slim rays which leaked through the owl holes cut in the gables of the loft: *The Diaries of Ambrosius Pomposus, Founder of the State of Chinanga.*

Constanzia's reading was interrupted frequently by the need to look up words with which she was unfamiliar. I went to and fro with her as she searched for references in various volumes written in a multitude of tongues, a process which ate up the hours. She had managed to get only to page one hundred forty-two of *The Diaries,* and she muttered to herself that it had taken the better part of three rainy seasons to read that far. A sense of fiery purpose emanated from her, like heat from the sun.

When I grew weary of reading, I explored the castle, finding the Viceroy soaking in his tub, a steaming towel wound around his head, leaving only his nose to quest for air, like a tapir's snout, while an intermittent procession of water carriers dipped out portions of the cooling water and poured in equivalent ewers of hot from the boilers in the kitchens below. Obviously, the plumbing no longer functioned, and certain smells wafting from lower regions indicated the drains, too, might be endangered.

Captain Jemez sat on a chair by the window, reading the *Nacifia Noticias,* remarking occasionally upon its contents, while the Viceroy muttered comments from under the towel. After a time, the Viceroy seemed to fall asleep, and Captain Jemez went to the window.

I peered over his shoulder. In the marketplace the fruit stalls were bright with mangos and pollarels, bananas and cuscumbres and chinangarees. On the hills behind the town the goatherds played their pipes, the sound coming faintly over the bleating of their flocks, borne by the soft warm winds down from Baskarone.

"Ah, Baskarone. Sun-kissed Baskarone of the thousand delights," the captain murmured, beginning to sing in a strong tenor voice, "I found my love in lovely Baskarone."

He crossed to the other side of the room to look out across the river, far among the drowned trees where the land sloped up to the range of jungle hills. After the rains, the river would fall, I had been told, into its narrower channel, leaving behind ten thousand little lakes and pools to reflect the blossoms and give a homeland to the frogs.

The captain had similar thoughts. "Bless all frogs and other helpful amphibians," he intoned in plainsong, switching to his baritone register.

"Captain," said a firm voice behind us.

"Madam," he bowed, flushing. I slipped to one side, not to be trampled by the visitor. Flatulina had come into the bathroom and stood considering her husband's recumbent figure as the steam rose gently about him.

"How long has he been in there?" she asked, arms akimbo, massive shoulders raised in inquiry, huge head cocked, its generous features dwarfed by the mane of black hair which boiled from her skull in an uncontrollable torrent.

"Most of the morning, madam."

"Get him out. He'll be all wrinkled." Flatulina's full lips twisted in distaste.

"Madam . . ."

"Get him out. There's an ambassador come. Ambassador Israfel from Baskarone. Tell him I said." And she was gone, leaving the captain to consider how he might best disturb the Viceroy without running the risk of that gentleman's wrath. I followed the woman, much desiring to see Ambassador Israfel from Baskarone.

And he was there. Though I was wrapped tightly in my cloak, he looked up and smiled at me as I came into the room. He was only slightly more marvelous than I supposed any other man might be, anywhere. Looking at him, I felt that I had been changed forever. The thing that burned at the center of me came alight, a fine white flame.

And he went on smiling at me, seeing me though the cloak was tight around me, seeing and approving that flame before he turned away and greeted the Viceroy. I leaned against a pillar in utter confusion. As soon as I could move, I returned to the *Stugos Queen.*

I lay upon my bed, wondering what I had seen, what I had felt. I had loved, still love Giles. That is a human affection, a love that desires, at least partly, some physical consumation: a touch, a glance, something that speaks from one body to another, one heart to another. Even if we were very old, Giles and I, we would want that. We would want to lean together in the gloaming, our cheeks next to one another, our hands clasped, letting our selves say to one another that we loved. I think that would be true. Remembering him now, I think that would be true.

This thing I feel in the presence of the ambassador is something else. This is what I sometimes felt in Westfaire, at certain times when the light fell beneath hovering clouds onto the windows and the grass, lighting them with a mysterious and marvelous effulgence, colors so pure that they made one's eyes ache, or at certain times when the rain dropped in gauzy curtains of mist to half-hide, half-disclose the fine, soaring lines of the castle. It is a longing so deep, an appreciation so rare . . .

In the twentieth I felt it a few times. I went to an opera and heard a woman's voice, like a stream of falling water, the orchestra behind her in a cataract of sound, and I felt it then. I felt it a little when I set my eyes on the jungles of Chinanga for the first time, a kind of perfection that sings inside.

They are both love. If Father Raymond were here, perhaps he would say this other thing is the love of God. But I was not thinking of God when I felt it at Westfaire, and when the woman sang, and when I saw Israfel. I don't think I was.

Night came to Nacifia. The riverbank bloomed bright with torches. The day had been long and hot and full of sights and sounds and tastes. I had no wish to engage in conversation or be introduced to anyone else. After supper, I put on my cloak and moved like a shadow along the quay, looking here, listening there. Captain Karon and his crew scattered themselves among the waterfront tavernas; the people of the town scattered themselves likewise. Constanzia approached the captain with a curtsy and a request from her mama. The captain was known to have certain special luxuries aboard. Would he be inclined to display them?

Display his wares tonight? the captain asked in nicely feigned disbelief. Who would look at his poor goods after sundown?

Certain people, she said, had indicated that they might be persuaded.

The captain demurred. Surely not.

There was so little amusement in Nacifia, she persisted, with a flounce, a sidelong look, and maidenly laugh.

Until, at last, the captain gathered up a dozen torches and set them around the *Stugos Queen* while ordering three of his men to open the hatches of the small, forward hold and bring out what was there.

Cages of silver peacocks and lengths of shining silk. Incense and carved sandalwood boxes. A half-lifesize mechanical ballerina who danced upon her toes, click, click, click, like a cricket, coming to the edge of her stage and raising her tiny hands in mechanical fright before turning to begin her dance again. Pots of perfumed ointment and hand-blown bottles of cologne. Monkeys with gold collars and iguanas in jeweled chains. Lace from the convent at St. Mole and confections from the monastery of St. Cloud. How so many things could come out of the little hold was a wonder to everyone, no less to me. Each thing brought out smelled, too, that old, mysterious smell which I had never identified: the chapel smell, the smell of Westfaire.

Coins changed hands. The Viceroy's wife went home with lengths of sparkling fabric. Other wives contented themselves with the piece goods Flatulina had overlooked. Daughters sniffed at the crooks of their arms where drops of ointment deliquesced in silken folds. The robust Malisunde carried off an ape in a cage, as a substitute for a husband who was never home said someone, not meaning to be heard. Only the shadows and I heard, and only we laughed.

In the half-darkness, at the edge of the torchlight, a young lieutenant stood with Constanzia, murmuring, "His Excellency, your father, has been somewhat distraught of late."

"Do you think so?" Constanzia asked. "I had thought he was rather less irritable than usual. This business in Novabella has quite set him up. He hasn't tried to kick Grandma for at least a week. Even when she got soap under his feet and knocked him down in the long gallery last Friday. And he is sending Mrs. Gallimar as plenipotentiary. With a provisional permit!"

The lieutenant agreed that the issuance of even a provisional permit betokened the possibility of novelty, even, perhaps, of change. He was gazing at her as at a wonder, but she did not seem to notice.

Constanzia nodded thoughtfully. "I believe the people of Novabella have promised him a virgin with a difference. He has all the ingredients but that one. Think what it will mean if she truly is what they say she is!" She smiled on the young man, at which he blushed red as a rose. But then, just as he put out his hand to touch hers, she excused herself and went trotting off up the street toward the citadel. He turned away in confusion. Poor boy.

I stood sleepily by the gangway of the *Queen* as the place emptied and night settled. Only a few persons remained when I, with considerable surprise, saw Constanzia peering around a corner near the square. I thought again, as I had several times during the evening, how lovely she was. Her face had a spontaneous liveliness about it. Very dark. Very sexy. Very sly, at the moment, and cautious not to be heard or seen. She came out into the street, carrying a basket from which protruded the dusty cover of the book with the word "Forbidden" stamped upon it. She came nearer, slipped up the unguarded gangway onto the *Queen,* opened a hatch cover, and disappeared below. When the boat left in the morning, evidently she intended to be aboard.

I heard the stumping footfalls of the captain moving along the quay. I followed him onto the riverbank, where Mrs. Gallimar still sat as she had throughout the evening, bidding for nothing at all, dreamily watching the torchlit flow of the water. The captain was not content to leave her so. He carried a bottle of ruby glass in which, so I heard him say, she might find a wine which a master vintner would envy.

Mrs. Gallimar was so touched with his gift that she suggested they share it then and there. They sat in the flamelit night, watching the reflected flares shimmering on the Stugos, avenues of silken light reaching away from them away into unimaginable darkness where the flood moved silently in the night. As they watched the light, ignoring their glasses, I drank their wine. A divine vintage. One of the wines, perhaps, of Baskarone.

"We are at the center of the universe," purred Mrs. Gallimar. "See how the light reaches out from us in all directions."

Silently, I agreed that it was so. In daylight, things seemed to vanish at the horizon, joining there. Here in the firelit dark, all lines plunged toward us across the waters, ending at our feet, a fan of radiance with ourselves at its center. All things centered upon the observer. I was the axle of a wheel of light. It seemed important to remember this moment when the universe wheeled upon my hub, the moment in which I was impaled upon a fan of light.

"Remember this," said a voice. It was the voice of the ambassador from Baskarone. "Remember this. All things end here, with you, Beauty. Remember this."

"Remember," whispered an old woman's voice. Senora Carabosse. I looked around, but she was nowhere near.

It was a fantasy, no doubt, brought about by the darkness and the wine. Still, I would remember.

"We are," the captain said in a strangled voice, "the very center of everything."

"Until now," sighed Mrs. Gallimar with a softly amorous tone, "I had not looked forward at all to this journey."

"Until now," growled the captain in husky honesty, "neither had I."

I left them there, my lips sweet with the wine, my mind full of wonder at the circled paths of light, resolving, as I returned to my cool cabin on the *Stugos Queen,* never to forget this night. The old woman was standing at the railing, just outside my door. "Good night, dear Beauty," I thought she said, but the wine had made me too giddy to hear her aright.

"Good night, Senora Carabosse," I replied. Though the monkeys were screaming in the flooded jungle once more, I knew that, on this night, I would sleep.

19

Captain Karon, by threats and shouts and hiring a few layabouts to help with the unloading, got the last of the publicly acknowledged cargo off the ship shortly after sunrise. Three inmates from the clownery showed up to see the boat offshore, which delayed matters a bit as they insisted upon helping the passengers with their baggage.

The stokers bent their backs before the boilers, the whistle began to bleat, and the passengers trickled toward the rail to watch the departure. The chaperone emerged onto the deck to motion with one languid hand. Colonel Esquivar, a tall person with sharp squinty eyes, an enormous moustache, and very brown skin—riven by long exposure to the elements—had come aboard during the night, and he staggered out of his cabin bleary eyed, bowed to Mrs. Gallimar, sneered at the chaperone, and said something mildly insulting to the captain before staggering back into his cabin and slamming the door behind him. With a final toot, the *Stugos Queen* moved out into the flood, breasting it with a great shuddering clatter of both monstrous wheels, while the clownery inmates hurtled along the shore in a series of giant cartwheels and balletic leaps, ceasing to follow the ship only when it came opposite the swamps at the mouth of the tributary Rio Apenado.

The stewards began laying the tables in the first-class dining room. The cooks were already ladling out stew for the second-class passengers, the crew, and that part of the cargo needing to be fed at midday. (Was I the only one who noticed food being carried twice each day into the holds? No, the old woman saw it, too. She gave me a significant look and a wink. Who is she? What does she mean?) First-class luncheon would be later, which gave the kitchen boys time to decorate the dessert table with a frilled lizard carved from ice and garlanded with poppies carved from halves of blood-red chinangarees.

I settled easily into the routine of the voyage. Each morning I arrived in the dining room before Roland Mirabeau, who—

shaved, dressed, with his hair arranged and moustache trimmed by his servant—arrived shortly after me to drink a glass of cuscumbre juice before sitting down at my table with a steaming cup of coffee or maté or cou, all of which were available, each in several varieties.

Since I was not in the mood or market for a lover and had made this fact clear, Roland accepted me and talked freely in my company. I listened, seldom making any comment that required a reply. The old woman, Senora Carabosse, usually emerged from her room a little later to sit at a neighboring table with her tea, eavesdropping on our talk as she blinked and muttered to herself. Poor old thing. I felt ashamed of my animadversion. She was harmless enough.

[Really!]

After a time, Mrs. Gallimar would come down to breakfast, usually with either the captain or Colonel Esquivar in attendance. There would be a flutter of ribbons and a rustle of sweet, scented flounces, a titter of laughter and a softly modulated voice calling good morning. I would see Roland preparing himself for appropriate reactions, for smiles and courtly bows, for admiring nods and glances, all of which Mrs. Gallimar would expect. One morning he confessed to me that he felt there was something missing in his responses. He felt the lack, as one feels something missing in a flavor which does not fill the mouth but merely lies there upon the tongue as though in anticipation of some more complex savor. So Roland felt a certain lack of sincerity at the core of his acquaintance with Mrs. Gallimar. He did not, in fact, lust after her, although, on an intellectual level, he could appreciate all her lustworthy qualities. She left him chill and untouched, his flesh like tallow, stiff and unwarmed by her welcoming sensuality. So he said, supposing I would understand. This was an unflattering supposition, though I made no remark upon it but merely smiled, cocking my head to solicit further intimations. Behind me, Senora Carabosse chuckled quietly to herself.

Had this been a new sensation, Roland went on, he would

have been disturbed by it, but in fact it was his usual feeling with regard to women. Flowers could move him. Sunsets could bring tears to his eyes. The sight of the wind bending the trees at dawn could make him cry out in luxurious sensitivity, but women moved him not at all. There was something about them, some inherent fleshiness, some excess of corporeality which turned him cold. And then there was their smell, whether masked in perfumes or alive upon the air as itself, that fecund stench, that earthy aroma, that mephitic scent, which seemed to come upon them with womanhood.

(I leaned toward him, wondering if he would catch my aroma. Evidently he did not. It was then, I think, that I began to understand the world in which I found myself. I was beginning to find a certain lack of consistency. As though natural laws only partially applied.)

Little girls smelled otherwise, Roland said. He quite liked little girls. He loved their breastless little bodies and their wee buttocks, like two eggs laid side by side. He loved their elven haunches, their dimpled knees, and pink soled feet, but all this adoration was in his eyes only. He did not lust after them. He merely worshipped them, as he worshipped the egg icons in the sanctuary of St. Frog, for what they symbolized, not for what they were. Purity. Oh, Roland adored purity. Purity and beauty. It was why he had become a chaperone, after all, in order that he might adore it. Serve it. Preserve it. And though there was much beauty, there was little enough of purity in Chinanga, so he said.

"I sometimes wonder," he remarked to me over his second cup of cou, "what we would have been like had we not been condemned to live here in Chinanga. What would we have been like had we been allowed to settle in holy Baskarone?"

His remark was overheard by Captain Karon, who snorted and said, "Better ask what Baskarone would have been like if we'd lived there. Can you imagine the Viceroy ruling Baskarone?" Then the captain flushed and looked around himself quickly to see who might have overheard. "Meaning no disrespect," he mumbled, catching Roland's eye. "No disrespect, Chaperone."

"None taken," mused Roland. "In fact, I apprehend your question, Captain. Are we what our environment makes us? Or do we make our environment what we are? If the latter, then one might ask who really lives in Baskarone. Do we not say 'Blessed Baskarone'? Do we not speak of Joyafleur as a heavenly city?"

It was the first time I had heard those words. They set up a reverberation within me, a humming, as though some great tuning fork had been thrust down my spine. A holy city. A blessed country. And the ambassadors from that region, ah, what were they, then? I inferred what they were and flushed as I felt myself longing for angels. Had the ambassador from Baskarone been an angel?

The captain made a face as though to spit, then thought better of it. "Well, sir, since we're speaking frankly, how by all the serpents would I know? Not having been there. We look up toward Baskarone from these sweaty lowlands and see it all stretched out there like some great, feathery wing, full of color and design, but who's been there? None of us, that's sure. The border posts, they don't let tourists from Chinanga go up to take a look, now do they?"

I caught Senora Carabosse's eye. She was listening unabashedly, her mouth slightly open, as though ready to bite at some intimation she desperately desired.

Roland murmured, "There have been visitors from there."

"Ambassadors. Oh, yes. Once in a while. Closemouthed as turtles, too. I met one once, at Mrs. Gallimar's."

"Did you indeed? An ambassador from Baskarone?"

"A great tall, tan fellow with a sunny smile and a ready laugh, not a feather in his wings out of place, and no more information in him than there is good intentions in a woodtick."

Was it the same ambassador from Baskarone? Had he had wings? I could not remember.

"Then what was he doing here?" asked Roland.

"Flew down to find out how many cases of wine we wanted lowered from Joyafleur. Come to find out what we had to trade. Come to find out whether any contraband was getting through, had I been bothered by pirates. Asked if Chinanga was stable, if it was safe if someone wanted to leave something here for a while. Complained a little about a few hunters climbing the wall and falling off. It messes up the trails through there, so they say, and since the wall is known to be impassable, creates a foolishness. That kind of thing. Full of questions, he was. If you ask me, he was here spying, finding out about us, about Chinanga."

"Did you ask him about Baskarone, directly?"

"Well, you know how people will, at a dinner party. 'How're things in Baskarone, Your Excellency?' 'Had any interestin' happenins in Baskarone?' 'How's the weather been in Baskarone?' That kind of question."

"To which he replied?"

"Not at all," said the captain. "Far's I could tell, nothing ever happens at all in Baskarone. He said about six words."

"I wish I'd been there," Roland mused. "I would have asked him directly, 'Tell me about Baskarone.' "

"No you wouldn't," said the captain. "You think you would, but you wouldn't."

"I suppose that's true," sighed Roland, with a sidelong glance at me. He sipped the cooling cou as he stared across the undulant waters, letting the silence settle between them.

I thought of the captain's words often in the succeeding days. Did we suit our environments or did we change them to suit ourselves? And in that case, what were we who had lived in the twentieth? And in that case, who were they who lived in Baskarone?

Late that night the *Stugos Queen* tied up at what had once been and would be again, when the floods had passed, the riverbank. There, under the motionless branches of great jungle trees, Captain Karon conducted some hours of quiet business. All the passengers except myself had long been asleep before the captain and the mate opened the hatches to the forward hold and lifted out a number of cages. During the earlier hours of the evening small boats rowed by persons claiming to be from Tartarus and Tophet and Eblis and Gehenna had drawn near to the *Queen,* and now they surrounded the ship. Natives came aboard a few at a time to pick up consignments or to offer Captain Karon bids for his unconsigned merchandise. Cages were lowered into the waiting boats. To unsuccessful bidders, the captain offered his hand and the suggestion that they might have better luck next time. As the first fingers of dawn stroked the sky, the last native boat departed, skimming the water like a swallow, away and into the drowned forest and up one of the tributary rivers, Rio Lamentarse, Rio Abrasador. The cage tied to its hull shaking from the agitation of those enclosed.

"Is that the lot?" the captain asked the mate.

"That's it. Thirty-seven big cages and thirteen small ones. Only ones left are in the after hold, a dozen of 'em, consigned farther upriver. Erebus, if I remember right. Oh, and there's one little box for Abaddon, up the Rio Desmemoriarse. What do the natives do with them, anyhow?"

"No idea. Long as they do it out of sight, I don't much care. I get paid to ship 'em, and ship 'em is what I do. Load 'em aboard at the Edge and take 'em wherever they're consigned, if they're consigned. Sell the others. Any we don't sell, we drop off in the Great Swamp, but I get paid anyhow." The captain took a deep breath and sighed. "You took a look down in the forward hold, did you, to see none of them got out of the cages?"

"I always do."

"Wouldn't do to have one of those wandering around the *Queen,* now would it. Ugly things. Scare Mrs. Gallimar out of her pretty shoes."

I, who had seen all that the cages contained, had not found them that ugly. Pitiful. Angry. Hopeless. But not ugly.

The mate answered, "No, no escaped ones. I did find something else down there, though."

The captain turned and fixed him with a stern eye. "You found . . . ?"

"This," said the mate, beckoning to one of the boatmen on the lower deck who came up the ladder tugging a struggling young woman along behind him. It was the Viceroy's daughter, Constanzia. I had wondered when she would show up.

"Stowed away," said the mate. "And she's the Viceroy's daughter, to top it all." If he had intended surprise, he had achieved his goal. The captain stared at the young person as though he could not believe it.

"What in the . . . ?"

She shook herself, thrust wild hair back from her broad, low forehead, then smoothed her dress and stood erect, glaring at him. "I have brought money to pay for my passage. The only reason I went down into the hold is that I couldn't let anyone see I was aboard."

"Your father will be very annoyed with me," said the captain throatily. I knew he was thinking of beheading, or of quartering, or perhaps of both. "He was annoyed with me last time, and he will be annoyed with me again."

"Papa will not even know I am gone if you do not do anything foolish, Captain. I have come to see the virgin with a difference, as I seem to remember having done once or twice before, though this time there may really be a difference, which has not happened before now. I thought I might get to know her a little on the return voyage. When we get back to Nacifia, I will disembark quietly, and Papa will think I was merely avoiding him for a time, which I often do."

Captain Karon shook his head, then nodded, then shook it once more, conveying the confusion of his thought. "We're full," he muttered. "There's no cabin space."

"Oh, yes, Captain," I murmured, having taken off my cloak and folded it over one arm. "The young lady is welcome to share my cabin with me."

And so it became possible for me to read even more in the diaries of Abrosius Pomposus.

["She's getting too involved!" I cried to Israfel. "She's thinking too much. How can this be a safe hiding place if she starts analyzing it? She'll pull it to pieces!"

"Hush," said Israfel. "Imaginary lands are hard to destroy."

"They are not hard to disbelieve in," I told him. "She's reading, studying . . ."

"She learned to do that in the twentieth," he said. "It's not something you can stop her doing."

"We may have to talk to her," I said. "Tell her."]

"Wait a while," he said. "See what happens."]

"There are slaves down there in the holds," Constanzia cried to me later that night as we prepared for bed, tears coursing down her olive cheeks. "Slaves."

I nodded understandingly. I had seen them.

"Women and children, too," she sobbed. "And men, young ones and old, old ones. It's dreadful."

"Dreadful," I admitted. But there was nothing she could do, nor I. She had evidently not understood the implications of the book she carried with her.

Kindhearted child. She cried herself to sleep.

I went out onto the deck. The old woman, Senora Carabosse, was standing there. I nodded and smiled good evening. In the saloon, I heard a clock strike. Suddenly, with a rush of memory which was almost a physical blow, I knew where I had heard the name before. Carabosse! It was the name on my clock. She was the fairy who had cursed me!

"Is it you!" I said, raising my hand as though I would ward her off or strike her, one. I don't know whether I would have struck her or not. I felt like it.

"Hush," she said, raising her own hand. Mine fell to my side as she gestured at it. "Whatever you think you know about me is probably false, so don't do that."

"You cursed me," I said.

"If you call that a curse. As it turned out, I cursed your half sister, Mary Blossom," said the old woman. "Which I meant to happen, right from the beginning."

"Why?" I cried.

"To get you away without anyone knowing," she said. "Away from Westfaire. Away from England. Away from the middle centuries. To hide you somewhere safe."

"Here?" I looked about me at the wallowing riverboat and laughed. "Here?"

"No one knows you are here," she whispered to me. "Jaybee doesn't know. The Dark Lord doesn't know."

"What Dark Lord?"

"Hush. Men like Jaybee do not spring into existence like

spring spinach. They are aided into being by the Dark Lord. The evil power. The Devil. He who has taken his portion in horror and pain. That one."

"And you would hide me from him here?"

She repeated patiently what she had said before. "No one knows you are here. No one knows *here* is here."

Staring into her old eyes, I suddenly believed her. I had read Pomposus's books, just as Constanzia had. The difference between Constanzia and I was that I had understood what they meant. I knew that Chinanga was an imaginary world. All the people in it were imaginary people. It had been dreamed up by Ambrosius Pomposus—or by some creature or person calling himself or itself Ambrosius Pomposus. He had packed it full of all manner of strange things and characters. He had borrowed from myth and legend and other worlds for some of them.

How would anyone except Ambrosius himself know anything about this world? And he, I thought, had possibly died long since.

As though reading my mind, Carabosse said, "I used the secrets of time to find this place and explore it. No one else could find it in ten million years. All my effort, all my care has been directed at bringing you here. Believe me, Beauty, here you are safe." She patted my hand.

Safe? Why should Carabosse care? I opened my mouth to ask these questions, and others.

She shook her head at me, much as my aunts had used to do when I asked questions about sex. No, no, no, her expression said. You must do without knowing. She drifted away down the deck, leaving me to wonder at what she had said.

What did I believe?

I believed that I was safe. I believed that she cared greatly about my safety, though I did not know why. I believed there was something more she had not told me. I did not believe, could not believe who it was she said I was safe from. What would the Dark Lord, under any name, want with me?

The *Queen* arrived at Novabella about noon. Among those assembled for the arrival were a squat and swarthy couple, Emilia and Domenico Sandifor, charged with conveying an official welcome to the Viceroy's plenipotentiary and the chaperone, and, of course, to the captain. Constanzia and I became part of the party by virtue of the fact that no one saw fit to deny us that privilege. If anyone had done so, I am confident that Constanzia would have been equal to the occasion.

"I hope you'll consent to stay with us," Emilia bubbled at Mrs. Gallimar. "Don Masimiliano, the perfect of our province, has requested the honor of your company at the castle, yours and the chaperone's, but I thought you'd want to stay here in the town for convenience's sake."

"I will not have time even to dine with Don Masimiliano," said Roland in a severe voice. "I am to be taken to the person at once for a preliminary survey."

"She's been staying with us," admitted Emilia. "With Jorge on a mat outside her door every moment that she's in her room."

"Windows?" snarled Roland. "What about the windows?"

"They have very heavy gratings, Senor Mirabeau. Quite impenetrable, I assure you."

"Senora, if you had seen some of the things I have seen." He shook his head gloomily to let us know that he had seen the worst that life in Chinanga afforded.

"Well, why don't we get along there now?" Domenico offered.

We strolled along the cobbled street to the Sandifor house, the official delegation in the fore, we unofficial hangers-on following close behind. A tall iron gate admitted us to an acre or so of garden with orange trees and orchids. The house bulked beneath its tiled roof; an outside staircase led us to an upper floor where we found the manservant, Jorge, curled in stupified slumber before a metal-bound door. His bulky form stirred as Emilia took out a large black key, and he woke enough to move aside as she started to insert it into the lock. The key was taken from her by the chaperone before she could turn it.

"If you don't mind," Roland smiled. "I believe this is my affair from now on."

"Not quite," smiled Mrs. Gallimar. "It would be fair to say, our affair. *Quis custodiet ipsos custodes?"*

"Really!" The chaperone was outraged. "I am a licencee of the Bureau of Public Morals!"

"And I am the Viceroy's personal representative. Shall we go in together?"

Which, after a lengthy simmering glance, they did.

Left in the corridor, the Sandifors looked at one another in awe. "What was that she said to him?" asked Domenico.

"I have no idea," his wife replied.

"A quotation," I murmured from behind them. "A question once asked in a similar connection. 'Who will chaperone the chaperones.' "

"Oh," he replied. "Do you suppose we should wait here for them?"

Emilia shook her head. "I want to see what's happening."

She had spoken all our thoughts. We went quietly into the room. Mrs. Gallimar and Roland stood side by side, their backs to us. Before them, sitting on one of the luxuriously padded window seats, a young woman sat reading. She looked up when the two stepped forward.

I was astonished. So astonished I could not move. It was as though I had looked into my own face in a slightly distorting mirror. My hair. My eyes. She looked less like me than Beloved had, but she resembled me in ways Beloved did not. I knew who she was. She was the one I had been seeking. Elladine of Ylles. Who else could she be?

Roland sank to his knees before her. I moved to one side so I could see his face. He was looking at her hair, at her feet, at the delicate rose of her cheeks. At her eyes. The swell of her breasts, like petals belling before spring wind! I saw his eyes flicker. The smell of her! I saw his nostrils dilate.

"You must be the virgin," smiled Mrs. Gallimar with a slightly sceptical tone.

For a moment the young woman could not or would not answer. Then she murmured, "Indeed. At the moment I must be. Are you the Viceroy's representatives?"

"I am the Viceroy's representative. This gentleman is Roland Mirabeau, licencee of the Bureau of Public Morals, a registered chaperone, first class."

The young woman smiled, unspeaking, nodding once. Oh, but she was beautiful. But then, so was I.

"Now." Mrs. Gallimar smiled again, licentiously. "We need to ascertain that you are as represented . . ."

"No," Roland announced, firmly. "It is not necessary to do anything at all. The young woman *is* as represented. As a registered chaperone, I can tell."

Mrs. Gallimar stared at him, unbelieving. He took her firmly by one arm and drew her away. "I can tell, Mrs. Gallimar. By the smell alone. She smells like a six-year-old child after a bath."

Mrs. Gallimar sniffed. "She may, in fact, just have bathed."

"I assure you, I cannot be misled."

"She may have used scent."

"There is no such perfume. She is as she is, Mrs. Gallimar. I know it!" And he turned to confront the young woman who sat looking at him with a lively and precocious interest. "My nose cannot be misled!" It was obvious he believed it was so, and yet this young person was looking at him with unmistakeably sexual interest. "She is a virgin, and with a difference," he murmured abstractedly, turning and looking straight into my face with an expression both of doubt and anxiety. I knew he was wondering whether he was indeed the best person to protect that virginity all the way back to Nacifia.

"Tell me about her," he demanded from Emilia and Domenico, when we were all sitting in the Sandifor courtyard.

"She says she was married to a duke. She got tired of being married to him and left him to go home. Something interrupted her journey to or from, at that time or some other, and she ended up in the jungle. She says she has the feeling she was there for a very long time. The natives picked her up and brought her here. That's as far as we've got."

Roland stared at Emilia in disbelief. "This is all you know? But you've had her for days!"

"She talks a great deal. I can tell you all about the duke, and his sisters, and where they lived. She puts in a lot of detail."

"You haven't tried to hurry her any?" Mrs. Gallimar asked.

"Madam. Senor Mirabeau," Domenico interrupted, "perhaps things are different in Nacifia. Perhaps there are many interesting events in Nacifia. Not here. Things are dull in Novabella. We examine what we can see of Baskarone through our telescopes. We eat. We take a nap. We go down and stare at the river, wondering whether it will rise or fall. We see the little boats from Abaddon, and we fervently hope they will keep their distance, or, at worst, try to sell us fruit or monkeys from the jungle. We eat something else. We wait for Captain Karon to arrive with something new in the cargo. We play cards. We grow frightfully . . . how shall I say? *Pococurante.* You understand what I am saying?"

"Bored," murmured Roland, who had told me he was very familiar with the feeling.

"Exactly. Anything new, any new tale, new jest, new trick, new dress—anything new is delightful to us. Why would we hasten it away? We have let her take her time, tell the tale in her own way."

I wondered how much my mother remembered. How had she come to be lost in the jungle of Chinanga? How long had she been there?

"You have not heard the end of her story?" I asked.

Domenico shook his head. "There may be no end to it. Better if we are left with a little still between our teeth to chew upon after she is gone."

While the others went on talking, Constanzia and I went back to visit the virgin. She welcomed us as she might have welcomed any fairly interesting strangers. Seeing her face, even younger looking than my own, I suffered from doubt and fear that she might reject me when I told her who I was.

"Since my arrival," she confided to us, "I have been asking what country I have come to, but aside from telling me the name of the place, the people here are remarkably evasive. What is it about Chinanga that occasions such restraint?"

"They are ashamed of their origins," said Constanzia with a blush.

My mother regarded her with the liveliest interest. Without thinking, I said I felt no origin, however lowly, should shame a population for more than a generation or two. Constanzia shook her head at me.

"There has been only one generation, Lady Wellingford. I believe that Ambrosius Pomposus, father of Chinanga, must have been a warlock who traveled in far and wondrous places, only to fall under the spell of his own memories, his recollections of tropical lands full of languor and splendor and luxuriant vegetation, full of incestuous entanglements and erotic desires, a place in which time seemed damped in its passage. He determined to create such a land of his own, so laid claim to this milieu along the eternal rivers and created in it, Chinanga!" She gestured widely, signifying all and everything, a great, inclusive gesture which stopped only at the farthest reaches of her fingertips.

"How do you know this?" asked Elladine.

"She read about it in Pomposus's book," I replied, to Constanzia's amazement. She had indeed read it there, though she still did not understand what she had read. "Though Pomposus may have been only a writer, not a warlock. Writers, too, can create such places."

"I see," breathed Mama.

I went on, "I believe Constanzia has also read that Chinanga is to remain changeless until the Viceroy, while in the company of a virgin with a difference and after the celebration of a certain rite which Constanzia has not yet been able to translate, decides differently."

"I see," said Elladine, who did indeed see, turning to the girl. "Your father wishes to change the country? A revolution, perhaps?"

"A devolution, I believe," whispered Constanzia, coming away from the windows as though suddenly aware of ears which might be pricked at those windows. "He wishes to attain mastery over Baskarone. He speaks of it metaphorically, as the

ascent of the lover onto his mistress's balcony, claiming he will
do it with love."

"There is ravishment of that kind," said Elladine, dispas-
sionately. "And then there is rape."

Constanzia nodded. "I know. Daddy has grown insensitive
and mulish with the centuries. He wishes some great apotheo-
sis."

"I, on the other hand," said Elladine, "merely wish to get
home to Ylles."

"Ylles," mused Constanzia. "Ylles. I have heard of Ylles. It
is mentioned in *The Diaries*. It is here, in the continuum, part of a
larger creation, not far away."

"Roland told me it was an unachievable distance away.
Surely he would not lie?"

"Nonsense. A chaperone wouldn't know the truth if it
waved its wings at him." Constanzia patted my mother's shoulder. "Never mind. I'll find Ylles for you. When we get home, I'll
look it up in the great encyclopedia, if you will only tell me how
to spell it."

"*Wy,*" I said to her. "Double *el, ee, ess.*"

"How did you know?" Mama asked me.

"I have seen reference to the place in certain family papers," I replied cunningly. "In Westfaire. My home."

"Westfaire," brooded Elladine. "I remember Westfaire.
Then you . . . you must be . . ."

"Your daughter," I answered softly, watching her face.

She gave me a long look, a troubling look. As though she
could not believe who I was. At last her lips trembled open, and
her eyes lit with . . . was it love? Was it something else?

"Beauty," she cried. "You got my letter!"

Constanzia watched in amazement as we embraced. The
embrace itself was not what I expected. It was awkward, a little
embarrassing. Mother did not cling. She gave me a brief, almost
perfunctory hug, and then stood away from me, looking intently at me, as though trying to find in me some resemblance
she had expected. Perhaps our meeting would have seemed
more natural if Mama had appeared to be only a little older.

Almost at once Constanzia increased my embarrassment by commenting upon Mama's youthful appearance.

"She's a fairy," I told Constanzia. "I imagine she'll always look that way. On the other hand, I am only half fairy. I'm already older than she is." I smiled fondly at Mama. At least, it began as a fond smile. Mama's reaction to it was to turn abruptly away from me with a sigh. Something was not as I had planned or hoped, but I didn't wish to consider what it might be at that moment.

"You're very lovely," said Constanzia, patting me upon my cheek. "You couldn't be prettier even if you were only twenty-three."

Since I thought I was only nineteen or twenty, at least as I counted elapsed time, her words did not greatly cheer me. And, though I considered myself only nineteen or twenty, there were unmistakeable signs about the eyes that I might actually be somewhat older, which reminded me suddenly of what Mama had said in her letter to me. The bit about coming in haste, before I got any older.

My mother reached out a hand to touch me, felt of my breast with her fingertips, drew her hand away as though burned. Perhaps she had felt the mysterious fire within me. Perhaps she could tell me what it was!

Before I could ask her, she spoke, almost abruptly, to Constanzia. "I simply cannot figure out what I am doing here! I had returned to Ylles, I remember quite distinctly. Then something came up, some necessary journey back to Westfaire. I think I was with Aunt Joyeause. Then we were returning to Ylles once more, and suddenly I was caught up, as in some whirling vortex of wind, and deposited on a small, uncomfortable outcropping in the middle of a jungle."

I started to tell her why she had gone back to Westfaire, then realized that would require lengthy explanation. I was saved from saying anything by Constanzia.

"It might have been Daddy who trapped you there," she said. "He's been making black magic to summon a virgin with a difference for years. He may have hit upon something that worked."

I thought this exceedingly unlikely. The Viceroy had not struck me as a competent sorcerer. The spell had been cast by Carabosse, to catch and hold my mother here, to bring me here to join her, to keep me safe. Why was my safety so important?

"But why? Why this obsession . . . ?" my mother asked.

This was a safer subject than the other, and I had been thinking about the matter ever since we left Nacifia. I had come to certain conclusions, and in order not to think about other things, I shared them with Constanzia and my mother.

"Ambrosius Pomposus had only the compass of his own mind to invest in his creation. Each of the beings he placed here in Chinanga partook of his sensitivity and his feeling, and each is, therefore, similar to every other, or if not similar to, at least totally comprehensible by. There are no foreign thoughts, no strangenesses entering from outside. The mystery of the exotic is lacking. The lure of the peculiar, the alien, the inexplicable, all are missing.

"Even in the clownery, which I visited during a stop in Nacifia, the patients are not truly insane within the totality which is Chinanga. The actions of one are offset by the actions of another; what one creates, another destroys, precisely as errant thoughts in one's own mind are corrected by other thoughts until they result in a personality which, though undoubtedly unique, is entirely familiar to itself. It occurs to me that after long time, all of Chinanga must feel that it knows itself far too well, that it exists as one entity, bound about with invisible and inexorable ties of familiarity, alone, without contrast, in solitary confinement for endless time."

"Years of solitude," Constanzia murmured, nodding in agreement. "Mother has often commented upon it. Endless solitude."

"I first thought of this," I continued, "when I saw how delighted Mrs. Gallimar was to meet me and how little surprised she was about virtually anything else. Everything that can happen in Chinanga must have happened before." I paused for a moment, reflecting that Mama and I—and Carabosse and the ambassador—might be the only real, non-Ambrosius creatures currently in Chinanga. I did not want to say this to Constanzia.

She had obviously not considered her own reality or lack of it, and I did not wish to upset her.

I finished my peroration lamely, "Chinanga, though very lovely, remains a singularly inhibited creation."

My mother regarded me with wonder. "The way you talk!"

I chose to take this as fondness and smiled modestly. "I was a college student, majoring in literature."

"What is literature?" she asked.

It was not the time to discuss such things, so I replied only briefly.

"Still," she yawned when I had finished, "if I take your meaning correctly—which is, darling, somewhat difficult to do when you use all those strange words—it might explain why Constanzia's father has summoned me up. The poor Viceroy is simply bored out of his senses."

"I have not yet been able to translate the rites mentioned in *The Diaries,*" Constanzia murmured. "But I think Daddy has done so. He is not alone in being bored. Mother is bored. Colonel Esquivar is bored. Even Roland Mirabeau is bored. I have tried to deny it to myself, but I am bored also. What have we to look forward to except things we know are going to happen but which happen less frequently than others? The *Stugos Queen* arrives less often than do the seasonal festivals, and her arrival is therefore cause for more excitement. The river rises less often than the *Queen* arrives, and the rising is considered cause for celebration. A gallivant causes depredations only once in a very great while and brings, therefore, almost a quality of surprise. I'm amazed the people here at Novabella want the gallivant hunted and killed, for even the woman whose buttock it ate admits it has made an interesting change."

[We did not foresee this. I had never thought the place would be boring. So much life and color and exotic splendor should not be boring. And yet, I suppose, given sufficient time, everything becomes boring.

"We should have known," said Israfel. "We, of all creatures, should have known."]

Constanzia's voice trailed away into silence. She shook her head somewhat petulantly and excused herself, the tiny frown on her face betraying troubled thought. Perhaps she was beginning to realize that Chinanga was an imaginary land, and what the implications of that might be. I reproached myself silently for having said anything about Chinanga within her hearing. I had wanted to impress Mama with my intelligence, and all I had done was make Constanzia apprehensive. It would be better if Mama and I could leave Novabella at once, before I was the cause of any further disruption. I suggested to Mama that since I had the seven-league boots in my pocket, we might depart together, dispensing with any ceremony. She said it was worth a try, so I put them on. "Boots," I said, holding Mama tightly about the waist and refusing to acknowledge that she shrank slightly from my embrace, "take us to Ylles."

[Israfel and I held our breaths. She was not supposed to do this. She was not supposed to try to leave Chinanga! We muttered enchantments and held fast!]

At once the boots attempted to depart with my feet inside them. Mama, however, remained rooted in place. It was as though I had taken hold of one of the great forest trees, a mighty monarch rooted deep through the swampy soil of Chinanga into the eternal substance of whatever lay beneath. Mama could no more move than such a tree could move, but I was being whipped to and fro like a flag attached to an immovable mast, feeling my grip slowly loosened by the force of the fairy shoes.

"Boots," I cried in a strangled voice, "desist!" I fell to the floor, for a moment unable to stand, feeling as though my legs were made of water.

"It will do no good," Mama murmured in my ear. "Whatever spell has caught me here in Chinanga will not let me go. We must find out what the enchantment is before it can be broken."

I did not think it was the Viceroy who had done it. I thought it was more likely Carabosse. I determined to talk to her the next time I saw her, to learn what she was doing to me and why.

In any case, it seemed we must defer our departure until later, and we could not return to Nacifia at once. We had the choice of joining the *Stugos Queen* as it completed its voyage upstream to the wall below Baskarone, or of remaining in Novabella. Since we were assured by everyone that nothing in Novabella was worthy of our attention—except the hunt for the predacious gallivant in which Colonel Esquivar was even now engaged, but which we, as non-hunters, could hardly share—Mama, Constanzia and I decided to go on upriver with the Captain and his remaining passengers.

We shared a large cabin. Roland and Mrs. Gallimar accompanied us upon the trip. Whenever Mama emerged from the cabin, one or both of them were in attendance. Though I was certain Senora Carabosse had been on the ship when we came to Novabella, she was not there when we left.

[I had gone home, to attempt to find out what we were doing wrong!]

Upriver from Novabella, the aspect of the country began to change. The river became swifter and less spread out; the land on either side sloped away more steeply. There were fewer drowned trees and more great rock pillars, accumulating as we traveled into ramparts, escarpments, and pinnacles of stone set well back from the flow but still visible whenever the mists lifted. During the entire voyage, Constanzia scarcely left the rail or the window. Each turn in the river made her exclaim.

"Then there is something new in Chinanga," I teased her, wondering if I had been mistaken about the country's reality. "You have not seen this stretch of country before."

"Oh, yes, yes," she replied. "There have been virgins with a difference reported before, though none were ever genuine. I have stowed away before. Before I knew it was all there was, I traveled all of Chinanga. But those journeys were so long ago I have almost forgotten them."

Once, late in the evening, we looked up to see the stars

occulted by a vast shadow with a line of light along its edge and knew we gazed upon the incredible heights of Baskarone.

"I want to go there," Constanzia breathed. "I can think of nothing else. Since I first saw an ambassador from Baskarone, I have longed to go there. It is why I started reading *The Diaries*. To find a way!"

Mama shook her head, biting her lip. "I'm afraid that is impossible, child."

"You don't understand. If you'd ever seen one of them . . ."

"I have," Mama said, her nostrils flaring, her mouth grim. "Several, as a matter of fact. What you say is true. Seeing them makes us long for Baskarone, but we may not go there, no matter how we long. They will not let us in." She turned abruptly and went into her cabin, leaving Constanzia and me to stare after her, wondering at her tone.

I wondered often at her tone. When I was honest with myself, I realized I had expected a mother, my mother, to be like Dame Blossom: a little severe, but unfailingly affectionate in a kindly, nurturant way. Mama was not that. Sometimes I thought she was not even very like the woman who had written the letter. Oh, it was nothing one could put one's finger on. We talked together, took tea together, confided in one another. I told her about Giles. Her eyes filled with tears, and we cried over that together. She understood. She said she had felt that way about my father. I held her hand and was happy. And then, just as I thought I was beginning to know her, I saw on her face an expression of remote untouchability. She looked through me, as though I did not exist. Then, some hours later, she became my affectionate mama again.

This happened more than once on our voyage. I could not explain it. I feared, from time to time, that something I had done or, more likely, had not done, sometimes came to her mind, damaging the feelings between us. Or I feared that something about me put her off. I didn't know what it was. When she was being my mama, I felt as secure as a child held in loving arms. When she looked through me, I felt wavery, as though my very existence was in question. I actually wished for Carabosse, so that I could ask her what she thought was happening.

Another night, with the *Queen* moored at the edge of the water, I saw the last of the cages disposed of. Several times during late-night hours of our journey I had left Mama and Constanzia sleeping and had sneaked into the hold to hold converse with those in the cages. Ambrosius had read or traveled widely, and had been interested in the religions of the world. Each cage had been consigned to a particular hell, and each cage was full of beings Ambrosius imagined had learned to fear that special hell, whether one of fire or ice or eternal separation or mere time-serving prior to some later reconciliation with whomever or whatever they considered responsible for their fate. There were many espousing fundamentalist Christian faiths, all babbling of the love of God while seething with guilt and resentment. I suggested to them that, if they could bring themselves to disbelieve, they might free themselves from their confinement, and a few must have managed to do so, for several of the consignees from Erebus complained of light weight when they received their shipments at last.

When I came up on deck after the last such conversation, the captain was standing at the rail. I was not wearing my cloak. He nodded at me and grinned apologetically. "Can you believe I used to bring them all across from the Edge in a rowboat?" he asked. "Of course, that was before I came to Chinanga. I suppose it's more interesting now."

"Where did Ambrosius borrow you from?" I asked.

"The Greeks," he said. "I am their ferryman."

"Of course," I said, remembering things I had read. "You rowed a boat across the Styx."

"For the coins on the dead men's eyes," he said. "The work has not changed much."

"And where do the souls come from in the cages?" I asked.

"Where do the trees come from," he smiled. "And the snakes and the orchids."

I nodded, thoughtfully, taking his point. "Are you bored?" I asked. Everyone spoke much of boredom here in Chinanga.

"Oh yes," he said in a grumpy voice. "I am bored. So much so that occasionally I long for the simpler days."

Two days later we reached the falls which came down from Baskarone and moored along the riverbank, well back from the plunging torrent. We could not see the top. The roar of the waters and the clouds of spray extinguished any appreciation of the enormousness of the fall.

In a clearing some distance from this pool the captain found the expected stack of kegs and crates, let down from above, I supposed, by some unimaginable windlass. While the crewmen were loading, several passengers departed, quiet persons with purpose writ large upon their faces. The captain shook his head after them as they went off toward the great wall.

"Going to try for it, they are," he told me. "Going to try and climb it. Every time I come up here, there's a few. Silly creatures. Even if the wall wasn't unclimbable, which it is, them from Baskarone aren't going to let anyone climb there."

I shook my head with him. Poor vagrant creations of Ambrosius Pomposus, destined to climb so high to so little purpose.

While they were getting the cargo aboard, Mama and I hiked to a hilltop some little way apart where we might see the falls entire. Even at this distance, I could see only the lower half, though Mama's fairy vision could see far more than I. She had some ointment in her pocket, one of the things, she said, that she always carried with her. She annointed my eyes with it, telling me to blink several times and wait until the tears stopped. It stung, but only for a moment. When I looked up again, I caught my breath in wonder.

The wall was wreathed in rainbow, not puny arcs such as we sometimes see after a shower, but great circles and bows, one within another, like the radiance of a butterfly's wing or the feathers of certain birds where the light breaks its own color through barbs and scales to make a glorious aureole. The waterfall was a silver marvel, tumbling in sprays and droplets, each catching the light, separating and rejoining in a myriad braided saults. Above, upon the height, I could see trees and towers and color where great tracts of flowers bloomed. The angle was wrong, I should not have been able to see anything there. It was as though the light itself bent, as it does going around stars, to give me a glimpse of what lay above.

The vision was more like taste than sight. When I looked away, my eyes longed for me to look back, as the tongue longs for savor. Each tree upon the height was the epitome of tree. Each tower the quintessence of what towers could be. Everything there seemed to be the design from which earthly things were made. I was conscious that the burning presence in my chest was still. I did not feel it. It was at rest.

In a moment my eyes stung again, perhaps from the ointment, more likely from tears, and when I looked back, the vision was gone.

"The ointment is stale," Mama said in an annoyed tone. "I waited for rescue overlong in that jungle. Never mind, my dear. When we come to Ylles, you will learn it is as beautiful as Baskarone." Her words sounded confident, but her smile, when I turned to look at her, seemed forced.

I believed her, but still I wiped tears from my eyes as we returned to the *Stugos Queen*. We were not alone. Several of the passengers had come along for the sightseeing, and they, too, seemed depressed and sad. It seemed almost willfully malicious to let us see what lay upon the heights and yet forbid us access to it, but when I said this to Constanzia she rebuked me.

"Such is not the case. It is only from such visions and temptations that fantastic longing comes. Out of that vision, a thousand worlds are built. I have heard it said in Nacifia that it is better to be a climber who falls to his death from the walls of Baskarone, than to be king in any other land." She sounded somewhat doubtful, as though the source of the quotation was not a trustworthy one. "Any other land," she repeated, as though to convince herself.

"Except Faery itself," I commented to Mama, as a quiet aside.

"Except Faery itself," she agreed. "Oh yes, dear. Of course."

When the cargo was aboard, the *Queen* turned downriver, and we raced with the current instead of against it, achieving in one or two days what had taken ten or twelve to accomplish on the way up. Our speed was such that we felt quite giddy. Before we knew it, we were at Novabella once more, having dinner with Don Masimiliano *(sopa de limon, filetes des pesces del rio, ensalada de los helechos tropicales, plantain tostarse, quarto trasero de gallivant asado*— from the colonel's successful hunt—*pastelillos de frutas,* with *patito-chuleta* as a savory followed by coffee and liqueurs) and then away downstream toward Nacifia.

Mama did not feel well after eating the roast gallivant. She whispered to me that the fauna of imaginary regions were invariably poisonous to beings from her realm. Not binding, necessarily, as were fairy fruits or the pomegranate seeds of Hell, but simply unhealthful. I had felt no such trouble, and therefore decided that my digestive system was probably fully human. When I mentioned this to Mama, she said in a tart voice that it had taken me some little time to arrive at that conclusion. Only then did I realize that she had not had recourse to the personal cabinet at the rear of the ship once since she had come aboard.

"In many imaginary lands, as here, they shit and piss," she advised me. "As on earth, though rather less copiously. But not in Ylles nor, I believe, in Baskarone. Never mind, dearest. When you eat fairy fruits, you will not be bothered with such grossness any longer."

I had not precisely been bothered up until this time, though afterward I seemed to give a great deal of unaccustomed attention to the matter. No doubt this was one of the differences that Roland sensed in Mama. The implications were shattering. How refreshing to have all the joys of love (I write in a literary or conventional sense, rather than from experience) sans consequent familiarity with those anatomical proximities which humans find both so unfortunate and so teasingly attractive. I came to the conclusion that there would be no perversions in Ylles.

We arrived at Nacifia late one night and tied up at the pier with no sound from the whistle. I thought it might be thoughtfulness on the captain's part until I saw him and Mrs. Gallimar tête-à-tête in the dining room and realized he simply had not wished to interrupt their last evening together. Last, one assumes, for a time, for a long time, though not for all time, since everything in Chinanga repeats itself. Constanzia had already gone ashore. It was one of those evenings when Mama and I felt close and familial, a dear feeling, one that left tears brooding in the corners of my eyes. We stood at the rail with Roland close behind and looked at the sleeping city while we whispered to one another all that we knew, thought and imagined about it. On the pier several escapees from the clownery presented classical tableaux vivants for our edification. They had chosen to portray an ascent to Baskarone, as though achieved by certain historic personages, each tableau occasioning a tiny frisson, as of surprise. If one were not continuously aware of Chinanga's origins, one was continually agitated by little shocks, only to say to oneself a moment later, "But what else would one expect in Chinanga?" Tableaux vivants, of course.

"Beauty," Mama said to me in a serious voice, "when we are taken to the Viceroy's palace tomorrow, stay close to me and do not be surprised at anything I may say or do."

[*"She's going to do something stupid,"* I said to Israfel.
"Who?" he asked. *"Beauty."*
"No. Elladine. She's going to do something silly. I can feel it."]

I kissed Mama on her beautiful cheek and promised her that I would not. We went into the cabin together and so to bed.

·
20
·

I had no further thoughts until the morning when the whistle, so long delayed, woke us as well as every living thing within hearing of it. It was not long after breakfast that the Viceroy sent a cart for Mama, one draped in fringed velvet, its curtains held aloft by a tottery framework of gilt staves. I guessed the cart had appeared in festival processions for many seasons, and when I saw the priest from the cathedral wringing his hands on the sidelines, I knew I was correct. Mama had merely replaced St. Frog in being hauled up the cobbled streets by a succession of devotees, including many inmates from the clownery who seemed in a state of unusual excitement.

I walked at the side of the cart, behind Mrs. Gallimar, who moved along with ladylike little steps, acknowledging the plaudits of the assembled citizenry. Beyond her was Senora Carabosse. I resolved to keep her in sight until we had a chance to talk. On the other side of the cart strode Roland Mirabeau, his fine features drawn together in an expression of concentration and resolve. Behind us came another cart bearing the head of the gallivant, preserved in a barrel of Baskaronian wine for this occasion. Colonel Esquivar strode beside this tumbrel, his moustaches waxed into spiral magnificence, with several of his ragged children tagging at his heels. Behind the colonel came the captain and his crew, and after them the ragtag and motley of the town. Outside the gates to the citadel there was a momentary hiatus in our progression, soon remedied when the great gates swung open to the accompaniment of fanfarons and vorticals. Inside the gates a blood-colored carpet led up the vast stony flight to the massive portal, just outside which the Viceroy waited.

He had dressed for the occasion in cloth of gold with diamonds. Flatulina was no less marvelously accoutred, and various of the viceregal children stood here and there, observing our approach with scarcely concealed incredulity. I was not surprised to see Constanzia between two of them, standing attentively immobile, as though she had been there all along. We paused at the foot of the stairs.

"Senorita," the Viceroy began, sweeping his hat before him in the first gesture of a very complicated reverence.

"Senora, actually," Mama said.

The Viceroy came erect all at once, like a poker. He glared at Roland Mirabeau, who shrugged elaborately.

"She is a virgin," the chaperone said. "No matter what she calls herself."

"With a difference?" hissed the Viceroy, coming down the stairs sidewise, like a crab, one hand held threatening before him. Flatulina edged down behind him, her head held slightly forward, like a snake about to strike.

"As you will observe," Roland said calmly, indicating Mama with a nod of his head. She sat at ease, awaiting the Viceroy's approach. When he had come near enough, she held out her hand for him to kiss. He bowed over it. I saw his nostrils quiver. Perhaps he scented the odor of . . . of whatever Roland had sensed. Over the top of his head she gave me a look of sceptical disdain, but when he raised himself again, her face was all sweetness.

"I have been told you require my assistance," she said. "So happy to be of help."

I scarcely heard her. At the top of the stairs, the ambassador from Baskarone emerged from the great doors. My eyes became fixed upon him. They could not turn aside. What business had kept him here so long? What business had brought him here at all? Why ever he had come, his stay had not changed him. The thought occurred to me that ambassadors from Baskarone were, perhaps, among the eternal things which did not change.

He became aware of my stare and smiled at me as though we were friends but lately separated. I blushed and cast down my eyes, released by that smile to come to myself once more. Resolutely I turned my eyes on Mama and the Viceroy. That was where any business pertinent to me would transpire, and Mama might at any moment need my help. When I glanced up a moment later, the ambassador had gone, perhaps away, perhaps inside the castle, who could say. My heart stopped for a moment, then resumed its steady thudding.

The Viceroy awarded a medal to Colonel Esquivar, to much tantara of trumpets and huzzah from the populace. The gallivant head was turned over to representatives from the firm of Pelasges y Plumas, *rellenadores acclamados* to the hunters of Chinanga. The head would hang in the viceregal dining room, said the Viceroy. Considering both its bedraggled state and the bestial glare remaining in the glassy eyes, the *rellenadores* would have their work cut out for them.

Mrs. Gallimar and the chaperone were rewarded and dismissed. A benefice was awarded Captain Karon. Alms were given to clownery inmates loose along the street. Sweets were tossed to the crowd. There was a general departure, and we were left in relative quiet, scarcely more than a two-family party: the Viceroy's numerous one; plus Mama and me. The Viceroy rubbed his hands together and put on a new expression as he winked and nodded at his wife. "I have everything ready," he chortled. "Have had, simply forever, just waiting, don't you know." His eyes glittered with hectic abandon. He was not the same man I had seen before. He was transformed by excitement.

[''I don't like this at all,'' I said. ''This wasn't supposed to happen.''

''Carabosse, it will happen, whether we like it or not,'' sighed Israfel. ''It has been inevitable, ever since Elladine arrived. This world does not appear in our futures; we misinterpreted that fact, that's all. We had no way of knowing.''

''I should have read all The Diaries, *'' I confessed. ''I should have been more careful.''*

''Shhh,'' said Israfel. ''Be ready to salvage what we can. . . .'']

I looked across at Constanzia, who shrugged. Evidently her father had gone further in *The Diaries* than she had. Following his urgent beckoning, we entered the castle and paraded down a long, stone-floored corridor between files of uniformed guardsmen, climbed several flights of rocky stairs which twisted and coiled about in the walls of the place, and arrived at last in a tower room set up for the study of astrology, alchemy, or some even more esoteric science. I stooped to one great brass telescope as we passed it, finding it focused upon the heights of Baskarone. The mechanism had not the power of Mama's salve, but one could make out the effulgence of the place.

"At last," the Viceroy said, lighting candles and setting alembics to bubbling. "At last," as he thrust a sword through a ring and suspended both above a chair. "At last," as he bustled about opening books to proper pages, laying out indescribable things upon a stone set in a pentacle. He motioned for Mama to seat herself in the chair. She looked at the suspended weapon with a suspicious eye, but complied even as she summoned me nearer, taking me firmly by the hand.

"If I am not mistaken," she murmured. "The Viceroy is about to turn his universe inside out."

["This world has lasted for centuries," I sighed. "Oh, Israfel, why. Why? Just when we had need of it."
Israfel didn't answer me. He had no time to answer.]

Various members of the Viceroy's family were assigned parts in the rite. They were already well-rehearsed. The telescope was evidently part of the ritual, for it was sprinkled with liquids from the alembics, censered with fragrant and bitter smoke, and Mama was asked to put her eye to it as the final words of the spell or invocation were spoken. The words were in no language I knew. I could not even have begun to spell the sounds which issued in gutteral imperatives from the Viceroy's throat.

Silence.

A wind came up from somewhere. Mama gripped my hand. A voice from behind us said, "May I drop you ladies somewhere?" I turned to see the ambassador from Baskarone, smiling at us both. Senora Carabosse stood at his side, looking like a rider whose horse had just died unexpectedly, her face a puzzle of chagrin and impromptu resolution. I looked back at the Viceroy, only to find him vanished, his place taken by an amount of empty and chilly air. So with Flatulina and the children. Constanzia whirled past, her hair a wheel of dark and light as she spun and was gone. She held out her hand toward me, her face pleading.

I cried out to her. "Constanzia . . ."

The ambassador shook his head. "Ambrosius Pomposus did not intend his imaginary world to exist forever. He included in his creation a procedure whereby the inhabitants, when they grew sufficiently bored, could accomplish the rite of dissolution. Some such rite is part of all creations, Beauty. Of Faery. Of the world. It is our misfortune that our own actions have helped un-create this one just now."

He took Mama on one arm and me on the other and began to stride across the clouds that suddenly stretched before us, Senora Carabosse walking effortlessly beside. I thought, irrele-vantly, that if she walked so easily, she could not be so old as I had previously thought. My fingers tingled where they touched the ambassador's arm. I heard Mrs. Gallimar's voice saying faintly to someone, "Such a lovely wine. Such a lovely, lovely wine," and then came the retreating wail of the *Stugos Queen*. The clouds opened below us to let us see a great, edgeless river where a lonely boatman looked up from his oars and waved. Chinanga had departed, but the river was still there.

"The Styx was imagined before Chinanga," said the ambas-sador. "It will be there through many creations yet."

"Ylles, Israfel, if you would be so kind," Mama said in a strained, polite voice.

"Glad to be of service, Elladine," he replied. There was something weary and ironic in his voice.

We were very high up. For a moment I saw the beautiful heights of Baskarone, clear as day. Then they were gone, and so was he.

.
21
.

I write the truth when I say that Ylles is an almost-Baskarone. When one eats fairy fruit, one sees it as glorious, lovely, utterly beyond compare. Since I had eaten no fairy fruit prior to arrival, however, my first glimpse of it was disappointing. It looked rather like a waste of moorland with some pigpens and hovels scattered here and there. The moment we arrived, Mama darted away into the bushes, and Carabosse, who was standing quietly beside me with an expression of deep pain upon her old face, leaned forward and said, "Come see me as soon as you can, Beauty. Ask Puck to bring you." Before I could ask her who Puck was, she took a step or two down the path toward some pigpens, sidled a little to the right and was gone. It was a method of coming and going I was to see much of in Faery.

Mama emerged from the shrubbery with a handful of berries which she thrust upon me, urging me to eat them all as quickly as possible. While I did so, she gathered others for herself. She chewed them as though famished, eyes rolled up, jaws working furiously. It was an astonishing sight which kept my eyes fixed on her for several minutes. When I looked at my surroundings again, I found myself in true Ylles. Parkland had replaced moorland; castles stood where the hovels had been, and over all stretched a sky of late-evening blue spangled with early stars. The grasses were also starred with tiny five-pointed flowers of silver, umbels of golden bloom, and tinkling sprays of bluebells. Though I saw it all quite clearly, Mama was not content until she had uprooted a small, hairy stemmed plant and rubbed the juice of its root into my eyes. It stung horribly for a time, but when the pain vanished, my eyesight was like that of a falcon.

"Elvenroot," she explained. "It grows only in Faery, nowhere else. It enables one to see all our marvels."

"Ylles is in Faery?" I asked stupidly, sniffing at an odor which had caught my nostrils, a familiar scent.

"A province," she said, nodding. "One of many. It goes from those hills over there," and she pointed, "to the ocean over there," pointing once more. "I am the ruler of it, when I'm here. When I'm not here, another of the Theena Shee takes it over."

I had not understood the word she used. She said it again, then smoothed a patch of ground and spelled it out with her finger, in Irish, evidently the only human language in which the word was written. "Daoine Sidhe," she said. *"Theena Shee.* My people. The people of True Faery. One of whom takes over rulership of my province when I am away. Here, I'll show you the boundaries."

She turned me to face a direction I thought of as north,

where loomed a range of shadowy mountains, their ridges making a jagged line against the stars. At the foot of the mountains
lay dark folds of forest. Mama turned me widdershins from the
forest to see the land sloping down to a starlit sea, the white
combers rolling endlessly toward us. Widdershins from the sea
was moorland, covered with low growth and extending as far as
I could see. Widdershins from the moorland brought me facing
uplands, where many fantastic and marvelous palaces stood,
though none, to my surprise, as lovely as Westfaire. Whichever
direction I turned, the familiar odor came past me on the wind,
as though blown from every quarter.

"Oberon's and Mab's," she said, pointing to the two closest
palaces. "And mine, and a dozen more. It doesn't really matter
which part belongs to who. Oberon's realm is next to mine, and
he would look after it if I left."

We stood beside a copse which was more or less at the
center of all this: tall trees, lacy, silvery, softly susurrant.

"Why would you ever leave it?" I asked, staring in wonder
around myself. Truthfully, it was very lovely.

"Oh," she said vaguely. "Sometimes one wants a change."

Every view was one a painter would sell his brushes for.
Every aspect thrilled. Every structure was perfect from every
angle. The scent of the flowers alone was enough to make one
drunk, though it did not mask that other scent. . . .

"Mama, what is that smell?" I asked.

"Smell?" She sniffed delicately. "The flowers?"

"No, the smell on the wind."

She sniffed again, her ivory nostrils dilating to take in the
breeze. "Not the sea? Not the pines of the forest?"

"No. The smell . . . the smell that's everywhere."

She laughed, liltingly. "The smell of Faery, silly child. The
smell of magic!"

As I was about to pursue that matter, we were interrupted
by the sound of horns, tiny horns pitched high as a wasp's buzz.
Mama gestured to one side, and I turned to see a troupe passing
by, little men mounted on mice, butterfly-winged maidens riding hedgehogs saddled with roses. Elladine called and they an-

swered, their voices like infant bells, waving tiny hands, calling a greeting but not turning aside from their processionary way.

"Trouping fairies," she told me with an indulgent smile.

"Where are they going?"

"Nowhere. Everywhere. They simply go. They camp on the mosses and dance. Then they move on. They are not serious creatures. They have only small enchantments, small as themselves. Sometimes they are seen in the human world, sometimes they are heard. Sometimes their dance floors are seen."

"Fairy rings?"

She nodded. "They are the only fairies with butterfly wings, the only fairies to inhabit human gardens. Once they were as large as we; once they were worshipped as gods and goddesses, long, oh long, long ago. They had mighty names then: Pomona. Naiad. Dryad. Aurora. Over time they have shrunk. They get smaller with every passing century. Eventually I believe they will vanish into the atmosphere, and we will hear them for a time, like midges, then they will be entirely gone." There was something careless and remote in her voice, a tone I had noted before, a tone I had shuddered to hear.

"Won't you miss them?" I asked, wanting her to say yes, yes, she would miss them because they were fanciful and marvelous.

She didn't answer the question I had asked. "We Sidhe do not need wings, nor mice to serve as steeds. We have our own hunt, our own ways." She sounded eager, almost voracious. There was something uncomfortable in her voice, something like an edge of grass, seeming so soft, cutting so deep, the life's blood following it almost invisibly so that one does not know one is cut until one sees the red. I drew in my breath, waiting for the wound to gape, but she walked away over the verdant meadow, and I followed her, drawn like the tail of a kite, wondering what had happened to her. Even in Chinanga she had seemed more . . . more human. But then, I told myself, Chinanga had been a human imagining, while Faery was not.

We had gone only a little way when we saw the Sidhe coming toward us, a host on horseback, the first among them leading two riderless horses by their bridles. Oh, the horses were fine! All the horses I had seen as a child were nothing to these, and all the tack I had cared for was nothing to what they wore. Milk-white steeds, they were, shod with silver and bridled in gold, with gemmed frontispieces over their foreheads and jeweled taches across their chests. The skirts of the saddles were dagged, with gilded edges, and were gemmed in patterns of flowers and leaves. Broad in the chest, those horses were, and their nostrils flared and their eyes gleamed as though made of fire.

The riders wore green mantles fringed with gold and bright helmets feathered with green plumes. Each one had in his hand a golden spear from which a long, narrow banner flew, the banners coiling across the sky like the writing I had seen on leatherwork brought back to Westfaire by Papa's father, the liquid writing of the heathen in the Holy Land.

"Read the banners," Mama instructed me, laying her hand on my eyes, and in that instant I could understand them, for they spelled words and paragraphs that slipped into my mind as a hand into a well-worn glove. They expressed the language of the djinni, the banner language of the slow-winds which all in Faery know. The words told me it was the King of that place coming to welcome Mama, and with him a whole host of other elvish peoples, all curling their banners to make her name: Elladine.

Behind these male fairies the females rode, clad in bright silks of colors and designs I had never seen, their hair bound in circlets of oak leaves tied with ivy, the ivy leaves dangling beside their pure white brows. Most among them had golden hair, and this was obviously the color preferred. Others, male and female, were smaller, swarthier folk who rode at the sides of the procession, and at the rear, mostly unheeded by the golden-haired. The King wore a high crown tipped with diamonds like drops of dew glittering with inner lights.

Mama bowed when he approached, tugging me into a similar obeisance. He got down from his horse and bowed in return. There was much talk as I was led forward and introduced. Beauty. Daughter of Elladine. Only half fairy, but true to her mother's line. Much murmuring among the ladies. "Elladine's child? But so old!" I tried not to let the shock show on my face as I tucked that away to think on later. There were many glittering eyes among the men. "Elladine's daughter. Still young enough!" No one explained, but it was not long before I learned why this difference in their perceptions.

We mounted the white horses brought out for us. I had never ridden a horse like that. His feet fell like feathers upon the grass. His mane tossed like silver floss, floating upon the air. His gait was smooth, firm, and steady as a stone, and his eyes were full of intelligence. I had no need to ride. He carried me. Mama touched me, and I found myself clad as they all were, silken gown, green mantle, and wreath of leaves. We rode toward the djinni castle nearest us, one with towers impossibly narrow and high, with conical roofs so tall I did not know how they could have been built, topped with banners which reached to the stars.

A fairy woman rode up beside me, and another on the other side. "Well met, Beauty," they called to me. "We are your grandaunts. We were at your christening." They waved and rode on, looking at me curiously over their shoulders with something of the same expression Mama had first shown me. That slight narrowing of eyes, that barely noticeable discomfiture.

Another took their place. "I am your Grandaunt Joyeause," she introduced herself. "When your mother and I carried your sleeping body up to the tower, I had no idea the curse would seem to take such little time."

"The curse . . ." I faltered. So far as I knew, the curse was continuing. Mama and Joyeause had gone back to Westfaire to move my body into the tower, and it was then, returning to Ylles, that Mama had been caught by Carabosse's spell. But it hadn't been my body they had carried up to the tower of Westfaire. With sudden pain I admitted to myself that they hadn't known the difference!

I turned away, trying not to think of that. "Is it morning or evening," I asked Mama, gesturing at the sky.

"It is as it is," she said. "As it always is in Faery. The sky a dark and glorious blue. The stars just showing. The flowers still visible, and their perfume lying soft on the air. The grasses cool with evening. The air warm from day just past and the warmed leaves of the trees exuding fragrance. As it always is, in Faery."

What was the emotion in her voice? I could not place it. Not sadness, not quite. What? I was lost among these people. I could not tell what they were feeling, or why!

"Look there!" cried Aunt Joyeause.

There were whisperings among the host. "Mab. Queen Mab. Come to greet Elladine."

A single rider came toward us, clad all in silver with a crown of pearls. Far behind her white horse was another steed ridden by a dark-haired young man. He was dressed in silver, also, but he was not her son or her brother or her lover. They appeared to be of an age, but this was only seeming. She was old as the hills and lovely as the dawn, and he was something other than that.

"Young Tom-lin of Ercildoune," they whispered. "See, she's brought young Tom-lin."

"He fell from his horse, hunting," Mama whispered to me. "In time to see Mab riding by. He greeted her, and she snatched him up. She brought him here to Faery, and here he's dwelt since, almost seven Faery years. She longs for him, but though he gives her every reverence, he'll have none of her." Mama's nostrils flared, as though in disgust at such ingratitude and impertinence.

"Maybe he longs for home," I suggested.

"What has home to compare with this," Mama said.

"Why do they call him Tom-lin?" I asked.

"Because he has ceased to be Tom," she said. "Though when he speaks of himself, he calls himself Thomas the Rhymer, still, and writes verses down on bits of paper."

Mama greeted Queen Mab, evidently a higher ranking queen than herself, though Mab was kindness itself when she spoke to me, welcoming me to Faery.

"You've been long away," she said to Mama.

"A hundred mortal years, evidently," Mama said gaily. "Else my daughter would not be with me."

So Mama hadn't known the difference between me and

Beloved. So what. I'd been asleep. Or rather Beloved had. And
Mama hadn't seen me since I was a baby. How would she have
known? Inside me, something said, "Somehow, she should have
known."

Queen Mab turned to ride with us to the palace and Tom-
lin turned to follow. I caught the full strength of his stare, hungry and demanding. I was careful not to stare back, having the
feeling Queen Mab would not much like it, but something in
me responded to that stare. Something human and sympathetic.

There was a feast prepared at the castle. We ate and drank.
The wine was wonderfully flavored and scented, but it did not
make one drunk. The food was wonderfully prepared, but it did
not make one full. One could eat and drink forever if one
wished, pandering, as Aunt Basil had used to say, to one's palate
with no thought for tomorrow's indigestion.

When everyone was weary of eating, we trooped outside. I
thought, perhaps, we would walk in the gardens or have music
or even dance, but no. In the glades behind the castle streams
ran into silver pools, steaming beneath the stars. The water was
warm, and my astonishment at this had not faded when I
looked up to see the inhabitants of Faery slipping into the pools,
naked as eggs, Mama among them.

She called to me in a bell-like voice. I sat on a stone and
fumbled with one shoe, trying not to stare. I could see them,
males and females both, slender, the woman almost breastless,
their vulvas naked of hair, their bodies like little manikins
carved from ivory. The males had a kind of sheath, like a dog, or
goat, coming from between their legs and a little way up their
bellies, and these sheaths seemed covered with golden fur.
Nothing dangled. Nothing protruded. Nothing seemed awkward or erotic. Their smooth buttocks folded gently together on
either side of a simple, unperforated crease. Mama had told me
the truth. They did not piss or shit in Faery.

But I was not built as they were. I had breasts. I had hair on
me. If I bent over, as some of them were doing, my parts would
show. I was overcome with shame. I blushed.

And every eye was on me, fierce and prurient. Out of
the doggy sheathes, little penises protruded, like darting red

tongues. On every female face a luxurious interest gleamed, and I saw their hands reach out to stroke one another familiarly.

I stood up and walked away.

Mama was beside me. "When our fairy children are reared here, they do not find our habits strange," she said with a little tinkle of laughter which did not cover her distress. Her tone was as it had been sometimes in Chinanga, when she turned remote and still. "Grown-up children have too much of the world in them. Perhaps, in time . . ." She patted me on the arm and went away, leaving me to walk among the flowers.

Thomas walked there, too, evidently as discomfited as I at the naked licentiousness of Faery. He glanced at me, but did not offer conversation. After a time the fairy folk came to get us, and we went into the palace, to our own rooms, to sleep on beds where soft moss grew instead of mattresses, and coverlets sewn of rose petals kept off the drafts. If there had been any drafts, which there were not. Fountains played in that place, and their music was an unending melody. I was glad to be left alone.

The blue of the sky seemed to deepen, only a little, as though in awareness that most of us slept. The stars crinkled and winked, as though talking. I lay awake, lost in wonder. After a time there came a scratching at my door. I went on silent feet and opened it, and it was Thomas the Rhymer there. He touched me on the arm.

"I did not dare speak to you in the gardens," he said, softly as a whisper, with great longing in his voice. He stared at me closely. "It's true, you're human!"

I let him in and shut the door behind him. I was dressed in a full, silky robe. I needed only imagine what I wore, and it was there, around me. It had sleeves that fell away from my arms, floor long panels that wafted like spider silk. "I'm half human," I told him. "Elladine is my mama, but my father is human."

He nodded. "I saw those of Faery at the pool, lusting after you. You have a fine smell about you, one that arouses them. You smell of fecundity. They are almost sterile, you know. They seldom have children of their own anymore. They must steal children from cradles, or consort with mortals to bear them."

"Why is that?"

"I do not know. It has something to do with the way they were made, at the beginning of time."

"My mama is disappointed in me." It hurt to say that, but I was sure of it.

He nodded at me soberly. "You noticed that, did you? Well, it is because you are older than most children the Sidhe get. Most half mortals are stolen as babies or are born here, and they can become like the Sidhe, almost entirely. It is too late for you, however. You will never be one of them, and Elladine knows it. Though she longs to love you, she will not let herself become too fond of you. They lust after mortals, but they do not let themselves love them much."

"Not even her own daughter?" I cried in anguish.

"Not even their own children, no. Long ago, at the beginning of time, it was a different matter. They were noble and mighty then. They did not reject the nobility of suffering for love. But things are different now."

"Why?" I cried. "Oh, why?"

"Because they are diminished from what they once were. Or if not diminished, changed. They do not say so, but one learns of it, listening to what they say and do not say."

"I thought only the trooping fairies were diminished."

"Now. As these will be later. Once these were great as gods, but Faery is dwindling, even now. When it becomes small enough, perhaps I could step out of it, but it will be too late for me."

He sounded anguished. There were tears in his eyes. I started to ask him why the diminution of the Sidhe, but there was a sound in the courtyard outside my window, and he slipped away, closing the door behind him. I heard Mab's voice, asking him where he had been, and he told her he had been walking in the courtyard.

"In the courtyard, Tom-lin?" Her voice was like honey and silk, like fire and gall.

"If it please you, Your Majesty."

"You know what would please me, Tom-Lin."

"I cannot, Your Majesty. Such an honor is not for me."

"I could put a spell upon you, Tom, so you'd think it was your Janet you were making love to."

His voice rasped as he said, "Then it would be my Janet I was making love to, Your Majesty. In my heart."

I peeked out through the window. She stood there in all her loveliness, beautiful as a goddess. If she was diminished, it did not show, not in that moment. "If I cannot have your heart and your seed, Tom-lin, then you cannot have your Janet." She turned and went away from him and he stood there in the silence, his shoulders shaking.

I fell onto the bed, deeply disturbed by what I had heard, sure I would not sleep. The next thing I knew, it was morning, or so much morning as ever comes in that land. Mama and I drank little glasses of something warmly sweet and honey-smelling, then rode out in procession to attend a session at the King's court.

"Does the King have a name?" I asked Mama.

"Some call him Oberon," she told me. "Some Finvarra. Some call him the King of Golden Halls. Some, the King of the Hill People. Some the King of the Good Folk or the Gentle Ones. We call him He Who Endures, and we know when he is gone, so will we be." I heard in her voice again that slight remoteness I had heard once or twice in Chinanga, though now, having spoken to Thomas, I thought I understood it.

When we came to the King's court, the news came out to meet us that a delegation was soon to arrive, people of another sort. It was not Faery, according to what they said, and yet it was.

"It is not heaven nor earth," Mama told me mysteriously, "Nor any hell, so it must be Faery, and yet it is not the Sidhe." She would not tell me any more, but merely laughed. None of the folk of that place seemed to take this delegation seriously, yet when the time came for them to assemble in the great hall and hear the words of those who came as envoys, everyone was still and courteous and grave. The glamour lay about us so thick that I could smell it. Mama was on the dais among the royalty, and I stood along the side in dagged velvet and cloth of gold to watch the envoys come in.

Ah, but they were horrible. Hairy and twisted, fanged and dewlapped. Some among them were better-looking, more nearly straight, but as a general rule they gave the appearance of half-made things. One had long toenails that scratched upon the marble floors. One had an eye in the middle of his forehead. Some had batwings and others had rat teeth.

"Who are they," I whispered to my neighbor, trying to keep my voice from shaking.

"The Bogles," he replied. I knew the voice and turned in surprise to find Thomas the Rhymer standing close behind me. "Has your mother taught you to use the power of sight?" he whispered to me, seeing the fear in my eyes.

I shook my head at him.

"Narrow your eyes, and wish to see them true," he said. So I did, slitting both eyes and concentrating on the wish. In the moment I saw them differently, shorter, stouter people than those of the Sidhe, and darker-colored, but certainly not hideous. Somewhat like those who had ridden at the rear of the procession, though more open of face.

"They appear ugly to keep men at a distance," Thomas said. "Unlike those of the Sidhe who appear beautiful to make men come nearer. To men's eternal loss." His voice was bitter, though only a whisper, as he fell silent in order that we could hear the speeches.

My first view of them had been human sight, obviously. But once I had seen them true, I could not bring back the former vision of them. Most surprising, I had seen their leader before, every now and then when I was a child. He was my old friend, the pointy-eared boy! Of course! Puck.

"You've one among you seven years now," he challenged them. "Taken from human kind, Queen Mab. Time's near come for the teind, and you have him still. We've come to see the treaty complied with."

"It is no affair of yours what I do," the Queen replied in a silky voice. "Be back about your swamp dancing, Puck. We've had this talk before." I didn't know what a teind was, but his voice made it something serious.

"There's a new one come, as well," he went on in an even

voice. "And she's none of yours," and he turned and looked at me with a wry look as though to say, "Fancy seeing you here."

Mama rose on the dais and beckoned to me. I stepped forward uncertainly. Puck watched me with his green eyes, like water over stones. He had a brown face with great bushy brows and a wide mouth. My old acquaintance. I started to greet him, then, warned by something in his eyes, did not. Still, I was so taken with his familiar face I almost didn't hear what Mama said. "She is ours, Puck. My daughter. Beauty. Borne by me to a human noble and come to Faery to seek her mother."

He looked saddened by this, though why should he? He knew who I was, who I'd always been. Who had sent him to watch over me, back at Westfaire? I had always assumed it was Martin, or maybe Mama. Obviously not, but then who? Carabosse? He shook his head at me and turned to those on the dais. I stepped back to feel Thomas's hand rest lightly on my shoulder.

Puck tried again, "So, sad though it be, she's here by her own will, Mab. Still, there's Thomas the Rhymer who is not here of his own will. He's not been lastingly harmed as yet, but what use will you make of him?"

"I say it again, Puck. Take your Bogles back to the swamps and the streams. Get back to the crossroads. Tell your brownies to get to their sweeping, your leprechauns to their shoemaking, your kobolds to their mines. There are enough humans out there for you to cosset without worrying over mine."

"He isn't yours," said Puck, something strained in his voice. "Queen Mab . . ."

"All that is mine is mine," she chanted. "And all that is yours is mine as well. If I so choose."

"I beg you not to choose," he said to her holding out his hard, square hands. His words were an entreaty, but she merely laughed, then went on laughing with those about her as the Bogles conferred among themselves. Puck threw up his hands, then turned to leave, the others coming behind him. Except for one very small, plain one with a scythe over his shoulder, who slipped out of their ranks and took me by the hand.

"I am the Fenoderee," he whispered. "If you have need of a friend, call me." Then he, too, was gone.

Thomas spoke in my ear. "Unless you wish to see the Fenoderee destroyed, do not tell anyone he offered to be your friend."

"I won't tell anyone but Mama," I said.

"Then he is surely dead," Thomas said.

I turned on him angrily, but he had gone back into the crowd. Looking at Mama on the dais where she laughed with Queen Mab, however, I decided I did not need to tell her about the Fenoderee. I had not called for a friend, and the little Bogle's offer did not necessarily warrant mention.

The audience seemed to be over. The nobles were coming down off the dais, talking with one another in careless voices. Curiosity would certainly not be out of place, so when Mama came down to me, I asked her what all that had been about.

"Puck and his following tend to be officious," she said with her remote, careless look. "They have taken it upon themselves to be protectors of man."

"I thought angels were the protectors of man," I said in a puzzled tone, remembering things Father Raymond had taught me.

"Well then," she laughed, with a nasty twist to her amusement. "Puck has taken it into his head to become an angel. It's an old argument, going far back into time."

I hoped she would tell me more, but Oberon came up just then, and we both fell silent as we made our deep reverences to him. He invited us to join him in the hunt, and we went out to mount horses already standing ready in the courtyard. This was in accord with something I had already noticed about Faery. Food was always ready when one was hungry. Horses were saddled and bridled when one wanted to hunt. Water was hot when one wanted to bathe. Possibly the most altogether magical thing about Faery was that we did not have to wait about for other people to do things before we could do the things we wanted.

We rode out, the horses' hooves making a steady drumbeat as we crossed the bridge and came onto the road of velvety dust. I thought that all the soil of this place must be soft, else the silver shoes on the horses would not last. Mama rode up beside me and hissed, "Riding clothes, girl! Have some manners!"

I looked up see everyone clad in riding clothes with high boots and flowing skirts on the ladies and their hair done up in narrow caps with veils flying behind. As soon as I saw it, I was dressed the same as they, but it had taken my perceiving them to do it. I had done it myself. This gave me a momentary exultation followed by a shiver of fear. If I'd been a child when I came here, I'd have done it without even thinking. What else could I do, just by thinking about it?

We hunted white deer that day. Two of them, a stag and a hind. They fled like the wind, and we pursued like the gale. They fled like the hawk, and we came after them like the eagle. They fled like the flame of candles, and we burned their trails like the fire in a forge. At last they wearied and we came up to them. Oberon shot them both with bright arrows, and the huntsman cut off their heads. When the heads came off, I had a momentary vision of something not right, something frightening and horrid. I turned away only to find Thomas's eyes on me, as though in warning. The huntsmen put the carcasses over a horse, and we returned to the castle, our horses' equipment jingling, a lutist playing, the people singing. When we came near, I had fallen a little behind, and Thomas rode up beside me to say, "Do not eat of the venison served tonight."

I started to ask him why, but he rode on, faster and faster, until he came up beside Queen Mab. She turned and smiled at him, and he smiled in return. A very sad, hopeless smile.

Most of the people went to the hot springs where they bathed. I went to my room. When the door was tight shut behind me, I sat down on the bed and called, "Fenoderee! I need a friend."

He was there in the instant, standing beside me.

I said, "There was something frightening. I can't remember what!"

"Ah, weel," he said to me, "you've not the knack of the *seein'* yet, and your human sight comes through. It wasna only deer they lopped the heads from there in the wood. It was a man and his wife they hunted down, a man and his wife who'd refused to give their child to Queen Mab when she wanted it."

"And they'll *eat* them?" I cried, unable to believe it.

"Ach, no, lass. They'll eat venison right enough. They wouldn't kill or eat human flesh, for that would break the covenant. But it was human flesh they enchanted into deer. So, what is it they eat? Ah? Did they indeed break the covenant? They'll tell you it's venison, and they'll tell you true, but you know what you saw, don't you?"

"Thomas told me not to eat it."

"Then Thomas told you what was good for you."

"Then he saw it, too." What I had seen, that overlay of human flesh when the heads had come off.

"Aye, he sees. A man so fearful as that will see what's true."

"What's he fearful of, Fenoderee?"

Fenoderee turned himself around like a dog trying to find a place to lie down. "He's fearful Oberon will use him for something forbidden."

"And what's that?" I could not imagine what could be forbidden in this land where cannibalism seemed to be a matter of course.

"Long ago," said Fenoderee, "when man was made, the Holy One asked us of Faery to help man out, for he was a witless thing then, barely able to stand on his two feet. Some of the Sidhe assented, a few. But Oberon was King then, as he is now, and he told them to hold their tongues, that the Sidhe would do it only if the Holy One commanded it.

" 'No,' said the Holy One, 'I could command it, true, but I will not. I have not designed this universe in all its unpredictable glory in order to interrupt it with gratuitous commands and arbitrary miracles. If you honor my request, you do it out of your own will, out of goodness, in thankfulness for what you've been given.' "

"What did Oberon say?"

"He said no, as he'd said before. So then the Holy One said, 'I will not command, but I may destroy some parts of my creation if they threaten other parts. So I will make treaty with the

Sidhe. It is I who made the Sidhe immortal, and they may remain so only so long as no man comes to lasting harm at their hands.' And Oberon accepted that."

"Who were the ones who said they'd help man?"

"Israfel and his lot. Oh, and Carabosse. Oberon paid them no attention. They didn't even go on living in Faery; they went off to Baskarone. Since then, we Bogles have called them our Separated Kindred, or the Long Lost. Oberon calls them something else, but then he's not a forgiving sort."

"But the deer," I cried. "The enchanted deer! That was surely lasting harm to the man and his wife. To be eaten!"

"Sneaky the Sidhe have become," said Fenoderee. "Sneaky and sly. It wasn't the man and his wife that they killed, you see. It was only deer. Sneakiness like that has been going on for some time now. They've kept the letter of the treaty, no matter what they've done to the intentions."

"Why?"

"Because they're proud, lass. The creation of man was a dreadful blow to them. It needn't have been if they'd put their minds to understanding man rather than just resenting him. But then, after the Dark Lord went off and made his own place, he sent whisperers among the Sidhe, telling them how much their pride had been offended. And some time after the treaty was made, Oberon made another one, this one with the Dark Lord, who pledged to teach Oberon ways to keep the Holy One at bay —though the Dark Lord couldn't keep daylight at bay if the Holy One didn't allow it. The payment to the Dark Lord comes every seven years, and it's what is called the teind to hell, for that is what the Dark Lord has made for himself."

"*The* hell?"

"The only one I know of," he said.

"What's the payment?" I asked, my throat suddenly dry.

"The payment is a person," he said. "Of some sort. Oberon's been using us Bogles for the teind, when he can catch us, but we've grown too smart for him and he hasn't caught one of us in recent time. That's why there were so many of us come to court with Puck, to fight them off if they tried to take one of us by force. Oberon knows if he uses one of the Sidhe, it could cause rebellion against him. So he's thinking of defying the treaty and using a human. And the only human resident in Faery now is Thomas the Rhymer. And you, Beauty."

"But I'm half fairy!" I cried.

"No teind is better than half. Half a teind is better than a whole," he said softly. "And once he's used human, half or whole, then the treaty's broken." Then, "Whsst. I'm gone." And he was.

Outside in the hallway I could hear Mama's voice, along with those of the others. She, still laughing at something Oberon had said, came into the room where I was, her nose twitching, like a cat when it smells a mouse.

"I smell Bogle," she cried. "Has that filthy Puck been near?"

I shook my head at her. "I've not seen Puck since the audience, Mama," I said, truthfully enough. She looked me in the face as though to tell whether I was lying or not, and then she said, "We of Faery value truth above all else, Beauty."

"I know you do, Mama," I said, thinking over what I had said to be sure there were no lies in it.

She sat down on the bed beside me. "Do not put yourself in peril, daughter," she said.

"In peril, Mama?"

"If you make cause with the Bogles against us, no place or time will be safe from Oberon's vengeance. The Bogles are always snuggling up to mankind. They mix more than they should."

I thought this a strange thing for her to say, she who had married my mortal Papa. Was that not mixing? Or even snuggling, come to that. Evidently she did not feel the need to be consistent. I had noticed the same thing among the aunts. What they told me to do was not always what they told others, or what they did themselves.

Mama went on. "Oberon will find you if you offend him, no matter where you go."

"Why should I offend any of you, Mama?" I cried. "You're my mother. These are your people." And, indeed, why should I? What did she know that I did not?

Satisfied at what she saw on my face, she told me to create a marvelous dress and come to dinner.

I ate fruit and bread and clotted cream and none of the venison. I drank what would have been too much wine anywhere else. All around me others were eating the meat with good appetite. I don't think anyone noticed that I left it well alone. Once or twice I looked up to find Thomas's eyes upon me and my plate. Once or twice I looked up to see Queen Mab staring at me with curiosity. I smiled carefully back, and cast my eyes modestly down. If she had enchanted a man and his wife for refusing her their child, what might she do to one who entertained Bogles in her bedroom? All the time I was thinking about the doctrine of transubstantiation and wondering if the man and wife were still present in the venison, though they had been enchanted into something else.

After everyone had gone to sleep, I heard the scratching at my door again. This time I knew it was Thomas, and he slipped into my room like a shadow. He was clearly frantic, his hands trembling, his eyes flicking like hummingbirds from one place to another. "I have to get out of here," he said.

"I know," I told him, going on to tell him how I knew.

"Queen Mab says she will neither let me be used as teind nor let me go," he said, his voice shaking. "But Oberon says he will use me as he sees fit. Queen Mab says she will use you, instead, but Elladine is in favor with the King, so he will not permit that. Oh, Elladine is in excellent odor just now for having brought a half-human woman into Faery, even old as you are. They are all in a frenzy over you."

"Can't you just run away?"

"How? In what direction? Are we under the sea or high in the air? Are we deep beneath the earth under a barrow, as some say, or are we in some enchanted land beyond the bounds of earth? In what direction should I go? And when I have gone, what is to keep Mab from turning me into a deer and hunting me down as she did today with those others? I can escape from this place only by human help, and there is none human here but you."

"When is the teind to be paid?" I asked.

"Soon," he whispered. "Faery time is not the time of earth. It flows fast, it flows slow. Sometimes it almost stops, wandering like the tortoise, long hours in the space of a breath. Other times it dives like the hawk, a year in a moment's pace. I only know it is soon."

He left me then, as quickly as he had come, his face haggard with fear. I lay on the bed, looking out at the sky, scarcely darker now than in midday. Blue, spangled with stars. There had to be a way to help him. Had to be a way.

Mama and I had a picnic together in the meadow. I had asked her for it, as a favor, wanting to, as I put it, "know her better."

"You must tell me some things," I assured her. "Simply must, Mama, or I shall make the most dreadful mistakes. You must tell me what not to say in front of Queen Mab or King Oberon, or any of the others."

"Don't talk of treaties or Bogles and all will be well," she said, not looking me in the eye.

"Can I speak of the teind to hell?" I asked innocently.

She blanched. "It would be wisest not."

"Then you must tell me what it is, so that I will not mention some aspect of it inadvertently."

"It's a payment," she said impatiently. "To the Dark One. For guarding our borders. For keeping out . . . other influences."

"Angels?" I asked. "But, aren't you acquainted with angels?"

She looked around, making sure we were not overheard. "If you are speaking of those from Baskarone, Beauty, then be sure they are not angels. They are no more angelic than we. They are our own kindred who separated from us when man was created, over some fear they have that we or mankind or both of us will do something . . . something irrevocable. Foolishness. Are we not Faery? Are we not wiser than that? Our separated kindred dwell in Baskarone, but they are not angels."

Though I very much wanted to pursue that subject, I had other matters at hand which needed concentration. "I heard some of the Sidhe speaking, Mama. They said I might be used as the teind."

"Nonsense," she cried. "Who would say such a wicked thing." There were tears in her eyes, the first I had seen there on my behalf. So, like it or not, she was fond of me. Or she was afraid. Or she cried for some other reason.

I almost stopped then, not wanting to be disloyal to her, but something made me go on. Perhaps the anguish I'd heard in Thomas's voice. He had been so fearful, so terrorized, so very human. I said, "So I thought. They have a perfectly good teind in Thomas, do they not? And yet, someone said they thought he might escape."

"He cannot escape."

"How do you know?"

"Because I know the spell set upon him. The only way he could escape would be if a human woman were to see him riding by, were to ask for him and hold him tight, despite all the changes Mab could put him through, hold him fast from midnight to dawn, then he could leave Mab and return to the land of mortal men." She said it carelessly, as though it didn't matter.

"That's not very likely, is it?" I asked faintly.

"Not likely at all, which is why Mab thought it up," she said. "So you've nothing to worry about. It is not long until Samhain, All Hallows Eve on earth, the night when the teind is paid. Once that is done, we'll have no more worries for seven Faery years."

"Mama," I asked, changing the subject, "I think it's time I learned some magic. What am I half fairy for, otherwise."

That night I told Tom-lin what Mama had told me. "Have you such a human woman, Thomas?" I asked. "I could attempt it myself, but I'm only half and it might not work. Besides, it would so offend Mama and my other kindred, I could not stay in Faery."

"My fair Janet," he said. "Oh, yes, my fair Janet might well hold fast against all hell."

"Where will I find her," I whispered.

"Near Ercle's Down is a wood, named for the carter's house

which is there and, near the wood, a well. By that well, roses grow, and Janet will come there at sunset to pull a rose in my memory, for it was there I pledged her my love and gave her a rose in troth."

"In what country?" I asked.

"Why," he replied, "in Scotland."

So, in the midnight hours of Faery, it was to Scotland, to Ercle's Down I went, begging my boots in a whisper to take me quietly.

I came there on a late afternoon in summer. I begged directions from a passing shepherd, who directed me to Carterhaugh Wood, and I went there, quickly enough. The well was less easy to find, for there were a number of wells. Only one grew roses, however, the last one I went to, at the edge of the woods. I waited impatiently for evening, watching the shadows lengthen. As it was growing dark, when I had about given her up, she came walking across the downs toward the trees. I was about to go out to her when I felt a tug at my sleeve, and there were Puck and Fenoderee. "Now that you've led us here, best leave it to us," Puck whispered.

I bridled.

"Nae, lass, leave it to us," Puck admonished me. "Ye have none of the language needed, and it has to be set in rhyme."

"Why does it?"

"Because she'll not believe it's from him, otherwise," and he gripped my hand tightly for a moment. I could feel his hand there for a long time after he had gone.

The girl came to the well and pulled a rose, and I heard Puck's voice in fair imitation of Tom-lin's.

> *"The Queen of fairies caught me up*
> *in a far green land to dwell.*
> *And though it's pleasant in that land,*
> *I've a fearful thing to tell,*
> *For at the end of seven years*
> *they pay a teind to hell;*
> *And I'm a fleshy human man,*
> *that the Dark Lord would like well.*

The night is Halloween, my love,
the morn is Hallowday;
Then win me, win me, if you will,
as well I know you may."

It went on for some little time, but was clear enough for all that, despite being interrupted by the girl's questions every line or two. Puck told her how to recognize him, that is, Thomas: right hand gloved, left hand bare, hat cocked up and hair down, riding nearest the town. He also told her where she would encounter the ride (at Miles Cross) and what horrors he would probably turn into, and that she must hold him until dawn. When he had done, we watched the woman go running back across the downs, her hair loose and tangled behind her, then Puck took me by one hand and Fenoderee by the other while I commanded the boots to take me back outside Oberon's castle.

There we stood upon the terrace, looking out across the midnight meadows, listening to the night creatures and the stream, both murmuring.

"That was a courageous thing you did," said Puck. "To help your fellowman."

"Help fellowman, play Faery false," I said bitterly. "One is the same as the other. I am neither nor, Puck. I am confused and wishing myself other than I am."

"Would we could help you, Beauty. Will it help to know you are helping Faery, too?"

"How?" I asked, very sceptically.

"They break the treaty if they give Thomas to the Dark Lord. And that will harm them far more than losing Thomas will do."

I heard him, but was not sure he told the truth. "Would you take me to visit Carabosse?"

"Old Carabosse of the clocks?" asked Fenoderee. "Old tick-tock?"

"Will you?"

"I will," he said. "I will come for you soon," and with that he was gone.

It was Puck who came for me. I was alone when he came.

"Get yourself upon a horse," he said, "ride out and call for Fenoderee."

So I had a stableboy saddle me a lovely horse, rode out some distance from the castle, paused beside a large rock and said into the air, "Fenoderee, I need a friend." Immediately, both he and Puck were standing beside the rock, Fenoderee grinning, Puck picking at a toenail. He liked to stand storkwise, on one leg, his fingers playing with the toes of the upraised foot.

"The fairy Carabosse has invited you to tea," Puck informed me.

"Clockwork Carabosse," chanted Fenoderee, cutting a circle about himself with his scythe. "Old gears and ratchets."

"Who calls her that?" I wondered.

"I just did," said Fenoderee. "Lots of the Bogles do."

"Some," admitted Puck. "Not lots."

"Why do they?"

"You'll find out when we get there."

Puck got up behind me on the horse and held me around the waist. It reminded me of all the times Bill had held me in the twentieth, when I was tired or discouraged or didn't know what to do next. Both he and Puck were small, but wiry and strong. Capable. I relaxed and let him guide the horse. Fenoderee bounded ahead like a fawn, disappearing behind clumps of grass and then appearing again, far ahead.

We came to the forest, went along it to the left until we came to a small stream, followed the stream into the woods, up a narrow defile, and then out into a clearing where a cottage stood, smoke rising from its chimney. It was a fairy-tale cottage. Though I don't know much about tales of that kind, I had seen cartoons in the twentieth. This cottage could have appeared in "Hansel and Gretel" or "The Three Bears" or "Red Riding Hood" without any changes at all.

"We'll wait," said Puck. "Just in case you need us when you come out."

I was fairly sure I could find my way back, but company on the homeward ride would be welcome. I dismounted and walked toward the cottage, hearing as I approached a sound like the muttering of rain on dried leaves. It grew louder and louder, and as I stepped onto the stoop, a chime rang, followed immediately by a cacophony of bells, whistles, cuckoos, gongs, all telling the hour with indiscriminate fervor. After a time the noise died away to the murmur once more, which I now recognized as the ticking of countless clocks, and I knocked firmly upon the cracked panels of the door.

"Enter!" cried a cracked old voice.

She was sitting beside the fire, under her tumult of timepieces. They dangled on every wall; they squatted on every flat surface. They made a noise like a storm of rain until she raised her hand and the sound stopped. All the little pendulums swung, all the little hands moved, but they moved in silence.

"So you've come," she said.

"I've come," I agreed. "I've come because you are the only one who knows what's going on, and I cannot go on, not knowing."

"You weren't supposed to know," she muttered. "You weren't supposed to be bothered with it. All we intended to do was keep it safe, inside you, until the proper times comes. . . ." Her voice dragged away into the clock-silence, the endless movement of hands and swinging pendulums, and she stared into the fire.

I did not disturb her. If she would tell me, she would. If she wouldn't, there was nothing I could do.

"Long ago," she said at last, "when man was made, which was long after we were made, I looked into the future and saw an ending there. You have seen that ending."

I had seen it. Of course, I had seen it.

"At that ending is no magic," she said. "At that ending, all beauty stops. There may be some life after, bacteria perhaps. Small, senseless things moving endlessly on the winds and in the seas. No matter.

"I saw an end. And those of us who could—they were not many, for most of us have been less than diligent in learning what may be done—decided that a certain *thing* should be preserved."

"In Baskarone," I said, suddenly sure of it.

"*Of* Baskarone, partly. Israfel was one of them who did the

preserving. He and his kindred distilled a thing from. . . .
From the necessary materials. They made it. But then we had to
hide it."

And I knew then. "You hid it here," I said, putting my hand
to my breast. "It burns."

She looked at me pitifully. "Does it hurt you?"

I shook my head at her in wonder. No. It did not hurt.
"What is it?"

"It is what it is. It is what Oberon wishes for but has never
been able to hold. It is what the Dark Lord lusts for. We must
keep it from him."

"That's a riddle, Carabosse!"

"It is how we old fairies speak," she said, looking at me
from under her scanty lashes. "If you knew what was going to
happen, you could not behave normally."

"This thing . . . I suppose it's important."

She sat unbreathing. It was as though the universe had
stopped for that instant. At last her breath left her in a sigh.

"Important," she whispered to herself. "Yes. Important."
She sighed again. "We thought no one would look for it in a
child. Then we planned to entice you into some place where you
could live happily for a long time. We picked Chinanga, the
timeless land. No one had ever aged in Chinanga. Chinanga was
poised there in the always, and we thought it would go on forever. How long did we need, after all? Only a few hundred
years.

"We planned you would want to leave Westfaire, that you
would think of the boots, that you would make them and go to
Chinanga. Meantime, your mama would return to Westfaire to
move your sleeping body to the tower, and on her way back
to Faery she would be caught by our spells and brought to
Chinanga also. By the time you traveled upriver, she would be
there to meet you.

"But, you didn't make the boots, and as you were leaving
Westfaire, those people came. They came from the twenty-first.
We cannot even see into the twenty-first. And when they took
you away, we could not reach you. And when you returned you

were pregnant. We didn't want you to go while you were pregnant."

"But then Elly was born," I said.

"That was the first good opportunity for you to go to Chinanga," she murmured. "But then, by the time you got to Chinanga, you were too old for your mama to be easy with, and the Viceroy had already heard of this virgin with a difference. Between them, the Viceroy and Elladine, they destroyed the whole place. Imaginary worlds do not show up in my Forever Pool. Elladine has always done things that are quite unreasonable. And now you are here, where we had never intended you should come."

"Why me?" I asked. "Why did you choose me?"

She sighed. "People don't understand about magic. There are always certain limitations and proprieties: certain symbols which must be kept aligned; certain congruities we must observe. *It* was born of magic and could not live unless there was magic around *it*. *It* was born in truth, so the place we put *it* had to be named truly. *It* had to mature in a place where no ugliness is, and that was Westfaire. *It* could not have been set into just anyone or put just anywhere."

"Why didn't you just let it be me there in Westfaire, sound asleep? That would have kept it safe for you."

She shook her head at me. "The rarer a thing is, the more assiduously it is sought. As magic grows rarer and rarer, the more intent the Dark Lord will become at seeking it out. Eventually, Westfaire will gleam like a beacon, the last repository of magic. Do you think he would ignore that? No. Westfaire was intended as misdirection, Beauty. Legerdemain. Even if he seeks it there, he will not find it. Mary Blossom is only a decoy. You were to have been in Chinanga."

"But I'm really here. And so is it."

"True. For a time, I was deeply dismayed at that, but Israfel assures me all is not lost. Your being here is considered to be perfectly natural. You came to see your mama. Why not? Elladine left you the means to visit her, or she thinks she did, and so long as she thinks so, so does everyone else. As for Westfaire, either they believe the curse has run its course or they know about Mary Blossom, but in either case, everything is explainable. We went to great lengths, Israfel and I, to keep everything around you as natural as possible. The use of magic leaves an aura, like a fire leaves smoke, so when we used magic, we seemed to do it openly, obviously. Anyone sniffing the smoke could see our innocent little fire and dismiss it as trivial. What was it, after all? A sleeping enchantment, a cloak, a pair of boots. Mere bagatelles. Even Elladine's stay in Chinanga is explainable—she believes the Viceroy's enchantments brought her there. No one suspects anything odd about you. No one knows except Israfel and the others in Baskarone. And I."

"Puck?"

"No. He is my trusted friend and servant, but he doesn't know. Even though he has done much running about on your behalf, he doesn't know about *it*. None of the Bogles know."

"So what do I do now?"

"We can still preserve that which must be preserved. If you will simply go on, as you are, pretending to be what you would have been had we never met. I have seen that your visit to Faery will end soon. You will go away from here, very naturally. You will be in the world, being yourself, and meantime, Israfel and I will be searching for some other place—something like Chinanga, only less boring."

I didn't say yes, or no. After a time she reached out and took my hand. It felt like a mother's hand, like Dame Blossom's hand. I wasn't sure I believed the business about my visit ending soon, but I chose not to remark upon it.

"Mother doesn't like me," I said, needing her to say it wasn't true.

"That's not entirely true," she said. "Humans make myths about mothers and daughters, fathers and sons. The myths are very strong. I have counted on them myself, but sometimes the two generations are simply not sympathetic. Especially when they resemble, let us say, the other side of the family."

It was true. Except around the eyes, I most resembled Father. I resembled him in other ways. Fleshiness. Corporeality. The thousand stinks and farts that flesh is heir to.

"Can you go on?" she asked me gently.

"Can you take *it* out?" I asked. "Can you put *it* somewhere else?"

She shook her head. I already knew that. It had grown into me. I could feel its roots, down to my toes, down to my finger tips. So I told her I could go on. What else was there to do but go on?

She patted me. She still felt like Dame Blossom.

"I have this problem," I said. And I told her about Thomas the Rhymer. "If I tell him, I am betraying the Faery folk."

She smiled as though she already knew all about it and said what Puck had said. "If you don't tell him, you will betray them far worse." Suddenly, inexplicably, she asked me, "What would you like to do? Right now?"

"Go back to Westfaire," I blurted. "Go back home and find Giles there and be with him."

She gave me a weary little smile. "Keep that thought in mind. I will, too. We'll see how things work out. Until then, go on, Beauty. Just let things happen, as they will. Very naturally."

Puck and Fenoderee were waiting to take me back to Elladine's palace.

There was a time in Faery after that, neither long nor short, but of considerable importance, during which I learned to do enchantments and spells. Mama taught me how to weave magical garments and how to lay geas on swords or jewels to make them fit for questing. There is a good deal of questing in Faery, as a pastime. This one or that one will be enchanted into forgetting who he or she is, and will then be sent off after a sword or a grail or some other marvel. Or they'll do the same thing to humans and follow along, watching it as though it were a movie. According to Mama, nine-tenths of King Arthur was questing and the other tenth was politics.

Mab taught me the magic of trees and caverns and clearings in the forest. She taught me the dwindling spell, by which things may be made tiny, and the Great Spell of Bran, by which giants may be conjured up. Even Oberon, once or twice, taught me something of spell-casting, mostly matters of bewilderment. Oberon is very strong in bewilderment.

He also invited me to his couch, quite openly, making an

honor of it, though not demanding an immediate response, for which I was thankful.

Mama was quite excited about that, not least at the thought of my possibly bearing Oberon's child. I did not want to bear anyone's child.

"It wouldn't be private, would it," I half-laughed to hide my embarrassment. If I had imagined myself talking to my mama about anything in the world, it would not have been this. I could not have imagined her urging me to let Oberon . . . or cooperate with Oberon . . . or even enjoy with Oberon. . . .

"Private?" she asked. "If you didn't want anyone to watch, you could say so. I don't suppose anyone would care."

I sat beside him at dinner. He sniffed at me, my breasts, my armpits. He laid his head in my lap and smelled me through my skirts, almost as a dog does. If I had encouraged him even slightly, he would have thrust his nose into my crotch. I moved away, pretending not to notice. This sounds foolish, doesn't it, pretending not to notice. And yet, the others behaved in such very strange ways that it was not as noticeable as it sounds. Still, Israfel would not have behaved so. Perhaps that is part of what Thomas meant, when he said they were diminished from former times.

Later, I said to Mama, "I'm not like you! My body isn't made the way yours is. He'd be disgusted. Either that or he'd have to lose his memory as you did with Papa."

"He would not lose his memory," she said stiffly. "Not here, not in Faery. And the fact that your body is more fleshy, more earthy, that it has smells of animal fecundity, only adds to his interest."

I had been wrong about there being no perversions in Faery. Their perversion was to lust after human bodies, with all their stinks and scattish contiguities.

"Will I offend him greatly if I ask for time to get used to Faery first," I asked, the only excuse I could think of at the moment. "Will you explain to him about things like . . . like . . ."

She snorted, making it plain she thought me a fool, but she told Oberon something that put him off without angering him. I caught him watching me every now and again with a lustful little sparkle in his eyes.

In truth, my body was in rebellion. I felt constantly weak and tired. I could cast the feeling aside by a little concentration, but I often found myself simply sitting, doing nothing, not wanting to move. It was unlikely that lovemaking would have been even tolerable, and I certainly didn't feel in the least lustful. The people of the Sidhe often went about virtually unclothed. Their bodies were fair and glorious to see, but I felt no prurience or desire, though their couplings and uncouplings were very casual. Sometimes they seemed like show-offy children, staring around to see if someone was watching, more concerned with being seen than with what they were doing. I remembered Roland Mirabeau, wondering if I had caught his disease of sexual ennui, but he had at least adored little girls and I didn't seem to adore any of the Sidhe. There was nothing in the smell of them to move me. They smelled like leaves, like moss, like clear seawater, like glass.

One night I found myself walking near Thomas the Rhymer. There was no one else about, so I told him we had been to his true love, Janet, and had arranged for her to save him. He was to have his right hand gloved and his left hand bare when he rode on All Hallow's eve. "Cap cocked up and hair long," I instructed him. "That's what she'll be expecting."

"You saw her?" he breathed.

"Only in the dark," I said. In truth, I had not seen her well, though she had seemed older than I had expected. Thomas did not stay to chat. Hope lit his face as he left me there, and I stayed, watching the night until the others woke.

Time went by, and suddenly one morning Oberon announced that evening would be All Hallows Eve and we would ride to the Dark One to pay him his teind. There was a flutter of excitement at that. Mab gave Oberon an angry look, which he pretended not to see. Thomas shivered. I could see it across the room. Elladine stared at Oberon until he turned to her and smiled. So. So and So. It had all been arranged. Someone was going to be very angry if Janet was waiting at Miles Cross.

I can recall almost nothing that happened during the day.

Along toward evening a group of us walked in a grove we sometimes frequented. At its center is the Pool of Delights, crossed
by a carved stone bridge, over the rail of which the people of
Faery are wont to peer, admiring their reflections in the water. I
remember looking down at myself, smiling up at myself. My
hair was twined up in a net of sapphires, and the thin muslin of
my dress was embroidered with blue flowers. The face which
smiled up at me was very beautiful, and I smiled at my own
reflection, not happily, but in appreciation. Mama's face, no less
lovely, was beside mine. It is the only thing I can remember
happening, all day.

We rode out at evening. As we went from Faery into the
world, the sky lightened and turned to rose and salmon and
violet. The air suddenly smelled alive. There were sounds of
things living and dying all around us. We went down the road,
and people, seeing us pass by, crossed themselves and dipped
their heads. Oh, we were glorious to see, like smoke, like mist,
like visions of glory, the horses like the waves of the sea.

We went through Miles Village and toward Ercle's Down.
A mile from the village was the crossroad, with a large cross set
up at its center. The fairy host rode by, not seeing the woman
huddled there until she came running toward us to throw her
arms around Thomas's legs, pulling him from his horse.

"Thomas, True Thomas," she cried. "I'll never let you go!"
She was a middle-aged woman, with gray in her hair. Thomas,
suddenly no longer young, looked as surprised as anyone else.

Janet could not have said anything more guaranteed to
make Mab angry. Thereafter Janet embraced a dragon, a worm,
a snake, a spider, a giant many-armed thing from the sea. She
held bears and tigers and man-eating lions. She held dogs and
hogs and eagles which tore at her eyes. Held them all, crying the
while, "I'll never let you, never let you go," the muscles in her
arms knotted as though forever and the ugly tears raining from
her eyes.

Too much time went by. Oberon cried like a hawk, pointing at the sky. There was a line of gold along it, the night going
fast. "Come," he cried. "We must ride." And they fled away,
leaving only Janet to struggle with the monsters in her arms.

Janet and me. I looked down to see Puck holding the bridle of my horse to keep him from galloping after.

"Get down, my girl," he cried, "for it will not take them long to find you gone."

"I should be with them," I said stupidly. "Mama will miss me."

"And who will they use as a teind with Thomas gone?" Puck asked. "You, Beauty, be your mama ever so fair and ever so wise, and even fond of you a little, still they'll use you rather than one of them. Carabosse never intended you should ride farther than this. Carabosse sent us, and Carabosse says to go home."

I was sensible for the first time of how foolish I had been to come on this ride. "How will I get away? My cloak, my boots are back in Faery."

"They are here," said Fenoderee, holding them up for me to see. He pulled me down, slapped the horse on its rump to send it galloping after the others, and then shoved the boots on my feet and my shoes in my pocket. "They do not know you are involved in this. Better they do not know."

"Ah, Puck, thank you," I started to say, not really knowing whether thanks were due.

"Go, Beauty," he said. "We'll meet again," and he turned me about, whispering to my boots, "Take this lady home."

Then was the familiar whirlwind, and I was gone and so were they.

22

I stood beside the rose-mound of Westfaire. Tottered, I should say, suddenly dizzy, as though something in my head had gone awry. Embarrassment, I supposed, at the prospect of meeting

Edward once more. And little Elladine. She would be two, or perhaps even three by now. She would not know I was her mother, of course. She would think the wet nurse was her mother or, if she had been weaned, the nursemaid. I thought of my daughter as I had seen her last, asleep in her cradle beside the fire, her dark hair bubbling over the pillow, like black water in torrent, already long enough to reach her shoulders. A pretty child. Not one a mother should have fled from.

Though Carabosse had said that mothers and daughters might not be sympathetic. "Particularly if the child resembles . . . the other side of the family."

Well yes, but she was not a devil. Merely a child who resembled her actual father in some respects. Now she would be walking and talking, but her speech would be the speech of Wellingford. She could not possibly sound like Jaybee.

With these thoughts I calmed myself as I stood beside the shepherd's well, leaning against it almost, pulling myself up straight with an unaccustomed ache, looking myself over to see if I was well enough dressed to go straight to Wellingford. I picked at a fold of my gown, stared at it in confusion, caught in dream, nightmare, pulling the fabric through my hands. . . .

Aside from my cloak and the seven-league boots, I was dressed in rags. Scarcely one thread held to another. I put hands to my head in confusion, only to feel oily tangles and squirming locks. I had seen myself in the Pool of Delights only this afternoon, with my hair swept up in a net of sapphires and my dress of fine muslin, embroidered all over with flowers. How had I come to be dressed like this? And my hair so filthy? It stank. It smelled of smoke and grease and less acceptable things. My fingers found small hard specks caught in the coils: nits!

Shock held me motionless for a long, calculating moment. Hush, I told myself. Figure it out later. You are only filthy, after all. Filth can be washed away. Hair can be washed and the eggs of lice combed out. You have other clothes to wear. Hush now and do what needs doing. Comforted by decision, though not greatly, I tottered down toward the lakeside. Making myself look decent would necessitate getting into Westfaire, which meant a trip through the water gate. When I arrived at the water, I did not bother to strip. The rags I was wearing could be thrown away once I was inside. I bundled the cloak and boots atop my head. The water was cold. I thought it must be winter, then reassured myself that there were flowers growing in the woods and the trees were in leaf. Still, the water was very cold and very deep and harder to move against than when last I had come this way.

Inside the water gate the steps were taller, too, and more deeply covered with moss. Everything was more difficult than when I had last been there. The stairs to the attic seemed endless, but I had to go there to get a dress. On my way back to the kitchen I stopped in Aunt Love's room to snatch up a looking glass and the fine toothed comb made of tortoise shell she had used on me when, as a child, I had picked up lice from my acquaintances in the stables. The bath place was next to the kitchens, a small, stone-floored room with a stone-curbed well in the corner, a great wooden tub, and over the hearth a huge hanging kettle with a copper to bail the water in and out. Except for Papa, my aunts, and I, who had had tubs brought to our rooms for occasional use, everyone at Westfaire had bathed in this room, sometimes half a dozen of them at once. There was a similar arrangement at Wellingford, though I had never been able to use it when I was being Havoc the miller's son for fear of being found out. Once I was Edward's wife, there had been no need. I had had my own tub again, filled and emptied by sweating servant girls. At least, I assume they sweated for I did by the time I had filled the huge kettle from the well.

I lit the fire, already laid, tied the belt of my cloak around my neck to keep from falling asleep, took off the cloak itself, and sat down to comb my hair while the water heated. The tangles were deep. The comb pulled and the tangles caught in the teeth. I pulled the wad of hair out and threw it into the fire, combing again. The next time I threw the hair toward the fire, a draft caught it and blew it back at me. Gray hair. Not wheat straw, not silver, but gray.

The looking glass lay face down on the table. I polished it with the rags of my sleeve. An old face looked back at me. No . . . no, not an old face. Just not a young face. A thirty-fiveish, fortyish face. Not old for the twentieth, but old for the four-teenth, when people did not live so long. There were tiny lines around the eyes, not deep ones, but they were there. There were more lines on my forehead, between my brows, furrows, as though I had often thought deeply, worrying over something. Most of my hair was still gold, but at either temple the gray swept upward in silver wings around a face thin as a chicken's breastbone.

I had only been gone a little time! A few weeks in Chinanga! A few weeks in Ylles! Whence came this protruding skeleton, this skull beneath the wrinkled skin? Whence came this hoary hair, this hip-stiff walk, this pale reflection of beauty gone, beauty done, beauty over! I screamed, I think. It was as though I had found a snake in my bed, a spider crouched upon my food, a monstrous devourer slinking close at my back, death, worse than death, for with death it is done soon and over, but with this, with this, I was still alive to know of it.

Panic and tears and wailing. I came to myself later to find the kettle steaming over the fire, the lid dancing upon the roiling waters, a jolly clangor which seemed to say so you're getting old, you're old, you're old. So what? Hills are old and getting older, rocks are older than that, stars are older still, so what?

"So it's gone!", I cried, half in pain, half in fury. "My youth, my beauty, gone. I didn't even use it up and it's gone! I didn't have time to waste it, time to taste it, time to glory in it, and it's gone! Here I am all sunk-cheeked, droopy-chested, flat-butted, and it's gone."

Bingity-bangety went the lid. You're half a fairy, aren't you? You've learned magic haven't you? What does it matter how old you are?

What did it matter? If I chose to use enchantment, no one would know it but me. Was there a difference if no one knew it but me? Oh, yes, I cried to myself. Oh, yes. There was more weeping, more howling, coming to myself at last with my hands buried in my filthy hair.

Old or not, I could not bear the dirt on me. I filled the tub and stripped the rags away. When I got them off, I recognized what they were: the remnants of the dress I had worn when I left Wellingford. A simple kirtle of fine wool. I had stood on the sandspit in Chinanga in that gown. I had traveled to the wall of Baskarone in that gown. I had met the ambassador in that gown. Evidently I had also grown old in that gown. It was gone. Only tatters.

I heard a voice singing.

> *"Beauty and rag tag and motley are twins.*
> *When the one's gone then the other begins."*

Oh, Fenoderee! How could you be so unkind! I looked around for him, but he was not there.

Chunks of soap lay on the shelf beside the copper. Cook had learned how to make it from some Teutonic connection of his, from tallow and ashes and a lengthy stirring. The aunts had been dead set against soap in the bath, thinking it fit only for the washing of filthy clothes, but water and scented oils alone would do nothing for my hair. I washed it, combed it, washed it again. The body was filthy, too. Not "my" body. It did not look or feel like "my" body. When I was done, I pulled the plug from the drain, then filled the tub again from the kettle and the well, lying in it to soak myself until I felt able to go on.

When I was clean, I fed the body. The body, though not at all familiar, was not as bad as I had feared, only very bony and ugly, like photographs I had seen in the twentieth of starvation victims or one of those unfortunate women with anorexia. Whatever I had been eating in Ylles, or thought I had been eating, whatever I had consumed in Chinanga, it had not been sufficient to sustain a half-mortal person. I felt my breast, feeling a warmth there, as though something simmered gently inside. Being half-starved had not injured what I carried.

Damn, I said to myself, Carabosse should have known!

None of my clothing would fit. Aunt Lavvy had been, was, very thin, as I recalled. Wrapped in a sheet from the linen store beside the bathroom, I went upstairs once more to Aunt Lavender's room. I found the kirtle she had used to ride in, plus several more, all of very plain stuff, with full sleeves to show the tightly buttoned sleeves of the underbodice. Aunt Lavvy's underbodices were all the color of dirt or excrement. Mama's underbodices, in the attic, were of prettier colors: madder red, and dark indigo blue, saffron yellow, and hollyhock root, which is a pale blue. They were soft enough that their fullness did not matter. Thieving through other closets, I took Aunt Terror's new cote-hardie, and Aunt Basil's surcote, which was almost new. I had never worn a wimple and veil, but it seemed a good time to start. Particularly inasmuch as the soap had left my hair as wild as a lion's mane. I found some clean headdresses in Aunt Marj's room, along with a leatherbound box in which everything could be packed. I thought of using the boots to take me to Wellingford from where I stood, inside Westfaire, but the thought of what all those thorns might do to me *en passant,* as it were, dissuaded me. The boots might take me without injury, but *sapiens nihil affirmat quod non probat,* as Father Raymond used to say, and God knows I didn't know for sure. So I went out into the lake, naked as celery, with the box teetering on top of my head, dried myself off on the shore, and assembled myself as best I might.

I had remembered to bring the looking glass and a comb and I'd taken half a dozen tortoiseshell hairpins from Aunt Lavvy's cupboard. Mama's soft linen underbodice clad me almost to my ankles. I chose the one died with madder, soft and faded pink from washing, and buttoned tightly to the wrists and neck. Over that went Aunt Lavvy's kirtle, made from soft brown wool with a low scooped neck and wide, short sleeves. Buff linen for the wimple and veil, and then Aunt Basil's black and brown striped wool surcote with red lions embroidered in the corners of the front and back panels. When I was put together, I gave myself a looking over—as best I could with the small looking glass—and saw a bony-faced but passable woman, much too thin, who would be handsome if she put on about twenty pounds. I put on cloak and boots and commanded them to take me and my box to Wellingford.

I did not say "the Dower House." I said "Wellingford," and it was to Wellingford the boots delivered me. For a moment, seeing the ruins before me, I thought I had repeated my earlier journey to the abbey. When my eyes had had time to clear, I saw that the place was indeed Wellingford Manor, but that some walls were fallen and others barely standing, that one corner of the roof had partly burned, and that no one lived there anymore. Or perhaps someone did. In the ruined hallway, I saw the embers of a fire and heard a deep voice mumble angrily, as though awakened from slumber. "Boots," I whispered, "take me to the Dower House."

One stride brought me to the door. The Dower House stood, and though it had much need of a careful hand, it gave evidence of being occupied. Broken casements sagged crazily on their hinges, paving stones tilted, weeds grew around the door, but there was smoke coming from one of the chimneys and chickens cackled in the kitchenyard. *Deo gratias.* I put the boots in my pocket, replaced them with a pair of Aunt Marj's pointed shoes and knocked upon the door.

A voice screamed inside, words I could not make out. Instructions to a servant, perhaps? Abuse hurled at a dog? The door opened to disclose a surly maidservant in a dirty kirtle and filthier apron who stared at me with her mouth half open. It was the hall of a place which had been my home. It did not look like home anymore. There were chicken feathers on the stairs.

"Who is it?" came the screaming voice from somewhere off to my right where the kitchens were. "Who is it?"

Who was it, indeed? Who was I? Not Beauty, wife of Edward, mother of Elladine. I had not thought of using enchantment. I was what I was, someone else, old enough to be an aunt and dressed like one. I borrowed the name of one of Edward's own aunts, adding Papa's title for verisimilitude.

"Lady Catherine Monfort, Edward Wellingford's aunt."

The slovenly servant trudged away. There were further noises offstage, perhaps a slap, then a door slamming. There were back stairs. Perhaps someone had gone up. After considerable time, someone came down, hand trailing upon the bannister.

"Lady Catherine Monfort?"

She could have been a pretty lady. In her thirties somewhere, rather more late than early. Her hair was red as a bonfire, and her chest as white as chalk. Both owed much to alchemy.

Both could have benefitted from washing. Still, the expression on her face was open and concerned.

I nodded politely, wondering who this apparition was. "Come to visit my nephew, Edward."

"You hadn't heard!" She reached out her arms toward me with genuine compassion. "Oh, how dreadful. You didn't know that Edward had died."

"Died?" I asked stupidly. It had never occurred to me that Naughty Ned could die. Not so soon. Not in such a short time. Sweet man, dead? Is kindness and compassion rewarded so? "Not dead?"

"When the plague returned," she nodded. "In sixty-one."

"Year of our Lord," I murmured, putting out a hand to catch myself.

"Thirteen sixty-one," she said. "Yes. I am his widow, Lydia. We had only been married a short time when he died. But that was almost six years ago. How could you not have heard?"

"I've been away," I said, wondering where the intervening years had gone. I had left in fifty-one. "Far away. In . . . the Holy Land."

"A pilgrim," she chirruped. "Do come in," she took my arm. "Oh, what a shock it must be."

We went into the little sitting room. It had been my room, with chairs in it, not wainscot chairs against the wall, but real chairs one could move about, with carved arms, made for me by a man who worked for Lord Robert, given me as a wedding gift. They were still there, still with the cushions I had worked when I was pregnant with Elladine. Sadly soiled and worn, those cushions. The fireplace was deep in ashes. Everything was dirty and ragged. Evidently this lady, like my aunts, did not hold with soap.

"His daughter?" I asked. "Little Elly . . . ?"

"Elladine? Oh, she survived, yes indeed. Very healthy child, she was. Is, I should say, though she's not a child any longer."

"How old . . . ?"

"Elladine would be what? Sixteen? Seventeen? Hard enough to keep track of my own, such an army of them."

"Your own?"

"Gloriana, that's the eldest. Then my oldest son, Harold. Then my second son, Bertram. Then Griselda. Then comes El-ladine. Then the two Edward and I had together. Twins. Cather-ine and young Edward. Your nephew Edward named them. Why, I just thought! Catherine must be named after you?"

I nodded again, feeling lost. Possibly Edward had named his second daughter after his aunt. And possibly the twins were not Edward's children at all. "You were a widow when you married Edward?"

She threw her arms wide, miming woe. "Twice, now. Oh, it's very hard to bear. Very hard, Lady Catherine. Lord Robert died early in the year, then Janet and the children. Then the youngest brother, Richard. Then, soon after we were married, Edward himself. All of Wellingford has fallen to me. I've the care of all of it to see to, and no one to help!"

If her two sons were older than Elladine, then she should have some help. "Your sons," I suggested weakly.

"Mere children," she waved her hand to suggest something inconsiderable. "Striplings. Caring for nothing but gaming and the hunt. Boys. Mere sweet boys."

"Your daughters?" I suggested, a little more strongly.

"So talented," she said. "So very musical. And such grace-ful girls. A little tall, perhaps, but then so is a willow, and noth-ing is more graceful, moving in the wind." She mimed wind, swaying at me. "But then, I'm forgetting myself. You must be famished? Thirsty? Weary? I didn't see your carriage?"

"I rode," I said. "Hired a horse in . . . in . . ."

"East Sawley?" she suggested.

I nodded, inventing. "Two horses and a man to carry my box. Sent them back again."

And she was dismayed. "Then you plan to stay? Not that you aren't welcome. Oh, you're very welcome. It's just such very short notice."

I gestured vaguely, signifying that I would make do. "There's an extra room, surely."

"A very little one," she assented. "Over the kitchen."

It was the warmest room in the house. The one I had used

as a nursery after Elly was born. There was a narrow bed in it, as I remembered. Though, after sixteen years . . .

We got my box. I carried it myself. There seemed to be no one else to carry it. The bed was still there, full of mice. The whole room was very dirty. Why was my whole history one of being given dirty rooms to occupy? "If you'll send me up a serving maid or two," I suggested.

"Serving maid," she said vaguely, as though she should know the word but had forgotten it. "Maid?"

"Women. Who clean rooms, who sweep floors."

"Oh. Of course. Yes."

As we had come along the corridor, I had noticed that the little linen room was shut, just as I had left it when I had gone away with the key in my pocket. The key was still in the deep pocket of my cloak where I had thrust it when I left. Though it seemed a wild hope, I went back to the closet and tried the key. Inside were sheets and covers and two clean ticks, and pillow cases and the extra pillows I had made when we killed the geese the last fall I had been in the Dower House. The mice hadn't been at it, or if they had, the chunks of black hellebore root scattered along the shelves had poisoned them. The cupboard hadn't been opened in all those years! No one had wanted to break it open; perhaps there had been no locksmith available. Perhaps Lydia had simply been too lazy to bother. The linens still smelled faintly of lavender as I carried sheets and pillows and one of the ticks back to the nursery in time to meet two maids, one of them the girl who had answered the door, the other an older version. Slatterns, both. They regarded me with insolent immobility, jaws moving like cows.

"You will clean this room," I said quietly. "You will use soap. Scrub the floors. Sweep down the cobwebs. Scrub out the windows. Take that mattress away and bring me clean straw for this one."

They looked at one another, back at me, challenging me to make them move. Aha. Well and a day.

"Else," I smiled, "I will summon a dragon to eat you both." I snapped my fingers and made fire dart at them so that they

screamed. It was a fine, hard fireflight, which told me I was in a
time when magic flowed strong.

They had no more sense of how to clean a room than of
how to fly. I kept coming back and making them do it over,
getting a little angrier each time and they getting a little more
frantic at the fire biting them. The whole house was evidence of
their slipshod ways, theirs and Lydia's. As for Lydia, she had
gone upstairs to lie about on a disordered bed with her elder
daughters and the twins, playing the lute (tunelessly) and singing (less melodiously than Grumpkin had used to howl) and
talking of the future. I put on my cloak for a reconnaissance and
overheard them from the hallway. Their plans seemed to consist
of selling Wellingford and going to London to live on the fruits
of that sale. For a moment I struggled with this idea, certain that
Elladine was the heir if all the Wellingford brothers were dead.
But, of course, she was not. Young Edward was the heir: the six-
year-old monster whom I caught torturing a dog in the stables,
and whose britches I set alight to teach him better manners. He
looked nothing like Edward. Nothing at all. Edward, my poor
sweet fish, taken twice on the same hook!

And where was Elladine? Over an indescribably bad dinner, I asked again for my "grandniece."

"Poor Elladine," Lydia murmured. "Such an unfortunate
name to give a child. Not a Christian name, surely."

"But where is she?"

"She goes off. On a horse, sometimes. Sometimes afoot.
We're never sure where she is. Poor child. First motherless, then
fatherless, I'm sure she'll be so glad to meet any kin at all."

"You and Edward were married in . . . what year?" I
asked.

"In the year of the second Death. Almost at once after Robert and Janet died," she said, "together with Robert's youngest
brother and all their sons. Edward was the heir, and he felt he
needed someone to help him maintain the estate. And, of
course, I'd been left a widow and desperately needed someone
to help me, as well. Four fatherless children to rear, with people
dying everywhere, it is no pleasant Maytime to be alone in such
circumstance, believe me. Edward most wanted someone to care

for Ella. I told him I would maintain his daughter if he would maintain me. It was not a love match, precisely, though I was fond of Edward."

Poor Edward. Destined always to be a husband of convenience. "How did you meet?"

"Janet was my cousin. I was visiting here when the plague struck. Oh, there were many visitors, then. Robert and Janet had taken in half the countryside who were homeless. I remember Janet going on and on about being unable to keep the place clean."

Which is why the plague had struck Wellingford, I thought. Poor Janet. So charitable. Giving a home to the multitude, with all their fleas.

"Of the Wellingfords, only Edward and Ella were left alive when the dying paused for a time," Lydia said, leading me into the next room as we heard the maids breaking crockery behind us. She went on to give me the details of the dying, with an unnecessary relish in the recounting, interrupting herself to say, "Ah, here she is!"

A ravishingly beautiful young woman came through the door. Sixteen or seventeen, perhaps. Wild dark hair. Wild dark eyes. A bruise on one cheek. Hands coarse and scratched and black around the nails.

"Elladine, this is your father's Aunt Catherine," Lydia said in a kindly tone, edged with some emotion I did not quite understand.

"What would she have here, madam? What's left?" the girl asked insolently. It was the same tone in which Candy might have said "So?" or "Big deal!" in the twentieth.

Lydia flinched, giving me an apologetic glance. Discipline wasn't Lydia's forte either, poor thing. I had yet to find what Lydia's forte was. Surely she must have had something to recommend her to Edward. Or was he so distraught at all the dying, he had grasped her as he, drowning, might have grasped at a straw? Ah well, if discipline was not her thing, neither were manners my daughter's.

"Elly, my dear," I said, kissing my child on her unwelcoming face. "I am your great-aunt, from Ylles, come to visit you."

She gave me a look to tell me she did not care. Her face was Jaybee's face, made feminine, made soft, but with broken glass beneath it. Her hand, as she pushed me away, was as hard as his had been. Elladine remained with us only so long as we held her in unwilling conversation, then departed as quickly as she might, and I stared after her, wondering what I could do to make this situation tenable.

I thought, her mouth is wide and sensual. She has hooded eyes. Her figure is as graceful and lithe as mine once was. Her breasts curve like the swell of a sail, and her cheeks are softly rose. She is beautiful, not as I was, but nonetheless, beautiful. I cannot tell if she is intelligent. She is hard as stone.

I wondered, how much of her hardness is my fault? How much of this iron rancor came from doing without a mother's love?

There was no time to weary myself assessing guilt. Someone had to see to her, see to things, and it was obvious that Lydia could not see to boiling an egg. Though Elladine could use a parent, I could scarcely introduce myself as her mother. I had no idea whether Edward settled anything on her or not before he died. Without a dowry, her future would be unenviable. All I could do under the circumstances was to be her aunt, stay with her, and try to remedy the situation.

LATER

Later yesterday I met Lydia's four older children. The two daughters are awkward and ungainly girls, both with an intransigent dirtiness about them. The younger one, eighteen perhaps, would not be bad looking if she were cleaner, and if she would stand up straight and comb her hair. The older, however, Gloriana, a maiden of some twenty years, is taller than any woman I have ever seen. She has a face that could carve stone and hands as big as a large man's. I knew at once who was responsible for the bruises on Elladine's face. Gloriana's hands twitch, knot, twitch again whenever she looks at Elly, like creatures with a will of their own. She is as full of anger as Elladine is, though from a different cause. An ugly girl who hates girls who are not. When I heard her voice, it was no surprise. Hers was the knife-edged shriek from the kitchen. That both of the girls are slovens simply fills out the picture. Their shifts have not been washed in many a season, their nails are brown with unthinkable dirt, their hair, I warrant, is as full of lice as mine was when I woke at Westfaire.

The boys, Harry and Bert, looked slightly less dirty when I met them. I believe their relative cleanliness may be due to their having been caught in the rain oft times while hunting. Both are beefy boys, red in the face, big in the teeth, with small eyes and large noses. They are even taller than Gloriana. Though Lydia is a woman of average size, her first husband must have been a giant to have begot these monsters.

Of the twins, the least said the better. They have been spoiled so rotten that they smell of corruption. Neither has ever been forced to do anything he or she did not want to do. They have two voices: a whine; a scream. They have no graces at all.

So, if the family is of little use, what about the servants? There are serving women about the place, but I recognize none of them. Besides the two who eventually finished cleaning my room, I found several more, enough to do the washing, sweep out the filthy hall, bring in wood for the fire, heat the kettle and fill the tubs. Lydia's daughters could have bathed. Their clothes could have been scrubbed. I wonder why they choose instead to go about in dirt? Well, they could do as they chose, but the Dower House need not follow their example.

I slept last night in a clean chamber. I rose this morning at dawn. I found the maids still sleeping, routed them out, and set them to work, though they grumbled mightily when I told them to clean the fireplace in Elly's chamber, saying that she always did that herself.

"Elly," I explained sweetly, "is my nephew's daughter. She does not sweep chambers, carry out slops, or make up fires. You do. You do it well and consistently or you will be eaten alive by dragons!" I glared at them and they cowered.

Elly came upon me in mid-dudgeon, carrying a pail of ashes. She shook her head at me angrily. "It won't do any good," she sneered. "Stepmama won't keep after them once

you're gone. They're lazy sluts, all of them." I noticed again that
her nails were black.

"They certainly won't do it if you do it for them," I suggested. "Go wash your hands."

One of the maids sniggered behind me. I set a small imp to
pinch her black and blue, and her howling could be heard for
half a mile. It had a salutary effect on the others. I smiled at Elly,
who regarded me with dawning interest.

"You know what these sluts call me," she asked. "Ella of
the Ashes. Just because I carry out the ashes so I can get the fire
in my room to burn. The others are so lazy, they'd rather freeze.
They all pile in one bed together to keep each other warm. Like
pigs."

"Why won't Lydia exert herself a little?" I asked, truly interested in Elly's perception of the situation.

"She doesn't want to keep Wellingford. She wants to sell it.
That's why she doesn't take care of it. It used to be beautiful.
It's all ugly now."

"Whether she wants to keep it or not, there is such a thing
as pride," I said. "Only those without any are filthy and lazy.
Perhaps she needs to be taught."

"When pigs have wings," said Elly with an ugly snort, leaving me.

It was only later I thought what she had said. Ella of the
Ashes. Cinder-Ella.

"Puck," I cried.

He was there, looking at me sidelong.

"What is this?" I demanded, half hysterically. "I've been in
the twentieth, Puck. I've read books. I've seen Disney, for the
love of God. I know the Cinderella story. What is this?"

"Did you think the stories were made up?" he asked me.
"Did you think there was no real Beauty, no real Cinderella, no
real Goldilocks or Rose Red or . . ."

"But why me? Why my daughter?"

He shrugged. "Did you never notice, in the twentieth, how
legends gather around some people. There is the truth about a
man, and then the part truths that gather afterward, and then
the myths that follow later yet. A legendary man tends to have

legendary sons. Power attracts power, so power gathers. It is one of the truths of magic."

"Am I to expect, then, that there will be a prince?"

He shrugged again. "It depends on what story you learned, there in the twentieth. Was it the true tale, or the part truth, or the myth? Do you know?"

I didn't know, but knowing that Elly was at the root of a fairy tale made me have some hope for her future, at least.

ST. MARY MAGDELEN'S DAY, JULY, YEAR OF OUR LORD 1367

My daughter is the same age I was when I started writing this story of my life. She is not very like me, as I remember being. She is bad-tempered, quick to strike, eager to continue the fray. She hates her stepsisters and brothers with a hot, even anger. She doses their food with nutshells, boils their woolens to elf size, spreads oil upon the floor outside their rooms to make them fall. They detest her, and she glories in their dislike. Her animosity and their slothfulness seem to have kept her alive. If any one of them had been capable of decisive action, he, or she, would have killed Elly. I look at her and I marvel. So like her father. She would rather have passionate hatred than lukewarm affection.

"What are you looking at?" she snarled at me.

"The indomitable human spirit," I replied.

"Go domit somewhere else," she returned. "I'm sick of you always looking at me."

Perhaps I, too, would be sick of someone always looking at me.

"What was it like when your father was alive?" I asked her.

Pain, then, in her face, swiftly passing but sharp while it was there. "He was . . . he was very good to me," she said. "I think he loved me."

"I know he did," I said. "He told me so."

"She says he didn't," she gestured toward her stepmother's window. "She says he only pretended, because I didn't have a mother. She says nobody could love someone as bad-tempered as I am. He only pretended. He thought he owed it to me."

"That's not true. He loved you. Very much. I remember

once when you were a tiny baby, only a few months old, I saw him bend over your cradle and tell you that he loved you, and it was not owing, it was real."

She sat very still, like a cat that is too frightened to move, afraid I would take it back. Her stance made me think of an old friend.

"There used to be a cat here, named Grumpkin," I said. "He was a great favorite of mine. He must have died a long time ago. It's been sixteen years."

"He did die," she nodded. "He was my mother's cat, and Papa said she left him to me when the enchantment took her away."

I gulped. So Edward had told her that! Poor Edward. He had been curious, and knew it. He had blamed himself.

"Grumpkin slept on my bed sometimes. He lived to be very old. I cried when he died. But he fathered lots of kittens, and I've still got one of his sons. Daddy named him Grumpkin the Second as though he were a king." Her voice had changed. All the hostility had left it. It was for that one moment as open and communicative as a child's.

"Why did the enchantment take your mother away?" I asked, wondering if I'd been right.

"Because Papa got curious about her," she said. "He said it was all his fault."

Oh, Edward. Edward. "Let's go see Grumpkin's son," I suggested, getting up from my chair.

"I have to take out the ashes," she said, not thinking, merely expressing her habitual contrariness.

"No," I told her. "Not anymore. While I am here, I will be sure the maids do it."

Brought to herself, her lip curled into its usual sneer. "How come you can tell the maids what to do and what not to do?" she asked. "You're not the mistress of Wellingford. You're only an aunt."

I had figured out who I was that morning. Even I, who had never cared for children's stories, could not have failed to notice what role I was playing. In the twentieth, I had seen Disney, after all. Though Elly and I were not privileged to be attended by singing mice, it did not surprise me greatly that this segment of my life had gained a spurious immortality, a glossy, oversimplified and untruthful half-life.

I shook my head at Elly, trying hard to get her to smile. "No, my child. You mustn't tell anyone at all, but I'm your fairy godmother."

She laughed at me, thinking I was joking. It was a genuinely amused laugh.

ST. MARTHA'S DAY, JULY, YEAR OF OUR LORD 1367

I have my Grumpkin back again. The son is like Grumpkin I, except that he has one white foot. When I picked him up, it seemed almost that he knew me, for he reached out his paw to touch my face as the other Grumpkin used to do. As I write, he is beside me, purring, opening his eyes every few moments to be sure I have not gone away. Though Elly values him, she does not care for him. I saw her slap at him, for no reason except to see him blink. Strange. With her, the having is enough. She uses or ignores. She does not maintain. In that, she is more like Lydia than she would like to think.

Though Lydia is too lazy to take charge of Wellingford herself, she does not seem to resent my doing it. In any case, I have not asked her permission. During the past days the maids have ceased to grumble: they, the household, and the household linens are clean. Elladine has had several baths (as have I), the floors have been swept, and the cook has been instructed to feed us something besides porridge and meat pies. There is plenty of food—it has been six years since the plague came and went again—but acquiring victuals from the gardens and orchards, from the sties and the poultry house and the herds, takes a little attention and good sense, neither of which Lydia seems to be capable of supplying. The small caches of coins I left behind me are still here, for the most part, and I have used some of them to purchase necessities. I also found the warrant upon the usurers of London where I hid it before I left, but I have set it aside against later need.

I have gained several pounds and look less like a skeleton. Elly's hands have come clean. Her bruises have faded. I set a small spell upon Gloriana that she should get a painful cramp each time she tried to pinch. She, robbed of her usual prey, has turned to accusing a pretty village woman of witchcraft. I will have to do something about that, too. I have not yet decided what to do to extricate Elly from her current problem, but at least the situation has been stabilized, as they would say in the twentieth.

Carabosse asked me, before I left Faery, whether I could just go along, pretending I was only what I am. Here, in this house, I am only what I am. The thing burns beneath my breastbone, but it is no stranger than my heartbeat or the sound of my own breath. It is almost as though I had stayed in Chinanga. Here, as there, no one knows who I am. I am someone else. No one knows I am here.

ST. STEPHEN'S DAY, SEPTEMBER, YEAR OF OUR LORD 1367
I was not surprised when a herald came to the door yesterday with a pronouncement. I have been expecting something of the kind.

All inhabitants of Wellingford between the ages of sixteen and twenty-five are invited to attend a series of three evening entertainments given in honor of His Royal Highness, Prince Something or Other, by his parents, the ruling family in exile of some tiny kingdom I had never heard of.

I was surprised, however, at the herald's voice. There was something familiar about it. Something that raised gooseflesh, made echoes in my heart. I went out into the courtyard with a cup of wine and offered it to the man. When I saw him, I knew him.

"Your name is Giles, isn't it?" I asked him, keeping my voice even only with a great effort. I wanted to throw my arms about him. I wanted to cry on his shoulder. "You were a man-at-arms in service to the Duke of Monfort and Westfaire." My voice trembled when I said it.

"My lady?" he asked, getting down from his horse and bowing to me. "Have we met?" He looked just the same. Older, of course, but just the same. His eyebrows quirked in the same way. He had that little turn at the corner of his lips that I had used to watch for. There was a new scar at one side of his brow. "I don't remember . . ."

I waved my hand in front of my face. "Many years ago," I said. "I can scarcely remember the occasion, but your voice sounded familiar." Not only his voice. He stood as I remembered, straight and tall, feet together, one slightly turned out. As though he had been invited to dance.

"Fancy your becoming a herald!" I said. "Why did you leave Westfaire?"

His eyes shut, only briefly, as though remembering an old pain. "The priest there sent me on a journey," he said. "A kind of pilgrimage, it was. To bring some sacred relics back to the chapel at Westfaire. I had to go a wearisome way, and when I returned . . ."

"The enchantment," I murmured.

"The enchantment," he agreed, letting his eyes shut again. "I think . . . I think they're all in there," he whispered. "All of them. One of them got out for a while, but she had to go back. She'd be a widow now."

Well, of course that is what he would have thought. It is, after all, what Edward thought, what Edward told everyone. Not about my being a widow, but about my getting out of Westfaire. "Someone you cared about?" I asked.

"Oh, yes, ma'am. Yes, indeed. Someone I care about."

I breathed deeply, taking note of the present tense. "So then, what did you do?"

"I chose to stay fairly close by, but I sought service where I might. There was plague, as you know. It seemed wisest to stay away from the cities. I lived rough as a man can. I farmed a bit. At least that meant I'd have food. Then, when these little royals took the place over by East Sawley Mill, they offered me good money to be man-at-arms for them. Escort, mostly. And herald."

"Herald," I said with a tremulous laugh.

He laughed with me. "I've got a good loud voice from calling cows, ma'am, and I remember things."

Oh, indeed he did. And so did I. "Can you remember the

reason for this widespread invitation?" I teased, letting something of my old childish teasing come into my voice.

He cocked his head and smiled at me, recognizing the tone if not the origin of that flirtiness. "These little royals, they got driven out of their wee country, over near France or some such place so I'm told, but when they came, they brought a fortune with them. They bought land past East Sawley Mill and rebuilt the big old house up there. But they don't know anybody, ma'am. What with the plague and the unsettled conditions since, it's a wonder anybody's left. They told me to ride to all the noble houses in the surrounding land and pronounce the invitation. There can't be more than six or eight great houses left, and that'll be stretching it. Wellingford's not rightly great, not anymore, but I thought I'd stop." He flushed, thinking I might take umbrage, but I only nodded, telling him that I understood.

"Will there be a ball?" I asked, doubtfully.

"Close as they can get. They've got musicians hired. They've got cooks working away, making three days worth of feasts. The boy's coming of age, ma'am, and his mama wants him to have a celebration. She says they've had enough sadness recently."

He handed me back the wine cup. I watched him go with tears in my eyes and a great longing in my heart, or wherever longing resides. I felt it in my stomach, so perhaps that is where. I had wanted to tell him who I was. The only reason I had not was that he did not recognize me. When I looked into the mirror, it was hard for me to know myself. I was afraid he could not love who I had become.

I went to the kitchens to find Harry teasing his sisters. "It's him," he was telling them. "The prince who's giving the party is the man who came riding by the other day. He's the prince."

Gloriana said, "Oh, Harry, it's not. It couldn't be."

"I tell you it is. The boy with the yellow hair." Harry seized Griselda in one oversized arm and paraded her around the kitchen, stepping on her feet. His hands were the same size as Gloriana's, and even on him they bulked large. He had jowls already, blue as steel, and a bit of a belly sticking out. Not an altogether prepossessing partner for the dance. "The prince was the one with the yellow hair," he bellowed raucously.

"His hair wasn't yellow," said Elly. "It was gold." She was sitting in the chimney corner as she often did, and she said it so quietly that no one heard her. If they had heard her, they wouldn't have paid attention. I had noticed that. No one paid much attention to Elly. Except me, of course. I kept looking for something of Edward in her. His patience. His devotion. Surprising myself, each time, by remembering that he wasn't her real father. And yet he had given her so much. All to be wiped away like this, lost when he was lost.

"You saw the prince, too?" I asked her in a murmur.

She nodded, pressing her teeth together, making a tight-lipped frown. She has yet to smile at me, except at my embarrassments, and at those she laughs.

"Was he handsome?" I asked.

She took a deep breath. She did not need to answer. Her eyes were answer enough. She looked at me hatefully, detesting this self-betrayal.

"Are we going to the ball?" Harold asked his mother. "We'll need new clothes."

"All of you?" Lydia asked doubtfully. "Why, Harry, I don't know. I'm not sure we can even find anyone to make clothes."

"Have to go," he replied, significantly. "Have to show the girls off. You know what he's doing, don't you? He's looking for a wife. That's why all the young ones are invited."

"He invited men, too," Griselda commented.

"Who would the girls dance with, otherwise?"

"Mother, do you suppose he *is?*" asked Gloriana, face suddenly red as a boiled lobster, eyes hot with hope. Oh, poor child, I said to myself. Don't hope for it, no. It isn't fated. It isn't willed. Poor ugly thing. Her skin was rough as her hands, her hair was a jungle, and she smelled like vintage dirt. My heart swelled with pity for her, and for Griselda, and for all other barnyard geese who long to fly.

"Perhaps I can find a seamstress," I suggested. "I used to know the neighborhood rather well."

"Not only a seamstress," Lydia fussed, "but fabric. Since

the second Death, there haven't been the merchants there used to be."

"I'll try," I said. Edward had set a store of fabrics by, bought for me, bought in anticipation of Elladine needing dresses. He had ordered them from London or purchased them from travelers. He loved to see me in silk from the Far East, in damask and velvet from Florence. There were boxes of folded materials in the attic, set away in linen sheets, dosed against the mice with hellebore, against the moths with wormwood and southernwood, lavender and rosemary. Boys mix the ashes of southernwood with oil and use it to make their beards grow. Lad's Love and Maid's Ruin, it is called. When I unfolded the linen, I remembered that, remembered Janet telling me. She was full of herbary, Janet. Fuller than the aunts, despite having an ordinary person-name.

There is a great length of mustard-colored silk, enough to make a gown for Gloriana, and enough greeny-blue damask for Griselda. Edward bought both pieces from a merchant who had brought them from Italy. There are other Italian damasks, too, to make cote-hardies for the boys, and velvet for overmantles. There are silks from the Far East for underbodices, and spools of finer silk for the knitting of stockings, if we had time to knit stockings. It seems there will be no time for that, or for embroidered sleeves, but the fabrics are rich enough. There is nothing in any of the boxes that I like for Elladine. She needs something light, something bright with her dark hair. White. It will have to be white, with short, full sleeves and a slash at the hem to show a bright full-length underskirt. There *will* be flowers embroidered on the sleeves, if I have to bribe one of Puck's people to do it.

ST. OMER'S DAY, SEPTEMBER, YEAR OF OUR LORD 1367
The seven-league boots made it an easy trip to London. I went there late at night, stayed half a day, and returned with white satin and with pairs of silken hose from Spain. So far as everyone was concerned, I had found them all in the attics.

"Mama, keep Elly home or she'll spoil everything," I had heard Gloriana saying.

"I don't think Elly should go," Lydia said.

"Oh, I agree," I said to Lydia. "She's far too young."

"I'm not too young," Elly later screamed into my face.

"Of course not, child. But you don't want Gloriana pinching you black and blue between now and then. And she will, if she thinks you're going. She might even break an arm or leg for you, or pull all your hair out, so sulk and be still. All will come right."

She sulked and was still. I suggested to Lydia that it might be wise to start bathing her daughters a week or so in advance to get rid of some of the accumulated grime. She yawned and said she supposed so and did nothing about it. I began working on Elly's hair, brushing it every night, doing it up on rags, saying quiet prayers of thankfulness for Candy's ministrations which had taught me all this, even though it did not seem to matter what I did to Elly's hair. Her hair was a treasure, like tumbling black water, lightless in its ebon flow. In anticipation of the parties, her eyes were slumbrous and her lips seemed swollen with invisible kisses.

While village women struggled with clothing for Lydia's children, I summoned some help for my own child. Sitting on the side of my bed, late at night, I said, "Fenoderee, I need a friend," only to look down and see him there.

"You're lookin' older," he said impudently.

"You knew how old I'd look," I said. "You and Puck, when you sent me back. I heard you chanting at me. Ragtag and motley, indeed!"

"You can look as young as you like," he told me.

"As Elladine does," I said. "As Mab does?"

He looked down at his feet, suddenly discomfited.

"Fenoderee?" I asked.

"Don't bother him," said a voice, and Puck stepped out from behind the tapestry on the wall. "He's afraid to tell you."

"Tell me what?" I faltered.

"That with Thomas gone and you not there, Queen Mab went into a fury and used your mama as the teind."

There was a moment of soundlessness, and I came to myself lying flat on the floor with both of them bending over me and Fenoderee saying to Puck, "Ach, you fool, she didn't need to know that."

"Yes, she did," said Puck. "Lest she have her boots carry her back to Faery, expecting Elladine to be there. Lest she say something unwary where Oberon could hear. So far he blames us Bogles for getting Thomas loose. So far he doesn't know Beauty was involved. Nobody knows but Carabosse."

"What . . . is Mama dead?" I asked.

Puck shook his head. "Us of Faery can't be killed so easy, Beauty. She's even kin to the Dark Lord. He despises Faery, but it's not Faery he wants to destroy. Carabosse says to tell you like as not, he'll play with Elladine for a time, then turn her loose. He does that with things that amuse him."

They helped me sit up, and Puck gave me a bit of wine from the bottle in the cupboard. He went to it, as though he knew right where it was. As though he had been there before.

"There's nothing you can do about it," he said. "Carabosse says you are not to upset yourself or think of doing *anything!* She says you will understand what she means."

I did understand. If it came to a choice between Thomas, who was a fellowman, or Elladine, who was my mother but did not much care about that, I was not sure where duty lay. In any case, Carabosse was right. I could do nothing about it. Anything I tried to do would only draw attention to me.

"You wanted something or you wouldn't have called us," said Puck.

It seemed foolishness, then, but I told them what I wanted. Someone to make some dresses for Elladine's namesake, my daughter. I had thought of doing it myself, as I had made dresses in Faery, but I felt insecure with the idea. "I want someone who's done it a lot, who knows what they're doing," I told Puck. A kind of look went back and forth between them, and Puck said he'd send someone along. As he was about to go, I asked him, "When I was a child and saw you in the woods, was it Carabosse who sent you?"

He looked at me insolently. "Me?" he asked. "Why would I have been in *your* woods? I'll send you a seamstress."

She came. A Bogle seamstress, to make Elly's gowns. Three

bright white dresses: one embroidered with daisies over a yellow underdress; one with periwinkles over blue; one with roses over red. The trader had said the red silk was from the Far East, beyond the Holy Land. It was the only place where the dyers could achieve that color, so much brighter than madder. Cochineal, perhaps. It must have been China, I told myself. Even in the twentieth, some of the finest fabrics came from there. The seamstress also made three spider veils for Elly's hair. One with pearls, one with sapphires, one with rubies. I am keeping everything hidden as a surprise.

ST. LAMBERT'S DAY, SEPTEMBER

When the morning of the first celebration arrived, Gloriana and her sister decided to bathe. Though I stayed as far away as possible, I could not help hearing the screams as tangled hair refused to be combed, and long embedded dirt refused to let go. Elly sat in a corner of my room and smiled remotely, as though she were already far away, dancing with her prince. I spoke to her, cautioning her to keep her temper in check, to smooth the frown lines from her brow. I told her that men like girls who are sweetly spoken. She merely smiled, as though nothing I could say applied to her. It was as though she was fated, and knew it. A small, cold chill made its way down my spine. What could I do?

That evening Harry and Bert rode off with their sisters toward the manor, some seven or eight miles away. I told Lydia that Elly and I were going for a ride also. Instead we repaired to the stables where I had accumulated certain supplies. A pumpkin. A cageful of mice. Six lizards. One fat toad. I had already created a wand, to add to the drama of it all, though a wand is totally unnecessary. With what Mama and Oberon had taught me, I could have done it blindfolded and with my hands tied behind me.

The mice became horses, prancers, matched grays of considerable spirit. The pumpkin made a golden chariot, the like of which no one had yet seen, nor would for several hundred years. It was exceedingly well sprung, and in the fourteenth no one understood springs. The toad became a coachman, and the six lizards the footmen, the one in brown livery and the six in green. Getting the livery just right took almost the last bit of magic I had in me, and I was panting a little as I spoke seriously to Elly.

"Now listen to me. This equippage will get you there in great style. The only reason we're going to all this trouble is to get the prince looking at you. I've cast a spell of glamour over you to keep him looking, and to prevent Gloriana and her sister and brothers from recognizing you. However, none of it will last past dawn. Fairy things often don't. There's a monastery near the prince's dwelling, and when the monastery bell rings for Matins you must leave, or you can't be sure to be home before the sun rises." I was reminded of my listening for the bell when I had been wooing her father who was not really her father, Ned. Matins was supposed to be sung about midnight, but in my experience the monks were often late with it.

"The place is only two hours or so away," she argued with me.

"If you don't have an accident, yes. But if your coachman has to mend a wheel, it could take longer. You must leave a large margin for error."

"I could walk home," she shrugged, giving me one of Jaybee's intransigent, stubborn looks.

"If you don't want to go back tomorrow night, of course you could. It's about eight miles. But if you want to go back tomorrow night, then be home by dawn. I have to reuse what is here." Once things have been enchanted, it takes less effort to re-enchant them. Besides, it had taken me days to catch six lizards. I was not as agile as I had been as a child, and they do not, unfortunately, enchant until one actually has them in hand. I gave her the dress embroidered in daisies (which she examined critically before saying it would do), combed her hair for her, and told her to be on her way.

"Barefoot?" she asked me. "Fine fairy godmother you are. They'll laugh themselves silly."

I had not thought of shoes. I had extended myself on everything else and had not thought of shoes. There was not enough glamour left in me to create three pair. One would have to do.

One to go with everything. I meant to make them white. I was tired. They came out transparent, like glass. It shouldn't have surprised me, but it did. In the future, the story would include a hundred false details, but the damned glass slippers were really part of it.

I hated them. Silly, plastic-looking things. Elly had never seen plastic, so she loved them. "Glass slippers," she cried. "I almost believe you're really a fairy!"

I had turned a toad into a coachman, had turned mice into horses, had invented coach springs several hundred years before their time, but it took glass shoes to make her believe in me! I watched silently, wearily as she departed, then put on the seven-league boots and went where she was going. All I wanted to do, I told myself, was see her have a good time. Expiation of guilt, certainly. I would have done her better service to have had a serious talk with her about reality, but who was I to speak of reality? She was one-quarter fairy, as I was half. Perhaps I could even have taught her some of the things Mama taught me.

Better not, my conscience said. Better not. My conscience sounded much like Father Raymond. Elly would not use such power wisely. Or even kindly. Not until she was older, if then.

The prince's celebration was very minor stuff. A dozen local musicians, scraping and blowing, any one of whom would have made more tuneful sounds killing pigs. Still, there was a certain rude vitality evident which came partly from reliance upon the wine kegs, partly from letting the notes fall where they might, and partly from everyone's determination to have a good time. The tunes they played were well known. They could not have assayed anything else. They took my added voice as the effects of intoxication and played on, rather better than before.

The prince was yellow-haired and quite good-looking, in a sweet, almost feminine way. He had a straight nose and a gentle, delicate mouth, with dark eyes and brows to lend drama. He was slightly taller than Elladine and a head or more shorter than poor Gloriana. His nickname, given him by his mama, was Charme, or "Charming," as we would say in the twentieth, and he suited that name well enough. His mama was fat and fond and indulgent. His papa, the King or Prince or whatever, was taciturn and worried about other things. When Mama did not recall Papa to himself, he sat on his gilded chair and looked into distances I could not see. The loss of a kingdom, even a very small one, would weigh on one, I supposed.

The young prince dutifully danced with all the ladies, even the very ugly ones. Of these, Gloriana was the most, and Griselda a close second. There were three or four rather pretty girls, and the rest were what one might expect if one rounded up a sample of the countryside. Elladine arrived a couple of hours before midnight, driving directly up to the terrace beside the ballroom as I'd suggested. I'd made sure the doors were open, and no one could have missed her arrival. I had assured her that this could only add to the mystery and make her more fascinating. Not that she needed additional glamour. What I had given her was quite enough. In fact, looking back on it, what she had of her own might have been quite enough. She and the prince danced, and then again, and then yet again. Several of the young ladies cast angry glances at their partners and one another. Gloriana was quite red and unhappy. I put a quick spell on several of the young men along the sidelines, to make them attentive to her, but it did no good. Gloriana had eyes for no one but the prince.

After a time, I wearied. I went out onto the terrace, took off my cloak, and sat on a bench there, watching through the windows. The evening was still and warm. I heard the song of a nightingale among the trees.

"Will you dance, ma'am," said a voice at my shoulder.

I looked up. It was Giles. There was no need to speak. I simply rose and let him take me by the hand. We danced, as they danced inside, bowing and circling, only our hands touching. He looked at me, smiling, in his eyes something almost like recognition.

"I did meet you," he whispered. "I wish I could remember where."

"At Westfaire," I agreed. "On some occasion or other. Perhaps at one of the wedding banquets."

He shook his head, laughing. "Oh, ma'am."

"Catherine," I said. "My name is Catherine."

"Oh, Catherine." He bowed and led me in a circle around him, one hand on his hip, his soft shoes making a brushing sound on the stones. "I remember those banquets well. The lady Sibylla, her face all screwed up. Beauty, the duke's daughter, like a rose. All the aunts. If I'd seen you there, I'd have remembered."

When he said "Beauty, the duke's daughter," his voice had been soft and yearning. I could not help it. I let enchantment happen. Not a lot. Not to be sixteen again. But to be beautiful.

He smiled at me, his own face becoming younger. We danced. "You look like her," he said. "Like Beauty. Are you related to those at Westfaire?"

"Oh, yes," I said. "Edward of Wellingford's wife was kin to those at Westfaire. He was Elly's father. And I am her aunt."

"I didn't know anyone got out of Westfaire except Beauty," he said softly. "And she had to go back. I thought they were all there still."

"Some weren't there at the time," I said. "Elly wasn't born yet. And I was elsewhere."

His hand tightened on mine. His eyes feasted on my face. Mine were as greedy. We danced, and he drew me closer to him as hours spun away.

In the nearby monastery, the bell rang for Matins, and I drew away from Giles, reluctantly.

"Tomorrow night?" he asked me.

I nodded, smiling at him. Oh, yes, tomorrow night.

I turned to the window, saw Elly's head come up, listening. She wavered. She knew if she left, the prince would go on dancing with the others. She knew if she stayed, she might not come back the following evening. Prudence won, and she slipped out of the ballroom and across the terrace to the drive where the horses waited. The carriage got halfway to the main road before the prince realized she was not coming back. She, meantime, lay in the rocking carriage and dreamed, a curved and sensual smile on her face, while I watched invisibly from the opposite seat, wishing I were back there on the terrace, dancing with Giles.

We were home in time. I disenchanted my supplies, storing my mice and lizards away in a box in an empty manger and then sent Elly into the house to sleep. She did not want to rest, so I told her she would be ugly if she did not, and that decided her. I napped myself, then put on my boots about midday and went back to Prince Charming's home, desirous of knowing what he thought and felt and, perhaps more important, what his parents thought and felt. I had seen his papa staring at Gloriana last night and knew there might be some considerations of which I was not aware.

As there were. The prince was in full spate, screaming in a high, trembling voice at his parents.

"She's ugly. She's huge. She's dreadful."

"Her younger brother is heir to a large fortune. He would settle a good bit on her."

"He might settle the moon and all the stars on her, and I would not have her."

"Duty is not always pleasant. If we are to regain the throne . . ."

"Throne! Until the people throw out Uncle Richard, there is no throne to gain. And if there were a throne, would you want me to marry without any possibility of an heir? I swear to you, I could easier mate with a sow in a sty than with that woman, and if I were forced, I would sooner kill myself." He was sulky and vehement.

"But we have no idea who this other girl is. None at all!"

True enough, they did not. Nor would they, until Elly was safe from Gloriana's retaliation. I felt the matter stood well enough for my purposes and went home to sleep.

That night Elly wore blue. That night she begged to be allowed to stay until the bell rang for Lauds. It was too close to dawn, and yet I allowed it. How could I not when she begged me? How could I not, when I wanted to stay, myself. When she arrived at the ball, her eyes were dreamier yet, and her movements more sensual and languorous. The young cock might be pretty as a girl, but he had it in him to stir this little hen. I envied her. Oh, how I envied her. The only true attraction of that kind that I could remember in myself had been toward Giles and toward the ambassador from Baskarone. Even in Ylles, where I had seen what passed for love all around me, I had not cared enough to consummate it. Not so, Elly. If one touched her, she burned. I envied her lust, the lubricious waves she swam upon, the elegant titillation she was prey to.

Envied, and emulated. Giles waited for me on the terrace and we danced again. I taught him a new dance, one I had learned in the twentieth, where one does not parade at arms length but presses tightly against one's partner. I let enchantment happen, let us be wrapped in glamour. I was young, and so was he. We were together. Nothing separated us except the slow movement of the music, and even the music was enchanted. I held up my mouth to be kissed, drowning in his kisses. We put our hands up the sleeves of our outer garments so that nothing was between our hands and our naked flesh but one layer of thin, silky fabric. We pressed our thighs toward one another, between one another's, letting the hours pass in passion which climbed ever higher and was yet unsatisfied.

Matins rung and was ignored. Lauds rung. I tore myself away from him, seeing the dazed look in his eyes and knowing it was on my own face as well.

"Tomorrow," I said. "Oh, tomorrow."

Elly was already running down the stairs toward the carriage when I came out of the shadows in my cloak. I saw the prince running after her and made him trip and fall. We barely made it home before the sun rose, and if I had not been behind the carriage in my boots, hurrying the horses, she would have been too late.

It was early afternoon before she woke. "I need not leave early tonight" she told me. "This is the last night. I will walk home, after."

"If you are in that ballroom when dawn comes," I told her, "all the faery stitches will vanish from your dress and veil. The cloth will fall about your feet, and you will be there naked, with everyone sniggering at you. Best leave him at Lauds, as you did last night, and let me act the marriage broker for you."

"Early in the morning," she begged. "When the bell rings for Prime."

"When Prime rings, the sun is already coming up," I told her, pitying her, envying her. "When you hear it ring for Lauds, you'll know the dawn is coming. You must run, then, or be caught out. I do not think the prince's parents will want him to marry a girl who takes off her clothes in a ballroom."

She promised me. I scarcely heard her, thinking of my own lover. I went with her once again, and watched briefly through the windows before Giles arrived. Poor Gloriana had no hope and knew it now. The prince danced with no one but Elly.

And Giles and I lay in the grass below the terrace, hidden beneath my cloak.

"Beauty," he sighed, and I did not correct him. I was. He was. We were. Our bodies moved and touched and held one another, with nothing between us. We grasped at stars, once, twice, three times, falling exhausted at last into the warmth of our nest. My kirtle was somewhere in the grass. My underdress was around my neck. Giles wore only his shirt. Our secret flesh was still wet and entangled, one with another's.

A bell rang.

"Matins," I said drowsily.

"Lauds," he said as drowsily. "Matins was hours ago."

Above me on the terrace, I heard a sound and looked up to see Elly in the prince's arms.

The little fool was going to let her clothes vanish and stand there in her skin, begging him to take her, as well he might. I could not blame her. How could I blame her? And yet her chance to marry him would be over. His parents would not permit such an impropriety. Princes had to have virgin brides, lest doubt be cast upon their heirs. I moved with a strength greater than my own, wrenched myself away from Giles, wrapped myself in the cloak, distracted the prince with a faroff cockcrow, seized Elly up beneath the cloak and bore her away.

She struggled. She was a strong girl. I got her out to the driveway just as the carriage dissolved. The pumpkin rolled there, broken, spilling its seeds. Mice scattered in all directions as the toad hopped away into the brush with a disenchanted croak. Luckily, no one was looking at the assemblage. Everyone was staring at the terrace, where the prince was running about like one demented. Somehow I got the boots on. I put a spell of silence and compliance on Elly, gathered her up in my arms again and said, "Boots, take us to the Dower House stables." As we went, I heard the bell striking for Prime.

When I set her down, her clothing fell around her feet, as I had told her it would. Her breasts were still rosy with desire, her nipples like little rubies. She put one hand between her thighs as though something hurt her, then left it there. She gave me a slow, hating look. "Why did you do that?" she demanded, her hand moving slowly back and forth.

I snatched it from between her legs and shook her. "Do you want him for one night, once? Is that all? One time, then he will marry someone else?"

Her eyes did not focus on me, so I slapped her. That got her attention, and I asked her again what she wanted.

"I want to go to bed with him," she said in a voice like warm honey. "Over and over again."

"Then you must marry him."

She stepped away from me, stumbling. She still wore one of the glass shoes. The other had been dropped in our flight.

"They didn't disappear," she said. "I dropped one on the stairs."

As soon as she said it, I realized why. They were clear. They were glass. There was no appearance to disappear. They might gradually fade, over some weeks, but they would not disappear suddenly. Which is why they had been in the story in the first place.

"Go to bed," I said wearily. "I need to think."

"He'll marry me," she said as though she were God, deciding fate. "He will. He has to. He can't live without me. He said so."

I did not tell her that men often said such things. Even pretty princes said such things. Even Giles had said such things. I went to my room to think. To think and to get dressed. My hair was down around my shoulders. I had nothing on but a stained underdress. I looked like a woman who had been made love to on the grass all night. I could not let myself think of Giles, for whenever I did, I trembled.

While I struggled with myself, events transpired without me. The first I knew of it was when I rose to a sound outside, went to the window, and saw Giles himself below, flourishing a scroll from which he was pretending to read his already memorized message.

"Know all men, by these words, that Prince-So-and-So of Marvella announces his intention of marrying the maiden whose foot fits the shoe he found last night upon the stairs. The prince rides after me, bringing the shoe to try on all maidens of this house." While I watched, Giles accepted a glass of wine from Lydia and told her the tale, looking about himself the while, looking for me, I supposed. I hurried to get myself dressed, thinking betimes that the work of the marriage broker had already been done by someone else. This public pronouncement was almost as good as a betrothal. The prince was determined to have his way, but Elly had no dowry that I knew of and the prince's parents might still have much to say about that.

By the time I got my hair braided and got downstairs, however, Giles had already ridden away. I found Lydia in the garden, agog. When she had finished repeating the tale three or four times, with embellishments, I asked her what marriage portion Edward had settled upon Elladine before he died.

She flushed. "I'm sure he meant to," she said. "He didn't mean to die so soon."

"You mean he didn't provide for her," I challenged. "Surely, then, you intend to make up for his lack of foresight."

She pursed her lips. "I've thought of it," she said, not looking me in the eye. "But it's really up to Edward to say. As soon as he's reached his majority, I'm sure he will do something about it. He won't be of age, of course, for a number of years."

"Fifteen years," I said drily. "Elladine will be a bit old by then. Thirty-some-odd. A confirmed spinster."

"She could enter a convent," Lydia suggested eagerly. "I've been meaning to mention that to her."

Foolishly, I did not advise Lydia that she reconsider and talk with me again before making any such suggestion. While I went on thinking of ways and means, Lydia went straight to Elly and suggested she enter a nunnery. I heard Elly's scream of rage and got there just in time to prevent her killing her stepmother, though not in time to prevent the attack. The expression on Elly's face was one I did not want to see. It was Jaybee's face, as it had been when I had last seen it, full of towering fury and indomitable determination. She could have killed Lydia gladly, and I feared somewhat that she might do so yet, or do something even more dreadful.

The prince arrived with the shoe in midafternoon. Gloriana was first to try it on, able only to get her big toe into it. She retreated in tears, while Griselda tried. I was there, with Lydia. The prince was there, with a couple of his men, but not Giles. Casually, I asked after Giles and was told he had not returned from his heralding, which had somewhat surprised the prince. There was some courtly chit-chat, though not a lengthy conversation, and Griselda gave up the attempt.

I said, "There's another girl in the house who must try it on."

Lydia glared at me, but I sent a maid after Elly, whose voice I could hear in the kitchen.

We were waiting for Elly to appear when we heard the scream. Gloriana's voice. Lydia and I ran. We found Gloriana in the kitchen, the great meat cleaver still in her hand, her left foot cut half through and blood spurting in all directions. Gloriana had done it herself. In the corner, Elly watched with a remote smile.

"What did you do?" I hissed at her.

"I just told her her feet were too big," Elly said indifferently. "That they might fit if she cut them in half." She took the other glass slipper from her pocket and went out to the waiting gentlemen while we struggled mightily to stop Gloriana's bleeding. The huge girl was too strong for us. She fought us off until she had lost so much blood that it was too late to help her. While Elly melted into the arms of her prince outside in the garden, Lydia and those of us in the kitchen gathered around the body of her stepsister and wept. Gloriana was not a pleasant girl. She was a great cow of a girl, with a cow's mute and intransigent hungers. She had little intelligence. Still, there was something monstrously tragical about the manner of her death, not the least that it has shown me what my daughter is. Of the two of them, Elly had been the more brutish.

Gloriana was buried in the chapelyard at Wellingford. Elly lay on her bed in her room and dreamed lascivious dreams. The prince had a tantrum in his own suite at his own house, but his parents remained adamant that they would not allow his marriage to a woman without a dowry. It was no more than I had expected. I got the warrant out from the hole where I'd hidden it and took it to London, where I sought the man who had issued it, a Jew named Yeshua ben Levi. Yeshua was dead of plague. I found his son. His house had advised my papa, some years before the first great Death, to use the money in the purchase of grain. During the times of plague the price had soared. The two warrants were now worth so much that Papa could have settled all his debts and found it unnecessary to marry Weasel-Rabbit. I told the House of Levi to keep the other warrant upon their books, for some heir would come to claim it, perhaps hundreds of years later. They stared at me strangely, but one of the bearded sons made a note of it.

When I returned to Wellingford, I carried with me a more than adequate fortune for Elly's marriage portion. I went to the prince's parents and represented Elly's interests. I signed the documents as her guardian, as her father's nearest kin. I arranged the nuptials. I did it all without meeting with her or discussing it with her. The prince's father negotiated with me, his ponderous mind plodding after me, step by step. He was not quick, but he missed nothing. It was like being tracked by a bear. Still, I did not give him everything. I saved some for myself.

I attested to the fact that Elly was a virgin of noble birth. True. She would not have stayed a virgin long, but she was still, technically, a virgin. And yet I lied. I wanted to say, "I fear she is a monster. Her father was a monster, and she is like him. I fear she is both sensual and cruel, a succubus who will twine herself around your son and suck him dry, making him rue the day he ever saw her." I said none of that. For all his intelligence, the prince's father did not ask. He cared only about the money, her virginity, and that she was nobly born.

I should have stopped it, somehow. And yet, wasn't it

fated? Hadn't the story been told for hundreds of years? Wasn't my daughter to have her prince and live happily ever after?

While I was there, I asked again for Giles, saying I had known him for many years. He had gone, they said. He had never returned after delivering the glass-slipper message.

I don't know what has happened to him. I don't know where he is. I want more than anything to go looking for him, but I can't do that just now! First I must arrange this wedding. When it is over, I'll find him. Then he and I will come back to Wellingford. There are fields to harvest and geese to pluck. There are apples to store and cider to make. I can't decide what to do next. There's an old pain burning in me and a new love. Between them both, it's hard to decide what to do.

Was this what Carabosse meant when she asked me to be merely ordinary? Is being a mother ever ordinary? Is caring about one's children ever ordinary? Is there always this much pain?

FEAST OF THE HOLY INNOCENTS, DECEMBER, YEAR OF OUR LORD 1367

Elly became pregnant even before the wedding. I had not thought to tell her anything about that. Neither had anyone else. Now that she understands there is no way to escape it, she has settled into a sullen resentment at the facts of life.

"I don't want it," she told me. "I just wanted the other, not this."

I told her I understood. I did understand, for I had not wanted it either. At least she had enjoyed the begetting.

Her eyes grew dreamy. "I like the other," she said. "I like it a lot. More even than he does."

I think perhaps I blushed. There is something so frankly lecherous in her tone when she talks like this, an insatiable hunger totally untinted with affection or humor. I tried to change the subject.

"It'll be fun for you to have a child. If it's a girl, she'll probably look like you."

"She can't," Elly said flatly. "I won't let her. No one looks like me. She can look like someone else. Someone pale, like him."

"She'll have your dark hair."

"His pale skin. His red lips. This baby can look like that."

"Like that," I agreed, feeling sick inside. On several occasions I have tried to get her to talk with me about other things: religion, gardening, pets. She doesn't care about any of them. She has some lingering affection for Grumpkin, but it is only a passive thing. Except toward the pleasures of her body, she is closed away. She likes warmth and frequent good food, and, most of all, fucking. She does not read, does not think, does not care. She would ride twenty miles in bad weather for her lust's sake, and would not walk twenty paces down a hallway to do a kindness. She emptied her ashes, not out of any sense of cleanliness, but only so her fire would burn so she could be warm. If she wants something, she could kill to get it, and if she does not want something, it might as well not exist so far as she is concerned.

I blame myself for her nature, though I keep coming back to the real cause. She is not like me. She is like Jaybee. Elly should never have been born, and but for him, she would not have been. But for him and for the fact I remembered too well the things Father Raymond used to teach me. I had told myself it was God's will when it was nothing of the kind. It was only man's stupidity.

Mostly, it was Jaybee's fault. I ask myself if I want Jaybee dead, and tell myself, no. Not dead. Not necessarily. Simply . . . simply unable to do to anyone else what he did to me. The more I see of Elly, the more sure I am that he should never father other children!

She sends for me. Every day or so, she sends for me. When I get there, she takes my hand and holds it, as though it were a rope and she were drowning. She looks at her swelling body with terror.

Well, well, I know. She has heard what all women hear in this time, that babies do not come easily nor safely. Women die giving birth. Many of them die. Life comes through the doorway of death in this time, and Elly is in terror of death. So she sends for me, and I sit beside her and hold her hand. After a time, she grows calm, and her eyes grow soft and her mouth loosens. She begins to think of the prince, and then she sends me away.

I want to go looking for Giles. I cannot. Not so long as she needs me.

Daytimes, I go on about my self-imposed duties at Wellingford. Harry and Bert have gone off to London. Some weeks ago I suggested to Griselda that she might look into the convent where Aunts Tansy and Comfrey—"Acquaintances of mine, now dead"—had found so many pleasant years. She did so and liked it. There she will not have to worry about men or clothes or being ugly, though she will have to bathe. Lydia arranged a dowry for her, very quickly, too, considering that young Edward is still a minor, and Griselda left us. Lydia and the two young children are alone with me. I do what I can with the children. The boy seems past help, but the little girl, Catherine, is beginning to respond to consistency and affection, like a flower growing toward the sun.

ST. BENEDICT'S DAY, MARCH 1368
Little Catherine is dead. My so-called "namesake." Sweet Catherine. Winter came, and with it the diseases that always come, and she died and was buried next to her half sister.

From time to time I go to Edward's grave and talk to him, telling him I am sorry. I should not have left him and Elly. It was my duty to stay. Even as I say it, I know it's not true. Nothing I could have done would have changed things. What looks out of Elly's eyes at the world would have been there even if I had been with her every moment of her life, born in her. Her nature will have its way. Love and good intentions simply don't solve everything.

ST. JULIA'S DAY, MAY 1368
Last night I woke at the Dower House, feeling I had heard someone call my name. Elly's voice. I put on the boots and went. She was in a room overwarmed by a roaring fire, with the midwives all around her, wringing their hands. She was screaming as I had done when she was born, as all women do in this time, her eyes bulging. "Mother," she cried. She had never had a

mother, but she cried for one. I gave her my hands and would have given her life itself, but it was already too late when I got there. She had waited too long to call my name. She grasped at me, panting.

"White as snow," she panted, her eyes fixed on mine. "Red as blood. Black as death." She pointed to the child the midwives were holding, then died as I held her, sobbing as she had used to do when she was a baby and we put her down for a nap she did not want. The blood ran out of her in a wave. The baby girl had been born early, her white skin bloodied red all over. She did not want to live at all, but the midwives persevered and at last she cried. They washed her and laid her in my arms. Pale as a white rose, with Elly's dark, wild hair.

When I came into the outer room, Elly's young husband wept, but his eyes were full of some other emotion than grief. Was it relief? Was it gladness? He had the look of a man tried past endurance.

I knew what he was feeling. In college, I had read the Victorian poets. I was much enamored of Swinburne. He had spoken of this same feeling, "the delight that consumes the desire; the desire that outruns the delight." Elly's desire had outrun their delight. The prince did not ask how I came there, but his mother gave me a speculative look.

"There is no question of returning the dowry," she said plainly.

"I did not come for that," I told her.

"What then?" she asked.

What had I come for? "I came because she called for me. I would like Elly to be buried beside her father," I said. "He loved her very much. Perhaps if he had lived, she . . . things would have been different."

Red patches came out on her cheeks. She whispered, "I am glad she is dead. She was destroying my son. She was like an evil spirit, sucking his life." It was as though she had to confess it to me, had to receive absolution from me. It came out in a hiss.

I gave her the absolution she wanted. "I know," I said. "It is a hunger she was born with."

"Her daughter . . ."

"It is not in her daughter," I told her. "Her daughter is your son's daughter. You may trust in what I say." I knew it was true. I could sense nothing evil in the child at all. There was nothing there but sweet babyhood, innocent as dawn.

They let me take Elly's body away. I have found a priest to bury her in the Wellingford chapelyard, beside her father.

STS. DONATIAN AND ROGATIAN, MARTYRS

Only the prince came to Elly's internment, to stand dry-eyed while they filled in the grave. When it was over, he laughed, then he cried.

"We are going home," he said. "The people rose up and killed the pretender to the throne. He was my half uncle, Richard, and I am glad he is dead. They have sent word we are to return." His words had a childlike simplicity, and for the first time I really looked at him. He met my gaze innocently, without intention or guile. There was no large intellect there. He had none of his father's ponderous mind.

"Are you taking the child?" I asked.

"Oh, yes," he told me. "My daughter. Mama is very fond of her. So am I. Do not be concerned about her."

"Does she have a name?" I asked.

He gazed at me abstractedly, trying to think of the name. "Mama named her," he confessed at last. "After a spring flower that blooms through the snow. I cannot remember at the moment. Of course, she hasn't been christened yet."

He sighed, then smiled, without meaning, then said, "There was a man of ours you had an interest in. Father said you had asked after him."

"Giles," I said, my mouth falling open.

"He was killed. Someone saw the assault and sent word to my father. It was a group of men assaulted him, while he was riding on our business that day." He flushed, remembering that day. "Father said you had wanted to know."

Giles. Dead. Elly. Dead. Edward. Dead. Oh, God in Heaven. All dead. All I had loved. All I had tried to love.

"Where?" I breathed. "Where is he buried?"

"There," he said, gesturing vaguely eastward. "Where they killed him."

He left me and rode off with his serving men, still smiling his ineffectual smile, while I wept until there were no more tears. I had brought flowers for Elly's and Edward's graves, the roses they both liked. I gripped the bouquet until the thorns sank deep into my hands, knowing it was Giles's grave my flowers should lie upon.

I went back to the Dower House and got my boots. "Take me wherever it was Giles was set upon," I said.

And I was there, a weedy sunken spot by the side of an unfamiliar road, marked by a rough wooden cross. There was a man working in the field nearby, and he came to the fence, looking at me curiously.

"I didn't see you coming on the road," he said. "Are you looking for the place the fellow died?"

I nodded yes.

He pointed at the cross, at the sunken place. "I buried him there. I was over there, on the far side of the field. I saw him coming along, on his horse. They came out of the woods there, and set upon him. Eight or ten, maybe. Too many for me to fight. I saw his horse run off. I went to the village to get help. When we came back, the horse was there, grazing, and the body of the man. Dreadful cut about, he was. They knew him by his horse, though, for it had the King's arms upon the saddle."

I thanked him, and he went back to his work. I laid my flowers on the grave. They were marked with my blood upon their thorns. I sat there for a long time. When night came, I told the boots to take me home.

Perhaps in time I can find a stonecutter to make a monument for Giles. But why? In time even a monument will disappear. I remember the twenty-first and shudder. Why make monuments? Why build beautiful things? Why create anything when Fidipur's billions will tear them all down.

I don't know. I have no emotions at all except a sullen anger, which boils away inside me, building up the pressure. I want vengeance against the cause of all this pain. If I had not been pregnant when I came back, I would not have married Edward, I would not have had Elly. If I had not married Edward, I could have had Giles. We could have married, lived together, that ordinary life Carabosse wanted for me.

If I had not married Edward, if he had not had Elly, Edward might not have died, and he certainly wouldn't have married Lydia. Oh, what Jaybee had done when he raped me was more hurt than even he had planned!

When I left the twentieth—how long ago?—Jaybee was raging about, full of fury that he could not find me to do it all again. If I leave him there, he *will* do it again, to someone else. He will cause this pain again, generations of it, begetting sorrow as a cloud begets rain. It is not fitting that this should be so. I can do nothing for Elly. I can do nothing for Giles. Edward is gone. All I cared for is gone.

And Jaybee lives to make more sorrow.

Beauty can be disappointed of its children. The worst thing about being a woman is that things can be begot on us, things we do not want, cannot manage, cannot control. We swell to fruition with disasters implanted in us against our wills. We spew out tragedy. And all the disaster and the tragedy, though begot upon us against our volition, is part us. How much, we wonder. How much was me? What could I have changed?

Carabosse says I carry importance within me. A kernel of something incorruptible, no doubt. A seed. Yet one begot upon me without my consent. Can even Carrabosse be sure of the harvest? Can this seed grow bitter fruit? Can it be twisted and warped, as my own seed was warped?

And is this, perhaps, what the Dark Lord wants? What Jaybee wanted, whether he knew it or not? To beget horror on innocence? It cannot be borne. It cannot be tolerated. I cannot let it happen again, to anyone.

All my anger focuses upon Jaybee. Even though magic is thin on the ground in the twentieth, my powers will work there, so I believe, even if only weakly, perhaps enough.

Grumpkin is here. And my cloak. And my boots.

["What's she doing?" I asked Israfel.
"She's going back there. Back to the twentieth."
"Beauty! You mustn't. Please. . . ."]

.
23
.

JANUARY 4, 1993. WISDOM STREET

It is not Holy Wisdom, not Hagia Sophia, the street is named
for, but William W. Wisdom, who was Manager of Public
Works sometime in the forties. Still, I have always liked the
name of the street, and seeing it on the sign at the corner gave
me a feeling of welcome when the boots set me down only a
few feet from our front door. Our front door. Bill's and Janice's
and mine.

Bill had been so excited when we rented the house. To him
it represented everything he had ever dreamed of: unimaginable
amounts of room, safety, warmth, affection, plenty of privacy in
which to indulge himself in his harmless eccentricities; all of
the things so notably missing in the twenty-first. To me, accustomed to the vaulted spaces and elegant architecture of
Westfaire, it had seemed scarcely better than a hovel, though I
had agreed it was far better than the twenty-first.

It was, is, a small frame dwelling, white clapboard with
blue shutters and a blue roof, surrounded on its corner lot by a
white picket fence. Inside the front door a narrow hall leads
back to the kitchen. On the left is a combination living-dining
room, on the right, two tiny bedrooms and a bath. Some former
owner had built another bedroom and a half bath in the basement, and Bill had chosen those rooms for his own. There he
had his closet full of silky dresses and lacy underwear, his high-
heeled shoes and fluffy parasols, his full length mirror and his

private telephone. Though he never went "out" in his women's clothes, he wore them while he talked on the phone, endless high-pitched conversations full of flirtatious little interjections and giggles.

Though the basement rooms had been his place, he hadn't been stingy with his time and effort in the rest of the house. He and I had refinished the kitchen cabinets, taking endless hours to do it, more than the cheap construction was worth. He had sweated over the tiny lawn, fighting the weeds and mowing it twice a week. He had planted the junipers and the Seafoam roses on either side of the door. In summer they were a cloud of white. Now their brown canes poked through the rare light snow, like old bony fingers. I knocked. Janice opened the door as though she'd been standing in the hallway, waiting for someone. She said, "Yes?" in a tone of voice that told me she didn't know me. Well, why would she?

"I've come about Bill," I faltered. "May I come in?"

She stood back, rather grudgingly, to let me enter, her head tilted to one side, her bird's eyes fixed on me as though I were a bug. I had an almost uncontrollable urge to tell her who I was, but I fought it down. Telling her would involve too many explanations, and I couldn't guarantee she'd believe any of them. Besides, I could not depend on her good will. Her relationship with Bill and me had always been a reluctant one. I must have squeezed Grumpkin, for he protested at being held so tightly. I put him down on the floor and he promptly began to sniff his way around the hall.

"That's Dorothy's cat," she said. "Where did you get Dorothy's cat?" Once we had agreed that I was to be "Dorothy," Janice had never used any other name for me. Bill had always called me Beauty when we were alone.

"I'm a friend of hers," I said. "She asked me to come tell you what happened." I made the comeback sign. Janice would trust a comeback sooner than anyone else, though she didn't trust anyone much. She looked startled, but she made the sign in return.

"Where is she?" Janice wanted to know. "And where's Bill?"

"Dorothy's gone away," I said, breathing in deeply. There was no kind or easy way to tell her what had happened. "Jaybee broke in here while you were away. He told Dorothy he'd come for her, Bill got between them, and Jaybee killed Bill and attacked Dorothy. He hurt her . . . raped her. She's gone away."

She stared at me, unbelieving. "How did you . . . ? I don't understand how you. . . ."

"I was a sort of witness to it," I said. "I was here when it happened."

She fell back into the chair just inside the door, her mouth open. "Jaybee? Bill?" Her eyes filled with tears. "I should have known. Oh God, I should never have left Bill alone."

Her emotion seemed genuine, though to my certain knowledge she had only tolerated Bill and me.

"He was like my son," she cried, the tears making red tracks down her face. "My son I was bringing to God. Oh, I loved him so."

I started to say, "You never let him know that," remembering just in time that I wasn't Beauty, wasn't Dorothy, wasn't who I was. I was older. A lot older. In the hall mirror I caught sight of myself, a woman in her sixties, perhaps. All grayhaired. With crepey skin on my arms. I looked at my hands, seeing the spots on the backs of them. Time. I had used it up, going back and forth. Used it up. I started crying, too, partly for Bill, partly for myself. All I had seemed to do lately was grieve. Grumpkin came over and extended a paw, asking his "prrrt." How had he aged so little? I picked him up, to hug, for warmth, for something.

"Who are you?" she asked. "Do I know you?"

"My name is Catherine Monfort," I said through my tears. "I came because Dorothy asked me to, and because she thought you might let me stay here."

She threw her hands up, shaking her head, no, then realized how inhospitable that looked. Janice couldn't bear to look bad, though she didn't care what she did if no one knew. Finally she nodded, pointing at the front bedroom, tears running down her face. "He was here yesterday. He asked for 'Beauty.' He even asked for Bill. That bastard. He was laughing at me. Oh, God will punish him. Oh yes, God will punish him."

"Jaybee?" I asked, knowing already that's who it was. Yes. Jaybee. Still looking for Beauty. He hadn't given up.

Janice had her hands folded under her chin, her eyes closed, her lips moving. While she cried and prayed, I went into the bedroom. My bedroom. All my things were still there, except the few I'd taken when I'd run away. My clothes, young clothes, for a college girl. Well, I could wear the nightgowns. The panties. The jeans, maybe. The shoes. Not the brassieres. I had little enough to put a brassiere around. My chest had gone flat, not saggy, just flat, like the fairies. Fairy blood, I guess. Sylph blood. Better than flopping, I suppose. Somewhere, I'd have to get some clothes suitable to a woman my age. I hung up my cloak, set my boots in the closet, put away my book and Mama's box in the drawer of the bedside table. Grumpkin jumped up on the bed, kneaded a place soft and lay down, eyes slitted, just as his daddy used to do. I turned to find Janice in the doorway, staring at me.

"Do you have a job?" she asked. She had suddenly realized she might have to support me. Janice wouldn't do that!

I shook my head.

"What can you do?"

"Handle horses," I said.

"Nobody's going to hire you for that, at your age." The words were a sneer. Janice was sounding more like herself.

I nodded, telling her I knew, thinking of Wellingford. "I managed an estate for a family for a while."

"If you could get references, that might be useful."

"I met Dorothy at college. We were both studying the same things. I'm a fair Latinist."

"Maybe we can find something academic. Through the network."

She meant the comebacks' forgery network that provided social security cards, birth certificates, educational documentation, and even jobs for returnees. What I really wanted to do was find Jaybee and follow him around, until I knew what he was doing, what his vulnerabilities were. That might have to wait.

Janice was still crying, wiping her eyes. "What happened to Bill? To his body?"

I tried to tell her and I choked. It was as if it had happened yesterday, rather than a year, two years ago. I finally got it out, about Jaybee having carried his body away.

"That bastard," she whispered again. "Oh, that rotten bastard." Then she wiped her eyes and said firmly, "When the day of judgement comes, he'll be among the damned." Then she went out, shutting the door behind her, leaving me alone.

I lay down on my own bed next to the cat, so tired it was hard to think, hard to move. I was old. Funny, I didn't know where my youth had gone, but I was old. When I looked in the mirror, I expected to see someone else, that younger face, that smooth skin, that unlined brow. Mama was still young. I should be still young. Instead, there was this thin, slightly wrinkled woman with flyaway gray hair who had to lean close to the mirror to see because she was nearsighted. I sat up and stared in the mirror, squinting my eyes as Thomas the Rhymer had taught me, wishing to see true.

It reminded me of one of the songs they had sung in Faery, in Oberon's court. "Lovely the days of your youth, and fleeting as grass. Stay with me forever in Faery, my golden-haired lass. . . ."

And that reminded me of Puck and Fenoderee, my only friends. I said their names, wishing they were with me.

"Yes?" said Puck. He came out from the wall, from the bookcase, from somewhere near there. Grumpkin opened his eyes for a moment, yawned, then went back to sleep. He wasn't impressed by half-naked Bogles appearing out of the walls. Puck said, "I came to tell you Elladine is back in Faery."

I felt my heart thudding, like a weary hammer. "Is she angry at me?"

"Why should she be angry at you?"

"Because I ran off." I felt guilty about that, had felt guilty ever since I'd done it.

"I ran you off," he said. "Elladine is of Faery, and she's old

in years. Age is a powerful protection against such as he. He's
not really interested in those of Faery, so he let her go. He
wouldn't have let you go."

"Still . . ." I said, tears in my eyes.

"Still, nothing. She risked your life taking you on that Halloween ride. It was sheer arrogance, too. Elladine is arrogant
where humans are concerned. All that lot are."

I thought it must be true. "She never comes to me, even
though I know she can!" I cried. "She never came to me when I
was a child. The only time she came was after the Curse, to
move my body, and it wasn't even me!"

What I felt was the same longing I had felt ever since I was
a child. I needed someone to care about me. Stubbornly, I could
not stop seeking love. I wanted Elladine to love me.

"Beauty, you're such a child," he laughed at me. "Why
don't you take affection from those who'd give it to you gladly?
Me, for instance." He made a languishing face at me, enough to
make me laugh.

"Elladine told me you're trying to be an angel," I said. "Is
that why you're here, looking after me? And how come you
never came before when I was here?"

He chuckled ruefully. "I was here before. As soon as
Carabosse let me come. Who do you think pushed those boots
into your hands when that man was coming after you?"

"I didn't see you."

He shrugged. "I know. Carabosse thought it was dangerous
for me to show up, in the flesh, so to speak. You knew nothing
about Faery then, and she thought you might go silly."

"I wouldn't have," I said indignantly. "If I could get
dragged from the fourteenth to the twenty-first, and then back
here, if I could go through all that with Jaybee without going
silly, why would I go silly seeing you?"

"Magic's thin on the ground here," he said. "She thought
perhaps you'd stopped believing in it."

I sniffed to verify the fact. "I can hardly smell it at all. If I
put on my cloak in full sunlight, people can almost see me."

"So, don't put on your cloak."

"I need it," I said stubbornly.

"What are you going to do?" he asked.

"I must make sure Jaybee hurts no more women," I told him.

He made a face.

I said, angrily, "I know you think it's only for vengeance, but it's not only that! It isn't vengeance when you kill a poison snake in the yard where children play, to keep it from killing someone else. I need to make sure he hurts no more people, fathers no more children like Elly. After that, I don't know. Maybe I'll go join a nunnery somewhere." What else was there to do? What had been between Giles and me had been quite perfect. I could never love anyone else in that way.

"You should leave Jaybee to Fate, Beauty. It would be safer. Truly. Listen to me. You have a granddaughter, back then. You could live then, be with her."

I shook my head at him. "They don't know I'm her grandmother, Puck. They think I'm a fairly distant relative. I'd be an intruder. She has a grandma, a grandpa, a father. She'll be a princess." I shook my head, firmly. "Are you going to stay here with me?"

"I'll drop in from time to time. I can't stay, though. We're still trying to convert Faery before they all dwindle, though they're a stubborn lot. Well, so are we Bogles."

"Tell me about it," I asked him, curling up on the bed the way I had used to do when I was young. My bones protested, but I persevered, wanting that feeling of having a whole long time to just sit and talk about anything at all, with pillows softening the world, and maybe hot chocolate to drink. That feeling of being in a safe nest where nothing could hurt me. The way I used to cuddle into my tower bed, when I was young. Grumpkin half-opened his eyes, crawled over to put his feet up against my leg, and started kneading me as he went back to sleep.

"What are you and the Fenoderee and the others trying to do?"

He cocked one ear at me, like a horse might do, or a dog. "We want Faery to fight the Dark Lord. On man's behalf, and its own."

I laughed. "I can see Oberon's face."

Puck grimaced. "Well, he's not receptive thus far."

"Why do you want Faery to fight, Puck?"

He settled himself on my bed. "I'll give you my lecture, which I've given the Bogles over and over. I've given it to the Sidhe, too, but they pay no attention. Mind now. Fold your hands in your lap and pay attention:

"When Faery looks at mankind, it sees him as mostly animal, not immortal and far from perfect. Since those of Faery are immortal, it stands to reason they should feel sorry for mankind, right? Poor little sinful, short-lived thing."

I nodded. I'd felt sorry for myself, often enough.

"But there's this unexpected thing about man. He climbs. That's the thing about him. He climbs. Not all of him, oh no, or there'd be no more living with him than with the angels, but now and then there's one who does." Puck folded his legs and leaned against my bedpost, scratching one brown ankle and furrowing his brow. "And when a man or a woman climbs, Beauty, he or she can end up as high as the angels or higher."

"The saints," I nodded, thinking I knew.

"Oh, saints," Puck said. "Whsst. Saints! Martyrs and virgins and what all. Relics in churches, and both the relic and the churches dead as brass. No. I'll tell you who climbs. Gardeners climb. And farmers. And painters. And poets. People who build beautiful things without destroying to do it. The ones who designed Westfaire, them. And people who live with animals and learn of them until they know every twitch of a tail or an ear. Them, too. And those that study atoms and how they move, and stars and how they move. Those who learn about the Holy One by reading his own book of nature and creation, that's who climbs."

"How do you know?" I asked. "How do you know those people climb?"

"Ach," he said, rubbing his head. "You know how, if you sing a note, sometimes a wine glass sitting in a cupboard sings the same note back again?"

I told him I did.

"Well, sometimes you say the name of a man or a woman

and it comes back to you out of the air, singing, and you know that man or that woman has climbed up somewhere."

"Dead or alive?" I wondered.

"Either," he said. "Maybe it's only us Bogles that can hear it, but when you're in Faery next, you try it. Say the name of the ones who built Westfaire and listen for it to come back at you."

I didn't know their names, more's the pity. "Why is that, do you suppose?"

"Because that's the way the Holy One wanted things to be, don't you see? The Holy One created the world beautiful and manifold and complicated, and the way it was made was the way He *meant* it to be! He wasn't just playing, making a toy world with the real world somewhere else. No, this is *it!* Anybody with eyes can see the truth of that. The Holy One wanted mankind to understand creation so he could create in his turn, for man's the only one among us who can create anything at all! Angels don't! They burn with a pure flame, like stars, but they don't create. Faery doesn't! It grows and flowers, without much thought, and it doesn't create."

"Faery is beautiful."

He rubbed his head and looked at me with saddened eyes. "Ah, nah, nah, you know better, Beauty. It's all glamour in Faery. All fool-the-eye, like dreams. It's not real. Without elvenroot and fairy fruit, we'd see no palaces nor fairy steeds. In Faery, it's all in the eye, not in the heart or mind. You know that."

"What's the difference," I said, being stubborn. "It's still beautiful."

"The difference is that nobody builds it. It doesn't really stand there. If we leave it, it will vanish. You can't show it to a mortal man, lest you put elvenroot in his eyes, and you do that, he can't see anything else forever. You can't take a picture of it. Sometimes I wonder if even the Holy One can see it."

"You mean if someone mortal gets elvenroot in her eyes, she can see Faery, but nothing else?" I asked in surprise.

"It's only your fairy blood lets you see Faery and still see this world, Beauty, and your granddaughter hasn't enough fairy blood ever to use it safely. If she goes there, she must stay forever. She's only one-eighth, and that's not enough to go back and forth. If you're thinking of taking her to Faery, beware!"

I hadn't been thinking of my granddaughter. I hadn't been thinking of anyone, specially, though I suddenly thought of Jaybee, wondering what a view of Faery would do to him.

"So why do you want Oberon to fight the Dark Lord, Puck?"

"Because it would do what the Holy One asked of Faery in the first place! To help mankind! Help him instead of using him or ignoring him, which has been the usual pattern. Make common cause with him. Join with him.

"And it's so logical," he said. "Man is dying from being too many. Faery is dying from being too few. We need to mix more, to value our children more. Men have too many of them, they're cheap. The Sidhe have too few, and they seek them like treasure. Man needs what Faery has to give. Fewer children. Longer lives. Less speed. More thought. Mystery and wonder and glamour built in, so to speak, through the slow creation of marvelous things. Less haste and destruction. More appreciation for what's been given. Like man and Faery were two halves of one thing. If the Dark Lord were conquered, it could all come right!"

"Why won't the Sidhe listen? They lust after humans enough."

"Oh aye, they do. But it's that pride again, Beauty. They said no to the Holy One; you think they're going to say yes to a Bogle? And while a little fleshy stink is exciting to them, they won't accept it as a daily thing. It's common. It's not how they see themselves."

"So they won't."

"They won't. Perhaps it's the dwindle, the way our magic is leaking away. And our numbers are falling, too, one here, one there. A forest gets cut down, and the fairies who were born out of that forest are gone. At one time, the glamour would have been strong enough to protect the forest, but not anymore."

"What's causing it, Puck? Why do they dwindle?"

"There's some say it's the Dark Lord's doing. Every time he makes a new horror, it takes hideous magic to do it, all tied up in that terror, like gold dug out of the earth and hid away.

There's some say it's the human priests, sucking our magic away to use it in their religion, turning wine into blood and making spells to forgive sins. There's some who say magic came from nature, and with man destroying nature right and left, there's not enough of it left. Whatever the reason, we've been losing it for a few thousand years. The only ones who're holding fast are us Bogles. We can tolerate mankind better than most, maybe because we never went in for glamour like the Sidhe. We can even live in wasteland, where those of Faery can't. But it's hard times for us, too. We watch things dwindle and dwindle, and Oberon forgets what he once knew, forgets his majesty and his dignity and ruts like a goat, laughing and pretending all is well. As though time were forever."

"But you said they're immortal."

"All that means is they don't die. It doesn't mean they can't fade away. They're tied to the forests, Beauty. Tied to the moors. Tied to the seas and rivers. They were drawn from nature and will go when nature goes. They vanish if their forests vanish. Fade away. Like snow, melting."

His face was drawn into a mask of tragedy, the corners of his mouth pulled down with woe. I took his hand in my own and stroked it.

"Right now," he muttered, "if I went to Faery *in this time,* there'd be almost nothing there. It's all shadows and ghosts. No palaces. No enchanted places. What's left has been invaded by *him.* To reach the Faery you know, I have to go back and come in from hundreds of years ago."

I nodded, sadly. "That's what Bill and the crew were photographing when I met them. The end of Faery. The last enchantments. They were getting a picture of Westfaire with the roses growing up."

He sighed. I tried to think of something comforting to say, but someone knocked on my door. I looked up, startled, looked back to find Puck gone.

"Yes?" I said.

Janice opened the door. "I've made some tea. I thought it might do us good."

I nodded, trying to smile as I levered myself off the bed on aching old legs to go have tea, feeling less lonely but more lost than I had half an hour before. Grumpkin purred and stayed where he was. The end of the world does not impress cats.

Janice wiped her eyes and made small talk. She wondered how long I'd been back in the twentieth; she wondered how I'd been getting along, without a job.

"Oh, I had a job until just recently," I said. "Caring for horses. Then, suddenly, I got old. Up until a year or two ago, I wasn't . . . didn't feel old at all."

She sipped and nodded. "That's the way it takes us all, I think. Suddenly, you're not young anymore, and you don't know where it went. And people tell us they don't love us anymore because we're too old. And some of us fight it, and some of us realize in time that it's God's will." Her eyes blazed at me.

"So," I went on quickly, derailing a disquisition on God's will. "I went back to school, and that's where I met your niece."

"You said you were a witness? When Jaybee came?" Her mouth was tight, but her eyes were avid.

I had to make it up as I went along. "Dorothy and I had planned to have New Year's dinner together. I had just arrived, and I'd asked to use the bathroom. I was inside, with the door ajar, when I heard the man come in. I heard it all, but I was afraid if he saw me, he'd kill me. There was nothing I could do. Afterwards, he picked up Bill's body and went, and I helped Dorothy get herself together, then she decided to go away where he couldn't find her. I don't even know where she is." I had to say that. Otherwise Janice would be at me to get the address. Her mouth was still downturned. Was she angry that Dorothy herself hadn't told her? Or was she angry that Dorothy had gotten away?

"She should have called me," she said bitterly. "I'm terribly fond of Dorothy." Her tone belied the words.

"I don't think she was thinking about that." Besides, I didn't believe her. Janice had never approved of me enough to be fond of me. I equivocated, "I'm sure she'll call you. Before she went, she suggested I come here, that you might like the company, that you might not want to be alone."

"Where were you living before?" she asked suspiciously. I

knew she was suspecting me of having invented the tragedy for the sake of free rent.

"In an apartment downtown," I extemporized. "The building has been sold, and all the tenants have to move."

It was evidently explanation enough. Janice forgot to be suspicious of me and returned to her grief. "That bastard," she whispered, tears coming again. "Oh, that horrible man. What will I do when he comes back?"

"Nothing," I said. "Nothing, please. Dorothy said not to do anything."

"I couldn't do anything now anyhow," she said. "I have to get out of town for a while. The team I used to work with is coming from the twenty-first to photograph whales. They'll be —we'll be coming here, to this very town. I was with them. I can't be here when I come. Not this near or it might make a loop."

When I asked for details, she told me the team had come from the twenty-first on January 12, 1993, and had rented a boat named the *Sally Ann,* with its owner as crew. They had gone out into the ocean and photographed migrating whales. She remembered it clearly, almost yearningly. Her expression softened, as though something wonderful had been connected with that trip. "Martin's coming," she whispered.

"And Bill?" I whispered. "Bill's coming?"

"Oh, yes. Bill. And the others." She got up and went into the bathroom, closing the door. I heard her weeping, making loud gulping noises. I didn't think she was weeping over Bill. Something else grieved her.

Alice had talked about staying away from places that had previously been visited through time-travel. None of the team would want to be in this town when their former selves came back. None of them could be, but I could. They hadn't even known I existed on January 12, 1993.

JANUARY 8, 1993

Janice trusted me enough to leave me with the keys to the house, money to buy groceries, and the names of some comebacks I'm supposed to call and ask about jobs. She said she'd be back on the eighteenth.

"When you came this time, when the team comes back this time, will they know about comebacks?" I asked her.

"Oh yes," she said, disapprovingly. "We even talked to one. Or rather, Bill did. I hardly saw her, but I remember, she gave Bill some clothes." She sniffed. Even with Bill dead, she still disapproves of his clothes.

JANUARY 12, 1993: EVENING

I saw them all. Jaybee, of course. Younger, but with that same red light of destruction burning in his eyes. Janice and Alice. Martin, the director. He and Janice were obviously in love, and that's what she had remembered so longingly. The two of them had no eyes for anyone else. Janice was lovely, too, with a winsome fragility that could age very quickly and lose itself. Perhaps that evanescent beauty was all Martin had cared about.

Bill was there. Young Bill. Much younger than when I first saw him.

It had taken me most of the past several days to find the clothes I remembered Bill having. The sheepskin was the easiest part. I got that at a place they make sheepskin jackets. I finally found the skirt at the Salvation Army store. I took the tags off everything, put them in a paper bag and carried it with me when I went down to the dock, very early this morning, before it was even light. I found the *Sally Ann.* When the owner came along, he unlocked it, then went up on top, toward the front. While he was up there, I went down inside. A stowaway, I guess I was. Like Constanzia.

I heard their voices on the dock, heard their feet as they came aboard, felt the surging as the boat left the dock, the heaving of the ocean. I prayed I wouldn't be sick. After a while, when we were well out on the sea, I came up from inside. I pretended it was an accident. I'd gotten a migraine while fishing on the pier, I told them, so I'd borrowed the boat to lie down in for a moment, and fallen asleep. I apologized profusely and said I wouldn't get in their way.

Bill and Martin exchanged a look and shrugged. Their twenty-first cameras looked enough like twentieth cameras that they assumed I wouldn't know the difference. They were doing shots to be used early in the whale documentary, shots of healthy creatures. The starving mother and calf that appeared in the final shots wouldn't be photographed until later, sometime around 2025 or 2030, after Fidipur's ocean farms had been built and all the krill and plankton was being used up by man.

Bill and Alice and I talked. I told them I was a comeback. They asked what it was like. I told them it was far better than the twenty-first, the last good time. When Alice joined the others, I showed Bill the clothes in the paper bag, stockings, silk blouse, skirt, underthings. High-heeled shoes, the kind I never wear, never have worn. They were way too small for me, but I remembered them on Bill's tiny feet. The fleece was in there, soft and new now, not the way it would be when I cut the boots out of it. I said I'd found the sack on the pier, and I guessed I'd throw them away. He couldn't keep his eyes off the bag after that. I kept fighting down the urge to tell Bill I loved him. That would have confused him utterly.

The day wore on. Janice clung to Martin, not even noticing me. The whales spewed and basked, and Jaybee ran his cameras. He had one that went underwater, like a tiny submarine, guided from a little TV screen with controls. The man running the boat stayed up front and paid no attention to any of us.

All the time I kept arguing with Puck in my head. He had chided me for wanting vengeance. Father Raymond would have said that vengeance belongs to God. I told myself it wasn't vengeance, and it wasn't for myself. It was for some other innocent person. Then I'd argue with myself some more. If Jaybee hadn't been there, right in front of me, I might have talked myself out of it. Every time he looked up at me, though, it was with that dead-eyed, death-making arrogance, an expression that said he was above any law, outside any commandment. It made me hurt inside. Each time I fought down the notion of what I was going to do, he made it come back more strongly.

Finally, I couldn't fight it anymore. When the boat turned back toward land, I asked Bill to introduce me to Jaybee.

Bill said, "Jaybee, here's a comeback lady wants to meet you. She thinks you're fascinating."

"I didn't say that," I bridled. "I said I thought his photography was fascinating."

Jaybee looked up at me and sneered. He didn't care about old women. He was kneeling on the deck, busy packing up his cameras.

"Be nice, Jaybee," Martin said. He was a handsome man, a bit older than the others. He had that power that some men have, of being always center stage, no matter who else is there. He wore boots and a complicated jacket with many pockets. "Be nice."

"I'm busy," Jaybee snarled. "No time for chitchat."

"Bill and Martin tell me you're a fine photographer," I said.

"There's never been a better one," he said, peering at me, seeing nothing there to interest him, letting his eyes drop away. "I'm good. I'm very good."

"You use oculum root, then, I suppose."

"Never heard of it," he snorted.

"Oculum root?" Bill laughed. "Sounds like a sneeze. What is it?"

I acted surprised. "You don't know about it? Really? I thought all the really great photographers used it. Not that it isn't a bit risky, but all the biggies seem willing to take the risk."

"Oculum root?" Martin frowned. "I think I've heard of it." He hadn't, of course, but he was that kind of man. He ran one hand along the side of a boot, polishing it. Janice put her hand on his and mooned at him.

"For sharpness of vision," I said. "Sometimes it's called hawkeye root. It lets the human eye see things in a new, fresh way."

"I'd love to try something that did that," Bill laughed. "But I confess I've never heard of it."

"Well, of course," I said, as though surprised at my own stupidity. "Of course, you haven't heard of it. It doesn't exist in the twenty-first. Because of Fidipur."

"Oculum root," he said.

"It's rare, even now," I said, getting off the rail where I'd been perched and dusting my hands. "I understand the supply is extremely limited. Pity. With oculum root, you'd probably be exceptionally good." Then I went off to look over the opposite rail, leaving Jaybee glaring after me. He might not remember. If he didn't remember, well and good. If he didn't remember, and if he gave up trying to find Beauty, nothing would happen. I'd go home. That's the bargain I'd made with myself. It was really up to him.

When we got back ashore, I went off up the pier empty-handed. I had already seen Bill wearing the clothes in the twenty-first, so I knew he would take them with him.

I found an unoccupied alley nearby where I could put on the boots. I told them to take me to Faery. There was a whirling blackness that seemed to go on too long. Then it cleared, showing me the landscape under the evening sky. It was almost the same as I remembered, the blue sky, the spangled stars, the flower-sequined grass. It was more shadowy than before. There were no palaces. No people. From the woods against the mountains came a faroff howling, totally inhuman, with a tone to it that sent a shiver of pure terror up my back. I stayed just long enough to find two of the hairy-stemmed herbs Mama had squeezed into my eyes. They came up easily, soil clinging to their roots. I told the boots to take me to Wisdom Street. The same whirling darkness happened again.

When I got back to the house on Wisdom Street, Puck was waiting for me.

"That was foolish," he whispered to me.

"What was?" I asked him stupidly.

"You went into Faery," he said. "It doesn't take much magic to get there, Beauty. Not now. There's not much of Faery left, and what is left is very close, because it doesn't belong to us anymore. It belongs to him, and he is bringing it close to man. Close as he can."

I shuddered.

"I told you he had taken over," he accused me. "Carabosse is wild with grief over this. She says you've risked so much, and for what? For vengeance. I told you to let it go."

"I could not let him go on!" I said, suddenly angrier than I have ever been. "Who are you, or Carabosse, to tell me to let it go? It wasn't you he did it to!"

He sighed. He turned pale. He looked at the floor, at his bare toes. I was sorry I had spoken so. "Tell Carabosse I'm sorry," I said. "No harm done."

He shook his head. "That may not be so," he said. "Something saw you while you were there. Carabosse doesn't know who or what it was, but something saw you. She wants you to come home."

"I'll come home," I said. "Soon."

"Now," he begged.

"Soon," I said tiredly, looking at the plant in my hands. Evidently my tone of voice was final. I looked up and he was gone.

I went into the kitchen where I'd already put a sack of potting soil and a flowerpot. I planted the herbs, watered them carefully and labeled them with a large, white plastic plant label. If Jaybee has given up trying to find Beauty, he will never see the plant and I will go home. If he hasn't given up, it is likely he will show up here, at Janice's house, within the next three or four days.

JANUARY 17, 1993

Several days ago I went to the optometrist and got glasses, bifocals. I hate them. Whenever I eat the line is right where the food is, and I keep spilling things down my front. I went to the beauty shop, too, and had a cut and set to make me look different from the woman Jaybee met on the boat. Younger, a little, though perhaps it is really only neater.

Jaybee showed up this afternoon, drove up with a squeal of tires, parked by the curb, stepped over the picket fence. I was raking the lawn. A kind of memorial for Bill. Jaybee asked me where Janice was, and I told him she'd had to go out of town. He knew that. He'd been out of town himself. That's why he hadn't been here earlier. He asked me where "Dorothy" was, and I told him she'd moved. He asked me where, and I told him I had it written down somewhere in the house. He followed me into the kitchen where I made quite a drama of searching for the address everywhere but where I'd put it.

The flowerpot was sitting on the counter with its huge label. He couldn't miss it: black felt-tipped block letters on white. "Oculum Root," it said. His eyes flicked around the room, looking at everything, as they always did. Photographer's eyes. Always seeing. They came to the plant, flicked away and returned, fascinated, remembering something that had happened a long time ago, something someone had said.

By the time I found the address and gave it to him, his eyes were firmly fixed on the plant label.

"What is this?" he asked, putting one finger on a leaf, as though to be sure it was real.

"Oh, it's a very rare herb," I told him. "Janice learned about it in her research. It's extremely hard to obtain. She's been wanting some of it for a long time, and she located a man who grows it just before she left."

I handed him the scrap of paper with the address on it. He glanced at it and saw it was the address of the college "Dorothy" had been attending. "I've been there," he said. "She didn't come back there after the holidays. She must be somewhere else."

I pretended to be puzzled. "Janice did say something about another address. Maybe it's in Janice's bedroom." I went out into the hall and around the corner into the back bedroom, leaving him alone in the kitchen. I sat down on my bed and waited, stroking Grumpkin, my mind totally empty. Some time went by. Long enough. I heard footsteps, then his car leaving. When I went back to the kitchen, the plant was gone.

I have not done anything. I have not injured him. I have not met violence with violence. All I have done is to put something where he could steal it if he came hunting for a woman he had abused. Now, perhaps, I will not need to do anything else at all.

Am I revenged? It's very strange, but I don't know. Except for the tiny furnace behind my breast bone, I don't feel anything at all.

JANUARY 18, 1993

Janice returned from her trip with word of a job for me. The university needs a part time librarian to work evenings who reads enough Latin and medieval English and French to help students. I thanked her, not telling her I won't be here long enough to bother. I was going to leave last night, but my conversation with Puck had reminded me of something I wanted to find out from her.

"Janice," I said, "Dorothy told me how she met you and the others."

"Did she," sniffed Janice, suddenly suspicious once more.

"She told me you were doing a documentary on the last of the fairies, the last magic. You were the researcher on that, weren't you?"

She relaxed. "I was, yes. Piles of old books I had to plow through to find the answers to that one!"

"Where did all the magic go, Janice?"

"The Church took most of it," she said, giving me this strange, wild-eyed glare.

"The Church?" I asked stupidly. It was what Puck had said, but somehow I hadn't believed it.

"Making magic," she said. "All their sacraments are magical. Turning this into that. Making spells to forgive sins. They don't admit it's magic, but that's what it is! *The recitation of formulae by an elect, resulting in a condition contrary to reality, is magic.*' But there was only so much of it around. The fairies had it, then the Church took it, and now the Church is losing it to something else. The last days are coming. It's been foretold. It's been revealed. . . ."

And she went off into a tirade about the last days, leaving me sitting there with my mouth open, remembering the smell in the chapel at Westfaire. It had been the smell of magic. The same smell as in Faery.

Something she was ranting about caught my attention. "What was that, Janice?" I asked.

"We never finished it," she said. "We never finished that documentary. We tried, later, but they wouldn't let us."

LATER

Our conversation was interrupted by a phone call. It was someone in the comeback network, and Janice talked to them for
quite some time. I went in my room and took a nap. When I
woke up, hours later, it was evening. She was waiting for me
when I went into the kitchen.

"I've had some news of Jaybee," she said.

"Oh?"

"He's blind. Blind and crazy. He can't see anything, but he
thinks he does."

I shook my head at her, saying nothing. Janice drew her
face into the expression I call her holy martyr look.

"At least we can take this opportunity to cleanse ourselves
of hate," she said, staring me straight in the eye. "We are being
given a chance to forgive. We must figure out some way to take
care of him."

"We? Take care of him!"

"We comebacks must care for him. He is one of us and we
can't afford to have him talking about us."

"Talking about what?" I laughed, a little hysterically, certainly not amused. "If he's crazy, surely no one is going to believe him."

"We'd rather he doesn't talk about us at all," she said. She
gave me a sidelong look, that judging, weighing look. "When
they called this afternoon, I told them we'll take him in for the
time being."

I couldn't believe her. "He killed Bill! He raped Dorothy.
You can't be serious!"

She pursed her mouth and folded her hands. That pious,
martyred, holier-than-anybody pose. "It's just for the time being. We have Bill's room downstairs that he can stay in. You'll
be working evenings and I'm working days. The network will
pay you to look after him while I'm at work. If you're going to
pay your share of the expenses here, you'll need more pay than
the part-time work the library will give you."

"I can't be party to this," I said. "I saw what he did, and I
can't be party to it."

Janice wrung her hands, rolled her eyes, became St. Janice

facing the lions. "Either someone has to take charge of him or we have to get rid of him. I can't even consider that! I'm a religious woman. I couldn't kill him. We have to forgive him. If he was crazy, he wasn't really responsible for what he did."

"What makes you think I could control him," I said. "He's a hell of a lot bigger than I am."

"They have him on drugs," she admitted. "Enough to keep him quiet. He can take care of himself. It won't be like nursing him, or anything like that."

"I see," I said, sickened. I couldn't stay in this place if Jaybee were here. I'd end up killing him. Maybe that's what she wanted. I gave her a look, almost understanding her in that instant. Did she know what she was doing? "Give me a few days to think about it."

"No time," she commented. "I think they just drove up outside."

They had, indeed, just driven up outside, two men I had met when I was young Beauty, friends of Janice's and Bill's, with Jaybee between them, being dragged along. I was reminded of the way he had hauled Bill's body away, carelessly, dumping it in his car, driving off. I had been huddled on the floor, my clothes in shreds around me, blood on my face, blood on my hands, blood leaking between my legs, still able to see him out of the corner of the window. So I saw him now, out of the corner of the window, being dragged along. There was a bandage over his eyes.

I went to my room and got my robe on. I put Grumpkin in the pocket. Poor old cat. He was almost used to it. I put my things in the other pocket, the ones I needed. I put the boots on my feet. I heard Janice open the front door, heard her speaking in her pious, all-forgiving voice. "Poor man. Bring him in."

He came in. I went out.

Puck found me in the hotel where I had taken a room. He was panting, and he looked pale.

I asked him what was the matter.

He rubbed his face with his hands. "It's getting harder to

get here. Harder every time. When are you coming home? Carabosse wants to know, Beauty. This is getting serious."

"Does she think I'm in danger here?" I asked. I couldn't get interested in Carabosse, for some reason. "Can I still get back from here?"

"You're not in danger. Not immediately. And you can still get back, for a little while."

"Tell her soon."

.

APRIL 1993

It is easy to get on a board of directors. All one has to do is give money. Of course, getting the money out of a warrant over six hundred years old is another matter.

The House of Levi still exists, strangely enough, though under quite another name, and it still exists where I found it first, in London. Getting there from here was my first overseas flight in a plane. I chose to do it that way, remembering how thin the magic is in current time. Using the boots to go back, it gets stronger as I go. Going from place to place in the twentieth, the boots might work, but they might drop me off in mid-ocean, as well. I didn't want to risk it.

When I showed the investment house the warrant, they looked at it in disbelief. They admitted that the money had been with them all those years. One of their young men sat down and figured what it was worth, millions and millions of dollars. I had to prove my right to it, as the direct descendent of the daughter of the Duke of Monfort and Westfaire, which, thanks to the seven-league boots and enough gold to oil palms here and there, I was able to do. Puck and Fenoderee helped, rather reluctantly, and only in past time. They didn't have to come here to do it. I'm not sure they could have. But in former centuries they were able to forge parish registry entries and put false birth records among ancient files. Marriages which had never occurred were recorded. Baptisms were entered in faded ink in ancient books. Confirmation records were put there as well. And, above all, wills, passing the warrant down from generation to generation, seventeen generations in all, to the present day. To Catherine Monfort. I am an heiress. The people of the House of Levi have been considerably astonished, but they are standing behind their document, six centuries old or not.

I called Janice and offered to hire someone to look after Jaybee. Janice was so angry I could hear her voice shaking, which confirmed my suspicion that she wanted to make me responsible for Jaybee. She had transferred her dislike of Beauty —Dorothy—to this new person, me. In Janice's world, there must always be a sinner who is paying for her sin while Janice watches and judges. Since she could no longer get at Dorothy, she wanted to get at me. I was Dorothy's friend and therefore probably guilty of something. In the last analysis, it is probably her own sin she is forever expiating. I don't know what sin that was. Perhaps neither does she.

It turned out, I didn't need to hire someone to care for him. Within hours of the time I left the house on Wisdom Street, she had found another place for Jaybee.

I found an apartment in New York, and I am now on the board of directors of the International Environmental Crisis Committee, a group of very powerful persons dedicated to saving the world. They feel it is going to hell in a handbasket, and I know they're right, though I can't tell them how I know. Many of them have given millions of dollars to this effort, and so have I. I am privy to everything they are doing. They are attempting to put together a coalition of all environmental bodies, all the so-called liberal religious bodies who are more concerned with life than money, all people everywhere concerned with life on earth. We spend endless hours in meetings, trying to build coalitions, networks, trying to agree on lobbying strategies. We argue which candidates to support. I go to bed every night weary and yet unable to sleep. Grumpkin lies beside me and purrs, and eventually the sound of him lulls me into unconsciousness. Then I dream of the child named Elaine, and her mother, and the knife, and the sound of a mad voice singing "Down, down, down," and I wake up again.

.

JANUARY 1994

Almost three hundred species of flora and fauna have gone extinct since I gave my first dollar to IECC. On the front page of the newspaper tonight is the announcement of a Mother of the Year Award, given to a mother of eleven children. I wonder what Father Raymond would say? Her eleven children can eat hamburger made from cows who were fed the ephemeral grass that comes after rainforest is cut and burned. They can breathe the already polluted air. They can look forward to growing up and having spaces of their own in the new prefabricated apartment houses now being built in Japan which give each renter one hundred fifty square feet. The article about the apartments says all the conveniences are built in. Bill's apartment in the hive in the twenty-first had one hundred square feet. There isn't far to go.

.

MARCH 1994

Puck has been back several times, begging me to come home, each time more frantically. I might as well have gone. There is no point in my staying here. There was never any point. Carabosse must have known that. She knew it was too late. I felt I had to try.

We have been thwarted at every turn by god. Not the real God. A false one which has been set up by man to expedite his destruction of the earth. He is the gobble-god who bids fair to swallow everything in the name of a totally selfish humanity. His ten commandments are me first (let me live as I please), humans first (let all other living things die for my benefit), sperm first (no birth control), birth first (no abortions), males first (no women's rights), my culture/tribe/language/religion first (separatism/terrorism), my race first (no human rights), my politics first (lousy liberals/rotten reactionaries), my country first (wave the flag, the flag, the flag), and, above all, profit first.

We worship the gobble-god. We burn forests in his name.

We kill whales and dolphins in his name. We pave prairies in his name. We have retarded babies in his name. We sell drugs in his name. We set bombs in his name. We worship him everywhere. We call him by different titles and commit blasphemies in the name of worship.

We were given magic to use in creating wonder, and the gobble-god has sucked it dry. His followers reject mystery and madness and marvel. They cannot tolerate questions. They can believe any answer, no matter how false, so long as it is a certainty nailed firmly onto the cross of money. They yearn for the rapture to come, without knowing they have killed rapture forever. Fidipur is what is to come, and the Holy One, Blessed be He, will not forgive mankind for that.

LATER

I called Fenoderee or Puck. I sat on the side of my bed and called them. Neither of them came. After a long, long time, I heard a faint, far voice calling my name. "Not enough," it said. "Not enough magic."

I may have trapped myself. If I am to try and get back, it must be now. There is nothing I can do to stop things. I've spent the last few days turning money into gold and gems—gems mostly, they're lighter—and what antique coins of the period the dealers have on hand. I made up a story about a costume party and had a couple of outfits made, plain, wool, fourteenth-century style, wimple, veils, shoes. It took me an hour to find this book and Mama's box and my cloak and boots where I'd hidden them when I moved into this apartment. I've sewn the gems into the seams of the cloak. I keep thinking I'm hearing things, someone here with me. Grumpkin is in my pocket with the coins. We're going to try.

24

I didn't think the first jump moved me at all. I was looking at my watch, thinking the date would have moved significantly. After a moment, I realized the first jump had only taken me back two minutes. I didn't look around. I was standing next to the desk where a previous me was sitting, writing, and I knew the other me was there, at the desk. I didn't dare look. I fixed my eyes on the floor and walked into the next room before I tried again. The second jump moved me four minutes, the third a little over eight. I hadn't been in the kitchen all evening, so I went in there in order not to run into myself. The fourth jump took me back half an hour. The fifth a little over two hours. I lost count of how many it took to get me to the sixteen hundreds where the magic was strong enough to bring me back all the way. The huge mound of Westfaire looms against the stars. The smell of magic is strong. The smell of trees is like wine. I'm going to lie down wrapped in my cloak and sleep. I'm very tired, very sore. I feel very old.

LATER: SHORTLY AFTER DAWN
I look very old, at least my hands and arms do. Luckily, I had a good haircut shortly before I left, and that seems to have stayed with me. So did my manicure, nail sealer, no polish. My new clothes fit. I haven't lost any more weight, at least. I'm just a nicely groomed, quite-old woman, miles from anywhere. I have no idea what year it is. Grumpkin was hungry so he caught a mouse or mole, something small and gray, and ate it. He didn't offer to share it. It's all right. I have protein crackers in my pocket, enough to last several days. Someone is bound to come along, sooner or later.

["She's back," I said inadequately.
"So I see," said Israfel. He was as weary as I. "Do you think she'll go back there again?"

"No. She's done everything she can do. You were right. It's grown into her. The two of them have become one thing, and she when she fought for it, she was fighting for her own life. I can't blame her. I'd have done the same."

"What do we do now?"

"Let her alone for a while. While we try to see what's going to happen next."

"She looks very frail. I could send a cart, at least."

"Do that. Send a cart."]

ST. CYRIL'S DAY, MAY, YEAR OF OUR LORD 1417

A cart came by midmorning, driven by a tinkerish sort of man, with a blowsy woman and several snot-nosed children along. I begged a ride, offering him a halfpenny, which he respected. I was glad of that, not wanting to use magic unless it was absolutely necessary. It was he, the tinker, who told me the year. Fifty years have passed since I was last here. Seventy since the curse fell on Westfaire. By the count of elapsed years, I am eighty-six. There must be some kind of rule in travel of this sort. It doesn't seem to be the lived time that counts, but some other chronological measure. I don't feel eighty-six. Or as I imagine eighty-six should feel!

Elly's daughter, my granddaughter, will be a middle-aged woman, possibly with children of her own. I will introduce myself as an elderly aunt. A wealthy, elderly aunt. Wealthy relatives are always easier to take. That is, if I can find her. If the little kingdom is still there. The tinker says there has been no plague for a considerable time. Still, there may have been a war. Indeed, there is a war. The war that was going on when I was a girl is still going on. The English against the French. Our King trying to take lands there, or reclaim lands there, or hold onto lands there. Their King trying to drive us out, or keep us out. One would think someone could put an end to it, though as I recall from references I picked up in the twentieth, it is to go on for decades yet.

Henry V is King. He will not be king long, poor boy. Edward III was King when I left in 1350. He was succeeded by his grandson, Richard II, and he by his cousin, Henry IV, and he by his son. This current King Henry will die of a flux of the bowels in France, and his son will die in the Tower, having spent a good deal of time, on and off, as a madman. However, Henry Five's widow will have a grandson who will be Henry VII, and it is all very interesting and complicated. I must be careful not to mention any of this lest I seem to prognosticate. According to the tinker, they are still burning poor old women whenever some busybody gets a gnat up her ass and thinks she's been bewitched. I must also be careful not to seem a Lollard. They are also burning Lollards. I'm not sure I remember what Lollards are. I mean, I know what they are but not the things one must not say if one doesn't want to appear to be one, and I am afraid to appear heretically ignorant if I ask.

The other interesting thing the tinker had to say is that the peasants have left the land and gone searching for better pay. I had read about that, but it all seemed frightfully unlikely. Now, here, seeing the vacant fields, I can tell it has really happened. The nobles have tried to put a stop to it, of course, but it's done no good. It used to be that a man could not leave the land, for there would be no place for him elsewhere. Every lord had his own serfs and little need for more. Now, however, the Black Death has killed so many that there are places begging for any good man. Well, I remember that from Wellingford, from the Dower House. It was hard, even then, to get anything done, and the Death has been back several times since then. Strange, isn't it. Men are more valued when there are fewer of us. Which is what I tried to tell them back in the twentieth. Which is what Puck said, too.

The tinker is a youngish man, but he has traveled these roads since he was a child. All Wellingford is empty now, he says. He does not know where the people went who used to live there. He remembers hearing of the King and Queen who were driven from their home over the seas, but he doesn't remember where that home might have been. He will take me within a very short distance of East Sawley Mill, which still stands, and there I will ask about to see if anyone remembers.

ST. JUSTIN, MARTYR, FIRST DAY OF JUNE, YEAR OF OUR LORD 1417

I got down from the cart in front of an inn. What passes for an inn in these times. Outside it, sitting on a bench, was a straight, slender old man chatting with a friend. When he saw me standing there in the road alone, he came forward to offer his assistance.

He looked at me for a long time. I felt dizzy from that look. "Catherine?" he asked. "It is Catherine, isn't it?"

For a moment I didn't know him. When I did, I felt everything whirling, like a tornado of feeling, swirling me around with it. "Giles? Oh, Giles. Is it Giles? But, you're dead. They told me you were dead!"

He held me, and for that moment I was thirty again. My heart was as strong as it had ever been and that instant became an eternity for me. He wasn't dead. Giles wasn't dead. He knew me when he saw me, though I cannot imagine how. He called me by the name he knew me by, Catherine. He put his hand out to touch my face, and he smiled, as though he had expected me. He told me he had expected me every day for the past fifty years. He said he has thought about me every day during all that time, and he knew I was somehow his own lost Beauty come back to him.

I cried when he said this. I cry every time I think about it. We are of an age. He is still straight as a lance, though his stride is shorter than I remember and he does not see as well as once he did. His hair is as white as mine, but it is still full and soft and falls over his forehead as once it did. I wept and begged to know what had happened to him, and he told me a tale of being waylaid by an impress gang, one of whom he had killed, defending himself, before he was overpowered and dragged away. It was that man who had been buried beside the road.

I told him I had gone there and laid flowers on the place, and he laughed, saying I was the only one to grieve over that ruffian. Because the horse was there, with the king's arms upon it, the witness had not considered it might be one of the gang who had died rather than the man they had assaulted.

The impress gang was working for a merchantman who had a royal contract to carry supplies to France and not enough men to man the ships. They kept Giles for months, sailing back and forth across the channel, and when he escaped at last, I was gone. He had dwelt here about East Sawley since, he said, waiting for me to return, knowing that I would.

"If I'd known you were here, I'd have come long ago," I told him. And I would have. I'd have come long, long ago.

"After what had passed between us, no little wait seemed at all worrisome," he said. "I have lived all my life in the memory of those three nights."

What can any woman say to that? I went into the privy behind the inn and wiped my face, telling myself I'd been a fool to go to the twentieth for vengeance sake when I could have stayed for love's sake, a fool to stay there for pride's sake, thinking there was anything I could do. But then, I never said I was not a fool.

When I spoke of them, Giles remembered the little royals, and he also remembered the name of their kingdom: Ponte Marvella, somewhere in the high mountains where Aragon and Navarre and France come together in a tangle. I told him about Elly marrying the prince and their having a daughter, my granddaughter. He says he will come with me to find her. Here we are, two old pots, though seemingly fairly hale for all that, going off over the seas. The boots would have taken us there in a moment, but now that he is with me we will travel as other persons do, to see the sights. Giles might not like the idea of the boots. Explanations would be complicated, and perhaps too risky. He loves me for what he thinks I am. So I will try to be what he thinks I am.

Giles has taken some of my smaller gems to turn into coin. He will hire a conveyance to take us to Bristol, a three day's journey. Once there, I can have a few more gowns made. The styles have changed somewhat. More people are speaking English, though it sounds very strange to me, because of all the accents clashing up against one another. Before the Death, no one traveled that much. Now everyone moves about, going and coming, here and there. The vowels slide about with the speakers, some say *ae* and some *ai* and some *ao*. It is almost easier to read lips. Giles says some years ago the Parliament attempted to make English the official language, but the lawyers all refused, saying they couldn't argue in it. Pish. Even in the twentieth they say that! They spend their careers making up words so no one will know what they're talking about! If lawyers had to write in plain English, nine-tenths of them would be out of work!

ST. BONIFACE'S DAY, JUNE 5, YEAR OF OUR LORD 1417
Bristol. The only rooms we could find here are in the pilgrim hostel. There are no ships. King Henry has commandeered them all to carry his army to Normandy. There are pilgrims waiting who have been waiting for weeks, running about each time they hear a rumor that some new ship may have come into port. Remembering Papa, I said something to Giles about such travel being of little use, and he hushed me. Lollards disapprove of pilgrimage, and speaking so may make people think I am a Lollard. I asked Giles, in a whisper, what Lollards are, meaning what are they like, and he told me they are followers first of John Wycliffe, who translated the Bible into English, much to the annoyance of the priests, and later of Sir John Oldcastle, who was condemned for heresy but escaped the Tower and plotted against the King's life. Though his followers were caught and executed, the man himself remains at large.

As to what they believe, Giles says, to my dismay, they believe much as I do. They doubt the efficacy of the sacraments because they are magical, which is just what Puck said. Lollards read the scriptures in English, which I have done for years. They consider works to be as important as faith, and the pursuit of relics to be wasteful of money that could be used to relieve suffering. It is obvious I must not talk about religion or I will be taken as a heretic. I must be still and rather pious appearing. Giles is worried about me. I can tell from the way he strokes my hand when we sit outside the hostel in the evening, drinking a little watered wine and wondering if a ship will arrive tomorrow.

I remember the feelings we had on the terrace that night, that last night we were together. They are as clear in my mind as the sound of the bell from the monastery. I can remember each shudder of delight, each spasm of ecstasy, and yet my body sits calmly while I remember. My mind knows, but my body does not mind.

I told Giles what I was remembering and asked if he ever feels that urgency. He says he felt it last many years ago, remembering me. He remembers it still, sometimes, in dreams. In recent years, the greatest urgency he feels is early in the morning when he must get up quickly or risk wetting his bed.

Perhaps it was the way he said it. We laughed until our sides hurt.

CORPUS CHRISTI DAY

A procession in honor of the Blessed Sacrament came winding through the streets today. Outside the hostel a crazy woman had a fit when she saw it and had to be dragged away, screaming and yelling. I am told her name is Margery Kempe. In the twentieth they would probably give the poor thing tranquilizers and put her to bed, but in this time she is quite notorious. She goes on incessant pilgrimages, falling continually into these hysterical fits, and she has evidently been doing so for years. While there is no doubt she is seriously disturbed, she is also quite lucky about getting where she wants to go. At least, so Giles and I have been told. If we want to get to Aquitaine, it is suggested we keep close watch on Margery Kempe, as she will probably find a ship before the rest of us do. She wants to go to Santiago de Compostela, which is not far from where we want to go.

LATER

A ship has come in from Brittany and is loading for a journey to Coruna, in Spain. The madwoman has bought passage upon it, and so have we. Now the other pilgrims are muttering among themselves, plotting to keep the madwoman from embarking with us, as, so they say, her doing so is a sure invitation to disaster, storm at sea, shipwreck, and all manner of terrors. They have accused her of being a Lollard, so the authorities tell her she must go to Henbury to be examined by the bishop. The other pilgrims hope a wind will come up while she is gone, so they may depart without her.

LATER

Margery is staying with the bishop at his home in Henbury. Evidently he knew her father. There has been no wind.

THREE DAYS LATER

Still no wind. The pilgrims are beginning to regret their hostility. I heard one say today there would be no wind until Margery Kempe returned, that no matter what the pilgrims may think, God is with her.

LATER

We have been waiting ten days for wind. This morning Margery Kempe arrived, escorted by the bishop's retainers, and with her came a stiff breeze. There is no satisfying some people! Now the pilgrims assert she is a witch who can summon storm, and they threaten to throw her overboard if there is not a calm passage. I do not know what power Margery has, but I am tired of this nonsense. Mama taught me how to handle such matters. We will have a calm passage no matter how much I must weary myself in assuring so.

LATER

We have had four days of sailing south in light weather. Grumpkin has much enjoyed the ship. There has been good mousing, and the sailors approve of him heartily. The pilgrims have been put ashore here at Coruna, where some will go overland and some will take smaller boats down the coast to the port slightly nearer Compostela. Once there, they will ascend into the city, into the great Romanesque church where they can kiss the statue of St. James and receive the title "Pilgrim to St. James." I know all about it. Papa described it to all of us, over and over. It was Santiago Matamoros that most interested Papa, St. James the Moor Killer. Poor Papa. He did want to do something brave and dedicated against the infidel, but it never really worked out.

I told Giles there was no hurry in finding my grandchild and asked him if he wanted to go to Compostela, but he said no. He is no more interested than I in parts of people's dead bodies, saints or not. Saints' bodies are supposed to be incorruptible, but Giles says he has seen mice dried up in a grain sack who were also uncorrupted. We giggle, like naughty children. Old people find odd things funny. He told me about a time during those years we were apart, when he was in Italy to pick up a cargo which included a crate of relics. He was sent to the workshop where they were created, and there he saw them making miraculous shrouds.

"The workman smeared a naked man with flaxseed oil and wine lees," he said, "then the man lay down on a linen strip and it was folded over him and patted gently to take the print of his face and body. Then they hauled him up, without messing the print on the cloth, and put the cloth in the sun. When it had been in the sun for a time, they brushed off the dry lees and it was like a painting."

"Who was he supposed to be?" I asked.

"Oh," said Giles, "he was all different saints. In the crate I took back to the ship there was one shroud of St. Stephen, with lots of arrow wounds painted on afterward, and at least half a dozen of Christ. It was enough to make a man sceptical."

Well, since he does not wish to go to Campostela, we will stay on the ship for another few days as it runs along the south shore of the Bay of Biscay to Bayonne, where we will disembark to begin our search for Marvella. Bayonne, so everyone says, is as English as Bristol. We have had it ever since Eleanor married King Henry II, except for a brief time when the French took it back during the long war, while I was away. Despite our people being thoroughly familiar with the area, they do not seem to be familiar with Ponte Marvella. No one knows where it is. The captain of this ship has heard of it, but he has never been there. Certain other of the travelers aboard have heard of it. They have never been there. Surely in one of the larger ports near the mountains, someone will know how we can reach the kingdom where my granddaughter must be, by now, a plump and contented matron. Unless she was long ago married off to some petty kinglet. I hadn't thought of that before! She may not be there at all! Well, if she is not, we will go where she is. I hope it may be by horseback or in a carriage. Otherwise, I must use the boots, and we are having such a sweet and gentle time without.

JULY

While we search for someone to guide us to Marvella (and our quest so far has met with no success), I am enjoying seeing what is available in the shops. I have bought a warm mantle woven from the fine wool of Spanish sheep, as well as an illuminated book by one Christine de Pisan, *The Treasure of the City of Ladies,* which the bookseller highly recommends. He claims that his copyist is unable to keep up with the demand for this volume, though it is difficult to say why, since it is directed at "princesses," by which the author means the daughters of kings, princes, and dukes. Though she spares a word for women of lesser rank (including some of no rank at all!), her audience is to be found mainly among the nobility. Perhaps there are more of us than there seem to be. Or perhaps I have not been traveling in the proper circles.

At any rate, Christine reminds me very much of Miss Manners. I always read Miss Manners in the twentieth. Christine explains how to be polite and kindly and keep everyone happy and oneself in good odor with the world. It is a pity it was not written until a dozen years ago. If I had had this book in 1347, it would have told me at once what Weasel-Rabbit was up to.

SUMMER: ON THE ROAD FROM LOURDES

I have lost track of what day it is. Not that it matters. It is not so late in the season that I am concerned about the onset of bad weather. The land we are traversing is hospitable and not unlike home. There are fields and hedgerows and gentle rains and much burgeoning growth. We are ascending beside the torrent of the Pau, having not long ago left the town and castle of Lourdes, to turn toward the mountain called "Lost," which, considering what are going through to find Marvella, is not badly named. Pica Perdido, it is called. It is quite high, but we are not going to the top.

In Bayonne, we met with scepticism, not to say outright doubt, when we told guides and equipage purveyors that we wished to go to Ponte Marvella. No one knew how to get there. We spoke of it in English; we spoke of it in French. No one had ever been there. Finally, as we were about to give up in despair during the third or fourth day of quite concentrated effort—at our age it takes concentration to keep doing things over and over—a man presented himself to us and, speaking with a strange accent, told us he could guide us. He is, the French say, a Basque. His name is Echevaria, or Eskavaria, or some such. He speaks a language which no one else in the world speaks unless that person is another Basque. It does not derive from Latin, as does normal speech. It is not related to the languages of the heathen. It has no words in common with other European tongues. Eskavaria says it is the language used by the angels when they helped God make the world, the language of Eden, from which all Basques came directly. He was laughing at me, of course. I thought of teaching him it is unwise to laugh at one who is half fairy, but he is pleasant enough otherwise, so why make a fuss. Besides, he is a very little man, not four feet tall. He reminds me of Bill except that he is less childlike. He is not a dwarf, as my father's fool was. He is simply very small.

As to what he was doing in Bayonne, he did not say. He did say we could take a carriage to the town of Lourdes, not a very great town in this century, on the River Pau. In Lourdes, the river becomes a torrent, plunging down from the heights of the mountains. There, he told us, we would take horses and ride up beside the plunging water toward the highest peak, the "lost one." It is named "lost" in Spanish, that is, Perdido, but not in Basque. In Basque they call it something else. Halfway up the mountain, we will turn aside, so he says, along a valley, and in that valley is the principality of Marvella.

"Not a kingdom?" I asked. I had thought the prince's father was a king.

"It's maybe ten miles long. It's maybe three or four miles wide," Eskavaria replied. "There's two villages and a castle. It has some cows, some sheep, some goats, a few horses. I don't know is it a kingdom, or a duchy, or something else. What I hear them call it is a principality. Whatever it is, it's very small."

"You have never been there," guessed Giles.

"True," said Eskavaria, "but I been close."

"Why haven't you gone there if you've been close?" Giles wanted to know.

Eskavaria shook his head and gave us a half smile. "Perhaps when you get close, you'll decide not to go there." It sounded almost like a recommendation.

Thus far we have done almost everything that Eskavaria has recommended. We took a carriage to Lourdes. Most of the time, Grumpkin rode on top, with the driver. We spent a day sightseeing in the town. The river is very dramatic, as is the new castle set high above it. The next day we bought five horses, three for us and two to carry our supplies, and the day after that we started up the mountain. Grumpkin rides in a basket on one of the packhorses. They are small animals, scarcely larger than ponies, but they are sturdy. Because they are small, they are easier for me to ride than a big horse would be. My legs don't bend as well as they used to. Sidesaddle is actually easier than astride. Except for that, we get along well enough, Giles and I. We are brittle. We ache. But we get along. The early morning is the hardest. That and trying to get comfortable in our blankets at night. Eskavaria is so small he curls up as Grumpkin does.

Days we simply ride, hearing the marmots whistle, hearing the rocks rattle as herds of chamois flee from our horses. The marmots are very curious. They stand on their hind legs and wriggle their noses at us as we pass. Grumpkin stares at them and yawns, thinking them too large for prey and too impudent for acquaintance.

LATER

I asked Eskavaria what day it was. He doesn't know. He neither reads nor writes. He says no one writes in his language. I recall reading of the Basques back in the twentieth, but I don't remember a thing about the language or the people. All I can recall is something about a separatist movement from Spain with some of the terrorism separatists seem to consider requisite. I asked Eskavaria if he had ever blown anyone up, and he seemed quite shocked at the idea.

I have been reading more of the *City of Ladies* book. Christine would have frowned on my love for Giles. She talks of foolish love affairs and says, "If it happens that some young princess or highborn lady is so lacking in knowledge or constancy that she is unable, does not know how, or does not wish to resist the appeals of the man who is trying to attract her by various signs and gestures (as men well know how to do) . . ."

The only sign Giles ever gave me was the love in his eyes. The only sign I ever gave him was to blush when he looked at me, and for that Father Raymond sent him away. Christine would have approved of that. But she would not have approved of me. She has decided views on the conduct of virgins. When I was a virgin, I was argumentative and outspoken, which she deplores. I enjoyed eating entirely too much. And she says I should simply have relied upon Papa to have arranged a marriage for me, and should never have mentioned it to him or even have thought about it on my own. Her idea of a proper virgin is a bloodless one, I think. It's obvious that Christine de Pisan did not have Faery in mind at all when she wrote this book! That, or feminism.

I wonder what she would have done if a clock fairy and a putative angel had sunk some burning seed beneath her breast? Repudiated it, no doubt.

Oh, sometimes I wish I could.

LATER

About midmorning today we saw smoke rising over a ridge to our right. "Marvella," said Eskavaria, pointing.

"Do you speak their language?" I asked him, suddenly aware that we might not be able to communicate. Though that was a silly thought. I had communicated well enough with them when they were in England.

Eskavaria confirmed this. "They speak French," he said. "Or Spanish. Or English. They're not my people."

He left us at the ridge. Or rather, he stayed while we came on. He told us he would watch for us there, to guide us back. One day. Five. Ten. Whatever it took.

Giles thought it was strange he would not come with us.

As we started down into the valley, I smelled magic, and

knew why it was Eskavaria hadn't come. He might not know what it was, but he sensed the presence of it. This had a hot, wet smell, like metal doused in the forge. This was not merely magic, but something worse than that.

.
25
.

As we rode down into the valley, people looked up at us curiously from the fields. Some came to the road and wandered along beside us, feeling of our shoes, staring at the cat. We told the people we were travelers, going over the mountains to Spain. They spoke a kind of French-Spanish-English mix, which Giles and I could halfway comprehend, though evidently we did not speak it well enough to be clearly understood. Some of our followers ran on to tell others, and soon we had a crowd of them at our heels. Peasant people, ordinary people. Several quite good looking men. No women more than ordinary in appearance. A boy herding geese. A girl with a piglet in her arms. Men who had been cutting hay.

We asked if there were somewhere we could stay for the night. They pointed. We looked up to see the castle perched above us, on a crag. Oh no, we said, we're just ordinary travelers. And they smiled and pointed, pushing us, leading us, dragging the ponies along. Evidently we were to go there, like it or not. I looked at Giles, seeing nothing in his face but pleasant expectation. There was sweat along my forehead, next to my hair, but I kept smiling. Looking back the way we had come, I realized we could have seen the castle all along. If we had been looking for it.

I leaned over and whispered to Giles. "When we are asked for our names, old friend, do not be surprised at what I say."

He gave me a curious look, but nodded. I had originally

planned to introduce myself as Lady Catherine of Monfort, the name I had used when negotiating Elly's marriage. Now, something told me it would be better not to claim any former acquaintance with the prince or his daughter. Not until I knew how things stood.

The climb was a hard one. The ponies were sweating heavily when we arrived. Someone rang a bell at the high wooden gates. Someone kissed my hand and gave me a flower. Then they were gone, off down the hillside, chattering with one another, pleased at having delivered us. The gate opened and we were welcomed within. A chamberlain saw to us. He and a couple of serving men. He spoke French, and so did we. He asked if the cat could be taken to the stable, and I said no, it would stay with me. He asked if we were man and wife, and when I said not, he sniffed and escorted us to separate rooms. He told us the servants would bring bathwater. He said the Princess would welcome us at supper.

I laid my hand on his arm as he was ready to depart and said, "A moment. Long ago, I believe I met the ruling family of your realm." It seemed a neutral word, realm, since I did not know what kind of place it was. "The prince had just come of age. It was in England."

He raised his eyebrows at me.

"Is that family still here?"

"Prince Charme?" he asked.

I smiled.

"And his consort," the chamberlain said. "Princess Ilene." He said it *Ee-lay-nay*.

"His daughter?" I asked.

"He has no daughter," the man said.

"Never? Never had a daughter?"

"No children. Not in twenty years," he said. "I have been here that long."

"I am mistaken then," I smiled, trying not to weep. "It was another family." How many Prince Charmings could there be? More than one, obviously.

The chamberlain was as good as his word about the bathwater, and I soaked in the heat of it, letting it take away some of the soreness of the long ride. He sent a maid to see to our clothes. I had already hidden my cloak and boots away, under the bed. I wanted no foreign maidservants playing about with those. When time came for the meal, he sent a footman to escort us down the stairs and into the hall of the castle. Not the great hall, which we passed through on the way, but a smaller one, paneled in dark wood, with numerous candles, a fire blazing, and many trophies of the hunt hung in the high shadows near the cross-beamed ceiling. A dozen men and women, earls of this and countesses of that, introduced themselves and asked us about our journey. Though some of the men were quite handsome, all of the women were remarkably plain. The chamberlain came to the door and announced His Serene Highness, Prince Charme of Marvella; Her Serene Highness, Princess Ilene. We wouldn't use their names, of course. They would be called, "Your Highness, this," "Your Highness, that." She might be called "ma'am." They made their way slowly across the room toward us, stopping to speak to each of the other guests as they came. Each man bowed deeply, each woman curtsied.

He was much as I remembered him, sweet-faced, rather feminine-looking, though he now had a little gray beard and moustache to cover his gentle mouth and a little tummy to cover his gemmed belt. He was considerably fatter, much softer looking, much, much older. His eyelids made sad little swags of wrinkled flesh, hiding his eyes.

She was taller than he, very regal, very handsome, with a strange, exotic beauty, like a tiger. No. More like a serpent. Sleek. Also deadly. Her hair was dark, rising from a widow's peak to make a double bow of her forehead, a line completed by her pointed chin to make a narrow heart shape. She wore a close fitting gown of blood-colored damask. Her face could have been twenty-five, her body younger yet. Her eyes were several hundred. I thought of Queen Mab and knew that what I saw was not what was really there, then I carefully blanked out that thought and assumed the much excited smile of an elderly woman who was, oh, gracious mercy, right here in the room with royalty and all.

They came up to us. I curtsied. Lord, how long had it been

since I had curtsied? My old bones barely made it. Giles bowed.
He did it very nicely. He'd had more practice than I, so much
was obvious. The chamberlain announced the names we had
given. Lady Lavender of Westfaire. Sir Giles of Sawley. It no
longer mattered what people called me. Beauty. Dorothy. Catherine. Lavender. I'll be borrowing Aunt Comfrey's name next.
Though I had no sure reason why, I urgently did not want this
woman to know who I really was. Or what I really was.

"We are pleased to welcome you to Marvella," said the
Prince. His wrinkled eyelids rose, exposing his tender soul. Like
a quivering oyster.

"We are greatly pleased to be so charmingly welcomed," I
murmured. "We had not expected such hospitality."

"We have so few visitors," purred the Princess. "So little
news of the outside world." She looked me up and down, noting
the good though plain fabric of my gown—one of those I'd had
made in Bristol before we left—the simplicity of my wimple and
veil. I knew how I looked. Inoffensive. Her eyes cleared. I was
an acceptable dinner guest and nothing to worry about. She
gave Giles a quick look and dismissed him, as well. Too old, her
eyes said. Not worth the effort.

I felt his hand tremble on my arm. He had caught her look,
and it angered him. Well, it had angered me, as well.

We were seated near the middle of the long table, guests
but not honored guests. So much the better. I would not have
enjoyed conversing with the Princess. Or with the Prince. We
ate a salmi of duckling, fresh fruit, roast venison, bananas
(grown, so the Prince said, in the conservatory), salad, river
salmon, and finally a soup of almonds and chicken and lemons. I
asked my table companion to my left, an aged baron, if dinners
in Marvella always ended with soup and was told that they did.
"Always with something warm and liquid, to fill any holes previously unfilled, my dear." I remembered a dinner I had eaten
when I was young, in Chinanga, with Don Masimiliano. Had
that been any less real than this?

We drank wine. I watered mine and kicked Giles, on my
right, until he watered his. My left-hand companion was
watching me closely, and I murmured something about no

longer having the head for wine we had had in our younger years. He was as white headed as I, so we talked about that.

"I've outlived all my generation," he mumbled. "Charme's father, Prince William, was younger than I by a couple of years, but I outlived my half brother."

I had heard his name and title, but had not made the connection. "You're His Highness's uncle," I said. "I'm sorry, I didn't realize . . ."

"Nothing to realize. Uncles don't count for much. Especially half uncles. Prince William was my younger half brother. Our mother was a widow when she married Charme's grandfather, Prince Enrico. No, no," he waved the young squire away who was trying to pour more wine into his cup. "Go give it to the Prince, he needs it worse than I."

I decided to risk it. "I met the His Highness's parents. Years ago, in England."

"During the Usurpation," he nodded, putting a capital letter on it. "The usurper was my older brother, Richard. Richard and I were never in the line of succession, but Richard liked to pretend to have royal blood. Mama didn't have that. All she had was wealth she'd inherited when our father died. We were babies when Mama married Prince Enrico. Then she bore William, the heir apparent. Richard and I more or less grew up with William. He was the only proper heir, but after Prince Enrico died, Richard stirred up a bunch of malcontents and overthrew the throne.

"William and his wife and the boy fled to England. After they'd been gone a while, and after Richard started passing tax laws right and left, everyone here in Marvella realized what they'd allowed to happen, so they hanged Richard from a gibbet down in the market square and begged William to come home. He did, him and his wife and Prince Charme and the little girl. I felt very lucky to keep my neck unstretched, though everyone knew I'd told Richard he was a fool."

"Little girl?" I asked, trying to keep my voice only politely interested while my heart thudded away in a fit.

"Charme's daughter. Galantha. Beautiful little girl," he sighed. "She was about ten when William died. Charme ascended the throne, of course, and everyone was after him to get married again and produce an heir. Put it off a couple of years before he finally married Ilene. Not long after that the little girl got lost in the mountains. Eaten by beasts, they say. No one mentions her anymore, as hearing her name upsets His Highness."

"He's been married to Ilene for how long?" I asked. Giles, next to me, was listening to this conversation with great interest.

"Oh, it would be thirty-some-odd years now, wouldn't it? He was twenty or so when he came back. Around thirty-two when he ascended the throne. He must be seventy now. I'm almost ninety, which is a dreadful great age for a man."

"His wife looks very young," I said, casually, as though it didn't matter.

"Holds her looks," he agreed. "I'm told her family always has held its looks."

"A neighboring kingdom?" I suggested.

He snorted. "Marvella has no neighboring kingdoms, Lady Lavender. Except maybe Nadenada, and it's not really neighboring. We're a what-you-call-it, a holdover, a survival. Some crusader did a favor for the King of Aragon, I think it was, or maybe the King of Navarre. Whoever-it-was rewarded him by making him hereditary Prince of cowplop and sheepclip. The main road over the mountains is that way," and he waved toward the west, opposite to the direction we'd arrived from. "People used to have to hire porters to carry them down into the gorge, across the river, then up the other side. Prince William used Mama's money to build a marvelous bridge across the gorge, and now Ponte Marvella makes its living charging tolls. From pilgrims, mostly. Going down from France to Santiago." He sighed heavily. "I told Richard when he started all the fuss that if he wanted to risk his life taking over something, it should at least be something worth taking. Marvella isn't much."

I saw Ilene's eyes fixed on my aged informer, a tiny frown between her brows. He was talking too much, too intently, so I laughed with great vivacity, as though he had told me a funny

story. Her glance went on past, like the course of a comet, burning ice.

We drank wine. We ate fruit and nuts. We retired to another
room and played at cards for a time. The cards were from Ger-
many and were printed, unlike the painted ones I was accustomed to in that time. The Prince enthusiastically told me how
it was done, how the blocks of wood were carved and then
painted with ink and pressed onto the paper. I wondered if
Gutenberg was at this moment playing at games and being in-
spired by the unknown carver of playing cards. Printing would
be invented very shortly, and one thing always led to another. I
put the thought down resolutely and paid attention to my hand.

We learned a Spanish game in which players put together
"bodies," that is combinations of six cards making up a head,
two arms, two legs, and a torso, and then cried *"Hombre"* to the
others as they put down the man entire. It wasn't unlike
rummy, which I had played with Bill in the twentieth, so I
learned it rapidly. Giles caught on very quickly, too, and I was
glad to see that he had the same sense I did that it would not be
wise for either of us to win anything at all from the Princess.

Christine de Pisan hadn't covered the subject of manners
around royalty, but Aunt Lavender had. No one could leave
until the Prince and Princess left, and they seemed determined
to spend the night taking everyone's money. At last the Prince
yawned, everyone stood up, and the royal couple departed. One
of the earls fluttered about settling accounts. I paid what we had
lost, only enough to be polite, no large amount. I said good night
to the baron, my dinner companion, who was half asleep in his
chair by the fire, then Giles and I went up to our rooms, where
yawning servants waited our arrival and tankards of wash water
steamed gently before the fires. I told the maidservant she could
go on to bed, that I'd take care of myself after I had taken my
cat out. She did not like to let me go alone, but I insisted, and
when she had gone I put on my cloak, with Grumpkin in the
pocket, and let myself out an unlocked side door.

I waited about near the stables while Grumpkin found a
place that suited him. When he had finished, he went back in
my pocket while we strolled about, seeing what was to be seen.

All the lights in the castle were out except in one squatty tower, which was so close to the precipice it seemed to hang over it, like a vulture perched on a branch. The tower abutted the flat roof of the castle, so I slipped on the boots—when I wasn't wearing them, I habitually kept them in the deep pocket of my cloak—and went there in one step, interested in knowing who was still up, and why.

The room opened upon the roof through a casement window which stood ajar. Inside the Princess sat at a table brushing her hair. Her maid was putting her clothes away in the press. When the maid had finished with the clothing, she poured a cup of wine for her mistress and went away, shutting the heavy door behind her. The Princess got up and bolted the door. Interesting, I thought, wondering what interruption she feared. Certainly none from Prince Charming. I had seen no indication he would be inclined to invade her privacy. He had scarcely looked at her during the evening.

After a time the Princess stood up, walked to the far side of the room, and removed a veil or hanging of some kind. I saw her hand pulling the veil away, but I could not see what it had covered.

I inched closer to the low, crenelated parapet, which was the only thing between me and the valley floor, a quite dangerous distance below. By craning my neck, I got a better view of her. She was standing naked in front of a tall mirror with wiverns carved about the frame. I had never seen a mirror that size in the fourteenth or fifteenth. I didn't know they could make flat glass that size. The Princess put her hands out, beautiful hands, then stroked them down her face, and intoned:

> *"Lord within the glass, declare!*
> *Lord, who holds my beauty thrall:*
> *you have made me passing fair;*
> *am I fairest of them all?"*

A face formed in the glass. A dark face. Not dark in the sense of color, but dark in the sense of being hidden. It did not really show itself. It merely hinted at being. Despite this, I recognized it. It was Jaybee's face. Not precisely his, but the paradigm of what his face was and meant in its totality. Seeing it, I could say, "This is the pattern from which Jaybee's face was made." When the voice came, it matched the face, full of a mocking, horrid laughter.

> *"One time you were, and then were not,*
> *but now are fairest once again,*
> *while she whose beauty is forgot*
> *sleeps on among her little men.*
> *Snow white of skin, and black of hair,*
> *with gentle lips flushed sweetly red;*
> *full long has she lain sleeping there,*
> *with all believing she is dead."*

The Princess made a gesture, a stroking of herself, breast to hip, approving herself. She tilted her head, to get a better look at the line of her throat. "Full long she sleeps," she cried in a jubilant voice. "Oh, long time, yes. And will, forever."

In the mirror the dreadful being smiled and glanced my way. I gasped. Beneath my breastbone something flared into life, aware of deadly danger. My foot slipped on the roof, making a sound. The Princess whirled, like a great hunting creature, eyes wide, ears pricked. "Boots," I whispered, "take me to my room."

I was there! I slipped the cloak beneath the bed and myself into it with Grumpkin beside me, pulling my wimple off as I snuggled down, so my white old locks would show. I let the candle burn so she could see me there plainly. I shut my eyes, knowing she would come. Oh, yes, she would come down from her tower to see who had been spying on her. And she would come faster than any ordinary old woman could have come down all those stairs, thinking to find my room empty and me on the way. . . .

She was quick! The door opened. Someone peered in. I turned, as though sleepily, saying, "Whaa?"

The door closed, and she was gone. She believed someone had been outside her room, but she didn't know who. Down the hall, I heard her open Giles's door. And then close it. He really was asleep. I let time pass, scarcely breathing, pretending sleep. She might be watching. She might be hovering outside my window, like an owl. The candle burned to a smoky stub and guttered out.

Would she let it go at that? Would she ask that thing in the mirror who'd been spying on her?

More important, could it tell her?

"Fenoderee," I whispered, "I need a friend."

He slipped into bed beside me, yawning. "I thought you'd never ask," he said. His sickle rattled upon the floor. "Oh, you do need a friend, Beauty. Nastiness here. And you've got old Carabosse half sick with worry."

"Worse than mere worry," said a voice on the other side. Puck.

"What's going on here?" I said. "Who is Ilene?"

"A witch," said Puck, matter-of-factly. "She signed one of the usual witch contracts with the Dark Lord, her soul and body in return for being young and beautiful for a few hundred years. Of course, he threw a trick into it. He always does."

"A trick?"

Fenoderee nodded; I could feel his head going up and down on the pillow. "Ilene remains beautiful only so long as there is no other female in the kingdom as beautiful as she. She started out in quite a large kingdom, had to dispose of quite a lot of pretty girls, and the word got around. They came after her with hayforks and torches, the Transylvanian kind you use on monsters, you know? So she moved to a smaller kingdom, and then one smaller yet. Here in Marvella, there weren't all that many beauties to start with, and the last one she had to do away with was Galantha."

"Galantha?" I asked.

"Galantha. That little springtime flower, the white one that droops its head."

"Snowdrop?"

"That one, yes."

What a really odd name for a child! Hadn't one fairy tale been enough? Of course, that bit with the mirror had been a dead giveaway. Magic collects magic, Carabosse had said. "My granddaughter?" I asked, trying to disbelieve but not succeeding one whit.

"That's right," said Fenoderee. "Your granddaughter."

"Who isn't really dead!"

"No. Ilene tried, but she couldn't kill Snowdrop. She sent a huntsman to kill her, and he couldn't. She tried a cursed lace, then a poisoned comb, and that didn't work. Snowdrop is one-eighth fairy, after all. Witches can't be allowed to go around killing off fairies, even part ones. No, though Ilene tried several times to get Snow taken care of, everything failed except the apple."

"The apple?" I started to ask. There was a sound outside in the corridor, and my bed was suddenly empty of anyone but me and Grumpkin. The door opened, and I heard Giles whispering to me.

"Beauty? Catherine? Lavender? Are you all right?"

He came in and crouched on the bed beside me. We whispered together as I told him part of what I had seen. It took very little talk between us to decide this place was dangerous and that we wanted to be elsewhere. The Dark Lord had seen me, or sensed me, or at least caught a glimpse of me, so much was clear. What I wasn't sure of was what else he'd seen. In that moment the thing had flared up within me, and I'd felt like a lantern, throwing light in all directions. Had the thing in the mirror seen that?

"How did you get up there?" Giles asked me wonderingly, not waiting for an answer. "I'm not sure we can get out. There's a guard asleep downstairs in the hall, and another one walking up and down outside in the courtyard. And if she has some kind of captive spirit in that mirror. . . ."

I hadn't told him what was really in the mirror, but I was quite sure it wasn't captive.

"We'll get out," I said grimly. "As far as the stables, any-how."

I had Giles fetch his clothing from his room. I fetched mine out of the press. I put on the boots, held Giles tightly around the waist, with our baggage tied helter skelter and Grumpkin squashed between us, and said, "Boots, take us to the stables."

And there we were, standing beside the horses, an arrival which startled the horses almost as much as it startled Giles. I told him there was no time to explain, and he subsided unwillingly, full of questions we had no time for. Still, he had his wits about him sufficiently to suggest that we tie some sacks around the horses' feet, so their hooves wouldn't make a noise on the cobbles. We waited until the guard moved around the corner, then made a dash for it. Once we were past the courtyard (the gate wasn't even shut and there was no drawbridge), the road was mostly soft dust. We went down through the dark village, silent as mice, then up the other side. When we got to the top of a long rise, we saw a little campfire, and there was Eskavaria sitting beside it, waiting for us.

"Have you been here all along?" I asked.

"Thought you might not stay very long," he said. "Thought I'd take you along to spend the night with my brothers and me."

He wouldn't have thought of that on his own. Who had told him to stay? Puck? Still running errands for Carabosse? I didn't ask.

He brought our packhorses out of the shadows, mounted his own, and we went along through the starlight, with him humming a little song and the water making an accompaniment to it. We wove through rocks and trees. Once he got down and moved a log behind us, hiding the way. We came to the top of a long slope and could see below us the bulk of a house with windows faintly outlined in firelight.

Eskavaria looked up at the stars. "Midnight," he said. "Time we get under cover."

"What happens at midnight?" Giles asked.

"If she knows you're gone, she may come looking for you then," the little man answered, and we trotted down the long slope toward the house beneath the trees. A stable stood next to it, with a door connecting the two. We were beneath the stable roof when we heard the scream from above, a long, shrill cry that was not an owl.

Giles started to go out and look. Eskavaria grabbed his arm

and held him. "No," he said. "Never look up when you hear that cry, or she may see you. Faces show up in the dark more than hair or hats do." Then he led us through the door.

It was a simple house, though larger than it had looked from outside, with one big room downstairs and a large open loft. The brothers, all six of them, were asleep up there. None of them were any bigger than Eskavaria. I could tell from the size of the beds. If not dwarves, they were not far from it. I thought of the "little men" the Dark One had mentioned, and knew these were they.

"You know where my granddaughter is," I challenged him.

"I know where someone is. How can I be sure she is your granddaughter?" he challenged me in return.

I couldn't think of an answer. I was very tired. I hurt all over, and I started to cry. Once started, I couldn't stop.

Giles shouted angrily, "Now see what you've done. Damn it, Esky, she's tired! She's come all this way to find her grand-daughter, and you say a thing like that!"

This woke up the family, and they all came down, rubbing their eyes and asking what was going on. Among themselves they spoke the other language, Euskara. Evidently other people call them Basques, but they call themselves the Euskaldunak, which gives you a hint as to what the language sounds like. Except for an occasional word that sounded rather Latinish, I couldn't understand any of it, though the tone of the conversation was decidedly argumentative. There was a great deal of pointing up and making the horn sign and staring at us with a mixture of intense curiosity and obvious distrust.

I don't think there was ten year's difference in age from Esky, the youngest, to the oldest. The older ones had beards, the older the longer. Evidently they never trimmed them. The younger three or four were clean shaven. Esky told us all their names, and I promptly forgot them. Couldn't pronounce them, in any case. Not Sneezy. Not Grumpy. My eyes were falling shut. Next thing I knew, they were spreading some quilts on the floor and I was being invited to lie down and sleep.

I didn't wait for a second invitation.

When I woke, hours and hours later, it was full daylight

and the house was empty. The door was open. I could hear horses champing away in the stables and the buzz of flies. Otherwise, silence.

I sat up and fumbled with my hair. Giles must have heard me, for he came in from outside, bringing me a cup of something warm. Broth, I finally decided. With some kind of very fine grain cooked in it. Almost like grass seed. I leaned back against a nearby bench and drank it. Or chewed it. It needed salt.

Giles suggested, very sweetly, that since we had a few moments to ourselves, I explain to him what was going on. I did so, mostly. I told him my mother was a fairy, without dwelling on what that made me, and I said she'd given me certain fairy gifts. I said an inimical force was sort of following me around. I didn't mention Jaybee. I couldn't bear to tell him about Jaybee. In Giles's mind, I was Beauty and I was Catherine, both at once, and they were not necessarily the same person. He could accept that Elly had been Edward's child, and Galantha was somehow my granddaughter, without giving up his belief that his first love, Beauty, still virgin and pure, was asleep at Westfaire. I was her, and I wasn't her, so to speak. He had no trouble believing Galantha had been wickedly enchanted by a witch. He believed in witches. In those times, everyone believed in witches.

"I've been to see her," Giles said, looking at his feet.

"Her?"

"Your grandchild. Galantha."

I started to get up. He pushed me back, very gently. "She looks almost like she's asleep, Beauty. Very pale, but not . . . you know, not rotted or anything. They've put her in a kind of case, so nothing will chew on her. I don't think she's dead."

Giles had never seen Disney. This time I did get up.

"I want to see for myself," I said, pulling the pins out of my hair and trying to find my comb. Giles found it for me and helped me braid up my white locks. When I had the wimple pinned tightly, my veil on and my kirtle smoothed out, he led the way outside.

We went up a gentle hill, not the one we had come down the night before, and through a bit of forest, down a much used path, and into the gaping entrance of a mine. She was lying well back inside, in an area lit by torches. The case looked more like a reliquary than anything else, bits of rock crystal and faceted gems pieced together with gold to make a domed lid in a design of flowers and leaves. The leaves were emeralds, I thought. Or maybe jade. Through the flatter, clearer bits I could see her, only a child, twelve or thirteen, perhaps. She was very beautiful, rather like the child Elizabeth Taylor, in that horse movie they always showed late at night on TV in the 1990s. She was incorruptible, as saints' bodies are supposed to be. I thought of Giles and my conversation about mice and shrouds and laughed at myself.

Then I sat down beside the case and let some tears run, not many. After a while, Esky and one of his brothers came in and asked if I'd like the case opened. I said yes, and they unbuckled it at one side and laid the top back. She lay on a satin mattress, with a satin coverlet over her, her hands folded on her breast. She was dressed very simply, in a full white shift with puffy sleeves and a kind of laced bodice over it. Disney had got that part right.

The other brothers came from deeper in the mine, setting their tools down to one side and seating themselves on chair sized stones, one for each of them. From the wear on those stones, I could tell they had sat there like this time and again for years.

Giles took a deep breath. "She looks just like you," he said to me. "When I first saw you."

I looked at the child, considering. She looked something like Elly and something like her father, but a good deal like me. As though I'd passed on my own looks, skipping a generation. Her hair was black, of course, and mine had been gold, but otherwise, we looked much the same.

I nodded. Esky reached out to touch the bones of my cheeks and jaw and nodded. "I see it," he said.

He could see more than I, then, but his brothers all nodded, telling each other how much the child resembled me. The resemblance, whether fancied or real, seemed to allay their suspicions.

"How?" I asked, motioning at them, her, everything, meaning "How did it happen?"

Esky sighed. "One day we heard this screaming noise, so we went to see what it was. This big huntsman was down on his knees, crying. He said Princess Ilene had told him she'd kill him unless he took this little girl into the woods and murdered her. He couldn't do it. He said he was going to kill a deer and take its heart back instead. Then he went off and left the child behind. It was getting dark. Wolves was howling. We couldn't leave her there. We took her along home. She was a sweet, pretty girl. Not much sense, but sweet." He wiped his face with his hand, sighing.

"Well, some time went by. We got used to having her around. At first she couldn't do nothing useful. We taught her. Cookery a little. Gardening a little. If I tell the truth, Lady Catherine, all of us lusted after her even though she was just a child. With all of us living here, we agreed we'd behave decent. We may be hermits, so to speak. We may not be very civilized, but our ma raised us to be decent folk. Right then, we should have took her over the mountains into Spain. Or took her back to Lourdes, we could have did that. Truth is, none of us travels much, except me, and I didn't want her to go. She was so pretty. . . ."

He rose and went out of the cave. The brothers muttered among themselves, in their own language. No one said anything I could understand. After a time, Esky came back, his face wet.

"So one day we came home and seen her lying there on the floor. We picked her up and seen her bodice was laced up tight. It was a new lace."

One of the brothers interrupted, and Eskavaria nodded to him.

"That's right, a silk lace, one we hadn't seen before. So we unlaced her, and she caught her breath, all of a sudden. We asked her what happened. She told us a peddler woman come by. Well, we knew then what happened. The witch knew she was here."

The little men nodded, agreeing this is the way it had been.

"Gally wasn't real quick," Esky went on. "All of us knew

that. Even so, we thought since it happened once, she'd know next time. We told her no more peddler women . . ."

Another interruption, discussion, nodding of heads.

Eskavaria nodded. "That's right. No more visitors, no one. We said stay in the house until we come home. We said then we'd walk with her if she wanted to pick flowers or something.

"Well, wasn't a whole week passed before we come home and there she is again. All limp on the floor. We thought she was dead. We picked her up, and then a comb fell out of her hair, and she woke up. It was another peddler woman. Talked her way around the child, like the first time.

"So we knew we couldn't trust her alone. Right then we should have took her over the mountains, fast. We didn't do that. We decided that one of us would stay with her, to protect her. Then that didn't seem decent, so we said two would stay, to keep an eye on each other along with her. And that went along for quite a long while. . . ."

He turned to his brothers and asked them a question in their own language. They argued for a moment, then responded. "Almost a year," he went on. "It was almost a year. Then one day Euskaby found a big gem deposit back in the mine with a rock in front of it. Big rock. All of us had to move it. Maybe an hour we left her, but when we got back she was on the floor again. This time was no lace, no comb. We undressed her, took everything off, looked at everything, put everything back. We combed her hair. We cleaned her fingernails and toenails. We looked in her mouth, in her nose and ears. Nothing."

"The witch said it was an apple," I said. "I overheard her." It hadn't been the witch who had said it, but I wasn't about to explain about Fenoderee and Puck.

"If it was an apple, it's inside her belly," said Esky. "There's no way to get it out of her with her living."

And he was perfectly right, of course, in the fifteenth. In the twentieth, it would be minor surgery. But if I took her to the twentieth, I might not be able to get back. Or, if I got back, too much time might have passed, and I might never see Giles again. I sighed and bit my lip and decided not to decide, not just yet.

"We're still within the borders of Ponte Marvella, right?" I asked.

They talked it over and decided that we probably were right on the border, not really in, not really out.

"Then we need to get her out," I said. "Once we're outside Marvella, maybe the witch won't bother us, and we can decide what to do. I don't think my granddaughter's dead. Not really. Perhaps there's a way to remove the enchantment." In the story it was a prince's kiss, wasn't it? Or was that only my own story? Or was it Disney? I simply couldn't remember!

More argument. They weren't sure they believed me. I wasn't sure it was true. Esky waved his hands and shouted. Eventually they agreed. Two or three of them were crying. One thing they did agree upon. Daytime was the time to move. Nights were dangerous.

So we started out. Galantha's coffin was bound about with ropes and slung between the two packhorses. Our supplies went on Esky's horse. All seven of the little men came along, to be sure we got out safely, Esky said, but I think they simply were unwilling to let her go. She had become something more to them than a sleeping little girl. They decided the safest thing to do was to go down the south side of the mountains into Spain, since we were nearest the southern border of Marvella. Also, we had to avoid the toll bridge the baron had told me about. If the Princess wanted to stop our leaving, that bridge would be watched.

The idea was good, but the trails were simply not wide enough for the two horses with the coffin between. This became obvious very quickly, and a shouting match broke out among the little men. Two of them kept pointing to the ropes and screaming at two others. I could read their faces if not their words. "You didn't tie it right. It's all your fault." And the others: "You don't know a damned thing about knots. What do you mean it wasn't tied right?" It went on far too long, and Giles stopped it by bellowing at them, dismounting, untying the coffin, opening it, wrapping the girl in the satin coverlet, and taking her up in his arms. She was as stiff as an image carved from wood. In a way that was a relief. I had worried myself over what the little men might have been doing with her in that mine, all those years. They had done nothing, obviously, that they could not have done as well with an image carved from stone.

The little men muttered at Giles's picking her up, but decided to allow it. Still, they insisted on bringing the coffin along, the bottom and top tied separately onto the backs of two of the horses. It had been made with love, care, and endless hours of labor. The gems and gold alone were worth a fortune, not to speak of the workmanship. It was their gift to their Snowdrop, and they weren't going to abandon it. I shook my head at Giles, and he subsided with a growl.

After a time, we worked out a processional order that worked fairly well. Esky went first with one of his brothers, leading one packhorse, then Giles, then me, then the horses with the coffin led by two brothers, then the other little men coming along single file. We went up for a time, then abruptly down. Giles asked Esky where we were going.

The little man was breathing hard. "There's a place we can get across the gorge and onto the road to Santiago," he said.

Giles looked at me and shrugged. It looked like we were going to St. James's shrine whether we wanted to or not. I wondered if we would run into Margery Kempe. After that, I tried not to wonder anything or think anything except about hanging on. Riding a horse uphill is difficult. Riding a horse downhill is exhausting.

Night came. The little men went off in all directions, looking for a camp site, finding one at last under an overhanging ledge of stone where we could not be seen from the sky. I thought perhaps they were being overcareful. We must have come far from Marvella by this time. Then, late in the darkness, I was awakened by the same cry we had heard the night before. Around me I could hear indrawn breaths, silence. The horses stopped munching outside among the trees. After a time the cry came again, far away to the north, echoed by the howling of wolves. The little men began to breathe once more.

"What was it?" I asked Eskavaria.

"Night lammergeier," he said, not meeting my eyes. The lammergeier are huge vultures of the Pyranees, sometimes called "bone-breakers" because of their habit of dropping large bones from great heights to shatter them and get at the marrow. Ordinarily, I believe, they do not fly at night. I thought it wisest not to pursue the matter.

Midmorning, this morning, we came to the road to Santiago. The road is wide enough that the coffin can be slung between two horses once more. My granddaughter is in it. Eskavaria is leading the packhorse. His brothers have faded back amongst the trees, tears running down their faces. A traveler we met coming up from Spain tells us today is the fifteenth of August. We have time yet to get to Compostela before fall.

ST. HELENA'S DAY, AUGUST, YEAR OF OUR LORD 1417

We have traveled for several days on the downward road, very slowly because of the coffin, seeing no living things except an occasional herd of ibex, a few skulking foxes, or the ubiquitous marmots. Then, this morning, shortly after we began our journey for the day, we came upon a large party of noble men and women together with their servants, all camped among their wagons beside the road. It appeared they might have spare mounts, and Giles went to see if he could purchase a packhorse to carry the supplies carried by Esky's mount. Esky had been walking, and it had slowed our progress somewhat.

Several of the young men came over to us where we waited, looking us over in an insolent manner, until they saw the coffin itself. Then they became quiet. One of them, a boy scarcely fourteen or fifteen years old, pressed his face to one of the transparent bits of crystal and peered within. I thought it best, since he was surrounded by his fellows, not to antagonize him or cause any notice by using enchantment. I had seen similar gangs of young men, though not noble young men, in Bayonne, where they were said to roam the streets at night, seeking unprotected young women they might rape and ruin. It was a kind of game with them, and the insolence of these young nobles seemed also a game: cockiness pushed to its limits.

The coffin-peering youngster stood up, very arrogantly, and asked me who she was.

"My granddaughter, child," I said, unthinking.

One of the other young men started toward me, angrily, but another courtier, a very handsome, slightly older young man, put out his hand and said softly, "The young man who addressed you is Prince Edward. Fourth son of King Zot of Nadenada."

I bowed, as best I could from atop my little horse. "Your Highness," I said to the arrogant lad. The soft-spoken courtier regarded the prince with a worried expression.

"And you are, sir?" I asked the pleasant-voiced courtier.

"Vincent," he told me with a smile, taking his eyes from his master for only a moment. "Vincent d'Escriban."

Giles returned from the encampment shaking his head. No horse for sale. Well, it had been worth the trial.

I bowed again. "We must depart," I said. "It is a long journey to Compostela."

"Is she dead?" the prince asked, taking hold of my horse's bridle to prevent my moving.

"We think not," I said. "She may be under an enchantment."

The young man looked at Vincent and said, "I want her."

Vincent and I exchanged uncertain glances.

"I want her," the boy repeated. "Buy her for me."

"She is a person," I explained softly. "Not a toy. Not a mannequin. She is not something one can buy."

"Buy her for me," screamed the prince, growing very red in the face.

Vincent shrugged an apology toward me and moved to take the young prince in hand by distracting him from his madness. Esky took the right-hand coffin horse by the reins and led him purposefully onto the road. Giles and I followed, on our horses. The prince broke away from his keeper, dashed into the road and threw himself in front of the coffin horses. One horse stumbled. The rope came loose. The other horse bolted. The coffin fell into the road. The lid bounced off. My granddaughter's body rolled out of it into the road and lay there, coughing.

Beside her in the dust lay a piece of apple.

The mad young prince sat up, looked at my granddaughter

with great satisfaction, then smiled. "Buy her for me," he said again. "I want to marry her."

I had slipped off my horse and then had been knocked down in all the confusion. Giles was busy picking me up and seeing that nothing was broken. Eskavaria was cuddling Snowdrop and crying. Vincent was remonstrating with the mad young prince. Persons of great self-importance arrived from across the road to see what all the fuss was about and succeeded in making an even larger one. Questions were shouted at me, which I was too confused to answer.

We are now camped at the edge of the forest, being waited upon by the servants of King Zot of Nadenada while the mad young prince and my granddaughter play at shuttlecocks in the road.

"Who is she?" King Zot himself asked me, having been introduced through Giles and Vincent.

His tone was peremptory. I didn't like it.

"She is the daughter of the hereditary Prince of Marvella and his former wife, Elladine, who was the daughter of Lord Edward of Wellingford and granddaughter of the Duke of Monfort and Westfaire," I said with chill hauteur.

"Oh well, that's all right then," he said, glancing at me out of the corner of his eye. "Related to you?"

"My granddaughter."

"Ah," he said, scratching his nose. His manner changed to one of respect. "How old would you say she is?"

"I would say she is . . ." And I paused, wondering for a moment how old she really is. She had been born quite some time ago. "I would say she is twelve or thirteen," I said. "She spent some time under an enchantment, but she did not age during that time."

"Virgin, is she?"

I snorted. "Of course." Though I wouldn't have put it past Esky or one of his brothers to have tried.

"Ah," he said again, and then sat down, leaned forward, and began to tell me about his kingdom.

Nadenada, it seems, is a pocket realm just over the mountains toward France. It is larger than Marvella, but not by much.

The mad young prince is a pocket prince, not the heir, but still a prince, and at fourteen it is time he was married. So said King Zot.

"Undoubtedly you will think of alliances when you consider a wife for him," I said stiffly.

He stared gloomily at the dust between his feet, drawing circles in it with an ornamental dagger. "Not much of that kind of thing in Nadenada," he said, summoning Vincent with one hand. He sent the young man for wine and settled himself more comfortably on the chair he had brought over from his camp. Then he drew more circles. "France wouldn't care, far too big and far away. England wouldn't care, they've enough to worry about warring with France. Navarre wouldn't care, nor Aragon; everything is religion with them, and we're not that observant in Nadenada. And the same applies to Castile, come to that."

"Then you're not concerned with alliances."

"Not really, no."

"Some affair of state, perhaps, which could be helped along by a judicious match?"

"Haven't any affairs of state, either. There was the matter of the wool tax, but that's been decided." He gloomed into his linked fingers. "Shepherds said they'd go over the mountains into Spain, so we relieved them of it. Can't have all one's shepherds absconding to Spain."

"It wouldn't look well," I agreed. "No other affairs of state?"

"None I can think of," he said.

"The prince . . ." (I'd almost said "the mad prince," catching myself just in time). "The prince will want a large dowry, undoubtedly."

"Not . . . not really *large,*" the King murmured, giving me a straight look. "It's not as though he were in the succession, you understand."

"An elder brother?"

"Three elder brothers."

"Things can happen," I murmured.

"Yes," he said in a plaintive voice. "They can. Put it, then, that he's not *likely* to be in line for the throne."

"So he wouldn't need a very large dowry."

"Not *very* large."

I considered this. "Did you happen to notice the . . . ah . . . case that my granddaughter was traveling in? Before your son dumped her out into the road."

"I had noticed that, yes. Brass, is it? And crystal?"

"Gold," I said. "And gems."

"Ah," he said again. "One wouldn't have known."

I nodded in agreement. One really wouldn't have known. If one hadn't met Esky's brothers, one wouldn't even have thought it likely. I said, "Of course, your . . . fourth son is very young. Perhaps too young to think of marriage."

The King scratched his head again and sweated gently into his beard. "Let me be frank," he said. "Since the boy became a man, which happened just a year ago, he has been quite . . . quite . . ."

"Urgent?" I suggested.

"Urgent," he agreed. "We are having some trouble keeping maidservants at the castle. His mother and I are agreed it is time he was married."

We parted, each to think about that. Vincent came to summon the mad young prince to lunch. Snowdrop, thus deserted, came to sit by me in the shade.

"Have you been having fun?" I asked.

"Oh, yes," she said. "It's so nice."

"What about the young man?"

"He's so nice," she replied with a happy expression. I offered her some cakes which the King had brought with him, and she took one, eating it greedily. I was reminded of her mother.

"Tell me, Snow," I asked. "Why did you let the witch poison you with that apple when the little men had told you not to let her in?"

She gazed at me wonderingly, her little brow furrowing with the attempt at thought.

"Because I was hungry and it looked so nice."

Her father, Prince Charming, was never long in the brains department, either.

ST. FRANCIS'S DAY, OCTOBER, YEAR OF OUR LORD 1417

Giles and I are here in Nadenada for the wedding. We are honored guests. Since the Death ravaged all of Europe, no one wonders if fathers and mothers aren't present at weddings. A grandmother does quite well enough, even one so obviously old as I. The Queen even offered her dressmaker in order that I might be suitably clad for the occasion. Prince Charme and Princess Ilene have been invited to the nuptials. I mentioned to the Prime Minister of this place that Ilene was probably responsible for the spell which had been laid on Snowdrop. He talked with the archbishop, and formal charges of witchcraft are being considered. As a princess, she is not subject to the laws of a neighboring kingdom, but the archbishop believes the Church has authority to examine her even if civil authority cannot. I'm not sure how I feel about this. I don't like Ilene, but then I don't much like heresy trials, either, and I certainly don't like anything which might involve Ilene's patron in the mirror. The archbishop has sent someone posthaste both to Avignon and Rome to attempt to get a ruling from one or more of the popes on the matter. I can't remember whether there are three popes at the moment or only two.

If I were wise, and if I had the conviction wisdom should lend me, I would seize Snow up and take her somewhere away from this pathological child she is going to marry. And yet, one asks, where? Where does one take a gloriously beautiful twelve-year-old girl who has not two tiny brains to rub together to make even one wee warm idea in her head? And when one gets her there, what does one do with her? No monastery would take her. No, that's not true, given a sufficient dowry some monastery would, but she'd be miserable there. Marriage is her only hope. And yet . . .

Well. Beauty does not breed true. I said that before, when Elly died. Beauty exists in all ages, but it does not necessarily breed true. Mixed with dross, it becomes dross. I am only her grandmother, after all. I am not God, who presumably made her as she is for some reason!

ALL HALLOW'S EVE

Tomorrow is the wedding. Tonight I was sitting alone in my warm, tapestry-hung room, with my cat on the bed and Giles next door, remembering Mama. I saw her last on Samhain Eve, so long ago, when Thomas the Rhymer got loose from Faery. I wondered if she would care that her great-granddaughter was being married.

"Fenoderee," I whispered.

And he was there, sitting on the window sill, looking out at the night. Puck lounged against the bed, chewing at a fingernail. Call one, get both.

"I was thinking about Mama," I said.

"Ah," said Puck. "Well, she's in Faery, looking well."

I tried to think of something to ask about her, but I couldn't. Instead, I wondered, "Was it the Dark Lord I saw in the witch's glass?"

"It was," said Fenoderee.

"Did he see me?"

"Carabosse thinks he may have. Israfel thinks he did, also. They're both frightened for you, though they say it was probably going to happen, sooner or later. Once you went back to the twentieth, it showed up in the Pool that he would."

Puck added, "They think the Dark Lord will come looking for you, manipulating things. Be careful, Beauty."

"How much do you know about . . ." I started to ask, then shut my mouth, remembering they didn't know.

"About your burden?" Puck asked. "We've known since almost the beginning. It's not her fault, but old Clockwork Carabosse is one of the Sidhe, after all. She can't get out of the habit of thinking of us Bogles as slightly subnormal. She thinks we don't notice what's going on under our noses."

Fenoderee said, "I don't know what made her think we wouldn't see what she was up to. She and Israfel did it right there in front of us."

I sighed. "I'm getting old, you know. I won't last too much longer. They'd better start thinking of somewhere else to hide it."

Puck nodded deliberately. "They're cogitating, looking in the Pool, thinking deep thoughts, the way they do."

"And I'm still just supposed to go along, is that it?" I was surprised to find myself still capable of a little anger!

"For now," said Fenoderee. "Is that why you called?"

I shook my head. "No, it was just I was thinking about Mama. I was thinking of going to Faery to say hello, but when I returned here, wouldn't a lot of time have passed."

Puck nodded. "Oh, yes. No way around that. Your mortal part ages whenever you travel back and forth by magic."

I wanted to see her, but I couldn't risk that. If I died before Carabosse took away my burden, it might be lost forever. Besides, Giles and I couldn't look forward to that much time together. Nor Grumpkin, either. "Could you take a message for me?"

He smiled.

"Tell her . . . I love her," I said.

I think I do. Despite what she is and how she feels, I think I do. In my long life there have been few enough people, mortal or Faery, for me to love.

ALL HALLOWS NIGHT

Well, we have had a wedding. There was the mad young prince, all dressed up in taffeta and furs with a plumed cap, looking very handsome, and there was Galantha, Snowdrop, in silk and velvet, both of them standing outside the church door, exchanging their pledges. I had hired a local goldsmith to break up the coffin and melt down the gold into nice little ingots. That gave me a goodly sum for her dowry, and the King settled a house and land on his son. They have enough to live on; neither of them is bright enough to get into serious trouble; and I laid a happiness spell on them as a gift. It was the least I could do. The King is quite a jolly fellow, several decades younger than I, but gallant and well-spoken. He says to call him Zot, and that he'll send word to me in England how the children get along. He flirts with me and tells me I don't look a day over eighty.

After the pledging was done and the rings exchanged and

the papers signed, we went into the church and had the nuptial mass. And after that was done, we went to the feast, and there was Princess Ilene of Marvella. I'm not sure whether she knew who the bride was. I'm not sure the invitation mentioned the bride's name. If it did, she may have assumed it was someone else by the same name, or that Snow would have aged during the thirty years she'd been asleep, or something. At any rate, when Princess Ilene saw Snow, her eyes bulged. I've never seen that actually happen before, but it happened this time. Ilene was standing beside me at the time, her eyes bulged, and then something quite dreadful happened to her face. It sagged, melted, and began to fall off the skull. She raised her hands, just as she had when invoking the presence in the mirror, and they were all bones. Well, she'd said the Dark Lord held her beauty in thrall, and she'd been safe so long as no one around was prettier than she. However, Snow certainly was prettier and it seemed the Dark One was ending his contract and taking Princess Ilene for his own.

I was the only one who saw what was happening. Ilene crumpled to the floor, very slowly. I'd brought my cloak to the banquet with me, folded over my arm, thinking I might want to escape if things got dull. I spread it like a fishing net, to hide what was left of the Princess. "Fenoderee," I whispered, and there he was. "Take it away," I said. "And put the cloak back under my bed upstairs."

He was gone only for an instant. Then he was back. "Where did you put her?" I whispered.

"Under the church with the other old bones," he whispered back, then made a face at me and departed. Faery folk aren't very respectful, sometimes. That was consecrated ground!

Then I caught myself and realized that was merely another way of saying "magical ground." She could lie there as well as anywhere.

A few moments later, Prince Charming, the hereditary Prince of Marvella came wandering toward me with Snow on his arm and a silly smile on his sweet old face. He was looking for his wife to tell her he'd found his long-lost daughter, but

Princess Ilene was nowhere to be found. I helped them look for a while, until I got tired. Then I came up here to bed.

Giles brought me a cup of wine and asked where we would go now.

"Home," I told him. Meaning Westfaire. Or, at least, somewhere near there. I long for home.

NOVEMBER

King Zot of Nadenada gave us an escort to Bayonne. There we found it simple to join a group of travelers who were seeking passage to England. Good weather held. A merchantman presented itself in due course. Five days north, we landed once more at Bristol and found a carriage we could hire to take us to Sawley, where, after inquiries, I found the man who claimed to own Wellingford (though I much doubt his claim would stand a legal test). I paid him a few years' rent on the Dower House.

And in that house we have come to rest, Giles and I, keeping our old bones busy hiring people to refurbish the place and manage the farm land around it, and finding half a dozen women to keep it clean. It is not a wreck, not like some places in the countryside, but it is certainly dilapidated. I converted gems back to cash, and cash into investments with a certain House of Levi in England. This time, just in case I decide to go away and come back in five hundred years, the money is to be paid to whoever knows a few code words. I've had enough of darting about planting forged documents.

SPRING 1418

Winter came and went. Despite the cold, it has been the happiest time of my life. Strange to say that with youth gone and all the pains of age very much with me, but it is true. Giles is a loving, dear companion, a sweet and kindly friend.

A few days ago I decided I wanted to see Westfaire. I told Giles just enough for him to help me, and we went through the water gate together, floating on pigs' bladders, for neither of us is strong enough to push through that deep water. Inside it is just as I left it. We climbed slowly up to the tower, me holding the cloak, Giles clutching the boots to keep us from falling asleep. As we climbed, he paused often to catch his breath. He was not this weak when we were searching for Snowdrop. It must be a very recent thing.

Beloved is still there in the tower, still lovely, still sleeping.

"How long?" Giles wanted to know, reaching out to touch her face. "How long will you sleep?"

"You." Not "she." Oh, Giles. Giles.

Well, according to Joyeause, she will sleep thirty more years, until kissed by a handsome prince, though, according to Carabosse, that wasn't the real curse at all. Supposing that both of them are right (and I do not take Aunt Joyeause so lightly as old Carabosse does), at the end of a hundred years, someone may be able to take Beloved out of Westfaire and kiss her awake. If I am to see that event, I must live to be one hundred and sixteen years old. Looking at myself in the glass, I don't think I'll make it. Still, if and when that day comes, Beloved will know it was all worth it, being my friend. She'll have the best of it then.

I wrote her a note. "Beloved, you are Beauty. And Beauty is gone, long ago. Live her life as well as she would have lived it, or even better."

As I turned toward the stair, I saw my mysterious thing, still sitting upon the chest. It's a clock, of course. One of Carabosse's clocks. The hand has moved to half past fifteen. It does not measure hours but centuries. It ends, as the world will end, with the twenty-second. I leaned close and listened to the sound. The faint ticking. The tiny crepitation of time moving past. On the face of the clock is the word "Carabosse," entwined with the numbered centuries. She cursed me. But she left me this gift. Sometimes I wish it was all she had left me.

It was easier climbing down. When we got back to the lake shore, we were thoroughly chilled through. Such a stupid thing to do at our age!

LATER

Giles is very ill. I know what he has. He has pneumonia. I could get to the twentieth in an instant, I could steal penicillin, I could

be back before he knows I am gone. Maybe. I don't know if I
could. I could try!

I told him that. His being sick is all my fault. He would be
all right if I hadn't dragged him through the water and up that
tower. He must let me help him.

But he won't. He shook his head at me, smiling. "I saw you
sleeping in that tower, just the way you were. If I die, let me die
remembering that, sweet girl. I want you here, not off somewhere with your boots."

"Giles, we could have years, yet."

"Don't want years that badly," he whispered to me. "I've
had years. More years alone than I ever wanted. Don't leave me
alone now. I'm tired. It's enough."

He went off to sleep.

Oh, God in Heaven, I could not let him go. I wept and
screamed and threw myself about, while he went on sleeping,
more deeply, more deeply.

It was that gave me the idea. I called Puck and Fenoderee
and put on the boots, and we held him while all of us went,
holding onto him we went, through the thorns, through the
roses, into Westfaire. Oh, I could have used the boots anytime.
So foolish. So stupid. I let my love go through that cold water
when we could have used the boots. If they would go through
time, what were a few thorns!

I put him in Aunt Lav's bed. I took the boots away. He fell
even more deeply asleep. He slept, as all in Westfaire sleep. He
will not die. Nothing in Westfaire can die. I know it! That was
the curse Carabosse put upon Westfaire. Sleep! Not for a hundred years, but forever! It has to be. It's the only thing that
makes sense of everything that's happened!

I asked Puck if I was right, and he nodded, shuffling his toes
in the dust as though embarrassed. I asked him why, and he said
he didn't know.

26

With Giles gone from me, nothing seems worth it, somehow. Not that we were recent lovers, in a physical sense. All that sort of thing leaves you. You remember it, but your body doesn't urge you toward it. Your body wants comfort and affection and the sweetness of companionship. We weren't lonely, not so long as we were together, but now I am. I go to Westfaire often and sit there, talking to him as he sleeps. Sometimes I pretend he answers me.

It seems to me his breathing is easier. Is he healing? While he sleeps? It would be so easy to summon him up, not really him, you understand, but an enchantment of him. But I don't. I won't. It wouldn't be fair to him. It would be like Chinanga, all a dream, my creation, not really him at all. An enchantment Giles would be incapable of surprising me. He who always surprised me.

It was unfair of him to go before me. I believe I will probably live quite some time yet. Despite all the aches and pains, my heart sounds steady and strong and I breathe easily. I may have years yet to get through.

When I was a child, my legs used to hurt often. Aunt Terror, I think it was she, used to say it was growing pains. I have the same pain now. Perhaps now they are ungrowing pains. Whenever the pain wakes me in the night, I think of going back to Faery where I don't feel pain.

I called Fenoderee a day or so ago, and he didn't come. He always came before when I called. What's going on in Faery?

I need to talk to Carabosse. What's she going to do with this thing inside me? I would like to see Mama, too, to tell her how sorry I am for what happened to her. Besides, in Faery, I would at least look and feel young.

Remembering the condition I was in when I returned last

time, I'll need to make some provision for staying healthy and clean. Going to Faery will do no good if my human flesh is starved while I'm there. I'll have to figure something out.

The solution to staying healthy and clean in Faery is to come out of it every now and then, into the mortal world, and eat, bathe, and reclothe myself. I have hired a woman from the nearby village to go each evening to the kitchen of the ruined manor of Wellingford, to set out food and drink, to build a fire, and to heat water over it. Though the rest of the manor is dilapidated, the kitchen is whole and the roof over it is in good repair. The woman's name is Odile Kent.

Of course, she wants to know why. I have told her it was a promise I had made my husband before he died. A kind of memorial. Service for a ghost. Though the explanation makes no sense, she accepts it. People in this age believe in ghosts, and people in all ages do odd things in memory of loved ones. I told her, also, that the matter was secret, not something to be rumored about the countryside to bring beggars to eat the food she puts out. I called God to witness our contract and bring down fire upon her if she fails me. She looked suitably impressed. My agent in East Sawley will pay her, year on year. My agent in London will check to be sure that he does. Ever since Chinanga, I have put watchers to watch the watchers.

I have also instructed Odile to put a mark on the chimney face at each full of the moon, thirteen marks in a row, starting the next row beneath. In that way I will know how much time has passed. She's a sensible woman, strong and stout and still quite young. She should last longer than I do. I have already carried a pile of clothing over to the kitchen and stored it in a locked chest together with Mama's box. Looking through the box, I came upon that last hank of thread. When I see Mama, I must ask her what it is for.

The key to the chest is around my neck on a ribbon. As soon as I have taken care of a few things here, I am ready to go. I have told Odile to stay in readiness, that I will let her know when she is to start.

LATE JUNE

Surprise! Just as I was about to leave for Faery this very morning, I received a messenger with a letter from King Zot. He says
Snow is very pregnant. He says he's much afraid the father may
not be the mad young prince, but he's making nothing of that,
because it may be for the best. The messenger who brought the
letter is the putative father of Snow's baby: that nice young
courtier, Vincent, the one who tried so hard to keep his young
master in check.

"Well, this is a fine thing," I said, waving the letter at him
so the seals and ribbons flapped. "Why on earth?"

He shrugged, blushing. "I didn't mean to," he said weakly.
"She's so lovely. And she has no sense of the fitness of things.
And her husband was away, hunting, and I was rather drunk.
And she gets prettier and prettier."

I should have brought her back and locked her up in a
monastery. I know I should. "She's not intelligent, you know."

"Oh, I know." He sounded guilty about that, too, as he well
might. "One is constantly aware of that. It is like making love to
a beautiful talking doll. She keeps saying, 'Oooh, that's so
nice.'"

"What's the King doing about her?"

"He's sent me away," he said, shamefaced. "And he's ap-
pointed all women to look after them from now on. Old
women. You know. Past the age when . . ."

"I know," I snarled at him. "What will the King do when
the baby arrives?"

"The King plans to send it here to be fostered and educated.
The King doesn't want the baby around the prince, just on the
chance that . . . I mean . . ."

"I know what you mean," I said. "The child, if it's a boy,
might by some chance get into the succession, and the King
doesn't want him to be infected with madness. If madness is
infectious." It was no time to give Vincent a lesson in genetics.
"What are you going to do now?"

"The King heard that your friend died." (I had given it
about that Giles had died.) "So I'm to stay here and look after
you," he said. "For my sins."

Well! This postpones my return to Faery for a time. I can't wait to see the baby. Also, it will be nice to have a man around again.

FALL 1418

The baby arrived today. King Zot said I was to see to the naming of him and the rearing of him. The King is getting even with me for Snow, I'm sure of it. The baby's name will be Giles Edward Vincent Charming, honoring everyone who deserves to be honored and at least one who doesn't.

Since I knew the baby was coming, I've a wet nurse already hired. The one who came with him wants to go back to Nadenada. I also have a nursery maid and a pleasant young boy who will play with him when he gets a bit older. It isn't good for boys to have only women around them.

Since it is also not good for a young man to be alone, exposed to the temptations of the world, I have arranged a marriage for Vincent. She is the daughter of a local baron, fallen upon hard times, but of impeccable lineage. Her name is Elizabeth. She is quite pretty, extremely intelligent, and, thanks to her father, well-educated. We took her without a dowry, since the poor man had none to offer, and both she and Vincent feel grateful and relieved to be so well arranged for.

Since the Dower House is large enough for all of us, young Giles will grow up in a house with two parents and one old aunt!

CHRISTMASTIDE 1418

I am having such fun with the baby! Elizabeth is a treasure, such a sweet, helpful girl. I hope Vincent loves her as much as I already do. Both of them are quite sweet with baby Giles, almost as though he were their own. I feel fortunate that they are here.

WINTER 1419

Today, while I was telling cook at some length what I wanted prepared for dinner, I surprised upon Elizabeth's face an expression which was so familiar and yet so elusive that I spent a good part of the morning figuring it out. It came to me at last. With considerable shock I realized it is the same expression that I used to feel upon my own face when one of the aunts did something so outrageous that I could not believe it, yet had no recourse but to accept it. It is an expression of bemused fury.

Well, during my converse with the cook, I had changed my mind several times about the menu. I really had. There was a time when that would have annoyed me. The implication is inevitable. I am merely tolerated in my own house! The idea makes me waver between amusement and fury and grief. I have done everything for Elizabeth that a loving mother might have done. I thought she liked me. Well, she does. She simply wishes I were not so much about. If I were at a distance, she could probably like me quite well, or she could hate me without hindrance, whichever she was minded to do at the moment. When I realized this, I cried, then I thought vindictively of sending her and Vincent away—they are living here at my invitation, after all—then I cried again. Oh, I wish Giles had not died! It is only with our own loves that we are more than mere burdens. Neither of a mated pair should ever die first! Or even, as he has done, go to sleep!

Finally, after much weeping and self-examination, I decided that it is time for me to do what I had planned before Vincent arrived: return to Faery. The baby is not mine. He'll be happier if there is no dissention in his home. Tonight I will tell Vincent I am going on a journey. A pilgrimage. I will give him title to the Dower House and surrounding lands, which I purchased some time ago. I will advise him of the income he may expect to receive per annum. My investments, however, remain my own against my return. Unless I do not return.

LATER

"When will you be back?" Vincent asked. "Who are you going with?"

"A party of pilgrims," I told him. "At my age, I may not be back, my boy, but that is no concern of yours. If I do not return in—oh, thirty years, let us say—my great-grandson Giles Edward Vincent Charming will fall heir to what I have. Thirty is a

good age to inherit property. One is still young enough to enjoy
it, but old enough to have acquired elementary prudence."

"I don't want you to go," he said. "I don't want you to go."
Vincent's face was troubled, part duty, part affection. The larger
part affection, I think, though one is never sure, is one? Elizabeth had merely said farewell, without protestation.

"But I want to go," I told him with a smile.

I think I really do want to go. Before, when I was in Faery, I
knew too little. Now, I may know too much, but I want to see it
again. I keep worrying about what Carabosse may be doing. I
keep thinking of Mama. "I have lived long enough, having seen
one thing, that love hath an end." My favorite poet said that.
He was right. Before my end, I need to make it right with her.

I will take my cloak, boots, and book with me. The only
thing left to do is to send word to Odile Kent that she is to begin
her daily journey to the Wellingford kitchen.

"When are you going?" Vincent asks. "Soon?"

I will be gone before he knows it. One need not pack for
Faery.

FAERY, NO TIME, NO DATE

Most things done in Faery have no meaning in the world. However, as I know from when I was last here, words written here
are really written. When I go out of this place, they will come
with me into the other world. Promises made here are transfer-
able. Songs sung here can be sung out there. Meaning is meaning, whether in the world or in Faery. Only our outward seeming does not go from one place to the other. Here I am young
again, and very beautiful. Here I am Beauty once again.

It would be easy to forget to go back. Suppose my mortal
half died here, in Faery. Wouldn't my fairy half go on? Perhaps I
would be dwindled, as Puck says, but still immortal. Free to
dance here, and dine here, and while the endless time away with
hunts and feasts. Dwindle. Ride mice. Sleep in flowers. Become
one with the origin of my creation.

It is tempting. Enticing. Seductive. I try to summon what
Father Raymond would have called my conscience and deter-
mine that, whatever happens, I will go back, at intervals, to

wash and eat and dress myself and see what time has passed. Perhaps I can remember to do it. Perhaps not.

As I was leaving, I stood by the ruined hulk of Wellingford and peered back through the trees to see the Dower House well-peopled behind me. Its windows were alight and its chimneys sent up fine coils of smoke toward heaven. Let the smoke carry my prayer: pray God that Vincent and Elizabeth stay well, and so baby Giles.

.
27
.

WELLINGFORD: ONE STROKE ON THE CHIMNEYPIECE

A month already? I would have said a day or two. I am famished. I ate all the bread and cheese and drank most of the beer. After I have a bath, I will have the rest of the beer and the meat. My dress is a bit ragged, but it will do a while longer. I must have a clean underbodice. This one is covered with something dreadful along the sleeves.

Mama had returned to Faery, as Puck had told me. My boots took me to the flowery meadow at the center of that world. I put on my shoes and began walking toward the distant castles, and there she was, standing all alone. "Hello, daughter," she said, not at all surprised as she turned to walk beside me. "You've come back." She said not another word, nor did I, until we reached the castle. She kissed me on the cheek, an unmeaning kiss, like the kiss of an aunt, then pointed to a door and said, "Your room is there." How could one describe her manner? Neither warm nor chill. Neither welcoming nor forbidding. Merely neutral. As though it made no difference. As though I had been noticed, but only that. I did not know how to break through to her. All the words I had been saving were useless. I felt despair,

but then something stubborn in me said to stay and keep trying.
So.

Oberon noticed me, too—but only that. He bowed and
swept his hat widely, almost a satire upon himself, but did not
invite my company on his couch, nor did any of the others. Not
that I'd have consented, but it would have been nice to be
asked. After a few days of this treatment by all of them, I decided to find out why, not caring greatly except that I like to
know what is going on. I thought Puck would tell me, so I
wandered off into a copse of lacy trees and called him up. He
did not want to tell me, but did, finally. He says I smell differently now. Mortality, he says. Before, I was in the juice and fat
of life, but now I know what age is, I have a scent of sootiness,
like a candle burned down to its end.

"They can't see it," he said, kissing me on the cheek to take
the pain of his words away. "But they can sense it."

"I'm half mortal," I cried angrily. "I've wondered what that
means, really. Can't the mortal half die and the other half remain?"

Puck shook his head. "I've known several begot by mortals,
half fairy like yourself. If they were born here, or if they came
here as wee children to stay, then they seem to partake fully of
Faery. If they live in human lands, they seem to grow up mortal.
It's as though the heritage is the smaller part, and the rearing is
the most of it. You were reared to a good age in the real world,
so your fairy half maybe didn't have a chance to develop. Don't
ask me, Beauty. I grow less and less sure about things." He
looked older to me than he had in the past, if those in Faery can
be said to age. Perhaps Bogles do, if they choose.

"You don't blame me, do you?" I asked, needing him as a
friend and not wanting him to disapprove of me. "You don't
blame me for coming back?"

"Ach, no," he said. "I don't. The Fenoderee doesn't. None
of us do. Carabosse wants to see you, when you've time."

"Everything looks much the same," I commented.

"Thus far," he agreed. "Though Oberon is coming close to
changing his world. He's bored, I think."

The words set up a dreadful resonance in my mind. I had seen another ruler change his world out of boredom.

"He's gotten sneakier," said Puck, going on with his comments. "He's fallen into this pattern of evasion."

"Evasion?"

"Of the terms of the covenant. You remember his enchanting people into deer, and then killing them? Cleaving to the letter, but not to the spirit? He's doing more things of that kind. No matter what Oberon says, it's at least a small infraction of the covenant. It's like the agreement they made with the Dark Lord, a kind of slyness. It's unworthy of what he once was, is what it is, but you wouldn't dare say that to Oberon now."

"What would a big infraction of the covenant be, then?"

"Well, they almost found out, didn't they, seven years ago, when they set out from here intending to give Thomas the Rhymer to the Dark Lord?" He made a disgusted face. "They came close then!"

I went back to the castle feeling dismayed but trying not to show it. I needn't have bothered. The people of the hills simply weren't paying any attention to me. Partly because of my mortality, I suppose, but partly something else. Some great event due to occur, something that was known of and planned for even before I came back, something mysterious that even Oberon doesn't speak of. There is whispering, something I don't remember from my former visit. In a land in which everything is known, nothing really hidden, in which all veils are merely seeming, what is there to whisper about?

Finding out will be more exciting than sitting in the Dower House growing lame(r) and blind(er) while Elizabeth simmers. So, when I've had my bath and something more to eat, I'll return to Faery.

The Sidhe are as nervous as sparrows, twitching at every sound. Some great doings are abroad in the land, but they will not tell me what they are. There are tents set up in the meadow, as though the Sidhe were expecting guests. Everyone pretends not to notice them.

I have been left much alone since my return, full of doubts

and vagrant memories which sometimes overwhelm me. I spend much time thinking of Giles and of my life in the twentieth, wondering what I might have done differently with both. Sometimes I simply sit about, doing nothing purposeful, trying to make meaning of my life. It comes back to Mama, always. Why had I been born? For what? How had I failed her?

At last I begged her to walk with me in the flowery meadow, and among the copses I asked her to tell me what was going on.

"Going on?" She drew herself up and made her eyes glitter at me arrogantly. "Going on?"

"Come on, Mama," I said desperately. "You know what I mean. There's a definite mood of apprehension about."

"I don't know what you mean, Beauty," she said, striking a very dignified attitude. "I have no idea what you can be speaking of." She spoke as though to a stranger.

"Who is it that's coming?" I wanted to know.

She looked suddenly very haggard. "We're not sure who they are now," she admitted. "They were our kindred once."

"Then how do you know they're coming?" I asked.

"We just know," she said, the glitter in her eyes looking more like tears than arrogance. I tried to put my arm around her, and she pushed me away. "You should have come when you were young," she cried. "I told you to come to me when you were young! And when you came at last, you should have stayed. You went away, and now you stink of age and corruption. If you'd stayed when you were young, you'd have stayed young for a long, long time. So long, you'd have forgotten anything but Faery! I smell death on you, and it hurts me! I cannot bear it!"

Puck had told me about my smell, but hearing it from her was like being slapped. I felt totally mortal, unbelievably old. If I could have shrunk into wrinkles and ashes, I would have done. She stood apart from me, her back to me, and it was a time before I could answer her.

"Mama, I had to go away. Thomas the Rhymer was gone. I know you wouldn't have meant for it to happen, but it's likely

Mab and Oberon would have used me for the teind if I'd stayed."

"Better me than you, is that it?" She drew herself up, proudly.

"They didn't break the covenant with you, Mama. They would have broken it with me. And you survived. Puck told me when you came back."

"Puck!" she sneered. "I have a daughter who not only betrays me but also associates with Bogles."

"Mama!"

"I should never have given you the gifts I gave you. You're merely mortal! You aren't worthy of them!"

"Mama!"

She turned away, obdurate, angry.

"Take them back," I said. "If that's the way you feel."

She was sobbing. The Sidhe never cry. "No, the gift once made remains. You are what you are because of me. I try, but I can't hate you enough to take the gifts away." And she ran away, back to the courts, leaving me in the meadow staring after her, longing for a mother's strong love and seeing a child's weakness. Perhaps she could have loved a fairy child. She had nothing to give me. She had never had anything to give me. It was the other way around, and I understood for the first time what Puck meant. The Sidhe did not have children in order to give but in order to get. Mortals have a strength that they need.

Ridiculously, what came into my head then was the third hank of thread. I had wanted for a long time to ask her about the third hank of thread. Now I could not ask. She was hurt with me, but hurt with something else as well, something she had been worried about when I returned. Something great and mysterious had them all in an uproar. I had needed her, and she needed . . . what?

"Fenoderee," I whispered. "Take me to Carabosse."

He was there, holding the bridle of a horse. We went together, the same way I had gone before. Puck was waiting for us at the cottage door, and as I knocked I heard the susuration of clocks suspended into sudden silence.

"Come in," she cried. She sat huddled in a chair before the

fire. Behind her, all around her, the walls were still covered with clocks. More hung down a hallway I could see through a half-open door, while others stood on the window ledges and in the corners, hung from the rafters, or lay on the table before her with their gears and hands spread out before them.

The only thing I could think of to say was, "There are few, if any, clocks in the fifteenth!"

"Fifteenth what?" she demanded.

"Fifteenth century," I said.

"Fifteenth, twelfth, first, makes no difference to me," she said.

Puck squatted on the carpet and picked at a toenail.

"I don't keep human time," Carabosse said.

It looked to me as though she kept a great deal of human time, but it seemed inappropriate to say so. "What are they for," I asked.

"Amusement," she said. "Entertainment. A hobby." She got up from her chair, leaning heavily upon a gnarled stick. I sensed little glamour about her. She evidently didn't care what she looked like. Her hair was sparse; her eyes were bloodshot; her forehead was high and corrugated with deep lines. She had a hump on her back and walked bent in half. She pointed her cane to one of the clocks on the wall and said, "That's Oberon's. The one next to it is Mab's."

I looked at them more closely. They were fine clocks, very beautifully made. Italian, I thought, eighteenth-century, perhaps. Enameled bronze and gilt, a matched pair.

"They've about run down," she cackled at me.

"Would you like me to wind them?" I asked politely.

"Would I like you to wind them? Ha, ha. So, you're a jester, are you? Beauty. Come sit by the fire. Have some tea."

She stumped her way back to her chair, and I took the one across from her, a comfortable rush-bottomed chair which fit me exactly. I had a feeling it would suit any guest exactly. For all its small size and sparsity of furnishings, the cottage was warm and comfortable.

She poured and handed me a cup, cream and sugar, the way I like it. There was no tea of this kind in the fourteenth, either, at least not in my part of the world. It seemed unnecessary to comment on that. It was real human tea. So were the biscuits, real. She and Puck seemed determined to feed me real food.

"You're getting older," she said.

I nodded. "That's my inescapable conclusion, Carabosse. Are you doing something about it?"

"About your getting older?"

"About this package I've been carrying about."

"Shhh," she said, glancing sidewise at Puck.

"He's known about it since I was a child," I said. "Puck knows more about me than either my mother or father ever did."

She glared at Puck, and he made a face at her, like an impudent boy.

"More than your father, certainly," she agreed. "Stupid man. Couldn't think of anything but his ridiculous pilgrimages. Wandering about, gazing at pieces of rotted bodies, thinking that conferred some kind of grace, all the time letting Westfaire go to ruin."

"It really wasn't," I contradicted, a little angered by what she had said. "It wasn't going to ruin, I mean. The roof was whole. All the walls were sound."

"Oh, child, I don't mean the beams and the stones. I mean the people who could have kept it and preserved it. You were his only child, and he almost ignored you. He didn't find you a good husband to help preserve Westfaire. Westfaire deserves preserving. That and a good deal else."

"He didn't find me a husband because you had cursed me," I argued, growing a little pink in the face. I could feel it.

"No, no, no," she said, waving her cane. "Before I cursed you. I looked at what he would do if I hadn't cursed you, don't you see? I don't go around doing indiscriminate curses. Besides, it wasn't you I cursed, remember?"

"Wasn't it Aunt Joyeause who changed your curse from death to sleep," I argued, wanting to get this business of the curse straightened out at last. "That's what the letter said."

Carabosse shook her head, to and fro, sipping at her tea, smiling a knowing, half-toothless smile. "Joyeause doesn't have the wits of a bat. She couldn't summon up a fairy gift if her life depended on it. And besides that, she tells lies. She was the only one near when I cursed Duke Phillip's lovely daughter with sleep."

"Duke Phillip's lovely daughter, and Westfaire," I pointed out.

"Well, yes. And Westfaire."

"Forever?"

"Let us say without a stated time of wakening," she said stiffly, warning me with her expression to press the matter no further. "I left immediately thereafter. Joyeause must have gone to your Mama with some fay and follet story about what she thought I'd said or what she invented to say I'd said or what she would have said in my place. It's like her. Such a silly-shee."

"I used to think all fairies were wise," I said sadly. The thought that Carabosse might be lying never entered my head. She was telling the truth, and I knew it.

"Some are and some aren't."

"So, what's happening, Carabosse."

"The Dark Lord saw you, is what's happening. First, in Faery, picking that vengeful herb to get back at that man. Then, later, in that mirror in Marvella. The first time, it meant little to him. The second time, it meant more. Your showing up in both places has a certain resonance to it. He didn't really see what you're carrying, but he scents it perhaps. He wants to put his nose on you and sniff you up, find out what you are."

Hearing it like that, even though I'd known it, in my heart, made me shudder. "Well, Carabosse, you must find somewhere else to put it, that's all."

"True." She sipped and nodded.

I sighed. "I didn't mean what's going on about the Dark Lord, anyhow. I meant, what's going on in Faery."

"The Bogles did a thing," she said, cocking her eyebrows at Puck where he sat on the carpet. "Oh yes, they did a thing."

"What have you done, Puck?" I asked him.

"The Sidhe wouldn't listen to us, so we've tried the only thing left to try. We've sent a message out of Faery."

"How have you done that?"

"How haven't they?" snorted Carabosse.

Puck settled himself for oration. "We've cried out by every hob and boggart, by the gruagach and the selkies, by the killmoulis and every lob-lie-by-the-fire capable of speech. Every pixie and nixie, phouka and glashan have carried our summons. We've sent the aughisky and the banshee out to howl, the bogan and the spriggans out to screech. The gabriel ratchets have honked the call into the sky, and the fuath have bubbled it down into the watery places beneath the sea.

"In the towers of the north, the dunters are grinding our words in their quern until the message rattles the stones beneath the mountains. Even the duergar have been constrained against wickedness and made to write our summons in the smoke of their fires. The cait sith prowls the edges of the world yowling our yowl, and after her come the black dogs, barking our bark. In all the times of earth until now, no such call has gone out from the Bogle-folk, and if there are any left to answer it, surely they will." He finished up with a fine, broad gesture.

"If they'd asked me," said Carabosse, "I'd have told them it wasn't necessary. I'd have told Israfel, and he'd have told his kinfolk. A few quiet words. All this hullabaloo wasn't needed."

"We wanted a hullabaloo," said Puck in a dignified voice.

"And what answer have you had, Puck?" I knew the answer already. What else could it be?

"The Long Lost are coming home," he said. "They're coming back to Faery. The Sidhe don't much like it. Oberon's wrathful and that makes his people edgy. Elladine's people are in no good mood. They're snarly, and snarly folk do stupid things."

"They're snarly, right enough," I said, remembering how Mama had flown at me, over nothing.

Puck replied, "If things get very bad for you there, with them, call me. It might be well for you to come visit my places. I've visited yours often enough."

"Maybe you should come stay with me," suggested Carabosse.

I shook my head, feeling confused and alone. "What am I supposed to do?" I asked. "What will be best?"

"Just go on," she advised me, pursing her old, wrinkled lips, leaning forward to place her hand on my breast, feeling the little fire in there. "Just go on. Being ordinary."

"With the Dark Lord hovering in the wings, sniffing and waiting to pounce?"

"We've talked about that, Israfel and I. If he pounces, we'll be there. Don't worry, Beauty. We're watching. We're good at that."

I tried to get more out of her and got nothing. She was closemouthed as a turtle, glaring at Puck out of the corner of her eyes, as though he had betrayed the secret instead of merely finding out about it.

He and I went out into the world and rode back to the castle. When we came within sight of it, we stopped and merely sat, seeing what was there. Things change about in Faery. What is there one day is often not there the next.

"Why is Oberon's castle always there," I murmured.

"Because Oberon believes it is," said Puck. "As do his courtiers, of course."

"They all believe the mountains are there," I agreed, for the mountains never changed.

"And the sea, and the stretching moors, and the meadow. Yes. This is the land into which they were born. Originally, of course, it was in the world. Then, as men began to encroach, the Sidhe moved it, but this is the evening land of woods and sea that they were made for, and they believe in it."

"Do you?"

He shrugged. "It is the land into which I was born as well. Many of my people dwell in those mountains, beside that sea, at the far edge of that moor. Others of my people remained in the world when Faery was removed, and many of us chose to continue there, but this most resembles our ancestral home."

"But the trees move about. The copses in the meadow are one time here and one time there."

"The copses shift, perhaps, with those who think of them."

"I've noticed one sizeable copse that always stays," I said, pointing to one that shone silver against the dark bulk of the hills.

Puck paled, though I am not sure how I saw any change in his color in that long gloaming. "The Copse of the Covenant," he said. "It was there Oberon stood when he made the pledge to the Holy One, Blessed be He, that no man should come to lasting harm through the Sidhe."

"And everyone remembers it, so it stays there, in that place," I said.

Puck shook his head. "If they remember, it is not willingly. I have seen Oberon try to move that copse away. I have seen him send axemen to cut it down. He cannot touch it. It stands."

"Because everyone remembers it," I repeated.

"Because the Holy One remembers it," he said.

I could imagine how annoyed Oberon would be at that, how it would nag at him, reminding him. Puck forestalled further question by reaching out a hand to stroke mine, then he vanished as he usually does, not in a puff of nothingness, but with a sidle which seems to carry him behind something, even when there is nothing to go behind. It is so all the Bogles come and go, there one minute, gone the next, slipping into ways we mortals—or even half mortals—cannot see. I think they are ways that even full fairies do not often see, for, considering Oberon's hatred of them, if Bogles were easily followed and caught, there would be many fewer of them.

I walked back to the castle, wondering a number of things. Wondering if I could master the Bogle sidle. Wondering why one has to walk or ride in Faery, rather than simply "being" where one wants to be. Wondering, considering the empty feeling at my center, if it might not be time to come back to Wellingford and get something to eat. It seems too much effort. A needless effort.

I summoned all my strength of will and did it.

WELLINGFORD: ONE ROW ON THE CHIMNEYPIECE AND SIX STROKES BELOW
The boots brought me here and I stumbled, weak with hunger. Eighteen months since I was last here, though it seemed merely days, a few days. It was hard to summon strength to stagger to the broken-legged table where the bread was set out, covered with a linen napkin. I will stay here a day or two and eat. I may

even raid the kitchen at the Dower House. My clothes are rags. I have already discarded them for others. The warm bathwater was welcome. I soaked off dirt and scabs and washed my hair. Thank God I thought to leave a comb with my clothing.

I came so close not to coming back at all.

LATER

I eat like a starved dog, gulping the food down. I did raid the kitchen at the Dower House, sneaking around the dairy like a ghost before wraithing it upstairs in my cloak to have a look at baby Giles. Such a big boy, now. Vincent has made him a rocking horse, so he must be walking. Well, of course he's walking; he's almost two. Grumpkin III was curled beside the baby's cot. When I came into the room, Grumpkin woke and came to me, rubbing around my ankles, purring loudly enough to wake the house. I sat there and held him, softness beneath my chin, and he reached out a paw to touch my face. I hated to leave him there. I wanted to bring him with me. I cannot. He needs to be here, where there are mice to catch and queen cats to pursue. If I do not return again soon, I will find his child in his stead, and yet leaving him is like leaving part of me.

Now I have eaten, and bathed, and dressed myself. Now that I am fortified, I'm going back once again. Mostly because of curiosity. I want to know what's going to happen.

LATER

I had mentioned earlier that Oberon has largely ignored me since my return. This morning, or what passes for morning in the eternal evening of this place, he sought me out among the ladies of his court.

"Beauty," he smiled. "Well met."

"Well met, Your Majesty," I curtsied in a flourish of samite and lace.

"We have come to invite you to join the royal hunting party this evening," he said.

I curtsied again, wondering if this would be another expedition after enchanted deer, wondering how I could say no.

"We go to hunt the moonrise," he said smoothly, silkily, as

though he had read my mind. "In the lands of mortal men. Such a ride may not come again for a lifetime. We beg you to join us."

I acquiesced, smiling, dropping yet another curtsy. Hunting the moonrise seems innocent enough. I went to find Mama to tell her about the invitation, thinking it would please her. I could not find her, not in the castle, not in the gardens, not near the groves and pools where the ladies of the court like to wander. In the stables I found news of her, however. One of the lads told me the Lady Elladine had ridden out on some business of His Majesty's, some message to be carried somewhere.

I went back into the castle. Everywhere I went there were Sidhe walking about with torches from which a heavy, reddish smoke trailed, filling the air. "What's going on," I asked one of them, a tall, white-haired fay named Auspir.

"Smoking out the spies," he said crisply. "The King believes the castle is riddled with them."

"Spies?"

"Bogles," he said.

I started to tell him if the Bogles wanted to get into the castle, they'd do it, despite all the Sidhe could do against them. I thought better of it.

Grandaunt Joyeause came by, and I asked her what was going on.

"My dear," she trilled, "don't ask *me!* I'm always the last to be told, the last at any event. As you should well know!"

"Is it true that Oberon thinks there are Bogle spies in the castle?"

"Oh, very likely," she said with a high flutter of laughter. "He's always thought that, hasn't he?"

The smoke smelled harsh and resinous and made it impossible to stay in the castle. I went out into the paddock and spent the afternoon watching the horses and writing in this book. Soon it will be time to bathe and dress for the moonhunt. I'll take the book with me on the ride, just in case there is a pause during which I can record what a moonhunt amounts to. I wish Mama were here to go with us. It might make an opportunity for us to work ourselves back into sympathy with one another. Mothers care for their children even when the children are dy-

ing of loathsome disease, don't they? Though perhaps there is
no disease so loathsome as mortality, and that is why the old die
first in the world: so they need not see their children succumb to
it.

This ride is a strange affair. We began by trotting over the flowery meadows of Faery. Hoof-fall and bridle-ring jingle, a quiet
murmur of voices, the stars chiming like glass bells, the wind
coming up to blow in our faces and make us feel we are riding
faster and faster, fast as the wind itself.

Which we cannot be. Surely not. Surely not as fast as the
wind! And yet the meadow goes under the hooves like a great
carpet, smoothly pulled from beneath us, and we are suddenly
on the heath, where contorted stones come up through the
bracken and gorse to stand as enigmatic monuments upon this
high plain. I smell the glamour around us, thick as smoke. Afar
on one hand is the level line of the sea, glowing with dimly
reflected light from the gathered stars, while far ahead on the
other hand are barren hills and behind them a jagged bulk of
mountains.

Our ride has brought us out into the world. The air is moist
and chill. The horses' breath steams, making clouds around their
heads and ours. The rutted road winds along the flanks of the
downs, its pale track vanishing into a dark fold of hills. Dry
leaves skitter across the ruts. Hunched clumps of heather crouch
like toads in the lee of the twisted stones. I find myself counting
the months. I came to Faery in March. I returned to Wellingford
in April. I returned last the following April, plus six. Likely it is
October or November of that year here in the world.

The road winds, along this hill and another hill and another
hill. One twisted stone and another twisted stone. One glimpse
of the star-silvered sea as we come around a corner, then almost
darkness for a time until we wind that way again. Silence
among the riders. The horses champ and stamp, gusting their
breath in great sighs, and the silent hounds run red-eyed among
their legs.

At long last we come to a crossroad, with a crude cross set

up on a stepped pedestal, roughly squared stones laid by an inexpert hand. Have I seen it before? It seems familiar to me, and yet not, as though I might have seen it years ago, or in some other place. Oberon has dismounted and stands next the cross, staring at the sky, at the stars to see how they move, as though what he does next depends upon their movement. Perhaps the stars make the only clock Faery can depend upon to know when the moon will rise. I sit on the pedestal beside the cross and write, while the Sidhe murmur together like voiced shadows.

Oberon calls, relish in his voice, anticipation. We will ride again. He and Mab and a whole following of fairy folk. But not Elladine.

LATER

At the road's end is a great cavern, tall and dark as a tomb. Inside it is a fire the Sidhe have built, and behind the fire, a door. Oberon and his people are unusually quiet as they wait for the moonrise. There are so many of the Sidhe about that I do not feel I can call for Puck or the Fenoderee without endangering them. Instead I sit and write, an inveterate chronicler, recording each action. The Sidhe seem to me to be in no very contemplative mood.

Ah, now I see the first light on the eastern horizon. The edge of the moon pressing upward, a half-moon. Everyone murmurs at the rising light. As the moon comes higher, it illuminates the cavern where they are all standing, and they come out, into the pale light, leaving the fire behind them.

They murmur, I write. Now they turn toward the fire for some ritual or other. Oberon gestures. They fall silent.

The door is opening!

I see light within. A face in the light. A face I have seen before, in a tower room in Marvella, looking out at me from a mirror.

Oh, my God. My God. I've been a fool, a fool. Puck said it. He said, "Seven years ago, when Thomas the Rhymer got free!" It is still Halloween. Seven years have passed since Thomas was claimed by his fair Janet. The Sidhe owe another teind to hell, and this time no one has come between themselves and their intended victim. They have brought here the only teind they could lay hands on who is not wholly fairy. One stinking of mortality. An old woman.

"What have you brought me?" the voice in the doorway cries like a whinney, like a howl.

"Beauty," Oberon says, turning his glittering eyes on me where I sit, petrified, writing. "Beauty, daughter of Elladine."

I am glad she was not with them. I can tell myself she would not have let this happen.

And now they are all departing, taking my horse with them, and I have not cloak nor boots nor Mama's box; not Puck, nor the Fenoderee, nor Giles nor any friend but myself, here, all alone. And in the light the face smiles as only that face can smile, and a finger beckons.

A voice by my ear says, "We are here."

I look. Nothing.

"We are here," says the voice. "Do not fear."

Carabosse? Israfel?

The finger beckons again, and my body moves against my will. I cannot go on writing.

Barrymore Gryme is here. Jaybee Veolante is here. Others of their ilk are here. The things they created in their books and pictures are here as well, made real, embodied in flesh, or more than flesh, or less than flesh. It is not proper that they should be here, either the authors or their creations. It is not timely. I am half a millennium away from their time. There are no movies here, no television, no paperback books, no best-seller list in the *New York Times*. There are no publishing houses, no editors, no word processors, none of what it takes to create monstrousness and evoke horror, none of what it takes to record frantic lust as it edges its way toward death. And yet they are here. The ones whose names blazoned the bookstalls and the ones whose names were whispered over the counters; those who sold openly and those who sold covertly.

As I am moved through this place, I see some of them at desks, writing. Some are directing dramas. These are the willing ones who have always belonged to the Dark Lord. Others, the unwilling, who thought they could trifle with the Dark Lord's works for amusement only, they are held in cages until time comes to act out their stories, and then they are let out. They are costumed, false faces glued to their own, breasts nailed to their chests if that is needed, their own genitals cut away or modified as the plot requires, this one to play that one's wife or son or mother, another one to play the part of the character who will be slowly eviscerated in the third chapter, another one to be the child who returns from the dead with sharpened teeth or the child who is raped and then murdered, and then, then, they are set upon the stage, their memories wiped clean, and set to the play. Chapter after chapter, horror after horror, while the Dark Lord applauds and cries bravo, bravo, bravo.

Others are here, many of them from the twentieth. Those who forbade birth control and abortion, worshipping the fetus over all other of God's creations. They are here in their vestments, their religious garb, their Sunday robes or their everyday dress, carrying their picket signs and swollen in endless parturition, for so the Dark Lord commands that they shall be, endlessly pregnant, endlessly giving birth, endlessly suckling the demonic life that burgeons out of them, with no choice in the matter. Having allowed none, they are now given none, and the Dark Lord roars with amusement.

The nature destroyers are here, the tree-cutters and whale-killers, they are here, some of them willingly. They sit on bare stone and contemplate bare stone and eat bare stone for their sustenance. Surrounded by ten thousand of their like pressed in on every side, they gasp for air and beg for water. What they did, or wrote, or filmed, or believed in life has brought them here. Here there can be no undoing or rewriting. Here one is judged by the words already on paper, the picture already on film, the speech already recorded. Nothing new is written here. Only old things, redone. Old horrors, relived.

Still, I am able to think new words and distill new paragraphs out of the awful silences between the more horrible sounds. Between the screaming, the panting, the *uhng uhng uhng* sounds flesh makes when the pain and terror grow too much for comprehension. To shut out that sound, I think sentences, I spell them into happening, into my book, wherever my book may be, writing them there in shadow letters, willing them to exist, enchanting them into existing, somewhere, to keep myself sane.

Mama stayed here for a time. Mama came away herself still, or almost herself, still. Can I?

He has put Barry and Jaybee in cells next to mine. Cells. One could call them that. Obdurate cloud, frozen pain, structured agony, something not metal nor stone, something not permeable, not tangible, not anything one knows about substance. It isn't substance, but it's there, on all sides, below, above, opening nowhere except when He reaches through with his hand, his finger, his long, sinuous, lascivious, dignity-destroying tongue.

I hear Barry's voice. He says, "Help me, help me, please, oh help me."

I scream at him in fury and pain. "Nothing is happening to you you didn't describe, think of, imagine. Nothing is happening to you you didn't conceive of and write down. Why do you ask for my help?"

I cannot even help myself.

"We are here," say the voices. They come close, like a cloak, like a bandage, like a barrier between me and what other things are here. There is healing in them. There is quiet in them. Invisibly, they are here. Even when I am being hurt, they are there, between the core of me and Him. The torturer can see my flesh, but not the thing I carry. He can feel my flesh, but not what it conceals.

"We are here," they say. "Hold on."

Jaybee is next door to me, separated only by a veil. If he sees me, he will break through. If I move, or breathe, or blink, he will see me. So I sit, like a statue, immobile, while he prowls there. Clever of the Dark One to think of this. So much worse than merely being raped, or killed. To think one may escape, if one merely doesn't cough. Doesn't breathe. Doesn't move. Doesn't move. Doesn't move.

He is singing, beneath his breath, a happy little hum as he

wanders, brushing against the veil. "Down, down, down to hap-pyland . . ."

It would be easier to die.

Except for the voices that gather around me to protect me, to make all quiet. "Hold on," they say. "We are here." How do they stay invisible? Undetectable?

Who are they? Is it really Carabosse, old Carabosse? Is it really Israfel, come to this hideous place? Strangely, I hear more voices than theirs. I do not take time to wonder. When they offer sleep, I sleep.

Once in a while there is the sound of a great gong, the reverberations slowly dying away into nothingness. I tell myself the gong marks the passage of days, or weeks. It has rung twelve or fifteen times since I have been here. It must be to mark the passage of time. What time? Is it like Carabosse's clock, marking the time until the end!

Time. There was a time, I remember a time, when certain things were said to be unthinkable. Persons did not dwell on these thoughts, they cast them aside, exorcising them by crossing themselves, by prayer, by recital of some formula which would wipe out the unthinkable thing. It did not do to dwell on such things. The darkness was too close. The reality of death was too near.

Later came science and electric lights, a time when people sitting in well-illuminated rooms said, "nonsense, we can conceive of anything at all." Any horror. Any disgusting, vomit-making thing. Any garbage. Any offal. Any violence, blood, evisceration, ripping open, heads flying with blood spurting, things emerging from inside the heart with the tissue ripping like paper and the tender inner places laid bare, no defense, no place to hide. "We can think of those things," they said, with a chuckle. "We can think of them."

There were times, I remember, when we said certain things were unspeakable. Fantasies too horrible for words. Imaginings too gross for description. Violence too inhuman to be put in human language. And then came those who said, "We can speak it, we can say it, make stories of it, until there is nothing that is not there on the page for the eye to see, for the mind to comprehend, for the child in each of us to be corrupted and eternally tainted by."

Innocence. Gone, forever, with the unthinkable and the unspeakable. And innocent laughter gone as well. Now only the dirty giggle, the wicked snigger, the game of out-grossing, the playtime of the beasts.

So that when the real death stalks

When the real horror begins

It will all be familiar and we will be able to enjoy it.

Barrymore Gryme has been put in the cell with me.

"Do I know you?" he screamed at me.

One eye hung on his cheek, that cheek gnawed open so that the teeth showed through. I shuddered, sickened, put my hands out and healed him. I am half fairy. I can do that. He was naked. His white, pouchy flesh was covered with scabs and bruises. Parts of him are mangled. Touching him is like touching something long dead.

"When did you die?" I asked.

"Die. Die," he screamed at me. "I'm not dead. I wish I were dead."

"You're in hell," I told him. "The hell you made. Did you believe in it, when you made it?"

He turned his face into the corner of wherever we are and wept. I tried to find a way out, but I cannot get away from him. My pain and disgust are part of the teind. They amuse the Dark Lord who is disgusted at nothing, who feels no pain, but who relishes it in others.

"Hold on," the voices say, breathing cool, fresh air upon me. Offering me cool, fresh water.

Later I saw Barry watching me. "You're beautiful," he said in wonder.

"I am not beautiful," I told him, stripping the glamour away so that he could see what I really am. He did not see. The Dark Lord will not let him see. Or perhaps he sees too well.

"You glow. You shine. Don't be afraid," he whispered. "I won't hurt you. I am a decent man."

I laughed. I laughed until I cried.

The Dark Lord cannot create. Faery cannot create. The angels cannot create. Only God, and man. I told Barry this, carefully, making him pay attention to what I was saying. It was hard. The face glued to his own would not let him breathe, the false breasts fastened to his flesh pained him, the shoes he wore had somehow been made part of his feet so he could not take them off. One of the spike heels was broken, and a fractured end of bone protruded from it. He kept reaching down to feel the bone, trying to convince himself it was not there. It was there. I saw it.

He had been playing a character from one of his own books, a woman who moves into a house occupied by a terrible thing from some other dimension of reality. It kills her children, one by one, in horrible ways, then her boyfriend, then comes after her. Barry had played the role well, so I assumed, for I had heard the Dark Lord's bravos ringing through the substance of the cell. One of the added horrors of this place is that one hears everything.

"The Dark Lord cannot create," I told him again. "You have created everything here. You and the others. He has only borrowed it from you."

"It was only a story," he cried. "Only a story!"

I thought of Chinanga once more. That, too, had been only a story, and yet I remembered Constanzia's face as she twirled slowly into nothingness. What are stories, after all, but reflections of a reality we make? Before Jaybee did anything, first he told himself a story about it. First I will go to her house, then I will break in her door, then I will knock her down and lie on top of her, watching her scream, then I will let my weapon out of my trousers and hurt her with it.

"To those who read it, it was real," I told him. "They lived it, while they read it. Perhaps afterward, they lived it. Some believed it. Perhaps one of those who believe it picked up a weapon and did to someone else what you did to a character. Or tried. There was enough belief to give it reality. Otherwise you would not be here."

He won't believe that. He has stopped talking to me.

The cell is open. I go out. Barry comes behind me.

He is playing with us, of course.

We walk, and I think words. Somewhere they are distilled onto a page. We . . . walk. My feet shuffle along. Barry tiptoes, screaming when he does not get high enough on his toes to avoid the broken bone at his heel. This is part of it, of course. Tempting him to walk, to escape, so that he will try this ungainly, ridiculous gait which hurts him so. I shuffle, he tiptoes. Time goes by. We are still surrounded by others. We can feel them on all sides.

An opening. We separate. He goes one way, I another.

I found a river. I came upon a place where space breaks through into something almost real. Like the door in the cavern, like the mirror, this connects to the world. Or to some other world. It is hard to tell. Mists hang heavily over the flow, which is turgid and silent. Nothing moves in the water. There is no shore I can walk along, but only this one space where hell waits on one side and the water on the other.

Still, it is a change. I sit beside the flow, listening, hoping for a sound other than those I have heard for so long. At last it comes. A slow plopping. From somewhere to my right and behind me. Eons pass and the slow sounds are no closer. And then, at last, they are here, in front of me. A rowboat, a rower, a few other figures who are drawn up past me as though made of smoke, fleeing past me into the enormity of this place.

The rower turns to face me, his dark hood shadowing his face.

"Captain Karon," I whisper.

"Lady Wellingford," he smiles. "Fancy seeing you here." His smile is a death's-head grin, and yet there is something of the old captain there. "Back at my old trade, you see. Sometimes I miss the *Stugos Queen.*"

"I thought," I say, wondering what I thought. "I thought that you . . ."

"Would vanish, with the rest? With my lovely Mrs. Gallimar? With Constanzia and the Viceroy? No. No, I was not part of that story only. I am part of many things."

"You've thought about who you are, then."

"I've had an eternity of time to think about little else," he smiled. "Plying across the Acheron, the Styx, the Cocytus, the Lethe, the Dark Waters at the end of all things."

"Who made them, Captain?"

"Men made them, Lady. Made them with magic their religions stole from Faery. Made them and named them and peopled them, too."

"Along with Acheron and Abaddon and all the rest."

"Surely."

"And this hell behind me, Captain? Did men make this one, too?"

"Men and the Dark Lord, Lady. Each helping the other." He sighed. "Is there anything else I can tell you, or do for you, Lady Wellingford?"

"Would you row me away from here? For old time's sake?"

He laughed. "Where to, Lady Catherine?"

"To the other side."

"What other side?" he smiled again, and pushed his boat away. I heard the quiet plops of the oars recede and was then drawn back into the place.

"Never mind," said the voices. "It may be a way out."

Giles. I have found I can almost escape this place by thinking of Giles. The voices give me silence, and I think of him.

When one is young, one thinks of love in romantic or erotic terms. I did. When I was sixteen, I thought of Giles in romantic and erotic terms. Romance when we were in the dining hall. Eros when I was in bed alone in the night hours. There is no innocence so deep as to veil the urgencies of the flesh from one's own youthful awareness. I wanted Giles, very specifically, to do to me what the stallions did to the mares, what the stable boys talked of doing to their sweethearts. I had no experience of it, but my flesh knew. And then, twenty years later, when we did at last what I had longed for, my flesh knew once again. It was the single thing needed, the one thing wanted, the savor and marvel of life.

I could not imagine doing without it. Being without it.

And yet, all those years in the twentieth, I had done without it, been without it. Seventeen, eighteen years old. At the peak of urgency and desire, and yet I had done without it. Because there had been no Giles. I had remembered him, lusted after him, pleasured myself in my bed pretending he was there. He had been necessary to my joy. It would have been nothing without him. So I had thought.

And when we two had come together at last, we had been splendid, but it had been more than the splendor of the flesh. It was we who loved one another. We two. Old Giles laid his hand upon mine and looked sweetly into my eyes, and I loved him no less than I had loved him on the terrace outside the ballroom where Elly and her young prince moved in a dance of another kind.

Our love, mine, was made of such little things. When we traveled to Marvella, he would rise in the morning and find something warm for me to drink. Broth, perhaps. Some herbal concoction. A cup of mulled wine. He would bring it to me, knowing I wake grumpily from the pains of sleep—since I was a child, my legs have bothered me. They pain me especially at night, and many nights I spend half sleepless, turning over and over. So, he would bring me something and sit on the side of the bed while I drank it and call me Beauty, though I was an old, white-haired hag with pouches beneath my eyes and lines around my mouth even then.

And the love would come up from inside me like water rising in a well. Not lust, not romance, but something kindlier than that. The feeling one has watching a sunrise sometimes. The feeling one has watching kittens at play. The feeling one has seeing a rose bloom beside the window. The Baskaronian feeling. A perfection of being.

When we were on the way to Lourdes, each delightful thing that I saw I could not wait to turn to him to see if he saw it, to point it out, to make some jest, to evoke some wonder. Things I read that I wanted to read to him. How we laughed over Christine de Pisan together.

When he grew sick, he did not want me to go back to the twentieth to get the medicine for him. He did not want to go on living if it meant he might outlive me. If one of us died, he wanted to die first. He knew I was mean enough and grumpy enough to get along, someway. He did not think he could live without me. And he knew I would remember him. Perhaps he wanted to be remembered.

I wonder if he knew I would remember him in hell, and for that little time of recollection, hell could not exist for me.

There are men here. Sometimes, between the howls and screams and grunts of pain, I hear marching feet and voices raised in song. Sometimes I hear laughter. Sometimes I hear whispers, too soft to understand the words, but full of sly meaning. Sometimes I hear a shouted name, and know it is a name of someone real, someone I have read about somewhere. Not only one name, but several, in a questioning voice, as though a teacher calls a roll.

Often there is an answer. A voice raised, "I am here!"

And sometimes almost a chorus singing, their voices full of a terrible urgency and a dreadful joy, "Down, down, down to happyland."

I have been down to see Captain Karon once again, though he tells me simply Charon would suffice.

"Difficult to be captain of a rowboat," he said, as the newest cargo of ghosts streamed past him into the place.

"Charon," I said, "if there were another side, would you take us there? Or an ocean, maybe, that the river empties into."

"Would I go to an end if I could?" He smiled his death's-head smile at me. "Wouldn't you?"

"Are they dead?" I gestured behind me. "Are they all dead?"

"If not, they will be someday," he said. "Who lives forever?"

The Dark Lord, I started to say. Faery. But then I stayed silent, for he had given me the germ, the merest germ of an idea.

"Yes," said the voices in my ear. "Yes, try that. Those words are good words, as good as any."

"They are not magic words," I say, objecting. "They are mortal words."

"Any words can be magic," whisper the voices. "If they meet the need."

"Did you know that I am a fairy?" I asked Barrymore Gryme.

He laughed, spitting pieces of teeth in all directions. I reached out and healed him. He still laughed.

"How else could I heal you?" I asked him. "Fairies can travel through time. Fairies can be taken captive. Still, they are fairies, with powers of their own. I have magic, Barry."

"Much good it's doing you," he muttered through swollen lips, glaring through bruised eyes.

"It's because I'm alone," I said. "I am outweighed by all you others."

"So, you're stuck," he said. "Like the rest of us."

"My point is, I could get some of you unstuck, if you'd help me. There is some magic in each of you, as well. Man has been stealing it from Faery for thousands of years."

A wily look, perhaps hopeful. "How?" he asked.

"I'll teach you some words," I said. "When you see the others, teach them the words. Have them teach still others. When the gong rings the third time from now, everyone say them together and think of the shore of a river. The words are a magic spell. They'll get us out of here. Think of a river shore and a boat, a big boat come to take us away from here."

He does not believe me. Still, he has learned the words I have given him.

"I've heard this before," he complained as I recited to him.

"Spells do not have to be original to be efficacious," I told him. "This one will work. It will draw upon the magic of Faery. If everyone says it at the same time, it will free us. A great skeptic wrote these words. They will work." Perhaps they will.

Though, actually, it is hope that will do the most. Optimism. The undying desire of most men to make things come out right!

Time goes by. Eventually, the gong rings. Over its dying reverberations I hear a whisper, as though a thousand voices have said "One."

There is time here when nothing happens, when there are no voices, no sounds. My mind circles, like a dog, trying to find a place to lie down. It runs off in all directions, thoughts flying in and out like bats while I chase after them. I keep losing them, thinking, "What was the thing I was just thinking of," trying to trace it, trying to remember. I become exhausted, unable to think at all. I start to panic!

"Shhh," say the voices. "Lie down. You are soft, in bed. You are comfortable. Your hands are folded on your chest. You do not hurt. What would you like to hear, or read, or watch?"

One of Bill's documentaries, I think. And suddenly, it is there before me. Bill's documentary on the Last Radish.

Fidipur's farms.

Glass houses as far as I can see. The camera plunges down through the glass, and shows shallow tanks, full of green slime, constantly agitated by mechanical fingers and bubbles from perforated hoses. The camera dwells upon these things, tenderly, sensuously. Between the tanks walk robed acolytes, examining the soup, bending to a thermometer with a motion like a genuflection, adjusting a valve with the tips of sanctified, gloved fingers. There is soft, holy music in the background, a choir singing.

Bill's voice: not his regular voice, but his awed voice. "This is one of Fidipur's farms. Here, isolated from any organism which might conceivably interfere with a maximized harvest, the soup is grown from which our food is made. It is here, in this particular section, that green one and two are manufactured."

The voice guides the camera as it follows the green soup. It spills down transparent pipes to the great cookers and emerges as a flaccid mush onto a conveyor belt. Knives divide and texture it. The belt moves into drying ovens, emerges once more, goes through a machine which injects other substances.

"Here essential vitamins and minerals are added," Bill says. "Before the mixture goes on into the molding section and the ovens." He does not mention flavor.

The camera follows the belt as it dumps its half-dried goo into a hopper, from which plops of green-gray gum are extruded into depressions in a great steel band. Heated plates come down at the end of stems. There is a sizzle of steam, then the tops rise and the band curves over to dump its cargo of baked biscuits onto another conveyor beneath.

"Food for the billions," Bill says in a proud tone. "But in the past there have still been those who believe they are too special to eat what the billions eat. Until now there have been the elite, who ate old-style, natural growth foods, because of the status it conferred." Montage shots of fat people at tables, toasting each other, eating with knives and forks. Close-up shot of a jaw, chewing. "In the past," Bill says, "some people have robbed Fidipur, but the robbery is at an end. The new managers, elected by you, Fidipur's billions, are harvesting the last of the old-style foods. Tomorrow, one of Fidipur's farms will rise where they have grown."

Camera flies over the glass houses, flits across the multiple towers of a hive, darts downward into an open space where narrow rows of greenery show against brown earth. The camera turns to the side of the field where Martin, the director, stands beside a stout, wrinkle-faced man dressed as everyone dresses in the twenty-first.

Martin says, "It did not seem right that the managerial class be allowed to consume this last vegetable, and there are not enough such vegetables for all of Fidipur's billions to share. So a worldwide lottery was held to find one of Fidipur's billions to have this privilege." Martin turns, beams at the man next to him. "This is Mr. Walford Tupp. What words do you have for us on this occasion, Mr. Tupp?"

The man gapes, smiles, giggles. "Well, gee, I don't know. I mean, it's such a privlige to be here on this momous casion, isn't it?"

"Yes, it certainly is a privilege on such a momentous occasion, Mr. Tupp. Are you ready to harvest the last radish?"

"Well, I don't know. I mean, sure. I mean, that's what I come for, isn't it? Right?"

"Remember, Mr. Tupp. Slowly. We want to be able to catch every nuance of this historic event." Martin smiles his professional smile and pats Mr. Tupp on the shoulder.

Camera on the Tupp feet, walking over brown earth. He is pigeon-toed. The soles of his shoes are worn more on one side than the other. The earth gives under each footfall, little cracks run away around the edges of his soles, leaving prints behind. There is an ant on the ground. He steps on it. Behind him, the ant struggles out of the compressed soil. Now the camera runs ahead of him, finds the radish, brings it up until it fills the screen. . . .

Green leaves, as large as sails. Slightly crinkled, textured, glossy hillocks separated by darker-veined valleys, the veins running like brooks to join larger veins, these wandering toward the center to join the strong central rib of the leaf. It is like a rib in the vault of a cathedral, curving gently, its size diminishing toward the leaf-tip, growing larger as it plunges down toward the stem, the whole rounded on one side, cupped on the other, the proportions perfectly designed. Light fractures off the leaf. Light falls through the leaf. The rib is darker, becoming wine colored at its base.

And this is only one leaf. The camera pulls back to let me see two, then three, then four. Each a triumph of architecture. Each a wonder, a marvel. The camera pulls back, back, and suddenly the fingers come down. Grasp the leaves. Crunch them together. The microphone picks up that crunch as cells explode, as their tender juices run out onto those fingers. The fingers pull.

Soil shatters. Crumbs of moist soil rain down the sides of a growing cone. There is a volcano of disturbed soil. Out of its top emerges a flame-red, spherical shape, slowly rising, like a great balloon, like the sun, a gleaming ruby, a vast carbuncle brighter than blood, up, slowly, the long, white root trailing behind, tiny hairs on it broken from their home within the earth. It quivers. It almost screams.

The camera follows the fingers, up, and up, and up.

The camera sees a mouth. Opening. The radish is inserted, halfway. Yellowed teeth champ down. Saliva perks at the corners of the lips. The mouth opens again.

"Shit," says Mr. Tupp, spitting. "That's awful." The camera follows the radish as it falls, a bite out of one side, the other still glowing like martyr's blood, wet and miraculous.

The camera sees Martin walking away with Mr. Tupp, his arm around Mr. Tupp's shoulders in comradely fashion. For a moment the camera follows them. Then it turns downward, down to the last radish.

Jaybee always knew what made a good picture. As the camera draws away, and turns, and draws away, the radish becomes a sun on the horizon, an arc eaten out of it by a low brown hill; the leaves around it are a forest, and behind that forest the glowing ruby sun is setting. Forever setting.

The gong rings. Stronger this time, I hear a murmur, as maybe many voices whispering, "Two."

I am alone in my place. Barry is being tortured somewhere else. I am thinking of my mama. And of myself.

I was Elly's mother. Unwillingly. Without intention. Mama was my mother. If not unwillingly, at least without intention. She left me, left me to Westfaire and the Curse, a short span in her life, telling me to come to her when it was over. I left Elly, only for a few years, I thought, intending to return when they were over. So, perhaps, mothers leave children every day, intending to return, only to find they are too late, returning. The thing has happened. The hour has struck. The time has passed when it would have mattered.

So, are they to blame? Am I to blame, for Elly? Is Mama to blame for me?

And if the mother hovers, settles like a hen upon the nest, clucks to her chick beneath her wings and does not let it go; if the mother says, "No, the hour may strike, the thing may happen, and I will not leave you alone"; if the mother does that? What?

The chick struggles, and runs, and hides, wanting to feel the sun on its feathers, the air beneath its wings. And if it runs away and the hawk gets it, whose fault is that?

Is Mama to blame I am in hell? Was I to blame that Elly was in hell from the day of her birth?

The third gong. I wasn't expecting it. The sound came in a great wave. It left in slow vibration, and after it the almost hysterical gabble of thousands of voices moving from a whisper to a grunt to a shout: "Three, three, three."

Then the voices, saying the words I had taught them, words my favorite poet had made long ago, in some other place:

> *"From too much love of living,*
> *From hope and fear set free,"*

The words were ragged. I joined them, shouting, hearing Barry's voice rise up next to mine.

> *"We thank with brief thanksgiving,*
> *Whatever gods may be"*

The words came more strongly, more surely.

> *"That no life lives forever;*
> *That dead men rise up never;"*

A shriek from the Dark Lord. He had heard us. Was he too late to stop us? Did all the victims believe it enough?

> *"That even the weariest river*
> *Winds somewhere safe to sea."*

We were on the river shore! I heard the shriek, the cry, the bellow of the whistle of the *Stugos Queen*. We were standing on the riverbank in Chinanga, watching it come around the bend. From the high deck, Captain Karon waved at me. Around me lay the bodies of some dead, including Barry, who would rise up

never, and some living, who now knew they would surely die.
And before them was their transportation on their journey toward that final sea, the one the captain had long wished to find.

I heard a cooing voice and looked up to see Mrs. Gallimar
clinging to Captain Karon's arm. She looked like Bill. She was
Bill.

So, and so. The captain had done some dreaming of his
own. Or he had taken my dreams for himself.

There was a swirling darkness behind us. Out of this aching
cloud a figure lunged toward me, a scrambling monster, a hur-
tling shadow: Jaybee, alive. Well. He had not suffered here. He
belonged here, and he was coming to get me. It had been too
late, and useless. His breath touched my face, his fingers
touched me . . .

"May I drop you somewhere," said a voice from behind me.
It was Israfel. The ambassador from Baskarone. Jaybee's hand
slid away, an empty skin, a sack, something hollow and un-
living.

"Ylles, Israfel, if you please," I said in a fair imitation of
Mama's tone.

"Faery, Israfel," said another voice. Carabosse.

He took our hands and we went up.

I looked down to see the river winding toward a far horizon, an endless starlit sea. Behind us was a seething darkness
which no light penetrated. "He's still there," I said, disappointed
that he had not vanished, as Chinanga once had done.

"A great deal of creativity has gone into that hell," said
Israfel. "You and Carabosse and I, we made a spell that freed a
few of us, but it will take more than a few verses of Swinburne
to free him."

He meant the Dark Lord, of course. I meant Jaybee and all
who are like him. Perhaps we both meant the same thing.

"Did you plan for him to catch me?" I asked, wondering
now that it was over what it had all been about. "Did you plan
it?"

"No," said Carabosse. "Oberon planned it, and Mab. But
we knew of it and let it happen. If we'd stopped it, he'd have
tried something else. He had the scent and wouldn't give up

until he knew—or thought he knew. So we let it happen, but we came along to make sure he would not find in you what he was looking for."

"Will he try again?" I asked, wondering if I could last, again.

"No," said Israfel. "He thinks there's nothing there. He thinks he was misled, and he finds you troublesome. Besides, if things go as we believe they will, he'll be too busy." His voice was furry and throat-stopped with grief. He said nothing more.

·

28

·

Israfel and Carabosse suggested that I stop in the world. I did so. They waited while I ate, bathed myself, dressed myself. It took forever. I was so slow. I kept dropping things. Finally, I looked at my hands and cried out, hearing the sound of the cry, a tiny shrilling, like a lost bird. My hands were like claws!

"How long?" I cried.

"The bell rang once each year," Israfel told me.

How many times had it rung. Fifteen? Twenty? "How old am I?" I cried.

"About a hundred and three," said Carabosse, adding kindly, "Don't worry about it, Beauty. It won't matter in Faery."

I laughed, a quavery little laugh. "Odile may not live long enough for me to return again. I think I'll take my things with me this time."

"Things?" Israfel asked, smiling his radiant smile.

"There's still one hank of thread left," I said. "And the needles. I'll put them in my pocket."

When I had dressed myself, I got out Mama's box. It still had the letters in it, her letter, and Giles. I left them there. The time was past for letters. I put on the ring with its little winged figure. I put the needles and thread in my pocket. Then Israfel and Carabosse took me by the hands and led me back into Faery, back onto the flowery meadow where the tents had been set up. A dozen of so of the tents were clustered not far distant from us. Their occupants were standing outside, very quietly, as though they had been waiting for us to arrive.

Carabosse sidled sideways and was gone, but Israfel did not leave me as he had done when he brought me from Chinanga. He walked with me toward the clustered tents, holding my hand upon his arm. On either side, the Sidhe bowed, as though reluctantly, as though forced to do so. None of them looked me or Israfel in the eye, I noticed. I stared them down just to make them more uncomfortable, for among them were the riders who had used me for the teind.

My eyes were drawn to the Copse of the Covenant, where it sat afar upon the grass. There, too, a tent had been raised, and there was no question but that it, too, was occupied. The fabric glowed with a blinding effulgence. I looked away, my eyes watering.

"The messenger of the Holy One, Blessed be He," whispered Israfel, as he prepared to introduce me to those who had been standing by the tents. His fellows. His companions. Male and female.

Michael. Gabriel. Raphael. Uriel. They are the eldest, says Israfel.

Aniel, Raguel, Sariel, and Jerahmeel.

Kafziel, Zadkiel, Asrael, and Israfel himself. There are twelve of them all together. The Long Lost. The separated kindred. Twelve who assented when the Holy One asked Faery to help man; those who went away when Oberon said no; those who built Baskarone; those now returned to Faery. Twelve visitors. Plus Carabosse. Plus the Holy One's envoy.

The envoy is a seraph, says Israfel. Not a star-angel but simply a messenger. Come to deliver the word of the Holy One.

"When I was in Chinanga, I thought *you* were angels," I told them, my eyes on my shoes.

Gabriel shook his head. "Nothing so fiery. From time to

time men have seen us and have assumed we were angels, but we are merely ambassadors of Baskarone." His voice sank to a whisper. "To the worlds. Whatever and wherever they may be."

That whisper was familiar! It was like the whispers I had heard in hell, encouraging me, helping me find a way out. I realized suddenly that they might all have been there! All twelve of them! Their faces told me I was right. They had been there. Invisibly, they had followed me into hell, to keep me safe.

Israfel squeezed my hand, giving me a significant look, and I understood. They did not want me to speak of it, not even to thank them. They did not want anyone—anything—to know what they had done. They did not want anyone—anything—to ask why.

I tried to think of something inconsequential to say. "Are you ambassadors even to dreamworlds?" I asked. "Even to places like Chinanga?"

Gabriel laughed. "If one stretches time long enough, they may all be dreamworlds. The only differences may be in the length of the dream and the strength of the dreamer. Perhaps we call reality that which is dreamed the longest, that's all."

I had learned something of cosmology in the twentieth— what anyone who read a popular science magazine might pick up. "You mean the Big Bang?" I said.

"God breathes in, God breathes out," said Gabriel. "Blessed be the name of the Holy One."

"What is Baskarone?" I asked them. "I thought it was heaven."

"We have tried to make it so," said Sariel. "By copying what was here when man came, and the best of what has been created since. Much of earthly creation had already manifested itself and departed before men came, of course, but we wished to preserve the work of the creators, somewhere."

She sounded almost as sad as Israfel did, and I did not ask any further questions. Besides, there would not have been time. Somewhere a fanfare of trumpets blew, a silvery shiver of sound I had not heard before in Faery. More of the Sidhe came out of their castles and walked slowly down the hills to the meadow where we stood. These were all the kindred of Oberon, those who occupied this world. Behind them came the horses of Faery, tossing their lovely heads, their silver manes flying. The dogs came, too, the white dogs with their red ears and red eyes.

From the other directions, Bogles emerged, as they do, making that sideways sidle which brings them into one world or another.

During what followed, I stood with my hand on Israfel's arm, his kindred arrayed behind us, watching them come. Puck came up to us, quite unselfconsciously, nodding to Israfel as though he knew him well. While he watched his fellow Bogles assemble, he whispered to us both, taking an inventory, as it were, jigging from foot to foot with the rhythm of his voice.

> *"When the silver trumpets sound to every puck and peri,*
> *From the clustered hills around, come the folk of Faery.*
> *Brownies, brags, bugbears, hags,*
> *   big black dogs and banshees,*
> *Boggy-boes, hobby-thrusts,*
> *   imps and lianhanshees,*
> *Kitty-witches, hinky-punks,*
> *   clabber-naps and swaithes,*
> *Fachans, follets, fays, fiends,*
> *   gallytrots and wraithes,*
> *Selkies, scrats, spunks, spurns,*
> *   ciuthaches and cowies,*
> *Nickies, nacks, gholes, grants,*
> *   tutgots and tod-lowries,*
> *Melch-dicks and come-quicks,*
> *   cors and mares and pixies,*
> *Pad-fooits and leprechauns,*
> *   chittifaces, nixies,*
> *Sprets, trows, gnomes, kowes,*
> *   goblins and Peg-powlers,*
> *Ouphs, brags, nickers, nags,*
> *   nisses and night-prowlers,*
> *Lubbers, lobs, tantarrabobs,*
> *   cluricans and correds,*
> *Tangies, trolls, tatterfoals,*
> *   hobbits and hob-horrids,*

Mawkins, tints, gringes, squints,
  shellycoats and sprites,
Roanes and ratchets, pinkets, patches,
  grindylows and wights.
When they hear the summons sound, every puck and peri
from the clustered hills around gathers into Faery."

He grinned at me, cocking his eyebrows, and I knew he'd been trying to amuse me. I suppose I must have been amused, or at least interested, for I'd paid enough attention to note that he had not mentioned the Fenoderee in this inventory, which was not inclusive in any case. Puck had ignored thurses, knockers, kobolds, and a dozen other beings that Fenoderee had spoken of.

When all the Bogles had ranged themselves on the seaside in a vast half circle, the Sidhe began to arrive, gathering on the upland side and leaving a lane clear to the Copse of the Covenant, which stood toward the mountains.

I did not see Mama anywhere.

Israfel put his hand on my shoulder and said, "She'll be here."

And at last she came, from her own castle, which stood to the south of the upland. She came walking with one or two of her people, Joyeause and another aunt, I think it was. There were tears in my eyes. I was grieving and didn't know why. When she came close enough, I saw how very beautiful she is. She looked at me, shaking her head a little from side to side, tears running down her cheeks. Oberon looked at her, then away, flushing angrily. He had sent her away when they gave me as the teind to hell! She hadn't known he was going to do it.

And it was all right. No matter that I was a hundred and three and all my remaining years had been used up in hell. It was all right. She hadn't known. She hadn't wished me ill. Oh, didn't I know it's the best we can do, sometimes, simply not to wish our children ill.

"Get on with it," said Oberon, impatiently.

Gabriel answered him. "There's nothing to get on with, brother. We are not here to make judgements."

Oberon stared at the distant hills and said nothing. So proud. He would not beg for mercy. Behind me, Israfel was silent. All that host was silent.

"Had he told you lies?"

Still silence.

"Had he made you promises?"

No answer.

The seraph made a sound, or we apprehended a sound, or a feeling, a sound of infinite regret, like a harp string plucked and broken. "Too large a part of this woman's life has been consumed in your kinsman's labyrinth, and that was not of her choosing. She is mortal and has been used to her lasting harm, Oberon. Not only for this reason, for there are other reasons, but with this as the cause, the Covenant is broken."

Israfel's hands came up once more. The glamour came back. My strength came back as the seraph turned and went away. Too late to defend them now. The seraph went into the tent and the light went out. The tent stood empty. The trees surrounding it began to blacken. Within moments they had fallen to dust and the dust had blown away on its own little wind. This was the copse Oberon had tried so hard to destroy, and now it was gone. Seemingly he could not take his eyes from the place it had been.

When I looked back at the assembly, all were weeping and moving away. Only Mama came to me and put her arms around me, saying, "I didn't know. Oberon sent me away, Beauty. He fogged the palace to drive the Bogles away so they couldn't warn you. He didn't tell me. He just took you. . . ."

I patted her shoulder, hugged her close, crying, "I don't understand how Faery could make cause with the Dark Lord. I don't understand how they could."

She wept, and shrugged, looking in that moment like any grieved old washerwoman I'd ever seen at Westfaire, crying over a lost child, a lost man, a lost life. "I don't know," she cried. "He wooed us. He whispered to us. He told us we had enemies. He told us he would defend us against them. He told us of plots against us, and said he had confounded them. He pointed to the religions of men that were sucking our magic away, religions which pretended to worship the Holy One, and he told us the Holy One allowed the worship and had thus betrayed us. He told us he could lead us to victory against the angels, who would soon declare war upon us. Oberon believed him, perhaps, a little. Enough to give him the teind. A small price, we thought."

Simple paranoia, then? A fairy sociopath, crouched in his labyrinth, spewing lies?

I had been there. I knew there was more to it than that. A monstrous ambition. A death-loving ecstasy. A worship of pain. What dwelt in the Dark One's halls was not only of faery, but also of man, a dreadful alliance. Could it possibly be that there was some dark angel there as well? A hideous triumvirate, brooding destruction?

I looked at Israfel over her bent back and asked, "What's going to happen now?"

"The Covenant is broken. We had our immortality through the Covenant. I suppose we don't have it anymore. That's why Oberon is weeping. When he is through weeping, we will see."

"Baskarone," I faltered.

"Baskarone," he said, his voice breaking. "I don't know how long it will last. The seraph didn't say." I noticed for the first time that Israfel looked . . . not older. No. Worn, somehow. As though . . . as though he had spent himself protecting me. None of us had come out of hell unscathed.

"Before it . . . if it . . . can I see it?" I asked him.

He turned to look at the others. Michael nodded first, then Gabriel. Then the others. Israfel took me by the hand.

"Will you come back?" Mama cried, stepping away from me.

"If there's time," I said. "If I have any time left."

"Israfel," she begged, "I was never part of any of this."

He looked at her without expression. His face was calm but unforgiving. "When man stood up beside his fire and the Holy One asked us to help him, there were only thirteen voices who assented. Ours, and old Carabosse. Yours was not among them, Elladine. When Oberon laughed and walked away, you were at his side."

She bowed her head and wept.

Israfel said, "I'll bring her back if there's time."

What shall I write of Baskarone?

Everything that was lovely of the world when men came into it is here. Everything that men made beautiful while they were in it is here. None of the dross, only the glory. Some gardens. Some monuments. There is even an entire town, designed by a woman of great artistry. I had seen a film on it in the twenty-first. It was built early in the twenty-first and then destroyed by the nationalist terrorists in the Great Reunification War of 2043, the same war that killed all the people in Ireland, North and South, and half those in England and Scotland, as well as sinking the lands of Ireland forever beneath the sea.

In the long run, it didn't matter who destroyed the city. Fidipur's ocean farms now cover the place it once stood. If the terrorists hadn't bombed it and thereby started the war, Fidipur would have razed it anyhow. Mortal man is mad.

There are a handful of marvelous mosques in Baskarone, serene and beautiful. An Egyptian temple is here, crowded with painted columns. A mud fortress is here, its walls glistening with bright murals in tiles. There are structures in Baskarone from Ecbatana and Susa. There is a building from Troy. There are two from the States of America, quite small ones, sculptural houses which look as though they grew from the earth.

Cave paintings are here, fleeing horses and lumbering bison. African carvings are here, and so many things from the Orient I could not see them all, including a city from China, lacquered all in red and gold with dragons upon its roofs.

And all these things are set in gardens and woods and forests and prairies. The flowers that bloom in those gardens are the loveliest that ever grew. The trees in those woods are tall and straight. The grasses on the prairies have never been cut, and the little peeping birds run about among their roots.

There are people here as well. The woman who designed the city, the men who built the fortress, the carpenters who carved the dragons. All those who made beauty with their lives, they are here. Those who climbed. Those whose names ring, like a wine glass in a cupboard, hidden but sounding nonetheless.

The dreams of the men who tried to reach the planets, before Fidipur took everything, they are here. I don't know how they are there, but they glitter like sequins in the shade of that place.

"But you can't have the dreams of space explorers here. That hasn't happened yet," I said. "This is still the fifteenth."

"As Chinanga existed in the always, so do these things," Israfel said.

"Surely the Holy One, Blessed be He, won't let this perish," I said. "Just because of what Oberon did."

Sariel was beside us. She sighed. "Things the Creator Himself made have perished, Beauty, because of what someone else does. The Holy One makes a tree that lives for four thousand years, and someone chops it down to make paper to package chewing gum. The Creator makes whales who sing in the deep, and men kill them to put their oil in lipsticks."

"Enough, Sariel," Israfel said. "She knows. She has seen the end of it."

They let me alone to wander where I would. I walked into a great cathedral, down aisles of yearning stone, the great carved branches sweeping upward toward the traceries of the ceiling, so high above that it seemed impossible men built it and stones sustain it in those delicate arches. A bell rang, and the sound of it moved among the pillars, now soft, now loud, repeating and reverberating, plangent as a sigh. Incense burned, and the smoke of it rose in a pure, blue column in the light coming through high, painted windows. All of it, stone and smoke and sound, blending into one thing, one place, one instant in which the beauty of it stops your heart. Men did it purposely, made that space do that purposely. They knew how. They knew what beauty is.

I walked down aisles of trees that spoke of even greater loveliness. Green glades where light slanted down in golden spears, touching blossoms in the grass. There were oaks as red as stained glass, sifting the sun onto ancient groves. When I walked there, I walked quietly, seeing glory all around me. God did that. He knew how. He knew what beauty is. The cathedral was only a copy of this.

Even the Temple of Helpful Amphibians was there. Ambrosius Pomposus, also, had known what beauty is.

I remembered what I had left in the twentieth: gray concrete and miles of scabby houses, featureless towers of glass and miles of parking lots. The glades had been cut down to make pulp for horro-porn. There had been no holy silence but only the rant and howl of the machines the youths carried on their shoulders, a constant rape of the ears.

Here in Baskarone was a silence in which one could hear birds singing and the low of cattle from distant fields. Once on earth there was silence in which a child's laughter could be heard, or the cry of a kingfisher ratcheting overhead or the high shriek of a falcon. Once fish could be heard, plopping in their pools, and the splash of frogs and the hum of bees.

When I had left the twentieth there had been only the *whom a whom a whom a whom,* each sound hitting the ear like a blow, bruising the hearing so that when the sound was gone the ear throbbed with it still, like a wound. There is no birdsong left in that time, and if, by chance, the ear finds silence somewhere it can hear nothing, for it has been mutilated by what it listened to.

And the eye also. If it has never seen beauty, how can it know? It has been mutilated by ugliness, destroyed by horror. And so the mind.

I wanted to stay there, of course, but I had not earned the right. I did not ask. They did not offer. When I had seen all my heart could hold, they took me back to Faery, where I found Puck waiting amid preparations for war.

Puck was sitting on the ground near where Israfel left me. He got up to take me by the hand and help me seat myself on a convenient stone. I noticed for the first time that he rather resembled Giles. Not the face so much as around the eyes. But then he looked a little like Bill there, too. Strange how much there is of people we love in other people we love. He offered me a cup of something warm which he happened to have by

him. It tasted suspiciously like worldly chicken soup with bar-
ley in it, and he confessed he had stolen it from a mortal
kitchen.

"The cook will not miss it," he said. "She had a whole pot
of the stuff. Rest, Beauty, and tell me about Baskarone."

I told him what I could, waxing as poetic as it is in me to be.
I could see him noting it all down in his head, ready to make a
song of it. While we sat there, several Bogles gathered around,
including the Fenoderee. When I had told him all I could, I
asked him what had transpired in Faery since I had been there
last. I did not ask him how long I had been gone. I was afraid to
know that.

It was thus I learned of the war.

"Oberon's people are not happy with him," Puck said. The
Bogles all nodded at this intelligence, agreeing that indeed the
Daoine Sidhe were extremely unhappy with Oberon.

"He has decided, therefore, that it is all someone else's
fault."

"Not mine?" I said, horrified. "Not Mama's?"

Puck shook his head and laughed, shortly. "The Dark
Lord's fault, Beauty. If the Dark One had not tempted Oberon,
then Oberon would not have broken the Covenant on his behalf. Therefore, everything is the Dark Lord's fault, and Oberon
is going to fight him. Him and his close kindred, at least." He
sounded disapproving.

"But that's what you wanted them to do!" I cried.

"True, though not for that reason," brooded Puck. "The
problem is that Oberon and his kindred are not strong enough
by themselves to do more than irritate the Dark Lord, but the
rest of Faery is too annoyed with Oberon to follow him."

I asked, "What about you, Puck? And Fenoderee? And all
the Bogles?"

The Fenoderee answered. "He hasn't asked our help, and
fighting isn't our kind of thing. Bogles have never gone to war.
Even though there are a few tribes of us capable of violence, by
and large we are too individual and eccentric. I think most Bogles will return to the world and live out our lives, such as they
are. We may not be immortal any longer, but something tells us

we're a long-lived people. Likely even in the twentieth or twenty-first, there'll be folk thinking they've seen a Bogle, or heard one."

"Where will Oberon attack the Dark Lord?" I asked.

"The Dark Lord won't come out," one of the little folleti piped from the circle around. "So Oberon will have to go in after him."

"Will my mama go with him?"

They nodded, slowly.

"He has many demons there," I cried. Actually, the thought of the demons bothered me less than those other things in hell. Those horrors created by men in the future.

I told the Bogles about some of them, and they shivered where they stood. "I don't know if those things can be killed," I told them. "Men invented them, but the Dark Lord has given them a dreadful kind of life. They may be proof against anything Oberon can do. Can the Dark Lord himself be killed?"

Puck nodded. "He was of the Sidhe, Beauty. His pride led him to break the Covenant. He was so proud he did not realize he would lose his immortality when the Sidhe lost theirs. Both he and Oberon are like the sons of a generous father who are spendthrift with their father's fortune, treating it as though it were their own and limitless, as though they had earned it rather than receiving it as a gift. Then the time comes at last when the father says enough. Then, when the sons are left without the riches, they curse fate and their father, not willing to lay the blame at their own feet. Yes, the Dark Lord can die, just as Oberon now can die."

I stood up and brushed myself off. It was time I saw Mama. I had promised her I would come back. The Bogles took me part way, then left me as I started up the hill toward the castle of Ylles. As I approached, I saw her coming toward me. We met halfway, and she kissed me. This time she didn't mention my smell. I was careful not to mention hers, which was the smell of old flowers, drying and fading.

I told her what I could about the things they would find in the Dark One's lair and begged her not to go with Oberon. She shook her head at me, but she listened carefully to what I had to say, asking me one question and another. She said the things I described had not been there when she had been used as the teind. Barrymore Gryme and his ilk hadn't been there, either. There had been only fairy horrors, things Mama could handle fairly easily. When I had finished telling her, Mama was very pale and seemed rather frightened. I wondered if she would be able to convince Oberon that he should be careful. Oberon had always struck me as being both arrogant and precipitant in his actions.

Mama said she must go talk with him, but even as she turned to go, she clung to my hand. Finally, she pushed me away from her, pointing toward the place where Puck and the Bogles waited. "Your Grandaunt Carabosse wants you to come to tea. She says she will have no time, later on."

I knew she would not. "When does she want me to come?" I asked.

"Now. As soon as you can." Again she made the pushing gesture, telling me to go with Puck.

I didn't want to leave her. "Should I be leaving just now? With this business of Oberon going to battle and your going with him?"

For a third time, she gestured at me to go. "That's why you must go! Oberon is irritated at you. Oh, Beauty, he's irritated at himself for . . . well, you know what for. He looks at you, and it reminds him of how irritated he is. It's not a good time for you to be in Faery."

I stared at her. "It's probably the last time I will be in Faery, Mama. I'm really one hundred and three. Human people seldom live that long. When I go back, I'm gone. This is the last time you and I will be together."

She started to cry again, and I felt dreadful. I patted her on the shoulder. "Never mind. I'll go see old Carabosse. I won't stay long. We'll have some time to ourselves when I come back." As I turned to join the Bogles, she was trudging up the hill toward Oberon's castle.

Nothing had changed at Carabosse's cottage. The clocks still ticked and could still be silenced by her gesture. The only surprise was that Israfel was with her. They were both very quiet. When we had had tea, Carabosse suggested that I look into her Forever Pool and took me out with her and Israfel to the garden. The pool lay beyond it, among a grove of silver trees. The bridge which arched over it reminded me of the one arching the Pool of Delights, and its purpose was the same. We leaned on the railing, Israfel, Carabosse, and I, looking into its depths, seeing our faces dimly reflected on the black water.

Carabosse moved her hand over the water. Darkness. There was only darkness. Israfel moved his. Still only darkness.

Carabosse said, "Now you," and I did, moving my hands as she had moved hers, in a wide double arc above the surface.

Israfel sighed. "There," he said, pointing. I looked where he pointed and saw a glimmer of light, so faint, so dim, as though in the very bottom of the pool some treasure gleamed, softly and infinitely far.

"Well, so," breathed Carabosse. She and Israfel looked at one another, no expression on their faces at all, but I could feel something flowing between them.

We went back into the cottage. "What's going to happen?" I asked them.

"Something other than what we planned," Carabosse whispered. "It is almost as though someone else had done the planning."

"Whatever happens," Israfel said, "we have seen light at the end of time. I will carry word of that to the others. I think it will be enough."

And that is absolutely all he would say, though his hand lingered caressingly upon my shoulder as he bid me farewell. I stayed only a little while longer. When I went out, Puck was standing there with the horse to take me back. We rode through the forest while Puck sang ballads at me and the Fenoderee accompanied him on a lute.

We stopped on the way to have a picnic. More human food: sliced ham and fresh baked bread and fruit. Several of the more interesting Bogles joined us and vied with one another in telling strange tales of humans they had known. I think I slept. I seem to remember sleeping. We stopped in a wonderful glade to pick orchidlike flowers that grew in the trees. Several Bogles came along and lectured me on the flora and fauna of Faery. It was interesting that some of the creatures I had taken as Bogles, they took as animals, and that some of the creatures I had thought were animals definitely were Bogles. There seemed to be no clear way to tell. Black dogs, for example, are Bogles. The Hedly Kowe, however, is an animal. At least, most of the time it is. And so are the Gwartheg y Llyn. I may have fallen asleep again, during one of the lectures.

We stopped again, to look at a waterfall which Puck thought extremely beautiful. There he introduced me to a nixie, and she insisted that we try some of her water-moss wine, which was exceedingly delicious. Could I have fallen asleep again? It seems to me I did.

When Puck suggested we stop for the fourth time, I said, "Puck, you're preventing my getting back, aren't you? I think you should tell me why."

He shook his head at me. "Well, to begin with, there was some talk among Oberon and his close kin about your knowing your way about in the Dark One's halls. Oberon was talking about taking you along, as a guide."

"I don't know my way about," I said, astonished. "The Dark Lord is one of the Sidhe. They would know more about him than I. Every time I moved about in that place, it was different."

"We know that," said Puck. "And so does Oberon by now. We were just giving him time to become sensible, that's all."

"A very long time," I complained, suddenly worried that we had been away too long.

"We could have returned sooner," he replied. "But Israfel suggested we should allow some time for other developments to occur."

With all the picnics and wine tastings and zoological lectures, I felt we had been gone long enough for most anything to occur. When we came out of the trees, however, it was apparent that what Israfel had meant by "developments" was much more than I could possibly have foreseen. I had rather expected to see Oberon and his kindred making ready for battle, a few hundreds of the folk of Faery making a brave but futile array upon

the meadow. What I saw instead was a sea of lances, the assem-
bling of a mighty host, all in bright armor with banners coiling
slowly overhead.

And there at the center of the host were the twelve from
Baskarone, the Separated Ones. Israfel. Michael. Gabriel. All.
The great swans' wings they wore made them stand out, glow-
ing like stars.

"Why?" I whispered.

"Hush," said Puck. "Watch now!"

We stood at the edge of the trees as other of the Sidhe came
over the hills and kept coming, more and more of them, more
than I had ever seen or had known existed. Puck whispered into
my ear as they came, identifying them, telling me about them.
These were Faery folk, though not of Oberon's lineage, and they
came from afar: an army marching from Tirfo Thuinn, the lands
beneath the sea; a mounted troop of the Plant Annwn, led by
their King, Gwyn ap Nud, and another troop from the Plant
Rhys Dwfen; people of the Gwyllion; Ethal Anbual, the Sidhe
king of Connaught, galloping down the hill at the head of a
great host of his people, mounted all on golden horses.

The warrior Queen Tyton came. She was armed with an
ebon bow and silver arrows, and she wore the crescent moon
upon her helm. Around her gathered a host of warrior maidens,
all serious-faced and fell, with knots of red upon their breast-
plates to show they intended that their blood be shed to the last
if need be. Their banners bore the image of the hoodie crow and
they cried names of Neman, Macha, and Morrigu in shrill
voices. These are the three names of Badb, the goddess of war.

Came also the seven winter sisters, Cailleach Bheur of the
Highlands, Black Annis of the Dane Hills, the Loathely Hag of
the Midlands, the Gyre-Carline of the Lowlands, Cally Berry of
Ulster, Caillagh ny Groamagh of the Isle of Man, and Gentle
Annie of Cromarty Firth (where winter is softer yet more
treacherous than most), all in gray robes, their heads wreathed
with gorse, and their faces the color of blue-gray stone. They
bore triangular banners of gray with a tiny sun in one corner,
and their voices were the voice of winter wind calling death
upon the world.

"Why do they come?" I cried to Puck again. "I thought it was only Oberon and his folk! Are they all following Oberon?"

Puck shook his head and held my hand tightly. "They are following Israfel and his kindred," he said. "The Long Lost have gone among them, speaking of the end of time. They know why they are fighting, Beauty. See how they look at you out of the sides of their eyes, without seeming to. See how they glance. It is why we came late to this meadow, why we are posed here against the trees. It is so they can see you, Beauty. They will carry your image and your name into battle, like a flag. It is for you, all this array."

I had not noticed the glamour until then. It was around me as it had been when we confronted the seraph, as much, and yet a different thing. A truer thing. I was as beautiful, but they were not seeing me, but what I carried.

"Tss," whispered Puck as he saw the tears in my eyes. "Hold your head high and do not dare to weep. They are going for you, and they must not see you weeping when they go."

It was a very great host. Many faces in that array showed the determination to die quickly for some great cause rather than to die slowly for none.

I, who was dying slowly, could not find it in my heart to abuse them for that.

And still they came, from afar, from the new world as well as the old, from the islands of the sea, from the forests of Africa, from great chasms and mighty rivers, from all the places of the world where Faery had made a home. I did not know the names of a tenth of them. Even Puck did not know them all.

And when the last of them had come, Mama came riding out from the edge of the host, up the long slope toward us. She looked very wan and worn.

"I told Oberon you could not guide us," she said. "So he's left you out of it. Besides, with all this. . . ." She turned to gesture at the host and sighed. "It was funny to watch him when they started coming. He suddenly remembered who he was! He suddenly measured himself against Israfel and did not want to appear unworthy." She said it with a tiny smile, a tiny, mocking smile. "He is Oberon once more, as I remember him from the distant past. Here at the end of things, he is Oberon once more, perilous and puissant."

I threw my arms around her. "Where are you going?" I asked.

"The route we know best," she said. "To the cavern on the heath. The same place the ride took you."

"I'll go with you that far," I said. She nodded and turned back to join the host.

Puck pulled at my leg. I looked down and he whispered to me. "If you ride with them, Beauty, wear your boots, bear your cloak, carry everything that matters to you."

"I don't even know where my things are," I said. "I haven't seen some of them since I was taken to hell."

"They're here," said the Fenoderee. "I gathered them up for you and kept them safe."

And there they were: boots, cloak, and book. He stowed the book in the cloak pocket and slipped the boots on my feet. The cloak I tied behind me, where I could get it in an instant.

"The Dark One hasn't forgotten what you did," Puck whispered again. "You'd be wiser not to go at all."

"It may be the last time," I told him. "The last time I see Mama. I can't just let her ride away without going with her as far as I can. You have to understand about mothers, Puck. I'm one, and I know. You can't always do for your children what you'd like to do. Your children aren't always people you can do for. But she never meant me ill, Puck. Never once. She must see that the same is true. I've never wished her ill."

The sound of a great horn came thrilling over the meadow, that horn which is said to be Huon's horn, given to Oberon as a token of friendship. And the ride began.

It was so vast, that host, that the Long Lost had reached the world of men before the last of the Sidhe left the meadow. We rode at the tail, Mama and I, with Puck holding to my stirrups and loping beside us. Not far behind I saw Carabosse on a donkey, picking her way along as though going to a fair. Quick though we rode, she kept close behind, though the donkey never went faster than a walk. She waved her stick at me, and I waved in return.

Mama said, "Did you make it up with Aunt Carabosse, then?" And I suddenly recalled that Mama knew nothing of my long association with Carabosse. Nor could I tell her, now.

"She says she never cursed me to death, but only to a sleep. It was Aunt Joyeause who made that up."

Mama nodded thoughtfully. "Joyeause has never cared for truth much. She says whatever comes into her head. I never doubted her at the time, though."

"Once I thought all fairies were wise," I confessed to her as I had to Carabosse.

"Oh, no," Mama said. "Wisdom is not a great thing among the Sidhe. I have heard a legend about that." She settled herself in the saddle and told me the story.

"It is said that the Holy One, Blessed be He, first created mankind as he created the Sidhe, marvelously fair, and he set the first of them in a garden much like Faery except that day and night came there, spring and fall, warm and cool, dry and wet, and every animal which has ever been, and every bird and every fish."

"I think I've heard this tale," I said, remembering Father Raymond.

"Very likely. The story is very old. And it continues that He set in the middle of the garden the tree of the hunger for wisdom, and He told them what it was. 'Eat of it or not,' He said, 'as you choose. Except, you eat of it, you must leave the garden of ever-life, for wisdom brings a terrible price, the price of pain and death and loneliness. But if you will be immortal, do not eat of it, and you may live here forever in peace."

And she went on to tell me the whole story of Eden, as though she were reading it out of the Bible, as Father Raymond had used to read it to me.

"Until the first woman could bear it no more," said Mama, "and she went to the tree of the hunger for wisdom and picked a fruit from it and ate it. Then she sat down beneath the tree and cried, for all the questions of the world percolated about in her head, like fish she could not catch, and she knew herself and all her children forever would be adrift in mystery, that as soon as one thing was found out another would present itself to be discovered.

"And the man found her there. When she told him what she had done, he took the core of the fruit she had eaten and tasted it and put the seeds in his pocket. 'For,' he said, 'if you must leave the garden, so will I. And if you must die, so will I. I will go with you wherever you go, leaving all the garden behind. And of the tree of knowledge you have given up paradise for, we will take the seeds to plant in every land we come to, and we will find the fruit bitter and we will find the fruit sweet.'

Mama sighed. "And that is why man was cast out to be no better than a beast, dirty and itchy and covered by smuts from the fire. And it is why he creates, and why he may grow wise, and why he is numerous. Though it is said among the Sidhe that both wisdom and children are the burden of men, we have desired only children. We have not much valued wisdom, for we considered it less valuable than the immortality man gave up for it. Which is why I gave you the hank of thread, child. To sew a cap of wisdom if you liked, for you are half mortal and might care about such things."

A thinking cap! Oh, I should have known. Of course. What else could it have been?

We had come to the road which wound among the dun hills. I could see the moonlight on the lances far ahead, for the host was strung out for miles. Here and there I noticed huddled human forms, their faces in their hands, trying hard not to see us. We must have seemed very terrible indeed, awesome and fell. I wondered what stories those people would tell their children about the night they had seen the Fairy Ride, going out in their thousands from the lands below.

Something itched at me. Something I had seen, or thought I had seen. A flicker, perhaps, along the route we were taking. Something or someone upon the hills. I searched, seeing nothing. Mama's eyes were better than mine, and so were Puck's. "Look," I told them. "Along the hills. Is there something there that shouldn't be?"

Both of them scanned the horizon. At first they saw nothing, but then Mama stiffened and pointed. Then Puck saw it, too, and then I did. The gleam of moonlight on metal, high upon a hilltop overlooking the road we were taking. I knew what it was.

"The television crew," I told them both, barking unamused laughter. "Here to film the end of Faery."

"They may be here to film it," said Puck, angrily, "but it will not be filmed." He jumped up behind me and turned my horse aside, and we went behind the hill. I heard a snort behind us and saw Carabosse's donkey following. So there were four of us, Mama, me, Puck, and Carabosse. We circled around the hills, the horses picking their way through the gorse and the tumbled stones as we worked our way higher, toward the ridge. Evidently no one else among the host had seen them. When we came out behind them, they had no idea they had been observed.

"Let me," I suggested in a bleak voice. "I know their language."

Mama nodded. Carabosse snorted, sitting still upon her donkey. Puck sat down cross-legged and waited to see what I would do.

"This sequence," I said loudly, "is expected to complete the documentary on the last fairies."

Bill spun toward me, then Janice and Alice. The machine sat a short distance away, like a great stone tub. Martin stood up from the place he'd been kneeling behind a stone, watching the host pass below. Jaybee turned slowly, letting the camera rest on me. Carabosse did something with one hand, and he cursed, taking the camera off his shoulder.

"Damned lens fogged," he snarled.

"You are filming the departure of magic from the world. However, your premise is false." I was determined to say it, no matter whether it was true or not. Mama was there, and she needed to hear it. "This host, it is true, will leave the world, but magic will return."

"The hell it will," said Janice. "This is the beginning of the end." She laughed, shortly. "From here on out, it's all downhill.

Magic is gone. From here on out, it's religion, then romance, then horror, then the end!"

"Whatever comes when," I said, fixing Jaybee with a loathing glare, "you film nothing here today. Nothing at all."

He had the lens wiped off and raised it to his eye once more, only to curse once more, taking it down to stare at it. Carabosse had evidently fixed it so that he could not get a picture.

"Give it up," I told them. "Go home. We're not going to let you do it."

Jaybee got up and stalked toward Carabosse, violence obviously in his mind. When he got there, she wasn't there. She was a hundred feet away, sitting on her donkey. "No," she said firmly, "you'll not show anyone what happened here tonight. No one at all."

"You have no right," blustered Martin. "People have a right to . . ."

"Know only what others choose to let them know about private matters," finished Mama. "These are private matters."

". . . a right to know," he concluded.

"No, they do not," Puck said. "People have no right to crash private parties, pornographer. And this party is private."

Jaybee sputtered.

"You won't get a picture," I said. "Even if we go away, which we're about to do. You just won't get a picture, that's all. We have decided the world will never see this."

And we rode down the hill to the road, leaving them fuming behind us. Bill hadn't argued. He had just looked at me, stared at me, listening to every word that was said, as though he recognized me. This trip had happened the day after I got to the twenty-first. I remembered his returning from it, angry that we hadn't let them finish. His superiors must have been annoyed with him, laying the fault at his door. Well, the fault was not his, but there would never be a documentary on the last of the fairies. The last whales, the last dog, the last tree, the last radish, yes. No last fairy. Not yet.

We came back into the ride farther forward in the column. We passed the cross I remembered from last time. It was not long after that we came to the great cavern, the one with the door. Some of the Sidhe had already built a fire. Others were watching the eastern horizon. Evidently the door opened at moonrise, whether the Dark Lord would or no. When it opened, they planned to go through.

Mama shivered, and I got down from the horse and went to her. "You're cold," I said, idiotically. We were all cold. The night was crisp and chill. A winter's night. "Take my coat."

She shook her head. "You have nothing heavy enough to warm this chill. I know what's down there."

I stepped away, staring at the fire and at the door behind it. I was the only one who did know what was behind that door, though I had told Mama and she had tried to describe it to anyone who would listen.

"Father Raymond used to say, *'Una salus victis nullam sperare salutem,'* " I told her. "It means that victory can come out of hopelessness." She smiled, only a little.

Israfel came riding back through the quiet host, looking for me. When he saw me, he turned his horse and came straight toward me, bowing to Mama, to Carabosse, even to Puck as he came. When he reached me, he held out a hand and pulled me up onto his horse, then rode a short distance away. We both got down and stood together, looking at the assembled multitude. He was very quiet.

"I want you to have this," he said, taking a scarf from around his neck and putting it about mine. It was crimson silk, with bands of silver and gold at the edges. "It is real, not enchanted. I wove it, with my own hands. When we go in, put on your boots and your cloak and go home, back to Westfaire."

"To Westfaire? But Carabosse said he would look there."

Israfel kissed me gently. "He would have. Oh, yes, my love, he would have looked there. But now, we believe he won't have time."

"I can't let you go in there alone," I said. In that instant he was Giles, he was Bill, he was anyone who had ever cared for me. I could not let him go.

"We aren't alone," he said. "Nor are you. And you have

something to do yet, Beauty. Something more important than going into that hellhole again. Carabosse knows. I know."

A sound caught his attention, and he turned to watch. The moon was rising. The door was opening. He leapt into the saddle and drew me up beside him. He kissed me again. It felt like Giles's kiss, that night when we danced on the terrace. He laid his head against my breast, where the thing burned, whatever it was. At Mama's side he left me, then rode forward into the host.

"Someone will come to tell you about it, daughter," she said. "Puck, if no one else. Do not grieve over us. We've played the proud fools for a very long time." She leaned down and kissed me, too, on the cheek. My lips and my face and my chest all burned from fairy kisses. Then she rode off, down the hill, and I was left standing beside Puck, holding the reins of my horse in one hand. Carabosse jogged past, waving to me. Below, the horses were pouring through the doors like water down a drain. In no time at all they were gone. The door closed. The cold moon looked down at me, unsmiling.

I tied Israfel's scarf around my neck. If there was something left for me to do, I could not imagine what. I had very little time left in which to do anything.

Puck was kneeling at my feet, holding the boots. I slipped my feet in, one, then the other.

"I'll see you there," he said.

Perhaps I nodded. Perhaps not. Far off on the top of a hill was a shimmer, a shifting, as of a time machine going back to its own time. I, too, needed to go to my own time.

"Boots," I said, "take me home."

29

I tottered on my feet beside the rose-hedge of Westfaire. Beside me was the shepherds' well. I could barely see the cat's-head stone. I put out my hands to catch myself, and they were only bones with a little flesh bagged about them, blue veins running like rootlets across their backs and between fingers with nails all ridged and twisted. I sat down on the coping of the well and leaned against the post. Israfel had told me to go to Westfaire. What could I do in Westfaire? Besides, I had no strength to go anywhere.

I sat there for a long time, accumulating strength, or perhaps losing it. The boots were heavy upon my feet, and I slipped them off. The cloak was heavy upon my limbs, and I took it off as well, letting it lie behind me over the well coping. I sat there in a ragged kirtle, feeling the sun strike my skin through the rents. Ah, well. If I got a bit stronger, I could put the boots back on and go to the Dower House. There might be someone there who remembered me. Or who would take me in, out of charity.

As I sat up, almost determined to go, something dropped from the pocket of my cloak. I picked it up and looked at it, the hank of thread. I reached into the clock pocket for the packet of needles and found it with one unlucky fingertip.

Thread and needles. To sew, so Mama had said, a cap of wisdom, a thinking cap. If one wanted a thinking cap. Mama hadn't. Wisdom was the curse of man, she said. In seeking wisdom, we had lost our heritage. I didn't believe that. We hadn't sought wisdom diligently enough, that's how we'd lost our heritage. We preferred cleverness to wisdom. Instead of seeking the truth, we had preferred to believe in easy certainties. Always so much easier to take the lazy, easy way and then pretend God had commanded it. I sighed. I couldn't make a cap. There was nothing to make it of.

One hand went to my face to wipe frustrated tears away, encountering a corner of the scarf Israfel had given me. Such luxurious silk. Silk for a princess. Real world silk.

I could make a cap of that.

That is, I could make a cap if I could thread the needle. My eyes were weak, half-blind. The needle was small. I fumbled with the hank of thread, moving the almost invisible end of thread back and forth. The needle slipped in my hand; I grabbed at it, pricking myself; and the thread fell into the well.

I sobbed. Weakly. Without conviction. What had made me think I could do it in the first place? My back pressed against the post, I waited to die, believing I could cry myself to death if I just kept at it. There wasn't much to me anymore. I probably weighed no more than eighty pounds. I thought I would leak my life out through my eyes and then dry up and blow away. That would be the end to it, and I could quit trying.

"What's the matter, Grandmother," said a voice. It was a male voice, a young voice. I couldn't see who spoke.

"I've dropped my thread," I said hopelessly. "It dropped into the well."

"I'll get it for you, Grandmother," the voice said. I hadn't time to wonder how before I heard the plop of something sizeable dropping into the water. Not a big enough splash to be a person. Or had it been? A quite small person, perhaps?

I heard assorted liquid sounds, plashings and gulpings, then a scratching and grunting, and finally something wet and cool pressed the soaking hank of thread into my hand.

"I thank you," I said. "But I'm afraid my reach is beyond my grasp. I needed it to sew with and cannot see to thread the needle."

"It's a pity we do not have a fairy about," fretted the voice. "One who would give you keen eyesight as a fairy gift."

I started to agree with the young man, coming to myself with rather a start. I *was* a fairy, one who had been taught such spells, a long time ago. I had learned diminishing spells. The Spell of Bran. Spells for far-sight, sure-foot, keen-ear. Perhaps if I blended the former and the latter. Keen-sight was what was wanted.

I tottered to my feet, made a few graceless passes, and chanted the proper words. My vision cleared at once, and I stared at the well coping where a large green frog sat regarding me with bulging eyes. "How marvelous, Grandmother," he said. "We had a fairy after all."

"I am not your grandmother," I snapped. At my age it was not easy to snap. The few teeth I still had seemed loose.

"I know you are probably not really my grandmother," said the frog. "I was only being polite."

Indeed, he was a particularly polite frog. I could not recall, through the fog of my aged memory, that I had ever encountered a frog of such poise before. I cast about for recollections of other frogs, finding such memories sparse and unprofitable, mixed inexplicably with memories of dinners in Bayonne and Lourdes and garlicky servings of something I had preferred to think of at the time as chicken.

"Of course," said the frog. "I am not really a frog, either."

I had already guessed that. "You're a prince disguised as a frog," I hazarded. "To prevent your being killed by your enemies."

He shook his head. Since a frog has little neck, this involved shaking the entire body. The coping was slippery, and he fell into the well once more, emerging moments later very wet and out of breath.

"Actually," he said, "I am a prince enchanted into a frog for some reason which I am utterly incapable of understanding."

I was busy threading the needle and spared only a moment to look inquiringly at him.

"Since you are going to be occupied with your sewing, perhaps you would like me to entertain you with my life's history," the frog suggested.

I nodded. Certainly there was no reason why not. Until I got the thinking cap done, there was nothing else I could do but sit and sew. I was already planning how to make the cap, by folding the scarf into fourths, diagonally, as one does to make a cocked hat out of paper, and then sewing the folded side closed and turning it up to make a brim. Since the frog seemingly had not interpreted my nod as permission to go ahead, I repeated it more firmly as I tied a knot in the thread.

"Ahem," he began, clearing his throat.

"My earliest memories are of a childhood surrounded by

loving people. My foster father and mother, my nursemaid, the servants, the young man who was hired to play with me, later my tutor. When I was old enough to be told anything at all, I was told that my true father and mother, a prince and princess, lived far away, in another kingdom from which it was thought advisable I be excluded, inasmuch as I was not an heir to the throne and my presence might serve as an excuse for usurpers to cause dissention and unrest. I was told that this step had been taken in order to assure me a happy and extended life, since claimants to thrones, even legitimate ones, often live shorter lives than other, less exalted persons."

"I have known of such cases," I told the frog. "History is rife with them."

"So I was informed," the frog went on. "Since I am not ambitious, this explanation was satisfactory to me. The allowance my foster parents received for my care was sufficient to guarantee a pleasant life, and the maintenance of the estate on which I was reared was a sufficient career to interest me. I learned agriculture, beekeeping, cattle raising, dairying, egg production, fodder storage, gardening, horsemanship, independence, jar molding, kennel keeping, lamb raising, manpower management, nut growing, orchard keeping, poultry breeding, quarrel quashing (among the serfs), rabbit hunting, sheep grazing, timber cutting, usury, viniculture, wool clipping, xyloglyphy, yoke making, and zealotry."

"What is xyloglyphy?" I asked, amazed.

"Wood carving," he replied. "It was the only x I could think of."

"And zealotry?"

"One must be zealous, mustn't one. About something."

"And you learned usury?"

"To avoid it, Grandmother."

I started to remind him I was not his grandmother, but halted. Dim thought swam through my turgid mind. A fish I could barely see. Something he had said. "Go on with your story," I said.

"My foster father, a good man, and my foster mother, a good woman, though at times impatient, gave every attention to my education. I had the finest tutors from the time I was a child and learned Latin, Greek, French, and the common tongue as well as the trivium and quadrivium, including grammar, rhetoric, logic, mathematics, composition, and history. I learned to play four musical instruments and sing in a pleasing voice a great number of popular ballads and instructive songs."

"How many times have you told this story?" I asked, taken with the well-rehearsed tone of the verbiage he was spewing.

"Many times, Grandmother," he sighed. "More times than I can count. Has it begun to sound overly familiar?"

"A bit more spontaneity might be welcome," I said, turning the seam in the cap I was making. "However, whatever comes most naturally to you will do." I sighed, fretfully, suddenly overcome with hunger.

"What's the matter, Grandmother?" the frog asked.

"I'm starved," I said. "Literally starved. I have been too long in Faery, and my mortal body has not been fed."

"I can find you an apple," the frog said, leaping off the coping and hopping into the woods which surrounded the rose-hedge. I remembered then that there had been an old orchard there, one that had not been used for generations, except by lovers, lying on the sweet grasses. Within a little time, the frog hopped back again, removed a ripe apple from his mouth, and wiped it upon my ragged skirt, apologizing for the only way he had to carry it. I felt a sudden spasm of affection for the frog.

The apple was crisp and sweet. I bit into it, gently, in order that my teeth not come out in the sweet flesh of it, and the juice ran down my throat as the frog continued.

"It's interesting that you're not all fairy. I am not all prince, either. Though, as a child, I was told I had royal blood; the kingdom from which I had come was small and had insufficient fortune to keep me well all my life. Therefore, I was educated with a view to becoming industrious and independent. My foster father told me that, when I was twenty-one, he and my foster mother would return to the tiny kingdom from which he had come, and which he missed agonizingly from time to time, though I cannot say why. The stories he told of it were uniformly boring. It had no natural splendors that he could remember, and its architectural heritage he described as rural revival, though a revival of what, he could not say. Still, I looked forward to the day when I should be master of my own destiny, little knowing that such matters are subject to many reversals totally outside one's own competence.

"When I was about ten, I learned that my mother and father, whom I had never met, had died in an avalanche. I grieved, though not greatly, since I had never known them.

"As do all boys, I came to the age of physical maturity somewhat ahead of any mental or emotional stability with which the physical surges and urges might be controlled. I had a bittersweet and blessedly brief affair with a dairy maid, an unsuitable partner, one might say, though she had a lovely complexion, very pretty hair, and a vocabulary not exeeding one hundred words, most of them to do with cows."

The frog reminded me of someone. I couldn't tell who, but he did. His manner of speaking reminded me of someone.

"I then wooed and won the hand of the fair Elaine," the frog went on. "A very suitable match. We were to be betrothed on my eighteenth birthday. She was some years younger, and it was thought we would be wed when she was fifteen or sixteen and I about twenty-one. In the interim, my foster father was of the opinion I should seek sophistication through travel. While he did not recommend any attempt to go to the Holy Land, then, as you know, held by the infidels, he did recommend a journey to Santiago de Compostela, to which he had journeyed in his youth with great cheer and good company."

Through the murk of memory, the fish swam nearer.

"However," said the frog, "before I could depart on the journey set out for me by my foster father, with due regard for continuing my education and experience in ways that would benefit me, I happened to go riding into the forest and became lost. On attempting to find my way out, I came upon a tower in which a maiden sat singing. Her name was Rapunzel, as I learned when an old and opinionated fairy came out of the underbrush, carrying a clock, and insisted that the maiden let down her hair."

"Carabosse!" I said. "It could only have been Carabosse."

"However did you know, Grandmother? It was indeed the fairy Carabosse. Well, to make a long story short (for I see you have almost completed your sewing), the fairy tricked me in a very unpleasant way, and when I climbed what I thought was a rope of hair securely attached to the head of Rapunzel—a very lovely maiden, indeed—I found the old fairy instead. She harangued me at length upon the subjects of time and beauty, ending her discourse by putting an enchantment upon me that I should become a frog and remain so until kissed willingly by a princess!

"Since that time, it has been my hope that I would first be kissed, then returned to my natural state, though I fear that neither Rapunzel nor the fair Elaine will have waited. Some thirteen years have passed since then. Both of them will be old maids of twenty-five, or buxom matrons, mothers of many." The frog wept briefly. "Though I have spoken to my foster father about the matter, and he assures me the estate will be still be mine when I achieve manhood once again."

I finished the cap and put it upon my head. The elusive fish swam up and looked me in the eyes.

"You are my great-grandson Giles Edward Vincent Charming," I said.

"Well of course, Grandmother," said the frog. "I would not have addressed you so familiarly otherwise."

This was specious, but I did not argue with him. I had been one hundred and three when I had visited Carabosse. If, while I dallied returning to Ylles, she had come immediately to the world of men to enchant my great grandson, as she no doubt had, and if thirteen years had passed since that time, I was now one hundred sixteen years old. The century had passed during which Beauty was condemned to sleep. Or was that in the curse? And which curse? Joyeause's curse, or Carabosse's? Or Disney's? I started to blurt all this out, then stopped. Beneath the thinking cap, faculties long unused—nay, faculties never used before—began to stir.

"At one time," I said, "I think it was in 1417 or the year after, while in Bayonne, I bought a book by Christine de Pisan.

It was called, I recollect, *The Treasure of the City of Ladies*. Do you know of it, by chance?"

"I'm sorry, no, Grandmother. I am unacquainted with feminist literature."

"She directs her discourse toward princesses, including in that number the daughters of dukes. Would you agree with her inclusive idea of royalty?"

"The daughters of dukes are certainly very noble, Grandmother. Certainly they might be included among princesses."

"Then let me kiss you, child. I have not seen you since you were two years old."

I leaned forward and kissed the frog. The air shimmered. I felt dizzy. A small earthquake made the stones beneath us shift, ever so slightly. When I looked up, he stood there before me, stark naked, as fine-looking a young man as has ever been my fortune to see, except for his very slightly bulging eyes. No doubt he would outgrow them in time. I enchanted a few leaves into a long shirt for him and told him that would have to do until we got into Westfaire.

"Westfaire," he mused. "I thought Westfaire was mythical, like Faery, like Olympus, like . . ."

"Mythical things frequently aren't," I said tartly. "Focus your mind, boy. Grandmama has need of you."

With Giles Edward Vincent Charming's assistance along the way—let us be clear, mostly he carried me—I got back into my boots and, holding him firmly around the neck, told them to take us through the roses into Westfaire. Once inside, he let loose my hand and promptly fell asleep, as I should have known he would. I was carrying the cloak and the boots and had the magic cap upon my head. He had nothing to protect him from the spell upon the place. Retaining the cap, I thrust the boots inside his shirt and belted it around him with the belt of my cloak. Thus closely associated with magical influences, he woke once more to stare around him unbelievingly. If anything, the hedge had grown taller since I had last been there. Everything within seemed to glow with a light of its own. The glamour was so thick it seemed buttery.

He carried me upstairs for his first look at Beloved. Once he had seen her, he could not tear his eyes away. He wanted to kiss her, but I would not let him. "No, Giles," I said. "Not yet. We have some thinking to do."

He became almost uncontrollable, so I pulled the cap off my own head and put it on his. He subsided, his mouth falling open as his mental faculties underwent instantaneous enlargement. When he looked completely dazed, I removed the cap and replaced it on my own head. I felt it might take a day or two to explore the full ramifications of the headgear, and I had no time to lose. In passing, I examined Carabosse's clock and verified that it was almost half-past the fifteenth century. The numbers still ended with twenty-two. Though all of Faery had gone to war, nothing had changed. Or perhaps something had. After I had seen light in the bottom of the pool, she had seen fit to leave Faery and enchant my great-grandson. There had to have been purpose in that.

We went first to the barracks, to get Giles Edward some clothing, and then to the kitchens. He prepared food while I sat and thought and thought and sat. We ate together, ignoring the cooks sprawled across the floor. While we ate, I began to tell him the story of my life, referring from time to time to this book, my book, the book Father Raymond gave me so long ago, to remind me of the sequence of occurrences. So it was I found Carabosse's addition to my text and marveled over them. As I read, I realized who it was the frog had reminded me of when he talked. It was myself. I had been a loquacious youngster.

When I grew weary, I gave him the book and let him read for himself while I dozed beneath the cap, aroused occasionally by his exclamations as he encountered something strange or unbelievable or patently impossible.

"I know, I know," I murmured. "But it all happened just as I have said."

I was not really surprised to find that my account of my time in hell was in the book, as I had imagined setting it down. That kind of thing is, had been, usual in Faery.

When we had eaten, we were weary, so I directed him to Aunt Lavvy's room where I had slept before. I had forgotten my Giles was there, but it did not matter. I told young Giles who he

was, then lay down beside my love. My great-grandson tucked
me into a blanket and rolled himself into a quilt upon the floor,
asking if there was any danger we would sleep forever. The
question was too close to my thoughts for comfort. I assured
him we would not, and in a moment his youthful snores echoed
in the room.

I dozed. After a time I woke. The very old do not need as
much sleep as younger folk, though they need it more frequently. Like cats, we nap and wake, nap and wake. The
thought of cats reminded me of Grumpkin, and I missed him.
One of the first things I wanted to do was explore the Dower
House stables to see if he had left a son.

I felt somewhat stronger, and wanted to look about me a
little. I took the boots from my great-grandson's shirt, replacing
them with the cap, and bade them take me to the lakeshore
beyond the roses. Instantaneously, I stood there, the cool night
wind blowing in my face.

Across the lake were the villages of East and West
Moerdyn, where, evidently, they were having carnival time.
There were fires on the lakeshore and torches among the trees.
All along the lakeshore, from far on my left to far on my right,
the little fires flickered and burned and I could hear, as though
from another world, voices raised in jollity.

On the surface of the lake, windlessly calm, the reflections
of the fires and torches stretched to my feet like a hundred
golden roads leading to the edges of the world. I was at the
center of a fan of fire, a wheel of golden beams.

I heard, as though in a dream, the voice of Captain Karon
saying, "We are at the center of the world."

I saw myself, once again young and beautiful, at the center
of a wheel of light.

All light, all beauty, ends at my feet, I told myself. It comes
from everywhere, and ends at my feet. For a time a vision possessed me, a great wheel of light which could not be extinguished, which would roll and burn and roll forever.

At length, I came to myself. It was chilly with the moist
wind blowing, and the fires had been put out. I bid the boots
return me to my bed. There I lay quiet and warm and quite

awake, my hand on my Giles's chest, wondering if Carabosse had foreseen what I would attempt to do.

When my great-grandson woke, I told him to put the cap on his head while I explained what was in my mind. When I told him the world, or at least all life was to end in the twenty-second century, at first he protested. However, the thinking cap exerted its influence, and he admitted it was inevitable, given the nature of men. When I told him that Faery might end very soon, he wept. Despite having been turned into a frog by the fairy Carabosse, he had gentle feelings for most of fairykind. After that, he simply nodded, concentrating on my plan.

"It might be done, Grandmother," he said. "If one really wished to do it." He looked very wistful, however.

"You're thinking of the girl upstairs," I said.

He admitted that he was.

"I am sure we can work something out," I told him. "But everything else must be done first."

"It may take years," he sighed.

"I think not," I told him. "I'm sure help is available. But, even if it should take years, remind yourself that you are one-sixteenth fairy, a sufficient share of fairy blood to guarantee you an extremely long life."

"How old are you, Grandmother?"

"One hundred sixteen," I said, thinking what a brief time it all seemed.

He sighed, but he was a good, sensible boy. Thank God he was Vincent's son, and not the child of the mad young prince. Thank God he took after his father rather than his mother. Thank God he took after his great-grandma, at least a little. Perhaps beauty does, in time, breed true. I knew he would do as I asked.

I lent him the seven-league boots and the cloak of invisibility, taught him a few enchantments, and thereafter he came and went many times each day. I, meantime, kept the fire burning and food hot in the kettle, and stood ready to admire each acquisition as he brought it in.

Giraffes and lions and rhinoceri. Auks and dodos and passenger pigeons. Elephants, okapis, and pandas. Snow leopards, tigers, and ocelots.

Seeds of great trees and small. Shrubs and flowers and mere herbage, shoot and root, leaf and branch. Robin and sparrow, goldfinch and wren, eagle and falcon and kestrel, and all the birds of the sea.

Those creatures too large to be transported *in statu quo,* as Father Raymond would have said, were diminished. I taught my great-grandson the spell and he had no trouble with it whatsoever. Evidently even one-sixteenth fairy blood is sufficient for such elementary magic. Once the creatures were in Westfaire, I removed the spell while they lay sleeping two by two, or one by six, or however they properly divided themselves. Herd beasts came by severals, others by pairs, at least two pairs of each, for Giles Edward Vincent Charming had learned his husbandry well. "You have to allow extra so you don't get too much inbreeding," he told me. And "I only picked the ones with young, for they have proven fertility."

Such a good, sensible, intelligent boy.

One day as I sat by the kitchen fire, waiting for his return, I heard a voice calling my name. I tottered out into the garden and found Sariel there among the cabbages. She looked worn and tired. I was afraid to ask her how the battle had gone, but she took me by the hand and told me without my asking.

"We weakened him, but we have not yet killed him," she said. "All those creatures of horror that men invented have gained strength and a terrible life of their own. We are not fighting only our own darkness. We are fighting men's darkness as well. Oh, Beauty, the things we found down there! The engines of annihilation! The machines of destruction! The human engineers of hate, laboring in their dens to make greater horrors yet. The human writers, hovering over their pens, creating baser terrors of bigotry and persecution. Oh, we could not have made these things, Beauty. Only God and man can create. All that God makes is beautiful. Why did He give man the choice? In the labyrinth of the Dark Lord, man is his ally. Only time can kill him, and them."

"Our side?" I asked, barely able to get the words out. "What about our side?"

She smiled, a remote, bitter smile. "Horror is stronger than joy, Beauty. Particularly when it is encouraged to flourish. Still, we have beat him back. He has fled from us, out of Faery and into some other dimension of terror. We are pursuing him with what strength is left. Many of our people are gone."

"Mama?"

"Your mama. Yes. She perished bravely fighting a thing none of us could have imagined. And Oberon and Mab. And Israfel. And many more."

Israfel! Oh, such a pain by my heart.

"But not the Bogles?"

"No. Not the Bogles. Sensibly, they stayed out of it. Sturdy. Independent. A little cynical. They do not let pride lead them into folly. They have come behind us, blocking the earths as it were, to keep the horror from returning. They will live a long, long time yet."

"And Carabosse."

"When Carabosse saw there could be no victory in time, she left us. She said she had a greater task before her."

"But some survive."

"Some survive, yes. But it is the end of Faery. We must leave the world. We must pursue the Dark Lord into whatever place he goes, however long it takes. In the end, we pray the victory will be ours. . . ."

"Then Bill and Janice were right. It was the last ride."

"They were right."

"Will you ever go back to Baskarone? Those of you who are left?"

That remote smile again. "Who knows if we will ever come there again. Or, if we do, who knows whether it will be there to receive us."

"May I have it?" I asked her.

She was astonished when I told her why, but she smiled and told me I might have it if I liked.

Then she was gone. I wept a time for Mama and for Israfel, but weeping does no good, does it? Sitting down and weeping is what women have done for centuries, and it has done no good at all. Nor praying. God has given us the earth. He is not waiting in the next room, ready to fix it for us if we ruin it. If we do not care for it, no one will. On other worlds, other races of men perhaps do better than we have done. He cares for us, but he does not control what we do.

So. So. I called Fenoderee, and he was there, with Puck, and a dozen other Bogles as well. I told them what Sariel had said.

"We know," said Puck. "We heard."

"Baskarone won't last. Faery is gone. Mortal men will trash all life by the end of the twenty-first. That means . . ."

"It means this is the only hope," said Puck. "We know. We've come to help."

And so they have. They have brought beetles and butter-flies and moths. Orchids and hibiscus and frangipani. Tropical fruits and desert plants. Things that fly and crawl. They bring them all to sleep in my gardens, my orchards, my stables, my hallways. Every sconce is hung with spiders. The moat is filled with fish, there are mice in Papa's pockets and moles under Father Raymond's skirts.

The library is littered with great buildings made small, with bridges and monuments, all those from Baskarone, made small. We could not bring the gardens or the forests, so we have settled for seeds.

On two of their return trips, I asked Giles and Puck to take Weasel-Rabbit and her mama out into the world once more. They are doing no good here; they would not be good breeding stock; and we desperately need the space.

Days go by, and they shuttle back and forth. My grandson with them, they alone, they in pairs or triplets, coming and going. The grounds of Westfaire are capacious, but they are be-ginning to fill up. Sleeping bodies are everywhere, perched, sprawled, flopped. Bats and sloths are hanging upside down in the buttery. I put the koalas in my tower bedroom, clinging to the bedpost, and four kinds of foxes are curled at the foot of my bed, next to the Taj Mahal.

Giles Edward has emptied the fountain and filled it with saltwater from the sea. It took all of them to bring the whales, though when they arrived they were no larger than goldfish. Sperm whales and right whales and blue whales and white whales. Killer whales and dolphins. Gray whales and pilot fish. Sharks. I thought perhaps we could leave sharks out, them and mosquitoes, but Puck said no, the Holy One made it beautiful in its entirety, and it had to be all or nothing. I sit on the edge of the fountain and watch the whales sleeping on the water, blowing spray from their blowholes and dreaming of the songs they will sing. Perhaps. Someday.

Grumpkin IV is on my bed. Or perhaps he is Grumpkin V or VI. He sleeps on his back with his paws curled over his belly. His wife is curled on my pillow, with the kittens. Such pretty kittens.

And at last it is all done. There is not a species alive between year one of mankind and the twentieth that they have not found and brought here, alive or in seed. Mammoths and mastodons and all. There is not a creation Israfel and his kinfolk included in Baskarone which is not here. And beneath my breastbone the seed of beauty burns and burns and burns, stronger with each thing that comes. It will not burn out. It will never burn out.

Now is only the last bit.

"Where will you go?" I asked Puck.

"Here," he said. "A few of us are going to stay here. If the time ever comes, you'll need help with this lot."

"Grandmother," said Giles Edward, a youth worn and tired from his long effort, "I can stay, too."

I shook my head at him. "Oh, child, of course not. There's Beloved up there in the tower all this long time, waiting for her prince. We can't let her go on sleeping forever. That wasn't the idea at all."

"But . . ."

"But me no buts, child. No. Tonight we will all have a celebratory dinner. Ham and cheese and ale and wine, and fresh baked bread—Fenoderee has someone to do that—and we will sing songs and laugh. And then you will take Beloved out with you, well away from here, and kiss her awake." Once out of

Westfaire, she would wake on her own, but why shouldn't he have the pleasure.

"And then?"

"And then you will apply all your alphabet of industry and intelligence to living a long, prolific, and pleasant life." God grant that it is so.

"And then? What will happen here?"

I shook my head at him again. Who knows for sure?

I was getting ready for our celebration when Carabosse showed up, suddenly, sidling out of nothing.

"So here you are," she said.

I mumbled something at her, something about how hard I'd been working and everything we'd done, and offered to take her about the place and show her.

She looked at the animals in the corners and the bats hanging from the wardrobe door and laughed. She toured the stables and the gardens. Then she sat down in a corner and laughed, the tears running out of her eyes.

"I thought you knew," she said. "I thought you had guessed."

"Knew what?" I asked her. "Guessed what?"

"All this. This," she said, pointing at all of it, animals, fish, birds, Baskarone shrunken to tiny size. "You didn't need to do this. We already did it."

"You . . . ?" I couldn't figure out what she was saying.

"Israfel. And his kindred. They already did it. Long ago. Before you were born." She leaned forward to tap me on my chest. "What did you think was in there, silly girl?" And she went off laughing again.

After a time, I laughed with her.

"Beauty's in there," she said. "In Beauty, beauty. All of it. Here in Westfaire. In the beautiful is Beauty, and in Beauty, beauty. Silly girl." And her head sagged, just for a moment, as though she was too tired to go on. "Everything you have collected is beautiful, girl. But it was already inside you. All inside you, made tiny, like a seed. For you to keep safe, forever."

Well, I had known that, of course. But it wasn't enough

merely to take their word for it. They might have missed something! It felt better to have done it myself.

A little redundancy never hurts. Someone told me that once. I can't remember who.

Carabosse joined us for our celebration.

Candles. Every candle in the place alight. Music. The Bogles came from everywhere for that. Wild things. Benevolent monsters. They are a very musical people. Food, and wine, and dancing, and games. I sat quietly in the corner, writing in my book, watching them all.

It went on until dawn. Somewhere out in the world a cock crowed. Silence came, and most of the Bogles went.

Giles Edward Vincent Charming brought the sleeping Beloved downstairs and out into the courtyard. He put on my boots. He was crying as he told me goodbye, but he was sneaking glances at her, too. He will not grieve for long. He kissed me and then he went.

Carabosse kissed me. It felt like a mother's kiss. She didn't tell me where she was going, but I have a feeling it will not be far. She sidled into somewhere else and was gone.

Fenoderee and the others who are staying are out with the animals. Puck carried my Giles up to the tower and laid him on my bed. Giles looks much better, much stronger. This long sleep has done him good. Then Puck helped me to climb all these stairs to be with my love. Since I've been back this time, my legs have hurt such a lot, and of course I am very, very old. One hundred and sixteen! Think of it! I could not have climbed here without him.

From the balcony I can see the light of dawn and bright wings circling straight above. A dove, I think. Very high. On my bed, Giles snores and Grumpkin snores, little breathy sounds in the silence. When I stroke either of them, they move as though to tell me they know I am here. I sit on the edge of the bed to write, remembering Giles Edward's question.

What will happen?

Beloved will awaken once she is out of Westfaire. He will kiss her, of course, but that has nothing to do with anything. No matter what Joyeause said about a hundred years, this spell was laid forever. Westfaire will go on sleeping. Papa will sleep, and Doll, and Martin. The aunts will sleep, and the young maids, and the young footmen and stable hands, all will sleep until the conditions of this enchantment are fulfilled and someone or something wondrous arrives to kiss beauty awake once more. Not a prince. Or not merely a prince. More than a prince. A rebirth of some kind. And not soon. Not until long after Carabosse's clock has run down. Long after the twenty-third, I should imagine. Long after Baskarone is gone and all of Faery vanished. Long after the Dark Lord and all his minions have perished from the weight of time. The inanition of age will get him, finally, where nothing else can, and having no victims except each other will kill the rest. Perhaps in the twenty-fourth or the twenty-fifth, or perhaps long after that, life will come again. I have done everything a half fairy can to preserve it. Carabosse and I make a good pair.

And if it happens—why, then everything is here. The whales and the elephants and the radishes and the trees. Magic is here. And man, too. All those randy stable boys and giggling maids. And the Bogles. Ready to begin again. Ready to recreate what God created. And Giles, to greet me again in the morning; and I, to greet him.

And if it does not happen?

Then everything is here. Sleeping. Dreaming, perhaps, of what might have been. Perhaps others, on some other world will catch the dream, will wake from it astonished at its marvel, at its complicated wonder. Perhaps someone or something will dream who can create once more.

There is a bedtime prayer Aunt Terror taught me when I was a child. "Now I lay me down to sleep; I pray the Lord my soul to keep." Such an arrogant idea to go to sleep on, I have always thought. Why should God do any such thing, except that I've always loved His beauty passionately. All God's beauty passionately.

That time, so long ago, I would not allow the Curse to touch me. I did not want to spend a hundred years sleeping. I thought it unworthy of me. I thought it monstrously unfair that

Papa had let me in for such a fate. I evaded it. I escaped it, so I thought. Escaping destiny is not so easy as that. Funny, the way things work out. Even Carabosse and Israfel couldn't quite keep it from happening the way it did. As though someone else had done the planning.

Puck is holding out his hand for my pen. And my cap. He says he will sit by me, and rub the pains out of my poor old legs. Until I sleep.

"I pray the Lord my soul to keep."

Perhaps, instead, He will keep the fire that burns here; the fire that Israfel and Carabosse set here.

Perhaps that has always been my soul.